*J*UANA took a deep, steadying breath and lit the candle. Its flame flickered for a moment, showing the stair plunging down into blackness. Her breath was coming too fast again. But now there was no excuse for further delay. If she did not start down, quickly, now, this minute, she never would.

She made herself move forward at once into the darkness. She had just reached the door when the gong sounded. Shooting back the bolt, she saw that her hands were shaking. The doors were pulled outwards as soon as the bolt was free. In the light of two torches she could see the hooded members of the Star waiting.

"I am ready." She kept her voice steady with an effort.

"Then let us in."

It seemed an age till the gong sounded for the second time. This was the worst moment of all. For she was not what they thought her, their friend, the Handmaiden of the Star. They did not know that she had secretly become their enemy.

Juana opened the panel, praying they would not see her terror. It was indeed a dangerous game she was playing. How long could she keep it up?

Fawcett Crest Books
by Jane Aiken Hodge:

The Winding Stair

by Jane Aiken Hodge

A FAWCETT CREST BOOK • NEW YORK

THE WINDING STAIR

THIS BOOK CONTAINS THE COMPLETE TEXT
OF THE ORIGINAL HARDCOVER EDITION.

Published by Fawcett Crest Books, a unit of
CBS Publications, the Consumer Publishing
Division of CBS Inc., by arrangement with
Doubleday & Company, Inc.

ISBN: 0-449-23590-4

Selection of the Young World Reader's Club, March 1969
Selection of the Literary Guild, February 1969

Printed in the United States of America

21 20 19 18 17 16 15 14 13 12

TO THE READER

Who wants historical footnotes to a romantic novel? You may well ask. But Juana Brett's imagined story is so deeply embedded in the history of her time that I think a few brief notes at the back of the book may amuse some readers, solve problems for others, and be happily ignored by the rest.

Jane Aiken Hodge

The Winding Stair

CHAPTER 1

Moonlight lay like water on smooth grass. Cypresses cast strange shadows across the river that ran fast, deep, and cruel under its ornamental bridge. Pausing there, a moment, before he braced himself to enter Forland House, Gair Varlow lifted his head to listen. Somewhere, a late nightingale sang. Nearer, running feet crunched on gravel. A figure appeared from where Lord Forland's theatre stood at the far side of the house, showed briefly in black silhouette against ranges of lighted windows, then cut across the rose garden towards the river. Watching, Gair instinctively stepped back into the scented shadow of a huge climbing rose, listening now to the sobbing, hard-drawn breath that might mean exhaustion or tears.

The runner emerged from the shadow of the house, and Gair swallowed a gasp of surprise. This was a creature from fairy-tale, a slender boy all silver-white in the moonlight, whose doublet and hose belonged not to 1806, the age of odd old King George and Bonaparte, but to an earlier day when Queen Elizabeth sent out her fleet against the Spaniard.

While Gair watched, stock-still with amazement, the boy reached the middle of the hump-backed bridge. Still sobbing, he stopped for a moment to catch his breath, unaware of the watcher in the shadows, then began to climb on to the low parapet.

"Don't!" In a moment the dream boy was going to plunge into the river, and Gair had stayed, like a fool, amazed, too far away to intervene. He would have to do it with words. The boy was hesitating, surprised at the interruption, poised on the top of the low wall. "Don't," Gair said again, but casually now. "It's quite shallow under the bridge," he lied. "You'll look sufficiently absurd, head down, legs up, in the mud. Besides"—he moved forward into the moonlight—"this is my best suit of clothes. I don't at all want to spoil it hauling you out."

"Are you sure?" The boy's high clear voice suggested that he must still be in his early teens.

"Of course I'm sure." Gair risked another slow step forward. "I ought to know. But let me introduce myself. I'm

Lady Forland's brother, Gair Varlow, and entirely at your service."

"Oh! Mr. Varlow ... Yes, I suppose you should know." But he stayed perched on the wall and Gair did not dare move nearer. "Is it really so shallow?"

"In winter it might be as much as waist deep, but now—"

"I see." The boy sat down suddenly on the parapet, and Gair breathed a silent sigh of relief. "What a fool I am," the high, clear voice went on. "I might have known it would be no good. Nothing I d—d—d—" He stuck on the letter, and seemed to writhe, for a moment, in ruthlessly revealing moonlight, then began again. "Nothing I do ever is." He finished it in a rush.

While he struggled, Gair had had a moment of delighted illumination. Here, fantastically, was opportunity presenting itself to him unasked. This was the very person he had come to Forland House to see.

"Do you stammer too?" he asked as if it was the most natural thing in the world. "I used to when I was a boy." He had thought a great deal about what his approach was to be, but had never thought of this one.

"You d—d—don't any more?" It came more easily this time.

"Not the least in the world. I grew out of it when I was at the University. I expect you will too."

"The University? Me?" And then, looking down at the extravagant white and silver costume, "Good gracious! You can't think—" An irrepressible, delicious giggle ended the sentence. Then, sliding lightly down from the wall, plumed hat in hand, with a parody of a deep bow: "Your humble servant, Mr. Varlow."

"And yours, Miss Brett." He knew it for the crassest of mistakes the moment it was spoken.

"Miss—" She choked on it. "You knew all the t—t—t— You knew all the while." She was too angry to let even the stammer stop her. "I suppose your sister t—t—told you. My Lady Forland who thinks I'll make such a comic t—t—turn in her opera. Viola with a stutter." She turned away towards the river. "Why did you stop me? If I'd kept still, down there, I might have contrived to d—to d—" She stopped, stutter and words alike lost in a rush of tears.

As for him, he was almost too angry to think. What lunacy was this of Vanessa's? He had asked her to get the girl to her house party so that he could look her over. He had warned

10

her, too, about the stammer, and yet she had apparently driven the child to the point of suicide. If he had not happened to be here. . . . He shuddered at the threat to his carefully laid plans. And it was not averted yet, though he saw with relief that Juana Brett was making no effort to get back on to the wall, but merely leaned against it, her face in her hands, sobbing and shuddering.

"But what in the world possessed Vanessa to give you the part?"

His tone of simple enquiry was just what she needed. She raised her head to look at him, her thin face ravaged in the moonlight. "I d—d—don't stammer when I sing," she explained. "They said it was just a singing part. My stepmother said I must. It was why we were asked, you see, and she said it was such a chance for the girls—my stepsisters." It was a relief to her to talk about it, here in the cool anonymity of moonlight. "It's a new opera of Mr. Haydn's," she went on. "One they found in the poor D—D—"

He watched her writhe, stuck fast on the letter, his compassion mixed with despair. What use could this poor creature be to him? He had had no idea her stammer was so bad. Had old Mrs. Brett not known, or had she simply not chosen to tell him?

"The D—D—" She threw back her head, her strong features showing shadowed in the moonlight, and amazed him with a fluent stream of Portuguese bad language. Then, on the same high note: "They found it in the Duchess of Devonshire's papers," she said. "It's based on Shakespeare's T—"

It was going to start again. "I admire your command of Portuguese," he said in that language.

"Oh!" It took her aback. "You speak Portuguese?" She, too, spoke it like a native. "I didn't think . . ." Was she blushing? "Nobody else understands it here. It seems to help, somehow. It's only what the servants used to say at my grandmother's."

"I can imagine." Dryly.

"It's not so very bad either," she went on. "They're happy people, the Portuguese; they don't swear much, or drink either. I didn't know what life was really like, till I came here, to England."

"You don't like it here?"

"Who cares whether I like it or not? What's that to the purpose? You don't ask to be born. If you're a girl, you don't ask to be happy either. You just live. Or—you don't." She had turned away again to gaze down into the dark water.

"I don't understand"—anything to distract her. "You don't seem to stammer in Portuguese."

"In Portuguese? Of course not. Why should I?"

Hope welled up in him. "Then you'd like to go back there?"

"Don't talk about it! I can't bear even to think of it. In Portugal I was alive. I could talk, think, breathe . . . You know Portugal, Mr. Varlow? You must, to speak the language so well."

"I've been there." Careful, he told himself; don't rush your fences.

"Then you know what it's like. The sun, and the sea, and the quietness . . . All that time to be yourself, with no one to carp, and quibble, and wish you different."

"You're talking about your Grandmother Brett's house at Cabo Roca?" It sounded most unlike his own experience of the gossip-ridden English colony at Lisbon, but then, things were different in that extraordinary castle on the cliffs, where old Mrs. Brett, English herself, ruled a Portuguese household with a rod of iron.

"The Castle on the Rock? You know it?" Eagerly.

"Yes. I went there once. An amazing place. I was actually received by your formidable grandmother."

"Were you really? And the others—you saw them? My uncles, my cousins, my Aunt Elvira . . ." Her voice changed, softened on the last name. "I grew up there, you know. I was happy." She made it absolute. "And I did not even know it, till we came away, my father and I."

He knew enough about the circumstances of her father's disastrous quarrel with his rich mother, and still more unfortunate second marriage, to be able to fill out her bare sketch in his imagination. It brought him back to the immediate point.

"And they want you to sing Viola in some opera of Mr. Haydn's based on *Twelfth Night*?" he asked.

"That's it." In Portuguese even her laugh sounded different, richer and freer. "It's a difficult part—calls for an unusual range. They could none of them do it. So Lady Forland asked us over to her house party. We live quite near, you see. Mamma was wild with joy. She's been angling for an invitation ever since we settled here." And then, "I oughtn't to be telling you these things."

12

"Never mind." He made it matter of fact, casual. "Blame it on moonlight and roses. Can you smell them? I think we're both a little moon-mad, you and I. Besides, I might be able to help you. Vanessa—Lady Forland—sometimes pays attention to me. Your problem, as I understand it, is that you can sing happily enough in their opera, so long as you don't have to talk?"

"That's it." Eagerly. "Recitative's all right; I can do that, but now they want to write in some dialogue in the duel scene. They say it will just add to the comedy if I stutter. I could kill them."

"I don't blame you." He meant it. "Better them than yourself, though I'd be sorry to see you hang at Tyburn."

Her laugh really was delicious. "Thank you, Mr. Varlow. And I'm glad you stopped me. Though mind you"—she was looking down at the river again—"I think you lied to me. It's quite deep enough, isn't it?"

"Of course." And then, risking it, "Shall I give you a leg up?"

"Not tonight, thank you. Not if you think you can persuade Lady Forland about the part. I won't be made a mock of, but I like singing. It's heavenly music, Mr. Haydn's." She threw back her head, and moonlight illuminated the thin, pointed face, with its huge eyes and the undisciplined ringlets escaping from under the plumed hat. " 'Oh, mistress mine' " —her voice rivalled the nightingales— " 'where are you roaming?' " And down suddenly to earth. "They will be wondering, won't they?"

"Where you're roaming? I suppose they will." He was loath to end this strange, promising, moon-drenched scene, but turned, beside her, to start back towards the house. "Tell them it's all my fault. You came out for a breath of air, met me, and we got talking about Portugal. Of course you wanted all the latest news." He left it like that, hopefully. This was too promising a chance to let slip. He needed to know much more about this strange, quicksilver, stammering girl before he decided if he could use her.

"But I do." She took the bait. "You mean, you've been there recently?"

"I'm only just back. I work for the government, Miss Brett—for Lord Howick, the new Foreign Minister. You know—he took over from poor Mr. Fox. Oh, I serve him in a very modest capacity." More bitterness in his voice than he liked. "You could say I run his errands. My latest one was to

13

Lord Strangford, our representative in Lisbon. I'm sure I don't need to tell you, who are half Portuguese, that Portugal is our oldest ally. And one of the few we have left, just now, to help us fight Napoleon."

"Yes." He could hear the smile in her voice. "I can remember how Father and Uncle Miguel used to argue about it, back at the Castle on the Rock. And Grandmother too." This was a less happy memory. "Father thought the peace we made with France, back when I was a little girl, would give us—what did he call it?—peace in our time, he said. Freedom to expand the business, he talked about. Our wine business, you know?"

"Yes, I know. And very good wine, too."

"Thank you." Playing the great lady, she reminded him extraordinarily of her extraordinary grandmother. She sighed. "He wanted to come to England, to reopen the English House. It would have worked, I'm sure, if war hadn't broken out again so soon." She was trying to convince herself.

"Of course." He knew too much about her father to believe it for a moment. Reginald Brett had always been one for the easy choice, the quiet life. Surprising, really, that his daughter seemed to have so much character.

"How did you know I was half Portuguese?" Her question, harking back to something he had said earlier, was a new reminder that she was no fool, this girl with the stammer.

"My sister told me," he lied, and wondered if it was a mistake. "Besides, there's your name. Such a pretty name: Juana." He must not betray how much, in fact, he had made it his business to know about her.

"But that's not Portuguese"—she pounced on it—"it's Spanish, after my mother. Not that she was Spanish, thank God," she hurried to explain. "But she spelt it that way. It was some kind of a family thing." Again she laughed that delicious laugh. "If you've seen anything of them, you must know that my family—my family in Portugal—are given to 'things.' Oh dear"—it was a sigh from the heart—"how I wish I was back there."

"You really do?" Should he speak now? No, first he must write to her grandmother. After all, the final decision, like the final danger, was hers—and this girl's, he thought, with a qualm that surprised him. What was he doing, boggling at possible danger to an unknown girl? Ridiculous. He took her arm and felt it tremble, ever so slightly, through the silk

14

sleeve. "We must be getting in or my sister will have my head. But"—he found he really meant it—"you'll sing me the rest some time?"

" 'What is love, 'tis not hereafter,' " she sang, then laughed. "You'll hear enough of it if you stay."

"Oh, I shall stay," he said.

Lord Forland had built his theatre a little way from his house, and in the shape of a Greek temple. It was an admirable arrangement, said his wife, when the weather was fine. On this mild June night, the big doors behind the portico stood wide open letting out a blaze of light and a babble of voices, but no sound of music.

"Do you think they'll have missed me?" Gair could feel his companion shrink into herself.

"Well—since you're the heroine—"

"I? Good gracious, what an odd idea. Lady Forland—Olivia—is the heroine. I thought they would be working on her scene with Orsino for ages. Anyway—"

He could not help laughing. "Since you did not intend to return, it did not much matter? Don't look so frightened, Miss Brett. I'll stand by you." They had entered the broad pathway of light from the doorway and he saw that she was both taller and plainer than kind moonlight had suggested. Tall and strongly built himself, he had not noticed, before, that her head came nearly up to his. Her boy's costume suited her, he thought. In women's clothes she would be a beanpole. Was she always so pale? "Courage," he said in English. "It won't be as bad as you think."

"It will be worse. I shall have to speak English." This, in Portuguese, with the simplicity of despair. "I shall stutter."

"If you think you will," he said bracingly, "you're bound to. But don't worry: if you start, I'll interrupt you. It's 't' and 'd,' isn't it?" he went on in English.

"You've noticed!" She answered in the same language. "Yes, they're the only ones. If I can just keep away from them, I can manage." He felt her stiffen on his arm as they reached the wide doorway and saw the buzzing crowd of costumed figures inside. On the stage, his sister, Lady Forland, magnificent in Elizabethan ruff and sweeping black velvet, was appealing for silence. "Does no one know where she has gone?" she asked. "You, Mrs. Brett? She said nothing to you?"

"She never does." A faded blonde in the demure grey of a lady in waiting. Mrs. Brett spoke more angrily than she had

15

intended, looked angrier still as a result, and continued on a note of careful reason. "Did she not say anything to you, girls ... Daisy? Teresa?"

"No, Mamma." Two other waiting-women moved forward to speak in unison and Gair, noticing their likeness to their shrewish mother, thought he began to understand what the trembling girl on his arm had to endure.

"Vanessa!" He pitched his voice high enough to be heard across the hall. "Here's your truant. You must blame me for delaying her. But who could resist the chance of talking to Cesario in the moonlight?"

"Gair! I might have known it." But his sister's tone was indulgent. Three years older than he, she had been his first and was his most faithful slave. "Thank goodness you are here at last," she went on. "You can settle the point that's been vexing us. It's the duel scene between Sir Andrew Aguecheek and Cesario. There's no music for it, I don't know why. Perhaps Mr. Haydn never finished the opera; perhaps the poor Duchess of Devonshire lost it. The manuscript was tattered enough when it was found. But there it is. We can't leave the scene out; it's the cream of the whole jest."

"Quite impossible." Her husband emerged from the wings, Sir Andrew in flame-coloured hose. "I may not sing like Grassini, but I venture to think I can take a comic part without disgracing myself." He looked round for confirmation.

His guests murmured sycophantic agreement, while Gair racked his brains. Here was his chance, if he could only take advantage of it, to make Juana Brett his friend for life. He led her forward through the interested crowd and up the flight of steps on the left of the stage. "Here's your Viola," he said. "Or Cesario, rather. I found her outsinging the nightingale by the river and must congratulate you on your casting, Vanessa. But as to the duel scene: a pity, surely, to depart from Mr. Haydn's text? Why not mime it? Your audience, we hope, will be familiar enough with the play to understand, and surely your musicians can contrive some accompaniment, based on Mr. Haydn's own music, that will be more in keeping with the rest of the piece than a sudden intrusion of the spoken word?"

"Gair! You're a genius! Of course that's what we'll do. You'll not mind miming, will you, Miss Brett?" Without giving her time to answer, Vanessa turned back to Gair: "I only wish you could solve our other problem so easily." And

16

then, "Good God! How could I be so stupid! You'll do yourself! Don't you see the likeness?" She appealed to her husband, who was busy making practice passes with his foil at the potted plant in the corner of the stage.

"Likeness, my dear? I don't believe I quite understand you." His voice was querulous. "And as to mime: I'm not so sure about that. I've learned quite half my words already."

"And what a struggle that was." His wife did not quite manage to conceal impatience. "Be grateful, my love, to be spared the rest. You will be able now to give your full attention to the niceties of the duel itself—and, don't you see, I've found you your opponent. Gair will make an admirable Sebastian. He and Miss Brett are almost of a height; they're both dark and pale-skinned; It is but to dress them alike and they'll be a perfect pair of twins. How odd it is."

Turning to his companion, Gair saw angry colour along her prominent cheekbones to show that she had not missed the implication. He had always believed in facing facts, pleasant or otherwise. The fact of his own good looks was one he had early learned to take for granted and use at discretion. His appearance was, simply, one of the tools he must use to make his fortune. He might, at the lowest point of his London career, have gone hungry; he had never gone shabby. But the strong bones and dark, deep-set eyes that made him handsome made Juana Brett plain, and her unusual height, carried awkwardly, was the last straw.

Now her stepmother came forward to exclaim about the likeness and elaborate on the theme of Juana's height: "Quite unlike my own girls! Would you believe it, ma'am?" To Vanessa: "I have to order a whole extra length for her gowns!"

"What a disaster!" Vanessa's tone made it a ruthless snub. She turned back to Gair. "I'll have your costume made up tomorrow like Miss Brett's—but what are we to do about her hair? We had proposed to put it up under her cap but that will never do if she's to look like you. How could you have yours cut so short, Gair?"

" 'There was no thought of pleasing you' " he quoted, laughing, and then, to his silent companion: "Can I not prevail upon you to follow my example, Miss Brett? I have the strangest feeling that it would suit you admirably. Our expressive faces—since we must plead guilty to the likeness— were not meant to be obscured by ringlets—however stylish they may be."

17

His sister went off into a hoot of laughter. "I can just see you in ringlets, Gair!"

She was interrupted by an angry protest from Mrs. Brett: "And when I think of the trouble those curls cost me!" she concluded.

"Precisely," her stepdaughter spoke at last. "I'll have them cut d—d—"

"You'll do nothing of the kind." Angrily. "I'll not have you making yourself any more conspicuous than you are already! What! A shorn head to top off that beanpole figure of yours? What are you thinking of, child!" Behind her Gair could hear a chorus of amused agreement from her two daughters.

It made him angry, a most unusual thing. "She's thinking that style is more interesting than beauty, ma'am," he said. "And I, for one, agree with her. If you'll let my sister's man go to work on her, I think you will be surprised at the results. I suppose you have Antoine here with you?" This to Vanessa, with a wry memory of their bleak, north-country childhood when they cut each other's hair and, as often as not, had to take it in turns to go out in the winter, having only one warm cloak between them.

"Well, of course." Since she had married money, Vanessa had made the absolute best of it, and, he thought, the best, too, of her poor stick of a husband. "Antoine is a genius in his way," she told Mrs. Brett. "If you will let him look at your daughter's hair in the morning, I am sure he will know what is best to do."

"Your ladyship is too kind." Mrs. Brett would never say no to Lady Forland. "Say thank you to Lady Forland, Juana."

Juana Brett surprised them all, probably herself more than anyone. A long step forward into the middle of the stage and she swept a graceful bow to match her costume. "Your most obliged servant ma'am." She blushed up to the threatened ringlets as a little buzz of applause broke out among the audience in the body of the theatre.

"Very pretty," said Vanessa approvingly. "And you're quite right, Miss Brett, it's high time we got on with our rehearsal. We were waiting to do the scene where you and I first meet."

The hint of reproach in her tone was not lost on Gair. "And I was detaining her, selfishly, in the garden," he said. "Well, you must call it a brother's privilege, Vanessa."

She laughed. "I wonder if you mean my brother or Vio-

18

la's. Now, off stage all of you. The Countess awaits the Duke's messenger."

As the orchestra struck up, Gair retired to a secluded corner at the back of the hall with much to think about. A man of quick decisions, he was at once surprised and irritated to find himself so uncertain about Juana Brett. When she had first started to stammer, he had given up his whole mission as hopeless, only to discover, a few minutes later, that she was as fluent as he in Portuguese. And she longed to go back there. Telling himself this, he recognised the real basis of his doubt. It was not so much about her fitness for the job that he was worrying as about the possible —no, probable— danger to her.

It was fantastic. He, Gair Varlow, the devoted student of Machiavelli, the worshipper of enlightened self-interest, was worrying about possible danger to a lanky, stammering girl he had just met for the first time. What could be the matter with him? Anyway, was he not entitled to do what he liked with her? If he had not stopped her, she would be drowned by now, a modern Ophelia, floating to muddy death down the river.

Would she? Here was cause for thought. Impossible, of course, to tell how his Portuguese project might work out. His intention, so far as it was clear at all, was merely to use her as a tool, an informer; but suppose the situation developed unexpectedly ... He was old enough, by now, in the secret service, to know that that was how situations usually did develop. Suppose he should find himself compelled to take her, to some small extent, into his confidence, to make her his ally? And if, then, she should turn hysterical or even suicidal on his hands? It might be more than herself that she destroyed.

He was interrupted by her voice, rising clear and full above the violins:

> "Make me a willow cabin at your gate,
> And call upon my soul within the house;
> Write loyal cantons of contemned love,
> And sing them loud even in the dead of night."

No trace of a stammer now, as she stood, head thrown back, smiling a little, and her voice sent a hush through the chattering groups in the hall.

"But you should pity me."

The last notes died away and, once again, a buzz of spontaneous applause broke out so that Olivia had to pause on her cue.

Somehow, illogically, that settled it for Gair. He sat up late that night writing a long letter to old Mrs. Brett in Portugal.

CHAPTER 2

During the busy week of rehearsals that followed, Gair watched Juana Brett as closely and as unobtrusively as possible. This was easy enough, since her position as second heroine of the opera inevitably brought her constantly into the limelight, while his own short part as Sebastian left him plenty of time to lounge in the wings and watch her.

He soon decided that nothing could be much worse than her present situation. Her father was a cipher, whom Vanessa had dismissed as incapable of carrying even a walking-on part in her opera. Marrying for the second time late in life, Reginald Brett had surrendered himself, willingly enough it seemed, to the domination of his blond, bad-tempered Cynthia. The daughter herself of spendthrift aristocrats, she might, Gair thought, have forgiven her husband his connection with trade a good deal more easily if it had not been for his disastrous quarrel with his formidable mother, the head of the family. Insisting on reopening the London branch of the business, he had failed, pitifully and inevitably; had been cast off by his mother, and reduced to living on the tiny income inherited from his first wife. His second one had been, she suggested to anyone who cared to listen, much misled when she married him, and as for her two dowerless daughters, it was simply monstrous that he had never contrived to obtain any allowance for them from rich old Mrs. Brett. Daisy and Teresa were her pride and joy. Had not their father been the son of an Earl?

Gair did not think they actually tried to make their stepsister stammer, but the fact remained that she was always at her miserable worst in their company. Their names were no help: "t" and "d" were her bad letters, and here she was, with Daisy and Teresa for sisters. Someone, he thought, should, in mercy, have invented easier nicknames for them, but then who, in that family, ever thought about Juana!

And he had contrived, he recognised, to make matters much worse for her by his suggestion about her hair. Shorn of her girlish, unbecoming ringlets, she emerged not in the least as a beauty, but as a young woman of character. Her forehead was still too high, her nose too Roman, and her

21

cheekbones too pronounced, but when Antoine had arranged a negligently falling lock across the forehead—"Just like the Prince of Wales"—and brushed the short side-hair forward to give width to her lower face, the effect was, at least, arresting. She looked, Gair thought, like someone with whom one would like to talk, and then, inevitably, thought: a pity about the stammer. Surely, to arrange for her return to Portugal, whatever danger it might involve, would be the kindest thing he could do for her.

He thought this more than ever when he saw her family's reaction to her changed appearance. Her father, characteristically, noticed nothing, but her stepmother and sisters were something else again. Even Vanessa noticed their jealous teasing and took Gair aside to ask him to do something about it. "If they go on," she said, "they are likely to reduce her to a stuttering imbecile—and then what's to become of my opera? The Melbournes are coming, Gair, and the young Lambs, and Lady Jersey, and everyone who is anyone. I've let it be known that I've got a second Catalini. It must succeed, or I'll be a public laughing-stock. And it will be all your fault."

"Ungrateful! I found her for you, didn't I?"

"Yes, and you must keep her in line! If things go on as they are, she'll start stuttering when she sings, and then, good-bye! Gair, you must do something. Can't you make her fall in love with you, just a little, to take her mind off her troubles? You know there's not a girl can resist you, creature that you are! And I never could see why."

He made her a mock bow. "It's my charm, dearest sister."

"Well then, for God's sake use it. Put your spell on her, so she thinks of nothing else."

"No." It came out more violent than he meant and he hurried into further explanation. "Don't you see that for me to pay her any marked attention would merely make those cats of sisters more jealous than ever?"

She sighed. "You're right, of course. Then what can we do? Gair, don't laugh, it's serious! I can't have Lady Melbourne and her party, and Lady Cahir triumphing at my expense. You know what their theatricals are like."

"Oh, poor Vanessa, is it so important to you?" Suddenly he felt years older than his elder, successful sister.

But her opera was equally important to him. It was not part of his plan that Juana should be badgered into collapse.

"Don't look so anxious," he went on. "For you, Vanessa, I'll make the supreme sacrifice."

"Oh? And what may that be?"

"Why, to make love to those comic-opera stepsisters."

"Gair, you're a genius! But—both of them?"

"At once. It's the only way. They'll be so busy being jealous of each other, they'll forget all about poor little Cinderella."

"Cinderella? Oh—you mean Juana. I must say, Gair, 'little' is hardly the word I would choose to describe her."

"Ah, but then you're such a little thing yourself, Van."

She smiled at the childhood nickname and plunged into a question she had been wanting to ask him. "Gair, what is all this? Why did you want me to invite Juana Brett?"—she held up a warning hand—"Don't tell me it was all for my sake, because I won't believe you. Though I am grateful, mind. If all goes well, my *Twelfth Night* should be the talk of the town. But I know you too well to think you did it just for me. Besides, I've seen you watching her while you thought no one was looking. Not"—she paused for a moment—"not at all as if you cared about her. More as if she was some kind of a specimen, something you were studying. What are you doing, Gair?"

"Trying to earn my living, love."

She looked more puzzled than ever. "But—you said you wouldn't make love to her. Besides, so far as I know, there's no chance of that old tartar of a grandmother's relenting and giving her a dowry. I must say," she went on, "I don't blame her for washing her hands of Reginald Brett. He must have been a disaster as a man of business."

"He must indeed." Gair found himself oddly grateful for the change of subject. It was not like him to have missed a whole range of possibilities, but here, suddenly, he saw that he had. Juana Brett and a dowry? Well, nothing was more likely. If only Mrs. Brett reacted as he imagined she would to the letter he had written her, Juana would certainly have her chance of one. And, judging by the rest of the strange family who lived in the castle on the cliff, it would be a good chance. Nobody knew what old Mrs. Brett was worth, but, he suspected, most guesses would be less rather than more than the real total.

So, here was a possible heiress, and one with the added advantage, from his point of view, that she was unaware of the possibility. He had always meant, as a last resource, to

23

marry a fortune if he failed to make one. And here he was, twenty-six, and with his foot still only on the first rung of the ladder. Why hesitate?

"In a brown study?" Vanessa's voice roused him.

"Yes, I'm trying to decide whether to begin with Daisy or Teresa, God help me." But not Juana. Curious to find himself so decided about that.

He made it, in each case, the lightest of flirtations: a flattering word to Daisy balanced by a quick pressure of Teresa's hand; a turn in the garden with one, a long after-dinner tête-à-tête with the other. It worked to admiration. The two girls, once united in baiting their stepsister, now turned their small-arms fire against each other, while Gair caught their mother's eye, once or twice, fixed on him with a look of speculation he did not much like.

But he shrugged that off. He had dodged more formidable matchmakers in his time. Besides, realist as always, he knew himself to be too small a fish for Mrs. Brett's ambitions. So he went on ogling Daisy while he turned the page of Teresa's music or, during rehearsals, standing devotedly behind whichever one of them gave him the easiest view of Juana.

The mime scene was coming along admirably, since, being Lord Forland's favourite, it got very much more than its fair share of rehearsing. Watching his sister yield gracefully to her husband on this point, in order to get her own way on a score of others, Gair found himself oddly sickened by the whole business. If this was what marrying money entailed, was the game worth the candle?

"Are you happy, Van?" He caught her, for a brief moment, alone in the deserted theatre.

"Happy? What an odd question! And from you, of all people, who taught me to look always to the main chance. Of course I'm happy." She said it almost angrily. "My own theatre—everything I've ever wanted—and, my God, have I told you? Sheridan has invited himself to come tomorrow. I've a million things still to do, and you talk to me of happiness!" And then, on a milder note, "But I'm grateful to you, just the same, Gair. Your prima donna is going to justify it all, don't you think?"

"Mine?"

"Well, of course. I don't know what you did to her that first night in the moonlight, and I'm not asking, either, but anyone with half an eye can see that she sings for you alone. It's quite another matter when you are not in the audience."

And then, reflectively, "She's no fool, for all the stammering, that little Brett. She knows just what you're doing with those stepsisters of hers. I've seen her watching. I was afraid, at first, that it would spoil everything, but not at all; she takes it to herself. And I don't blame her. I've seen you watching her, too. You talk to me of happiness! You're not going to do anything foolish, Gair?"

"I? Good God, no. But are you sure?"

"Of course I'm sure. Remember, the looker-on sees most of the game. And now, I must go and read the riot act to those musicians of mine. Did you hear how they dragged in the last act?"

She left him with much to think of. It was true: he had wondered how Juana would take his advances to her stepsisters, but it had never for a moment occurred to him that she might fathom their real purpose. If she had, she must be accepted, more than ever, as a young woman to be reckoned with. And an ally worth having? At all events, if Vanessa was right (and she usually was on such questions) it should make matters in Portugal much easier, if he ever contrived to get Juana there. An intelligent ally, devoted to him ... what more could he ask?

And yet, a curious cloud of anxiety hung round him, all through the frenzied last-minute rehearsals next day. Luckily Sebastian's part in the opera was even slighter than in the original play, so that this state of abstraction was not observed. He merely had to stand about, in doublet and hose, ready for his few, brief, and silent appearances. He had plenty of time to congratulate Daisy on the new tilt she had given to her head-dress and to beg Teresa to save him one dance when the opera was over. And, disconcertingly, having done so, to catch Juana's amused eye taking it all in. What a miscalculation to think that because she stuttered, she must be stupid. She was quicksilver, gunpowder perhaps. Remembering the quick changes of their first meeting—the passionate would-be suicide flashing into a flood of Portuguese bad language—he found himself thinking of another of Shakespeare's heroines. She is "all air and fire," he told himself, and wished, as he did so, that it did not take so long to get an answer from Portugal.

Had he written enthusiastically enough to old Mrs. Brett? Suppose she were to change her mind, now, when everything was so well in train? It did not bear thinking about.

"Sebastian!" Vanessa's angry voice roused him from his

25

dream. "I thought, at least, we could rely on you." And he hurried forward to receive Sir Andrew Aguecheek's blows and return them in good measure.

The rehearsal was going well, he thought a little later. If the final performance, this evening, was anything like as good, Vanessa need not fear even Lady Melbourne's sharp tongue. They were working up for the finale now. It was almost time for the moment of silent recognition between him and Viola, the quick embrace, before she turned to confront the Duke and Olivia and join with them in Haydn's delicious trio:

> *"Now at last the truth is showing*
> *Now our happiness is growing*
> *Cups with gladness overflowing . . ."*

Who had written the words, he wondered, and who had explained them to old Papa Haydn whose knowledge of English, surely, had been fairly limited?

Incapable of singing a note himself, he could still recognise the extraordinary quality of Juana's voice as it soared and swooped towards the oddly moving moment of silence when Olivia would turn and hold out her hand to Sebastian, and he must step forward to make up the quartet in appearance, if not in song. There: the three voices died away, Vanessa turned towards him, and as he moved forward to take her hand and give it a congratulatory squeeze, he heard, from the two ladies in waiting who stood behind her, a carrying whisper: "I'll wager a pair of French gloves she sticks on 'triumph of delight,' " said Daisy. And, "Hush!" said Teresa.

Vanessa's hand was rigid in his own. He did not dare turn towards where Juana stood beside Orsino. The orchestra picked up the tune again. Vanessa squeezed his hand hard, and began:

> *"Now the day has banished night,*
> *Future joys are shining bright*
> *In our triumph of delight . . ."*

Oh, God, thought Gair, as Orsino came in on his cue, why had he never noticed that fatal line, combining Juana's bad letters? But, up to now, she had come through it without the slightest hesitation. "I don't stammer when I sing," she had told him, and, so far, it had been true. But now, after that fatal whisper which, surely, she must have heard?

" 'Now the day has banished night,' " her voice wove in with the other two and he breathed a sigh of relief as the hurdle of "day" was passed. They were all singing together, each line repeated over and over again, and he held his breath, waiting, until first Olivia, then Orsino came in for the climax: "In our triumph of delight." This was where they all took hands to move downstage together. He had to reach for Juana's, and felt it shiver in his own. She had heard. Ridiculous to have entertained the hope that she might not have. " 'Triumph of delight,' " sang Olivia, and " 'Triumph of delight,' " Orsino echoed her. Juana dropped Gair's hand and turned to face him. "I can't," she said quietly, her face blanched under the make-up. "I can't." Her lips were trembling. In a moment, he knew, she was going to turn and rush from the hall—back to the river? Back to where he had found her a week ago?

He caught her hand again. "Yes you can." The orchestra dwindled into silence. "If we change the words."

"Change them?" This was Vanessa, grasping at straws.

"Well, of course. I don't know what Grub Street hack put them together, but we don't have to treat them as sacred Shakespeare, do we? Just think about them for a moment! 'Triumph of delight,' indeed! 'I'll rhyme you so, eight years together; dinners and suppers and sleeping hours excepted.' As, for instance," he struck an attitude:

> *"Now the clouds no more are grey,*
> *Now our cares are flown away,*
> *Evermore keep holiday . . ."*

"Or, better still"—he had belatedly become aware of that fatal "-day"—"how about 'Evermore our hearts are gay'? I won't say it's great poetry, but it's not much worse than the original."

"It's better for singing," said Vanessa. "Don't you agree, Miss Brett? I never did like that run on night and delight. Let's see, how does it go? 'Now the clouds no more are grey—' " She sang it through once, unaccompanied, then signalled imperiously to the orchestra. "Once more!"

This time it went perfectly, except that Orsino mixed up his words and ended by rhyming bright with grey. But, "Good," said Vanessa with finality. "We'll leave it there. It's

27

going to be a great success. Be sure and get some rest this afternoon, Miss Brett."

"Yes, Lady Forland."

Her tone alarmed Gair. "Let's take a turn in the garden first, Cesario. A breath of air will help you rest. No need to change your costume"—he anticipated her protest—"the audience won't begin to arrive for hours yet, will they, Vanessa?"

"Of course not." She could be relied on to take her cue. "Yes, do go out for some air, Miss Brett. I'm afraid I've been working you much too hard." As Gair led Juana towards the side door, he saw his sister bearing down on Daisy and Teresa and spared a moment to feel sorry for them.

It was hot in the garden. Vanessa's prized roses drooped scentless in the sun. And worse still, other couples had had the same idea and were strolling among the formal beds, pausing here and there to admire, or to help themselves to a bud or two. Gair could feel the tension mounting in his companion. "I'll take you to a favourite place of mine." He spoke in Portuguese. "Have you seen Vanessa's maze?"

"No." Even in Portuguese, her voice sounded strained.

"It should be cool there. Or at least cooler." He led the way through the walled kitchen garden, where a few of Lord Forland's army of gardeners were busy among asparagus and early peas.

The maze, when they reached it, was deserted, its high yew walls dark against the sun. "Don't be afraid I'll get you lost." He opened the wicket gate for her. "Vanessa let me into the secret when she had it remade. It was practically a wilderness when she married Forland. It's quite easy when you know the way." And he led her rapidly to the heart of the maze, where Vanessa had built a tiny Chinese pavilion with bamboo seats.

But Juana would not sit down. "You'll have to explain to Lady Forland," she said. "I can't do it."

"Can't do what?" He would not understand her.

"Sing tonight. I can't, I tell you. I'd only ruin it ... for everyone. You must see that. Now I've started stammering when I sing, it's hopeless." Hearing her, furiously fluent in Portuguese, it was hard to believe in the stutter.

But this was worse even than he had feared. "Nonsense." Angrily. "You're imagining things. When did you stammer?"

"Oh—you saved me, and don't think I'm not grateful. But you know I could not have sung that line as it stood."

"You could have, if your sisters had not put the idea into your head."

28

"Perhaps. But they have, you see. It's no good now. I can't."

"You must." Which argument should he use? Fatal to pick the wrong one. And useless to speak to her of the success or failure of the opera. That would merely be to make matters worse. He bent down to pick a sprig of sweet-scented geranium from the tiny formal garden and hand it to her. "Why do your sisters hate you?" he asked.

"Daisy and Teresa?" She could pronounce their names in Portuguese. "Hate me?"—surprised. "They don't. It's just ... I don't know—a habit they've got into."

"Not a very nice one. I wouldn't be in their shoes for anything just now."

"What do you mean?"

"Didn't you see? My sister was bearing down on them with all sails set. If you don't sing tonight, they're going to be in such disgrace with her—and, in consequence, with your mother—"

"Not my mother!"

"I'm sorry. Your stepmother. She's not going to be very pleased with any of you, is she?" No need to elaborate on it.

"I can't help it. I've told you: I can't do it. Miss Corson will have to take the part."

Miss Corson was her understudy. "You know she can't do it," he said. "The whole opera stands or falls by Viola. Without you, it falls."

"Not half so horribly as if I try and fail. Just think of it—"

"Don't," he interrupted her ruthlessly. "That's the worst thing you can do. Think instead what this means to me." He had tried one line and got nowhere. Now he must try another, a far more risky one.

"To you? What in the world do you mean?"

"Did you not wonder, you and your family, how you came to be invited here?"

"Of course. You should have heard them. They're still baffled." She sat down at last on the shady bench and looked up at him eagerly. "Can you explain it?" The tension was going out of her.

"Easily, since it was my doing."

"Yours! But why?"

Here was the crucial point. A lie? The truth? Or, as so often, a little of each? "I wanted to meet you," he said, still playing for time.

29

"Me?" There was something rather touching about her amazement.

"Yes, you. Is that so remarkable? I know your grandmother, I told you. She's talked to me about you." And that was true enough. "And about your voice. She made me curious. I wondered how, with your background, your breeding, you would have settled in England."

"You know now." Bitterly.

"Yes. I'm sorry. But that's it, you see." Now, at last, he saw his way clear. "Mrs. Brett asked me to write to her, to let her know how you got on. I think she feels anxious about you, perhaps even regrets the quarrel with your father. I was at my wit's end, secluded as you live, to think how to meet you. Then my sister mentioned her project of this opera and her difficulty over a Viola. She had heard of your singing, but it was I who persuaded her to invite you and convinced her it was worth—forgive me—the plague of having to invite your mother and sisters too. If you fail her now, it's the last favour she'll do me."

"You mean, you did it all for me? Without even having met me? You took such a chance?"

"Not such a chance as all that." This was precarious ground again. "I'd made some enquiries about you, you see. Your grandmother asked me to. I knew that your voice was something quite out of the way." He paused.

"And that I stammered." She was on to it like lightning. "My God, you must wish now that I had never been born."

"Nothing of the kind. Believe me, Miss Brett, whatever happens tonight, I'll never regret having met you." Dangerous! This was to walk across an earthquake. "I'm a poor man"—he was picking his words with exquisite care—"I'm, simply, penniless, with my own way to make in the world." There, that should do it. "But—don't think I'll ever, for an instant, regret having met you."

"Thank you."

She was oddly mature for her seventeen years, he thought, or did she simply not understand how near he had sailed to a declaration? No. He saw the rush of colour transform her serious, downturned face. She understood, but was too much the woman of the world to admit to understanding.

Now she looked up to meet his eyes with her clear, dark ones. "Lady Forland will be angry with you, if I don't sing?"

"Angry! She won't forgive me. Well, can you blame her? I persuaded her to this. Miss Brett, if you won't do it for your own sake, do it for mine. You can, you know, if you decide to."

"You think so?"

"I'm sure of it." He made himself meet her doubtful gaze steadily, confidently. More confidently than he felt.

The three voices met at last, to sing in unison:

"Now the clouds no more are grey,
Now our cares are flown away,
Evermore our hearts are gay."

The four of them were downstage, hand in hand, as the first crash of applause broke over them. The members of the orchestra had stood up, their instruments forgotten, applauding wildly. Gair bent, in a spontaneous gesture that would trouble him in retrospect, to kiss Juana's hand, then pulled her forward for her ovation.

CHAPTER 3

If Juana had hoped for another *tête-à-tête* with Gair Varlow—one of congratulation this time—she was to be disappointed. The party broke up next morning, and he was one of the first to leave, having received, he told Vanessa, an urgent summons from Lord Howick. "News from Portugal, I expect." He was saying good-bye in her luxurious boudoir.

"Bad news? Do you think the French are really going to attack them?"

"Why would Howick send for me if it was good? Don't be surprised if you don't hear from me for a while."

"You'll not be going back there?"

"How should I know till I've seen Howick? Don't worry, Van. You know how well I take care of myself."

"Yes." Doubtfully. And then, "Gair, you'll say good-bye to that poor child?"

"Miss Brett?" He would not pretend to misunderstand her. "Why should I? She'll be thronged with flatterers this morning."

"For the moment. Yes, she is. And stuttering at them woefully. But, Gair, you can't go without telling her how well she did. It was all for you, and you know it."

He looked at her sombrely. "All the more reason for not seeking her out this morning. I said quite enough yesterday. Too much, perhaps."

"You've never committed yourself?"

"Good God, no. You should know me better than that. But"—he paid her the compliment of being almost as ruthlessly honest with her as he was with himself—"she might just possibly think that I had."

"Oh, Gair! The poor child. And when you think what she has to go home to. Her stepmother and those sisters of hers aren't going to forgive her last night's success in a hurry. I wouldn't be in her shoes, this next month or so, for all the gold in the Brazils. And if you disappoint her too . . ."

"What else can I do?" But she had given him pause. If all went well, and he did want to use Juana in Portugal, he must

32

not find her reduced to a stuttering wreck. "Would it help, do you think, if I was to go out of my way to say a fond farewell to the ugly sisters?"

"Poor things; they're not ugly at all." She thought it over. "I suppose it might, but it won't make Juana any happier."

"I'm not so sure. She's no fool." He was tired of the whole business now, this women's work, and anxious to be back in London, learning what new development in Portugal had induced Lord Howick to send for him so urgently. "There's no satisfying you today, Van. At least, admit I've made your opera the success of the season."

"Yes." She laughed with pure pleasure. "I wish you could have heard that old cat, Lady Melbourne, congratulating me. As if every kind word cut her mouth in the speaking! Don't think I'm not grateful, Gair, even if you did do it for your own inscrutable reasons, as you do everything. I only wish I could do something for you in return, but you know how it is ..."

"I know, Van," He did indeed. When she had made her brilliant marriage, one of her first and characteristic projects had been to get Lord Forland to provide for her beloved brother. She had soon discovered her mistake. Indulging her every whim, Forland would do nothing for Gair. Was he jealous? Or afraid, as he claimed, of being mocked for carrying what he inelegantly described as "a parcel of hangers-on"? It made no difference. Gair, whom she had loved and protected as a child, must come to her house like any ordinary visitor and take care not to outstay his welcome.

"Don't fret, Van." Gair was always quick to sense what she was thinking. "I'll come about in the end; see if I don't. And in the meanwhile, I will say good-bye to your protégée like the best of brothers ... and to her sisters too, rather differently."

"My protégée? I thought she was yours."

"Good God, no."

He found Juana, as he had predicted, the centre of an admiring crowd, and felt a moment of pure fright when her eyes caught his. He had got her into this, she seemed to be saying, let him get her out. Sighing inwardly, he made his way through the crowd towards her, with a greeting here and an apology there to keep it all casual. Coming up, at last, from behind her, he found her fending off Sheridan's enthusiasm as best she might. Sherry wanted to introduce her to

33

his friends at the Opera House. "You'll be the greatest thing since Mrs. Billington, Miss Brett. Why, the young Roscius will be nothing to it."

"But, Mr. Sheridan, I can't."

"Nonsense. Of course you can. I've heard you."

"But that was d—d—" Fatally, she stuck on the "d," writhed on it for a minute, then looked up at Sheridan and said, quite simply, "You see."

Sherry was a kind man. He took her hand in his. "I may see, my dear, but I don't pretend to understand." And then, with obvious relief, "Ah, Varlow, do I hear you've had news from town this morning? Any word of poor Fox?"

"No. And, surely, in his case, no news must be good news." Gair turned to Juana. "Miss Brett, I am come to thank you for the great pleasure you gave me—gave us all—last night, and, alas, to take my leave."

"So soon?" For an instant, her face was a disappointed child's. Then, admirably, she rallied, smiled up at him, and half-sang, half-whispered the words from the clown's song that had almost been lost, last night, in the storm of applause: "But that's all one, our play is done—" She stopped, blushing, as she remembered the next line.

"You could please me any day of the week, Miss Brett." Sheridan came gallantly to the rescue. "But I too must take my leave. There was talk when I left town that poor Fox may have to be tapped for his dropsy. I'd not like to be away ..." His departure brought on a little storm of leave-taking, in the course of which Gair contrived to find Daisy and Teresa, irritated ciphers on the fringe of their sister's success.

"I could not leave without saying good-bye to *you*." The emphasis, the little extra pressure on each hand was exactly right. Now what? "I shall count on seeing you next time I visit my sister." He was pleased with that, suggesting, as it did, both that he wanted to meet them, and that Vanessa would invite them again. Turning back towards Juana, he saw that she had been buttonholed by Lady Melbourne herself. "Make my adieus to your sister," he went on. "She is too exalted company for me."

It was only halfway back to London that he was swamped by an incomprehensible, an absurd feeling of loss because he had not had a chance to press Juana's strong brown hand in farewell as he had her sisters' too-willing ones.

34

The Bretts left soon afterwards, and Daisy and Teresa spent the short drive home in making sure, as they said, that their sister had not been totally spoiled by the flattery she had received. They declared themselves vastly amused at Mr. Sheridan's suggestion that she might become another Mrs. Billington and coined a good many phrases to describe her success at Drury Lane: the stuttering diva was one they liked, or the prima stammer.

Normally, Juana would have been in tears by the time they turned in at the shabby entrance to their own house. Today, she surprised her tormentors by merely smiling and saying nothing. She was busy with thoughts of her own. Of course, it had been disappointing that he had not contrived to say good-bye to her (there was, at the moment, only one "he" so far as she was concerned) but Daisy and Teresa had made a point of delivering his message, suggesting as it did, to them, that it had not been worth the effort to seek her out.

She read it quite differently. It was merely another instance of Gair's extraordinary consideration for her, of the instinctive understanding that had done so much to get her through the ordeal of the last few days. Sitting silent in her uncomfortable position, bodkin between her sisters, she was serenely occupied in going back over every word, every intonation, every look from each of their meetings.

She would probably never see him again. That had been clear enough from what he had said to her yesterday in the maze. But whatever happened to her (or for that matter to him) she would always know that he, Gair Varlow, the most attractive man she had ever met, would have liked ... if only things had been different ... She blushed, boggling at finishing the sentence, even to herself, and came out of her abstraction to hear her sisters arguing heatedly about which of them Gair had preferred.

"We shall see when he comes to call," said Teresa.

"Mr. Varlow call on us?" Mr. Brett surprised them all. "You must be moon-mad, you two. Gair Varlow call on two dowerless country girls! Do you take no notice whatever of what goes on around you? Or do you contrive to see only what you want to? Surely, anyone can see that young Varlow is on the catch for just such a lucky marriage as his sister made. And with her behind him, not a doubt in the world that he will bring it off. No, no—" The carriage had stopped now, and he rose, as the gardener-turned-groom let down the steps, to help his wife alight. "Don't waste your valuable time quarrelling about Gair Varlow, girls."

The pronouncement added the last touch to the gloom of that return. After Forland House with its trim shrubberies and exquisitely tended lawns, there was no denying that their own straggling laurel bushes and grass-grown drive presented a depressing enough spectacle. Indoors, it was no better. The narrow hallway smelled of damp, and cabbage, and stale orris root. "I wish we hadn't gone," said Daisy petulantly, throwing down her bonnet and gloves.

And, "I'm not sure you're not right, my dear," said her stepfather.

Even Juana, creeping away, unnoticed, to the privacy of her tiny room, found herself tainted with the general depression, and tried hard to pretend that it had nothing to do with what her father had had to say about Gair Varlow. The idea of his hanging out for a rich wife did not at all fit in with her picture of him. She sat for a long time staring at nothing before she could decide to her own satisfaction that her father was merely taking his usual refuge in cynicism. It was a fortune of his own making that Gair Varlow was after, and why not? After all (even she could not help contrasting this bleak little room with her luxurious bedroom at Forland House) it was no use pretending that money was not important. And she drifted off into a series of day-dreams, in which Gair made a fortune in India, went to sea and captured a Spanish treasure-ship, or even joined the church and was presented with a handsome living by his brother-in-law. This, suddenly, was too much for her: Gair Varlow in the church! She giggled to herself, took off her bonnet, and went downstairs.

In the next few weeks she needed all the comfort that daydreaming could give. The visit to Forland House had had a profoundly disturbing effect on the whole household. Mrs. Brett grumbled more than usual about their straitened circumstances. And even her husband found himself missing anew the civilised living he had lost when he quarrelled with his rich mother. If he had not insisted on coming to England, he might be a rich man now. At least, he would be living in the slovenly luxury he remembered as home.

So it was with a pang of almost unbearable excitement that he opened the postbag one wet July morning and saw a letter in his mother's unmistakable angular hand.

His wife had noticed it too and hardly gave him time to decipher the handwriting which had grown a good deal less legible since he had last seen it. "Well! What is it? What does she say? Has she come to her senses at last?" Mrs. Brett's staccato questions brought the girls' attention to bear on him too.

"In a manner of speaking." He knew, only too well, how angry the letter's message was going to make her. "She's been ill," he went on pacifically.

"Has she?" Cynthia Brett did not try to conceal the satisfaction this gave her. "And I suppose she has discovered what a useless set your brothers and sisters are. And about time, too!! Though I must say, by all reports, this is hardly the moment to be moving to Portugal. Suppose the rumors are true: suppose Bonaparte invades: What then? I'm not sure that I would be justified in taking my girls there. But after all, I suppose, blood is thicker than water. What does she offer, Mr. Brett? I'm not going to live in that drafty old castle of hers, that's one thing certain. If she wants us, she must find us a suitable house of our own in the district. Sintra would be best, by what I've heard. There's said to be quite a civilised English society there. Not like that grim castle by the sea where you grew up. It always sounded a dead and alive hole to me. Well: why don't you answer me? What does she say, Mr. Brett?"

He knew her too well to point out that she had hardly given him a chance to speak. "I was waiting to tell you, my dear," he said mildly. "It's not precisely what you think." And then, quickly, to get it over with. "It's Juana she wants."

"Juana!" His wife snatched the letter from him and read it through, literally trembling with rage as she struggled with the difficult handwriting. "Been ill indeed! Overeating again, I have no doubt. Needs someone to write her letters for her: well, that's true enough! I never saw such a scrawl. But what about those boys of your brother's? Oh, I see!" She turned the page. "They spend their time in Lisbon, do they? At the bullfights, I expect." And then, with a snort, "Lonely, is she! Wants female company! Tired of that crazy daughter at last? And never a word; never so much as a message for me! Not a word about my Daisy, my Teresa! I was never so affronted in my life. Of course you'll say no, Mr. Brett. It's not only an insult; it's nonsensical. Send Juana! A child of seventeen, who's never even been to London alone. And a stammerer, too. Just imagine her: 'P—p—please, sir, where's the p—p—packet for P—P—' "

"But, my dear, consider a little ..." His eyes sought Juana's in mute apology. "We don't want to do anything to make Mother angrier than she is already. Just think: if she liked having Juana—it might change everything—" And then, belatedly, "Would you like to go, Juana?"

"Oh, Father!" In her excitement, she had hardly noticed her stepmother's mockery. "Back to Portugal! To the Castle on the Rock! More than anything in the world." And then, conscience-stricken she jumped up to give him a quick, shy kiss. "Forgive me. That sounds heartless, d—d—" She gave it up. "That's it, you see," this in her quick, easy Portuguese. "I don't stammer there. Don't think I won't hate to leave you—" If there was the slightest emphasis on the pronoun, he did not notice it. "But—I was happy there—"

"Hoity-toity—" her stepmother cut in ruthlessly. "I thought we had agreed, Miss, that it was the worst of ill manners for you and your father to speak Portuguese in front of the girls and me."

"I'm sorry, Mama, but you see, I d—d—"

"She doesn't stammer in Portuguese, you know, my love," put in her father. "She was merely saying she would like to go, if we could see our way to sparing her. Do you think you could, my dear? I know what a useful girl Juana is about the house."

"Thank you, Father." Juana's eyes were suddenly full of tears. "Of course I won't go if you need me here"—this in English, picking her words with care—"but if you could manage ..."

"Oh, as to that! As to managing!" Mrs. Brett was on her high horse again. "I don't believe my Daisy and my Teresa are altogether incapable girls. I'm sure we can manage well enough without Juana if you really mean to let her go."

"I think I must, my dear." He was relieved to find it so easy. "My mother writes as if she needs her badly. Only, I wish I knew what to do for the best. Suppose the French do invade Portugal? There was a good deal of talk about it at Forland House. You're English, Juana, don't forget. You might even find yourself a prisoner of war like the poor souls who were in France when the war broke out again in 1803. I don't know whether I should let you go. And yet, I don't want to offend your grandmother."

"Of course not." Cynthia Brett had made up her mind. "I never knew such a man for making mountains of molehills. The French invade Portugal indeed! Why should they? There's nothing there for them."

"I don't know." He turned, wretchedly undecided, to Juana. "What do you think, child?"

"If you'll let me, I want to go, Father." This, carefully, in English. "If there really is going to be trouble, it's all the more reason, isn't it, why Grandmother may need me? And we'll be safe enough out there at the Castle on the Rock, surely?" She did not quite manage to keep the eagerness out of her voice.

"Quite heartless," said Mrs. Brett. "And after all I've done for you. But how in the world shall we get her there, Mr. Brett?"

"I shall take her to Falmouth myself and put her in charge of the captain of the packet. If they don't roll out the red carpet for her on board, things have changed a great deal since I last made the voyage. The Bretts are not quite unknown, you know." And then, seeing that this had made her angry all over again, "If you can really spare Juana, my dear, I think we should send her as soon as we can."

"Of course we must. The sooner the better, if you ask me. And if they find her shabby, she can just explain to the old—to her grandmother about the straitened circumstances we live in, and about my poor girls with no dowries. Why, depend upon it, that handsome young man Gair Varlow would have proposed for one or other of them long since, if he had not known them to be poor as church mice. You'll explain it all to your grandmother, won't you, Juana, my love?"

"I'll try, Mamma."

Juana did her best to conceal how she felt about going back to Portugal. But only now, when it was almost over, did she dare admit to herself what a misery her life in England had been. Her own fault, of course. If she had not been such a self-contained little oddity, her stepsisters might not have made her their butt. And if her Uncle Prospero had not encouraged her, back in the Castle on the Rock, to read wide and freely in the shabby, well-stocked library, she might not have irritated their governesses so much. But there had been something, she saw now, quite fatal about her combination of learning and ignorance. No wonder if Daisy and Teresa had joined one governess after another in making her life a misery with taunts that still echoed in her ears. And then all of a sudden she had started to grow, and found herself towering over plump Daisy and tiny Teresa. Hard to see, now, why they had resented that so much, but it had merely accentuated her general differentness. Even her name had been a cause of friction. They had wanted her to spell it the English way, and she had refused, in floods of passionate tears, to lose this one last link with her dead Portuguese mother.

Well, it was all over now. Her small box was strapped and ready. Her stepmother and sisters had said good-bye the night before, since she and her father must make an early start in order to pick up the Falmouth coach. She took one last look round the room she had hated, blew out her candle, and was asleep before the raw smell of tallow had ebbed from round her.

The journey was delicious adventure all the way and it was only when they reached Falmouth and found that the wind was fair and the weekly packet just ready to sail that her courage failed her for a moment.

"Father?"

"Yes, my poppet?" He had never dared use the old pet name at home.

"Say I'm right to go."

"I hope so." He was plagued with anxieties of his own. The talk in the Falmouth coach had not been reassuring, nor had the amazed glances that had greeted his admission that Juana was sailing to Portugal by herself. But of course it was all rumour and moonshine. Mr. Fox and his friends were men of peace. Lord Lauderdale was in Paris, as everyone knew, negotiating with Bonaparte's government. It was only a question of time before the armistice was signed. So why were their fellow travellers so gloomy?

Juana was looking at him anxiously. "You don't mind my going, Father?"

"Mind? Of course not. After all, we must think of your poor grandmother. I only wish the news was more encouraging."

"Oh, that." She had a girl's healthy disregard for world affairs. "You've been listening to those dismal men on the coach! Don't worry about me. After all, I am half Portuguese. And you know everyone loves Grandma Brett. Even if the French should invade, we'll be safe in the Castle on the Rock."

"Of course you will." He was glad to let her convince him. It was only on the coach going back to London that he realised just how much he was going to miss her.

CHAPTER 4

No French privateer interrupted their safe, swift voyage. Juana woke on the fifth morning to sense a difference in the ship's motion. Sitting up in her narrow cot-bed, she peered out of the porthole to see that they had passed Fort Saint Julian and were well into the first narrow reach of the Tagus. Though it was only mid-August, the hills were golden brown already, throwing into relief their fringe of white-sailed wind-mills. Now, as they slid along by the left bank of the river, she saw a country-house whose brilliant white stucco and blue woodwork stood out against the luxuriant green of a well-watered garden. They must be almost up to Belem. She threw herself into her clothes and hurried up on deck in time to see the Tower of Belem ahead, like some fantastic piece of confectionery served up for dessert at Forland House.

A sharp order and a scurry of barefoot sailors across planks already hot with morning sun reminded her that incoming ships must lie to and wait for clearance from the Tower. As the sails came down and the ship's pace slowed, she stood quietly at the rail, keeping out of the way and watching for remembered landmarks. There was the towering monastery of the Geronimos. She shuddered, cold in the hot sun. Somewhere along the shore here they had built the scaffolds, years ago, after the Tavora plot (if it had been a plot) against the life of Joseph I. It had been a story to be told, in whispers, at twilight, to a frightened child: the lonely road, the King's carriage, the volley of shots that wounded but did not kill. And then the long sinister silence.

When the vengeance of Joseph's formidable minister, Pombal, had struck at last, it had been cataclysmic, horrible, like the earthquake that had preceded the so-called plot. The families of Tavora and d'Aveiro had perished, dreadfully, on the scaffold here at Belem. Juana's own mother, a child at the time and merely a remote cousin of the Duke d'Aveiro, had been lucky to be immured in a convent outside Oporto. She had not emerged into ordinary life until Joseph's death and Pombal's consequent fall from power. Joseph's daughter, Queen Maria, had freed Pombal's surviving victims, and indeed her present madness was rumoured to be partly due to her doubts about the authenticity of the famous attempt on her father's life.

But the d'Aveiro family name of Mascarenhas was still an unlucky one. When the Tavoras were cleared by Queen Maria's courts, the Duke d'Aveiro's guilt was confirmed. His son was reduced to living on Tavora charity, and there was not much future for his kinswoman in the covent at Oporto. So the kind nuns were delighted when a young Englishman, Reginald Brett, on business there for his mother, had seen Juana de Mascarenhas, just emerged, like a gentle moth into the daylight, fallen in love with her on sight, and married her out of hand. Juana sighed. It was all history to her. Childless for ten years, her mother had dwindled away after she was born, and her own first memories were of her Portuguese foster-mother, old Anna, and of kind, vague Aunt Elvira who had brought her up as tenderly as her dread of her own fierce mother, the matriarch, Mrs. Brett, would allow.

The dream of the past was shattered by a shout from the Tower of Belem, and the quick exchange of question and answer, through speaking-trumpets, that cleared the ship to go on into the main harbour of the Tagus. Juana shook herself. These thoughts of the past were morbid, foolish ... Why, almost, for a moment, she had felt a twinge of fear at the thought of the return she had longed for. Nonsense, of course. Pombal and all he stood for were dead long since. There were no scaffolds now on the dutsy shore beyond Belem; only the gardens and menagerie of the Ajuda Palace. And why did that make her remember, as a child, being shown the pillar marking the spot where once the Duke d'Aveiro's palace had stood before Pombal had had it rased to the ground, and the site symbolically sprinkled with salt?

A shout from the masthead brought her back to the present. "Ships of the line! Ours. One, two ... six of them!"

Hurrying across to the starboard side, Juana saw the six ships anchored in formation just below the tangle of shipping in Lisbon harbour, lying, she noticed, where they could command a view both up river and down to the bar.

"Six of them!" The packet's captain joined her, an anxious little cross-eyed man with a hearty respect for the name of Brett. "I don't much like the look of that. It's the most we're allowed to bring in here, by treaty. I hope it doesn't mean the French have invaded—or are going to." He peered at them anxiously through his glass. "That's the *Hibernia*, Admiral St. Vincent's flagship, and flying his flag. What brings him

43

here from his station at Brest? I don't like it, Miss Brett; I don't like it above half. You won't think of going ashore till we know what it means. Not that you'll be free to do so for a day or so, if I know anything of the way they go on here."

"No. My father said I would have plenty of time to let my grandmother know I was here before we were cleared for landing. I have a note ready for her, if you'd be so good as to have it sent ashore by the first boat?"

He took it, still looking doubtful. "But, Miss Brett ... those six ships may mean that the French have invaded. If so, you will have no alternative but to return with me."

"No alternative? After coming this far? I am here because my grandmother needs me, Captain Fenton. If the French really have invaded, she will need me more, not less."

"Quite so." Her tone of authority had surprised him, but after all she was a Brett, if a young one. "I'll send your note, Miss Brett. I'm sure your grandmother will be the first to forbid your going ashore if there is really danger. At all events, we should know soon enough. There's a boat pulling off to us from the *Hibernia* now."

His verdict, after the young lieutenant from the *Hibernia* had been and gone, was not encouraging. "There's no invasion—yet," he told Juana. "But Junot's at Bayonne, with twenty-five thousand men, and the Spaniards are massing on the frontier. It don't look good, Miss Brett. Remember, Napoleon's no respecter of persons—or of the rules of war. He makes prisoners of civilians—look what he did three years ago. I'm sure I don't know what to do for the best. But"—cheering up—"we're invited to dine on the *Hibernia*. They'll advise you there, I'm sure. Lord Strangford, our minister, is to be there."

"Oh, what a pity." Juana really meant it. "But I'm afraid I am not well, Captain. I must ask you to make my apologies."

He did not try to hide his astonishment. "But, Miss Brett—"

"I'm sorry." She was not prepared to invent an ailment. "Say all that is proper for me." Back in her cabin, she unfolded and reread the note she had found on her pillow after the *Hibernia's* boat had left. It was short and to the point: "If you are invited on board the *Hibernia,* refuse. This is no time to be seen with the English. And, when you land, insist on saying a prayer of thanksgiving to Saint Roque. Whatever happens, your grandmother expects you. Remember Sebastian."

Gair Varlow? It must be. Who else would refer to Sebastian? But what in the world could it mean? Puzzling over it, she had obeyed, so far, instinctively. But—a prayer to Saint Roque? She could not see the church yet, on its hill above Lisbon harbour, but there could be no question of what the note meant. Nor would it be difficult to do. Her father's lapse from the Catholic Church had been a contributory cause to the breach with his mother, and, in England, she had gone, with the rest of the family, to the local church. But she had missed the strong framework of Catholicism and had already decided that, once back in Portugal, she would return to her mother's church. She was ashamed of herself for having left it, and would have much to say to Saint Roque, her own saint. Only—it was certainly not for that reason that the note told her to go there. Was it absurd to hope that she would find Gair awaiting her in the church on the hill?

She decided to recover and be back on deck by the time the Captain and her three fellow passengers returned from dining on St. Vincent's flagship. After all, as the only woman on board, she might allow herself a certain unpredictability.

They returned early since Captain Fenton wanted to take advantage of the evening tide to move his ship up to the main harbour. "I'll not waste a moment, once I've got my clearance," he told Juana. "The sooner I'm safe out at sea again, the happier I shall be. And if I were you, Miss Brett, I'd resign myself to making the return voyage. Disappointing for you, I know, but better than spending years in a French prison."

"Are things so bad?"

"They're not good. No one really *knows* anything, mind you. Those goddamned Portu—I beg your pardon, Miss Brett—the Portuguese have been keeping St. Vincent at arm's length. That Prince Regent of theirs—Dom John—is still up at Mafra hobnobbing with his monks. There's been no one here for St. Vincent to talk to—he only received *pratique* yesterday, when their first minister, d'Araujo, finally got back from Mafra. Polite as you please now, of course, and all apologies, but it don't alter the fact that St. Vincent's been cooling his heels here in the bay for the better part of a week, and you can imagine how the old fire-eater has liked that. And Lord Rosslyn too—they let General Simcoe ashore, as a great concession because he's ill, poor man. He's at Sintra, and not likely to recover, they say."

"Rosslyn and Simcoe are here too?"

"Yes. Their frigate must have passed us on the way out. You can see why I say it's serious. They're here to arrange for military aid, if it's needed. Which it probably will be. We've an army all ready at Portsmouth, standing by to embark the minute the French cross the frontier. Mind you, they'll have to be quick about it, if they are to do any good. The Portuguese army couldn't hold back an invasion of mice. So you see, Miss Brett—"

"You say yourself that nobody really knows anything. It may all be a false alarm. My father was sure that we'd hear, any moment, that Lord Lauderdale has signed an armistice in Paris."

"I'll believe that when I hear it! But no need to look so anxious. Judging by what happened to St. Vincent, we've not a hope of receiving *pratique* for a while. Plenty of chance to hear from your grandmother between now and then. And maybe time, too, for news from the frontier."

In fact, time crawled. Anchored well out from Pombal's handsome Praça do Commercio, they were still near enough to see the stir of life in the square and hear the innumerable bells of the churches scattered over Lisbon's seven hills. Standing at the rail, Juana was content, for a while, to make out the various landmarks, remembered from childhood visits to the city. There was the Castle of Saint George, up above the Cathedral and the tumble of red roofs that represented the old Moorish district, spared by the earthquake. And there, much nearer, was Saint Roque itself, reminding her of the question that lay, all the time, at the back of her mind. Was she really going to make an excuse to go up there when she landed? An excuse of her religion? She was angry with herself even for considering it, angrier still with Gair Varlow— if it was he—for asking her. She turned impatiently away, to look downstream to where a stream of small boats kept plying between the English warships and the shore. The sight made it all the more maddening that they themselves had lain incommunicado all the long, hot day, waiting on the whim of the Portuguese authorities.

"Mind you"—Captain Fenton stopped beside her under the canvas shelter he had had rigged for her on deck—"no news is good news. St. Vincent promised he'd let me know if anything happened."

"Yes." She had been pretending to work at her detested embroidery. Now she dropped it. "Look! There's a boat coming."

"The officials already?" He admitted it grudgingly, unwilling to find anything good about the Portuguese. "The Inquisition too, by the look of it. You've got nothing out of the way in your baggage, I hope?"

"You forget, Captain. I'm a Catholic."

"Good God, so you are."

Catholic or not, Juana could not help a little shiver as the black-garbed representative of the Inquisition came aboard. Ridiculous, of course, to find herself thinking of the scaffold and the wheel. The days of *autos-da-fé* were gone forever, so why did she feel this queer little shiver down her spine?

In fact, the formalities were accomplished with the greatest speed and courtesy, and the only objection was raised by Captain Fenton when Juana's papers came to be examined. "It's not sure yet that Miss Brett is landing," he said. "I can't let her if there's any chance of a French invasion. As an Englishwoman, she'd be in the gravest danger."

"An Englishwoman?" The Portuguese official looked up from Juana's papers. "Nothing of the kind. On the mother's side, Miss Brett is of the Portuguese nobility. We are proud to welcome you home, senhora." And then, as Juana curtsied her acknowledgement, he searched among his papers and brought out a note. "From the Castle on the Rock, senhora."

It was short and to the point. "Welcome home, at last. I expect you tomorrow, without fail." These last two words underscored several times. "Jaime will be on the quay at first light. Lose no time." Again these words were heavily underscored. And then, without more greeting, the familiar signature, a little more shaky now, "Charlotte F. Brett."

"She expects me tomorrow." It was disconcerting to realise that they were all waiting to hear what the note held. "She says nothing about danger."

"Of course not," said the official.

And, "Absurd," said the priest.

"Well, I don't know—" began Captain Fenton.

"I d—d—" Juana stamped her foot on the hot deck, stopped, and started again. "I've made up my mind, Captain. I may go ashore in the morning?" To the official.

"Of course, senhora. I have instructions to give you every assistance."

"Thank you." That settled it. Only, after the official boat had returned to shore, Captain Fenton tried once more. "You're sure, Miss Brett?"

"Quite sure. At first light. Please?" There had been something oddly urgent about that brief note.

"Very well. At least"—he was reassuring himself as much as her—"it's clear that you are powerfully protected. I understand now why I got my clearance so quickly."

"You mean—?"

"Of course. It's not for everyone that those jack-in-office Portuguese officials will act as messenger-boys. I reckon you'll be all right, Miss Brett. It's odd to think of you as Portuguese."

"Yes." Curiously enough, after all the homesick years in England, she found it a little odd herself.

But next morning she felt nothing but eager anticipation as she gazed shorewards from the packet's boat, straining her eyes to try and pick out Jaime, her grandmother's *camareiro mor*, or chamberlain, among the morning crowds in Black Horse Square, as she still was English enough to call the Praça do Commercio. Home at last! But first—what about Gair Varlow? She still had not made up her mind. Was she really going to visit the church of Saint Roque this morning? And what would she find if she did?

Still debating this, she looked up at the church on its hill above the harbour. It looked near enough, in the clear morning light, but would involve, she knew, a considerable delay if she decided to go. Jaime would not like that; nor would her grandmother. Besides, what right had Gair Varlow to order her about?

What right? "Remember Sebastian," he had said. He had been wonderfully good to her at Forland House. Did she owe him this? Or was she merely trying to convince herself that she did, because she wanted to go?

Would she? Would she not? The boat scraped against the quay and Jaime came hurrying breathlessly to shout a greeting and help her ashore. "Welcome home, senhora." His hair had gone grey and he was smaller than she had remembered. "*Deus,* but it's good to see you. The Castle on the Rock will come alive again, with you home. This is all?" He lifted her small box on to his shoulder.

"Yes, but should you carry it, Jaime?" Disconcerting to find him old like this.

"Who else? The carriage is here in the square. The boy is holding the horses." He turned to lead the way, and she paused for a moment to thank the sailors from the packet in English, then, in Portuguese again, "Jaime! You brought

48

Rosinante!" She had recognised her own mule, tied to the back of the huge, old-fashioned carriage.

"Yes. I thought you'd like to ride part of the way—when we are out of town."

"Bless you, Jaime. I would indeed. No"—he had opened the carriage door for her—"we can't start yet: first I must go up to Saint Roque."

"Saint Roque? But, *menina*"—unconsciously he reverted to the old name for her—"little one."

"It's a vow, Jaime. An old one. You know I was born on his name day. I was so homesick: I promised him my first prayer on Portuguese soil if he would only bring me home." She was ashamed of the lie as she spoke it.

Jaime was looking anxiously up at the sun. "It's early yet, it's true; and—a vow's a vow. But your grandmother said to lose no time. And you remember how it is, *menina*. The road goes miles round . . ."

"But I shall walk up the steps. That's part of the vow."

"You can't." He was horrified. "It's bad enough coming back like this, unattended. But you must remember, young ladies don't walk here. It was all very well when you were a child . . . but now—Mrs. Brett would never forgive me."

"I shan't be a young lady, Jaime." It was odd to find that part of her brain had apparently worked out the whole plan. She pulled out her purse. "Here! You will bribe one of those old women over there—the sardine sellers—to sell me her shawl. I'll be a penitent, in black to the eyes. Nobody knows me anyway. Only, hurry, Jaime, or Grandmother will really be angry. I'm going, you understand, so let's waste no more time in talk."

"Yes, senhora. You sound just like your grandmother." It was hard to tell whether he meant this as praise, but at least he took the money she held out to him and hurried away to the little group of black-shawled old women who were shouting their wares on the corner of the square nearest to the fishmarket.

Juana had not thought how the shawl would stink of fish and old woman, but she wrapepd herself in it without flinching as they left the carriage at the end of the Rua do Ouro. "You may come too, Jaime." She knew perfectly well he would refuse to be left behind. "But don't speak. I have my prayers to say." And, liar, she said to herself again as they started up the steep cobbled lane, part path, part staircase, part sewer, that formed the direct rout to Saint Roque. She had forgotten how dirty Lisbon was, and how one had to pick one's way through piles of rubbish, some still dating from the earthquake, some more recent and less sanitary. Had she, as a child, just not noticed?

The smell of the shawl she was wearing, familiar now, was almost a protection against the odours that assailed her as they climbed higher among the crazy conglomeration of houses, pigstyes, and cattlesheds. Lean, scavenging dogs snarled as they passed; a scrawny cat was tethered by a long rope to a doorstep rather cleaner than the rest; a woman leaned out of an upstairs window to empty her slops with a cry of "*Agua vai!*" Juana pulled her shawl more closely round her.

Jaime, who had been walking a step behind, partly out of deference, partly because there was only one path beaten through the piled-up filth of the lane, pulled almost level to speak quietly in her ear. "I told the boy to bring the carriage round to the church. It will be better so."

"Oh, thank you, Jaime." She could have cried with relief. It was bad enough this time, but to have to do it again . . .

They came out, at last, into the purer air of the ridge where the church stood. "You will wait here, Jaime." She made it a command, but was relieved when he made no difficulty about obeying.

"Right here, senhora. I'll watch for the carriage. It should not be very long. So say your prayers with a free heart."

"Thank you." She felt horribly guilty as she pushed open the heavy church door, and her first action was to go forward to the main altar and kneel there, praying for forgiveness. It was no use. She could not forgive herself. She rose to her feet and looked about her. Lit only by flickering altar candles, the church was dark, almost empty, and smelled of damp, of wax and old incense.

She stood there, irresolute. None of the shadowy half-seen figures moved towards her. Where was Gair Varlow? Had it all been some horrible practical joke? Had she made a mockery of her faith for nothing? And her grandmother was waiting, would be angry . . . She could not afford to lose time, standing here, doing nothing. She began to move slowly around the circuit of ornate little side-chapels, hating herself for having come.

She had forgotten how tawdry and cluttered the chapels were, each lit by its own range of candles and hung about with gifts, some absurd, some touching: a bunch of dried flowers, a baby's shoe, a miniature copper frying pan. Why? she wondered, and entered the Chapel of Saint John the Baptist, whose splendour of gold, and marble, and lapis lazuli had struck her, as a child, as a kind of heaven on earth. Now it seemed almost embarrassing in its excess and she found herself thinking, with an odd little pang, of their parish church in England, cool, high, and empty, decorated, if at all, with flowers in season, with primroses and daffodils and Easter lilies.

What was the matter with her today? She had longed to be home. Why keep thinking, now she was here, of England? She moved quickly by the last chapels, merely glancing in to make sure they were empty. It was time to go. She had been a fool to come. She turned towards the main door and a priest came quietly up to her out of the shadows: "You wish to confess, my daughter?"

Gair Varlow. "No!" Her reaction was as instant as it was angry. Bad enough to have come here to meet him. Nothing would make her pretend a confession.

"I'm sorry." At least he understood. "This way then." He guided her to a chapel whose lack of candles or offerings indicated that it belonged to one of the less popular saints. "We can talk here. Quietly." His Portuguese was as fluent as her own. There was no reason why they should be noticed. "I apologise for asking you to come," he went on. "I had to. There are things I must explain."

"Yes?" More than ever, now, she wished she had not come.

He must have sensed it. "I'm sorry. This is more important than manners ... conventions. You've not asked me why I am here."

"Should I have?"

"It would have made it easier for me."

"Yes?" She stirred on the stool where he had seated her. "My grandmother is expecting me, Mr. Varlow. I can't stay."

"I know," he said. "That's just it. I must get a message to Mrs. Brett. Will you take it for me?"

"Why, of course." Was this all?

"You must understand." He leaned close, to whisper, so that she found herself wondering, absurdly, whether he disliked the smell of her shawl as much as she did. "This is urgent business; dangerous business. I am here with Lord Strangford, the English Minister. Your grandmother has been helping me. No, that's not right: I have been helping her. Three nights ago, the messenger we've been using was stabbed, murdered, here in the streets of Lisbon. It may mean nothing, or everything. Murders happen here, often enough. And there was nothing on him for anyone to find; the message was always verbal. But I don't know. Until I do, there's no safety for any of us, not even for you, since I have involved you, God forgive me."

"I wish I had any idea what you are talking about." It was not true. Passionately, she did not want to know.

"You're not stupid. Don't pretend to be. I'm talking about spying—secret agents, if you prefer. I am one. Your grandmother has been for years. We brought you here in the hope that you could help us. Could help England. I wish to God I didn't have to ask you, like this, with no explanation, no time to tell you what is involved. But I must. It's too important. I beg of you to believe me, Miss Brett, and do as I ask you. Your grandmother will explain."

"She had better." She was cold with anger, at herself, at him. It had all been a charade, a pretence. Memories mocked her: their first meeting, the moonlight, the nightingale ... all false, a stage set to trick her. And that last day, in the maze. "I'm a poor man," he had said, implying that he loved her. "Penniless ... with my own way to make in the world." This was how he made it. And she was to help him. She swallowed a sick lump of rage, and took a steadying breath. "It was all your idea, I take it?" She was proud of her voice. "You had me invited to your sister's; looked me over; decided I would do. I cannot imagine why. So: here I am. Very well then, since I am here, what can I do for you?"

"No! It's not like that," he began to protest. Then, "Well, I suppose, in a way, it is. You must see: in the end, I hope, you will see that there is more to it than that. But now, there's no time: not to explain, not to apologise. You *must* get to your grandmother's at once. She'll tell you why. And you'll tell her about the messenger. Tell her that until I find one I can trust I shall come myself. Your presence at the Castle on the Rock will give me my excuse. Tell Mrs. Brett I'll come tomorrow. Ostensibly to call on you. You won't mind?"

"Mind? Why should I?" At all costs she would not let him see how he had hurt her. "Very well. I'll deliver your message."

"Thank you. And—carefully. When Mrs. Brett's alone."

"I'm not quite a fool."

"I'm sorry. Sorry for everything. Look!" He turned away—with relief? "There's your man at the door. He must not see me. Forgive me." And before she could answer he was gone, his borrowed robes brushing softly along the stone floor.

She waited a moment, teeth clenched on rage, trying to collect herself, watching Jaime peer about, his eyes still dazzled from the sunshine outside. Then she moved forward: "Here I am, Jaime."

"Good." He made his reverence to the altar with the casual friendliness of long habit. "The carriage is here, *menina*." And then, as he held the heavy door open for her: "*Deus*, but it's good to have you back. You were always the best of the bunch. As for those cousins of yours, they're never home these days. They're courtiers now! Hangers-on of the Prince Regent and his wife. You may see them today, come to that."

"Today?"

"Yes. The boy learned on his way up that Dom John has left Mafra at last and is on his way to town."

"In August?" She paused at the carriage door. "Jaime, things must be bad!"

"You've heard the rumours too? But this may mean nothing. He's coming to welcome the English Admiral, that's all. He'll doubtless be back at Queluz soon enough, with his poor mad mother the Queen. But we'd best lose no time, *menina;* I'd rather meet them the far side of there; the country's opener."

Safe in the musty privacy of her grandmother's carriage, Juana sat dry-eyed, dry-hearted, tearing her daydreams to shreds. She would never be such a fool again. Her comfort, for what it was worth, must be that she had betrayed little, maybe nothing of what she felt to Gair Varlow. He must never know how successfully he had fooled her, those sunny days at Forland House.

In England, she had dreamed, over and over again, of this longed-for return home. Now, she hardly noticed the familiar landmarks they passed: the graceful Aqueduct of Alcantara or the pink palace of Queluz where, no doubt, the old mad Queen was pacing the garden to which her kingdom had narrowed itself, with her heart-rending cry of "*Ai, Jesus!*"

She was roused, at last, from her gloomy thoughts by a shout from Jaime, who was riding ahead. Luckily, the road, which had been running for some time between the high stone walls round the gardens of noblemen's *quintas*, or country houses, had just emerged on to an open stretch of heathy mountainside. Working quickly, Jaime and the boy manoeuvred the carriage to make way for the royal procession as it approached. Invisible in the shadows of her own carriage, Juana had a glimpse of Dom John, ugly as an orang-outang in the royal coach, then saw two of the riders pause to speak to Jaime. Of course, her cousins would have recognised the family carriage. Now they were pulling out of the cortège to greet her.

"Peter! Robert!" She leaned out of the carriage window. "It's wonderful to see you."

"Not Peter!" Her older cousin had edged his horse up close to the carriage. "Pedro. And Roberto." Tall, with dark, heavily curling hair, he was at once handsomer and less attractive than she had remembered. "And I hope you've not changed your name to Joanna, cousin. This is no time to be too blatantly British. God knows, Brett is bad enough."

"Brett? Bad? What in the world do you mean?" This was hardly the reunion she had dreamed of.

"Oh, we can't drop it entirely, of course, but Roberto and I prefer, these days, to be known as Brett-Alvidrar. At least our *mother* was Portuguese." A quick glance at the servants. "It's not that I'm not proud to be half English, of course; it's just that—well, things are complicated just now."

"They must be if you are apologising for being a Brett, cousin."

He gave an impatient exclamation. "I can't stop to explain now, but, for God's sake, Juana, have the sense to keep quiet until you understand how things are here. I told my grandmother she was crazy to invite you, but try to make her listen to reason ..." He looked round to where the procession was still making its lumbering way past them. "I must go. Roberto, try if you can make her see reason?"

"Don't mind him." Robert was slighter and fairer than his older brother, his pale face dominated by the heavy Brett nose. "It's an anxious time for us all, Juana." He took her hand and pressed it warmly. "Personally, I'm delighted to see you. The old lady is feeling her age, you know. She needs some looking after . . . And of course Aunt Elvira—" He shrugged.

"Is she the same as ever?"

"Worse, if anything. Oh, she's harmless enough, useful, in her way. She runs the household, so far as anyone does." He laughed. "I hope you don't delude yourself you're coming to a life of luxury, cousin."

"No, Roberto. Just home."

"Oh, well." He too was looking anxiously after the procession. "I hope you don't live to regret it, Juana. Anyway, welcome home. And—Pedro's right, you know. Be careful what you do—and what you say."

She was impatient now. "I wish you'd *explain*, Robert. What's the good of saying, 'Be careful,' you don't tell me why, or what it's all about."

He smiled at her suddenly, and she remembered how much she had always preferred him to his bullying elder brother. "You're not stupid, Juana, never were. Keep your eyes open, and your mouth shut, and you'll understand soon enough. This is no place for explanations." He bent down, ostensibly to kiss her cheek. "Trust no one," he whispered, kicked his horse, and was gone.

The procession was almost past now. The last heavy baggage wagons were lurching by with the scream of unoiled wheels that Juana remembered so well. "Jaime!" She raised her voice to shout above the din. "Bring Rosinante. I'm going to ride the rest of the way."

"So you saw your cousins?" He made it a question as he put her up into the comfortable Spanish saddle.

"Messrs Pedro and Roberto Brett-Alvidrar. Yes, I saw them, Jaime." Here, at least, was someone she had always trusted. She kicked Rosinante into a reluctant amble so that they pulled away from the lumbering carriage. "Jaime, you must explain. Pedro told me to be careful what I said, and Roberto said I was to trust no one."

"It's good advice, *menina*. You were a child when you left; how should you understand? Besides, it's got worse, much worse. And—I've never been to England, but I've heard about it all my life, seen the Englishmen from the Factory, and heard them talk. *Corpo de deus*, how they talk! As if there was no such thing"—he looked round to make sure the carriage was out of earshot—"no such thing as the Inquisition, or the Secret Police, or—" He stopped. "I'm talking too much. It's because I'm so glad to see you. But—believe me, they gave you good advice, your cousins. If I was your true friend, I think I'd turn round and take you straight back to Lisbon, to the ship you came on. I don't know what your father was thinking of, to send you here, now ... But then, he was never— Forgive me, *menina*—"

He paused, and she had a chance to ask her question. "What did you mean, Jaime, when you spoke of the Inquisition, or the Secret Police, or something else? Surely, there can't be anything worse than the Secret Police?"

"Don't!" They were well out on the heathy mountainside now, with no cover but a far-off clump of ilex trees, but he looked round as nervously as if rosemary and lavender bushes had ears. "Don't ask me, *menina*. And yet, perhaps I should tell you."

"Of course you should." How odd it was, after the grey years in England, to find herself slipping back into the old habit of command. "It's your duty, Jaime."

"Oh, *menina*"—he turned to her impulsively—"I wish your mother, or my poor Anna, your foster mother was alive to hear you speak like that. And you're right; it is my duty. Things have changed here since you were a child. It's not only the Inquisition now, or the Secret Police ... You've heard of the Freemasons?"

"Why yes. We have them in England. They're a ... I don't know ... a secret society of some kind, aren't they? Do you have them here, too?"

"Yes. If it was only them. When Junot was here, two years ago—you know about him?"

"The French General? Napoleon's friend? Yes, of course."

"Well, he was Ambassador here. Such state as he kept; you should have seen it. A jumped-up nobody from God knows where! But he was a great one for the Freemasons—at first."

"What do you mean?"

"They weren't secret enough for him. Or"—another nervous look round—"violent enough. But there was another society. *Menina*, you'll not breathe a word of this—not to anyone, not even to your grandmother? Swear it?"

"I swear, Jaime." She had caught his seriousness.

"They call themselves the Sons of the Star." He whispered it, as if the larks, twittering high above them, might hear. "If they condemn you to death, you're dead. No one knows anything about them. Your own brother might be one, your father, and you'd not know. They take an oath of secrecy so dreadful—the Freemasons' is nothing to it."

"But what do they do, Jaime?"

Once again, he looked about him nervously. "It's hard to say, since their victims, even if they let them live, never speak of what happened to them. Oh—at first, I believe, they did a great deal of good. They were founded soon after the earthquake. Their doings were more open then, from what I've heard; it was only when King Joseph died—God rest his soul—and Pombal fell out of favour that they went underground. And ever since, they have been growing steadily more powerful. *Menina*, the prayer you whisper into your pillow tonight may be the subject of discussion at their next meeting. They have eyes and ears everywhere. And I've heard it said that since Junot's time they have begun to mix themselves with politics. Well, you know, it's not all love and roses between us and England. Senhora, anything could happen. They stick at nothing. That's the one thing everyone knows about them. If they decide to get rid of the English— why, every one of them might be found dead in his bed. Now, do you see why your cousins prefer to be called Brett-Alvidrar?"

"Yes, but I don't like it."

"Liking! What has that to do with it, in a country placed as ours is? Spain has always been our enemy. If she and France join against us, it's going to take more than the English navy to protect us."

"But you've a Spanish princess, Jaime. What of Dom John's wife? Carlota Joaquina? Surely her own parents wouldn't turn against her?"

"Stranger things have happened. And it's common knowledge, anyway, that she and the Prince Regent never meet if they can help it. Things are bad here, I tell you. I feel that we're working up to an explosion of some kind. I'm still not sure I shouldn't take you straight back to Lisbon."

"Nonsense! You know my grandmother needs me. But don't imagine I'm going to start calling myself Brett-Mascarenhas after my mother!"

"Good God! I should hope not. Don't mention that name, even in jest."

"You mean people still remember? But it was in 1759, Jaime, nearly fifty years ago."

"The memories of sovereigns are long, *menina*." And he put a firm end to the conversation by turning his mule to ride back to the carriage.

He rejoined her after they had passed through the green gardens and flowering groves of Sintra. "We'll be entering your own land soon. I think your grandmother would prefer it if you made your entry in the carriage."

Mrs. Brett's slightest whim had always been law to servants and family alike and this was practically a command.

In fact, Juana was stiff enough already from the unwonted exercise to be glad to yield gracefully: "Just wait till we reach the top of the ridge. That's where you get the first view of the castle."

The bare, windswept ridge they were climbing presented a remarkable contrast to Sintra's green orange and silver olive groves, and Juana was grateful for the sea breeze that lifted her short hair under her riding hat and cooled cheeks flushed with exercise. And even up here, the crevices of the rocks were green with rosemary and lavender and the air fragrant with their scent.

"There!" She pulled Rosinante to a halt at the top of the long slope. "There it is at last." The Castle on the Rock was built on a plateau at the seaward end of the ridge they were on. Below and to their left lay the fertile, sheltered valley whose vineyards had helped make the fortunes of the early Bretts. Looking down, Juana could see the neat rows of grape vines from which they made a wine even lighter and more delicious than the famous Colares wine. And, ahead, above them, stood the castle itself, sharply silhouetted against the western sky, a place of dream or even, maybe, of nightmare, with its strange mixture of spire and minaret, of Christian and Moorish architecture. It had been at different times in its history a Moorish citadel against the Christian invader, a pirate's base, and, briefly, an English stronghold when Richard Coeur de Lion's crusaders stormed it on their way to the Holy Land. Now, for Juana, it was home. "Hurry, Jaime." She let him help her into the carriage. "Grandmother will be waiting."

CHAPTER 5

Their approach must have been visible for some time from the castle, but when the carriage laboured up the steep slope to the plateau and lurched through the great gate into the courtyard, it was greeted only by the inevitable horde of servants and hangers-on. They made, indeed, an enthusiastic scene enough, with their kissing of hands and patter of blessings, but, returning their greetings amid the well-remembered odour of salt fish and garlic, Juana could not help a glance at unresponsive windows above.

"It's siesta still." Jaime had noticed. "Your aunt and uncles will doubtless be ready to greet you when you have refreshed yourself after your journey. As for Mrs. Brett, she seldom leaves her room these days."

"I see." Submitting to the warm, garlic-laden embrace of a plump matron, Juana recognised, at the last moment, a childhood friend and accomplice. "Maria! It's good to see you!"

"Maria has consented to come back as your personal maid." Jaime was formal now, and dignified, as befitted his role of master of the household. "She will show you to the rooms we have had prepared for you. I hope you will be pleased with them, senhora."

"Rooms! I'm sure I shall be delighted with them, Jaime. You'll have my grandmother told I am here?" It remained disconcerting to have come so far for so little welcome.

"I'm sure Mrs. Brett knows already." It was undoubtedly true. The uproar of welcome in the shady, vine-hung central courtyard of the castle must have roused the most indomitable sleeper.

Following Maria up one of the winding stairs that led from each corner of the courtyard, Juana found time to think that Mrs. Brett had made no effort to imitate her grandsons in appearing Portuguese. The daughter of an English Duke, Lady Charlotte Beauroy had decided, when she married James Brett, to sink her courtesy title in what she thought the more important one of Mrs. Brett. After her husband's death, the English appellation had become something of a fetish with her, and it had been an unlucky servant who forgot and called her senhora.

Maria threw open the heavy, metal-studded door at the top of the stair and ushered Juana into a room that made her gasp with surprise. Here were none of the dusty cut-velvet draperies she remembered from her childhood, when every table or chair had its flounces. This light corner room with its two sets of windows was furnished for a girl in pale wood and gay chintz. "You like it, senhora?" Maria crossed the room to draw a curtain more closely against the afternoon sun.

"Like it?" She, too, moved to the window to make sure that it faced the sea. "It's lovely, Maria. But I don't remember this part of the castle."

"No wonder. It was shut up when we were girls. Don't you remember, Ju—senhora? We found the door open once, you and I, and got on the stair. Mrs. Brett found us! (She pronounced the name very badly, as did all the servants) *Corpo de deus*, what a beating I got! Mrs. Brett had it done over last month. I wondered then—we all wondered what it meant. Oh, I'm glad it meant you've come back to us, Ju—senhora."

"I wish you could call me Juana."

"I can't, *amiga*, and you know it. But it doesn't mean I'm not glad to see you. It's worth leaving Tomas, and the children."

"Tomas? You're married, Maria?"

"Well, of course." Affronted. "What do you think? We have been married four years, Tomas and I. We live down there, in the Vale Allegre." She took Juana's hand and pulled her away from the window that faced the sea and across to the one over the valley. "Tomas works on the vines—he's a skilled man." Proudly. "But I'd rather be here with you. Three children in three years are enough, and my mother-in-law takes care of them better than I could. Besides, he beats me." She rolled up the sleeve of her black bodice to show a great range of livid bruises, then rolled it down again in a hurry as two menservants appeared with Juana's box. "Put it there, you idiots, and no need to stand gawping either. No one's been up here yet," she explained when they had gone. "The rooms were only finished the other day. It's been a nine days' wonder in the castle. Oh, I'm glad you're back, *amiga*. Do you remember—" The tide of childhood reminiscence flowed freely as she helped Juana out of her riding dress and

60

into an India muslin that shocked her by its cut. A shawl, perhaps, she suggested, to cover that low neck?

But: "I'm an English girl," said Juana firmly. "We wear them like this. And it's hot, Maria."

"You call this hot! You must have forgotten. No wonder if you look—forgive me—a trifle pale and peaked, if this is a hot day by English standards. But we'll have you in looks again in no time, with some of our good Portuguese sun, and our food and wine. Do you really live on raw beef and beer, over there? It sounds barbarous to me."

Juana laughed. "Well, not quite, but I did miss the sun. Yes?"

This time it was Jaime, knocking on the door, to summon her to her grandmother. Did he, too, look a trifle anxiously at her lowcut muslin? She smiled to herself. He should have seen Lady Caroline Lamb at Forland House.

Mrs. Brett's apartments were in the other seaward corner tower, but in order to reach them one had to go down to the courtyard and along the Moorish cloisters that flanked it on the south and west sides. The other half of the castle had been burned down by the Spaniards years ago and replaced by a comparatively modern block which housed the family's general living rooms and her aunt and uncles' private apartments. Peering up at them from the vine-shaded coolness of the cloister, Juana could see no sign of life, but then they mostly looked out the other way, towards the ridge road and the Pleasant Valley.

The heat and the smell of burnt lavender in Mrs. Brett's rooms took her breath away. Here, everything was as she remembered it: crimson velvet, dark in the corners, faded where the sun had struck it, dusty everywhere. Two poor relations and a waiting-woman were giggling in whispers in the anteroom, but stopped when they entered. Juana remembered them all, and did not need Jaime's introduction to tell her which to smile at and which to kiss. But there were none of the leisurely reminiscences she had expected. "Mrs. Brett is waiting for you," said her cousin Estella.

"She's impatient." Manuela was tall and thin, with an immense Brett nose.

"It's the full moon." Estella was plump, and soft, and smelled, as she always had, of stale orris-root.

"She's always at her worst then," added Manuela.

Juana had forgotten their habit of speaking in chorus. Now, as she accepted information from each in turn, it all came back to her, and with it, the very taste of childhood. How frightened she used to be when summoned, like this, to her grandmother's presence. Well: was she not now? And, honestly: a little, she admitted to herself. "In that case," she said, "we had best not keep her waiting."

"She's in bed," said Manuela.

"She aches all over," said Estella.

"Of course she never admits it."

"But we know." Manuela opened the door at the far end of the room and ushered Juana into her grandmother's presence.

If possible, it was hotter still in here, where damask curtains, drawn against the setting sun, filled the room with warm red light. The hangings on the huge four-poster were red too, and Mrs. Brett, propped up among pillows, looked like some ancient ivory statue in its shrine. She had always seemed very old to the child Juana, now she seemed beyond age, timeless.

"You were long enough getting here!" Mrs. Brett spoke in English, her voice deep and resonant as ever. "My orders were that you would leave at first light. I'm too old to be crossed, Juana."

"I'm sorry, ma'am. I came as quickly as I could." This, too, in English and, mercifully, without a difficult word. She crossed the room as she spoke and bent to kiss the paperwhite cheek and feel the bone beneath the skin.

"Don't stand gawping there." Mrs. Brett scolded the two cousins in Portuguese. "You may go." And then in English again as the door whispered shut behind them: "Draw the curtains, child. I want to see you. Are you as plain as they say?"

"Yes." Juana looped back the heavy damask with its golden cord and turned to face her grandmother.

"Plain enough." Ruthless eyes missed nothing. "Not that it much matters. But this stammer: I don't notice it."

"I d—d—" Juana's hands writhed together. She began again: "It's only on some letters."

"And in Portuguese?"

"Never."

"Well, that's something," said Mrs. Brett in that language. "Bring up a chair, child; sit down. I'll break my neck if you go on standing over me like a giraffe." And then, as Juana obediently pulled up a straight-backed chair, "You're huge,

62

aren't you? Taller than I was. And they called me Atalanta in my day. But I was a beauty!"

"And I'm not. Who wrote you about me, ma'am?" But she knew. It was Gair Varlow who had described her as plain. In her general fury with herself, with him, this was hardly even a last straw.

"Who? Well, at least you're not stupid. Why not your father?"

So many reasons. "Because he'd have said I was beautiful."

The old lady's laugh was as resonant as her voice. "Not at all stupid," she repeated. "You're right, of course. Poor Reginald never faced a fact in his life. But we're wasting time. The sun's setting already. What kind of person are you, child?"

"What do you mean, ma'am?"

"Don't hedge. Tell me about yourself. Are you a coward? Can you keep your head? What would you do in the face of danger?"

"How do I know? I've never faced it."

"No?" How piercing the old eyes were. "You sang them down at Forland House. And in English, too. Surely, in Portuguese, you'd be no coward." She seemed to be discussing it with herself. "You know, I suppose, that there's talk of an invasion of Portugal."

"Yes, I know."

"And you weren't afraid to come? That you might end up in a French prison?"

"I was a little."

"So why did you come?"

"Because I was miserable at home."

"Good girl! I was afraid you'd say: 'For your sake, Grandmother.' "

"I nearly did."

"Well, you're honest, by all appearances. How did you learn that, I wonder?"

"By watching—" She stopped.

"By watching your poor father, who's not? It could work like that. Your mother was one for facing facts. You don't remember her?"

"No, ma'am."

"No, you wouldn't. It was the convent for her, or your father. She chose your father. If she regretted it, she never let it show. Oh yes, she had backbone, that one, for all her ill

63

health. If you take after her ... But there's no time. You'll have to do. I can't manage alone any longer. And as for my family ... Trust no one, Juana. Before we go any further, get that into your head. No one."

"That's what Roberto said."

"Roberto? You've seen him?"

"Yes." She explained quickly about their meeting. "They couldn't talk long, of course, as the Court was on its way to Lisbon."

"The Court! Pah! My grandsons hangers-on to that priest-ridden cipher of a Prince Regent! Trade's not good enough for them! Not their family name. Brett-Alvidrar! I always thought they would help when my strength failed me. And now look at them! They hardly like to come home any more for fear of being accused of belonging to the English party. Well, they're no great loss: bullfights, and lounging under a lady's balcony, that's all they're good for. You should hear Roberto sing those Brazilian *modinhas* that are all the rage. And Pedro—he's a huntsman; almost as mad for it as Carlota Joaquina herself. I'm surprised he was with Dom John: I thought he'd attached himself to his wife. After all, she's a Spanich Princess—might be Queen if the Spanish invade instead of the French. Or along with them. Either way, God help the country. You understand what's going on?"

"Not precisely, ma'am."

"No wonder." The old lady snorted. "No one does. But something you must understand, for your own safety—and mine. Portugal's in greater danger now, I believe, than she's ever been since the bad old days after King Sebastian's death. There was no King then, there's none now. The Queen's mad; the Prince Regent's a well-meaning fool, and his wife conspires openly against him with Spain. There's no great man now, no Pombal to save the country. The government's made up of fools and idlers—" She stopped. "I'm talking too much, and about the wrong things. There's so much to tell you, Juana. But I've made us allies now. If you were to tell the Secret Police what I've said to you today, Brett or not, I'd be in prison tomorrow."

"Yes, ma'am." It was the opening Juana needed. "But, in fact, we are allies already. I have a message for you, from Mr. Varlow. That's why I was late. He asked me to meet him in Saint Roque. He said to tell you his messenger is dead, stabbed in the street. Until he can find another he will have to come himself. He says my being here will give him a pretext." Had she kept the fury out of her voice? "He's coming tomorrow."

If Mrs. Brett noticed anything odd about Juana's tone, she made no comment. "Stabbed? In the street. By whom?"

"He doesn't know. He said it might mean nothing, or everything. That we were all in danger till he knew. Grandmother, what does it all mean?"

"Danger, as he says." Somewhere, down in the centre of the castle, a deep bell sounded. "There's not time to tell you now. That's why I wanted you here early. But never mind, you were right to meet Mr. Varlow, though I wonder just why you did. " And then, on a new note altogether. "I'm sorry, child. You've much to forgive me already, have you not? But this is too important. You'll understand when I explain."

"I wish you would." Buffeted at once by anger at Gair's betrayal and excitement at returning to the castle, Juana had hardly had time to ponder his extraordinary statement that her grandmother was a secret agent. Mrs. Brett, who had been an old woman ever since she could remember? And—what in the world could she do, out here, in the deep country, at the Castle on the Rock?

But Mrs. Brett was shaking her head. "Not now. You must go and meet your cipher uncles and your mad aunt and behave as if nothing was the matter. I won't come down. I'd meant to, but I must save my strength. You do understand that I've trusted you with my life?"

"I begin to. I only wish I understood why."

"Because I've no alternative. And, whatever you think of him, because Mr. Varlow advised it, and I respect his judgement. Shall I show you his letter? No, perhaps not."

"I don't want to see it." And that was a lie.

But it pleased Mrs. Brett. "Good girl! I'm going to like you, Juana. I'm glad we're to be allies. And now—run along. Eat your supper; bear with your uncles; be good to your poor aunt; and come back to me as soon as you can leave them without arousing comment. We have much to do tonight, you and I."

"But, Grandmother—"

"No time now. Your uncles and aunt will be waiting for you. Nothing must seem out of the way tonight of all nights. Be off with you, child; eat a good supper and rest while you can. We've a long night ahead of us."

Juana found her uncles and aunt awaiting her in the big

65

drawing room on the east side of the castle courtyard. Kissing each one dutifully in turn, she thought that time seemed to have stood still with them. Perhaps her Uncle Prospero was a little solider and her Uncle Miguel a shade gaunter, but her Aunt Elvira was exactly the girlish figure she remembered. Her cheek was soft and fragrant as ever to the kiss, her smile still as sweet and impersonal as the touch of a butterfly's wing.

Only Juana herself had changed. She could remember finding Uncle Prospero a formidable and Uncle Miguel a sinister figure. Prospero was a scholar, who spent his days in the library working on what was to be the definitive edition of Camoens. Miguel was devout. He lived surrounded by indigent priests with whom he was to be heard day in, day out, discussing abstruce points of dogma. In the old days, these activities had filled her with awe, only now, listening to Prospero as he stuffed himself with preprandial sweetmeats and held forth about the deplorable translation of Camoens' *Lusiads* published by the British Minister, Lord Strangford, did she realise that it was all just talk. Probably, shut up in the library, he ate more sweetmeats, and slept.

As for her Uncle Miguel, even as a child she had had her doubts about his piety, having seen him look up from discussing the infinite mercy of God to ogle a maid or condemn a manservant to be beaten. She had never much liked her uncles, she realised now, and indeed it was hard to believe they were her father's brothers, so completely Portuguese did they seem. But that, she knew, had been old Mrs. Brett's plan. Their estates, their thriving wine trade, their entire wealth was in Portugal. Obdurately English herself, she had intended her sons to be Portuguese, and, with the exception of Reginald, she had succeeded.

Aunt Elvira put down her embroidery and rose to lead the way into the dining room. Here, too, nothing had changed. Solid family silver stood where it always had on table and sideboard; the hot air was heavy with scents of olive oil and garlic; a servant stood behind each high-backed chair, ready to pull it out when Uncle Miguel had said his elaborate Latin grace.

On his right, Elvira gazed vaguely downwards. Her own maid stood, as always, behind her chair and saw to it that she ate a few morsels from each dish. From time to time, she would smile to herself and whisper a snatch of song. She had been like this since the unlucky visit she had been sent on, as a girl, to her mother's aristocratic connections in England. No one had ever told Juana what had happened there. Perhaps no one knew. But she had been sent back in haste, the strange creature she had remained ever since. Her brothers ignored her, as they had done for years, and, this evening, came pretty close to ignoring Juana too. They treated her, still, as the child she had been when they last saw her, and she expected that at any moment one of them would ask her if she had been a good girl and done her lessons today.

The meal dragged out interminably, but at last Elvira's maid bent to whisper in her ear and she rose to her feet, smiling vaguely across the table at Juana. "The moon is full," she said. "The hour is late. My true love waits me at the gate." And then, for the first time, directly to Juana. "Come, child, away; the full moon rises; we must not stay."

"We'll be with you directly." This was Prospero, on a note of reassurance. "We don't stay long over our wine, Miguel and I."

Coffee after supper was always served in the Ladies' Parlour, a room old Mrs. Brett had had made over for herself on the southeast corner of the house. Protected from the sea winds by the whole bulk of the castle, it opened onto a vine-covered loggia that overlooked the Pleasant Valley. Tonight, the huge silver tray of coffee and sweetmeats had been carried out on to the loggia, where not a breath of air stirred. "You will pour out, senhora?" Jaime was waiting to guide Juana firmly to the appropriate chair.

"I? But Jaime—" And anxious glance at her aunt, who had drifted over to the edge of the terrace and was picking herself a bunch of carnations.

"Those are Mrs. Brett's orders." This phrase had been final in the household ever since Juana could remember. She sat down obediently and lifted the heavily embossed coffee pot with a hand that shook just a little.

"The moon is rising." Elvira drifted back to put her flowers into a coffee cup. "The night has come. Shall we go out, child, and dance on the cliff? The witches meet there when the moon is full. I've seen them, in their black robes, often enough. Why can I never see their faces?"

"Nonsense, Elvira!" Juana had forgotten how quietly her Uncle Prospero moved, despite his vast bulk. "You're imagining things again. We shall have to send for Father Ignatius if you do that, you know."

The cup Elvira was holding splintered on the paving

stones. "No, no, please don't! I'll be good, you know I will. I'm always good. I see nothing, nothing, nothing. I see nothing, because I'm good."

"That's my girl." This with a brotherly tap on the shoulder. "Well then, say good night to Juana and off to bed with you. She's always at her worst when the moon is full," he explained to Juana as Elvira took her maid's arm and withdrew.

"Really? I'd forgotten. How do you like your coffee, Uncle Prospero?"

"Black, thank you." He settled heavily in his own large chair with its wide view of the Pleasant Valley. "No, you'd not remember. You were a child when you left, in bed before the moon rose. You'll find we still keep early hours here."

"Elvira been misbehaving again?" Miguel emerged from the shadows at the back of the loggia. "I met her on her way up; crying poor girl. I hope you weren't hard on her, Prosper. She's harmless enough, God knows. Yes, black thank you, Juana. How pleasant to have a lady's company for once. Mother seldom joins us now, even on her good days. How did you find her, Juana?"

"Older, of course, but just the same otherwise."

He laughed a little. "Still ruling the roost? She'll do that till her last breath, will Mrs. Brett." His tone now was in such contrast to the one he had used at dinner that she could only suppose the two of them had compared notes after she left them and reminded each other that she was grown up.

"Yes." Prospero, too, addressed her now almost as an equal. "You'll find she still likes her own way, our splendid mother. I hope you'll bear it better than my boys did, Juana. I believe you met them?"

"Yes, with the Court. I didn't know they'd left home."

"It made Mother angry, I'm afraid. But she's a fair-minded woman ..." Was he trying to convince Juana, or himself? "She won't hold it against them. After all, everyone knows the steward, Macarao, runs the business brilliantly. The old lady would not have let the boys interfere, even if they had wanted to. She must be proud to have them in such favour at Court."

"Yes, of course." She kept doubt out of her voice as best she could, and looked up with relief as Manuela came out, softfooted, into the rapidly darkening loggia. "Coffee, Manuela?" Where did they eat, she wondered, Manuela and Estella?

"No thank you, *menina.* Your grandmother is asking for you."

"Oh, in that case!" It was a relief to say good night to her uncles and follow Manuela back across the central courtyard to her grandmother's tower. The sudden Portuguese night had fallen, and Manuela took a candle from the shelf by the door to guide her up the darkly winding stair to her grandmother's rooms. "The senhora is impatient, *menina.*" Advice, or warning?

Mrs. Brett was dressed now, in the widow's black she had worn for forty years. She was sitting in her bedroom, bolt upright in her chair, only the rigid fold of her hands betraying tension. "There you are at last, child. Thank you, Manuela, that will do." And then, as the door of the outer room closed behind her. "Have you a black dress, Juana?"

"Black? No, ma'am."

"So I supposed. Well, for tonight we must manage as best we may. Look in the closet over there; quickly; we're much of a height you and I. There should be something that will do." And then, as Juana moved obediently over to the big clothes-press that occupied almost one whole wall of the room, "Thank God, you've got the sense to do as you're told without a lot of questions. Start at the left. You'll need one of the ones I wore when I was younger."

Obeying, Juana saw that a whole life's history was hanging there, from the bride's tissues and gauzes through a gamut of changing fashions in black. Clove oranges, here and there among the dresses, gave off their pleasant, aromatic odour. She reached in and pulled out a voluminous black cloak. "Would this do?"

"Don't want to wear the old woman's clothes, eh? Well, I don't blame you. Put it on, child, and we'll see. My domino! Lord, that makes me feel a thousand years old. Yes——" She rose to adjust the cloak so that it entirely covered Juana's pale muslin. "That will do admirably. Now, sit down, and listen as if your life depended on it. Which it may. But, first, lock the outer door. No; leave the inner one open. So, it is impossible for us to be overheard." She laughed. "You think I've gone crazy like poor Elvira?"

The thought had just whispered through Juana's mind: "Oh, no, ma'am," she began to protest, but was interrupted.

"Don't lie to me. Ever. Of course you do. And I don't much blame you. But I'm not mad, child, only very old, and very tired. I must have help. I never thought, when I began,

69

that it would go on so long. We neither of us did. Well, there it is. No good crying over spilt milk. And no stopping either. Not now. I've racked my brains as to where I could turn for help. No trusting those sons of mine, or my grandsons either. So I asked advice. I won't say I wasn't surprised at the answer I got, but it may do yet. At least you're not a fool, nor a coward. So sit down, and listen."

"Yes?" Juana pulled a stool close to her grandmother's chair.

But the old lady was silent for a moment, gazing past her into the shadowed corner of the room. At last she spoke: "It goes back a long way. To your grandfather. You know he and I were loyalists, of course?" She sighed. " 'Charlie is my darling!' Young fools that we were."

"I knew you were exiled in '45, ma'am, but I didn't know about Grandfather Brett."

"Why should you? It's ancient history now. George the Third's as safe on his throne as if the Stuarts had never existed. But when I was young, it was different. We still hoped for a restoration. My husband worked all his life for it. He founded a society: Catholic, loyalist, deadly secret. At the time, it spread all over Europe. There are advantages about being a merchant. You have connections everywhere, reasons for traveling ... But he worked himself to death, my poor James, with the business in the daytime and the society at night. We won't talk about that. After he died, the others lost heart; they met less and less often. I thought it was all over. In a way, it was. It had become more of an old men's dining club than a secret society. Then, much later, after the Revolution in France, something happened. It all began again, only different. It got taken over by another society, the Sons of the Star. Some people say Pombal founded that one, that it went underground after his death, became dangerous. It's dangerous enough. What is it, child?"

"Jaime warned me about them today—the Sons of the Star. He was terrified, even speaking of them."

"He was right to be. No one speaks of them if they can help it."

"Jaime said, 'If they condemn you to death, you're dead.' "

"That's about it. Luckily they need me alive. And you, Juana. Was your ship's captain surprised to get his clearance so quickly?"

"Yes. You mean ... ?"

"I told them, at their last meeting, that I must have you

70

here for this one. They think me an old fool, but a useful one. They need me, you see, to let them into their meeting place. I'm part of the ritual. James arranged it so that they could meet when he was away on business. That ritual!" Her laugh was only a whisper. "Men are children in some ways, Juana. They won't change it, however inconvenient. Or only to make it more complicated. Never to simplify. So they need me. When I realised what they were doing, I got in touch with our minister—secretly, carefully. My God, but I was careful. Isn't it odd to think that for over ten years now, I, of all people, have been working for King George."

"Ma'am, I don't understand."

"No wonder. I'm an old fool to ramble on so. And there's so little time. They meet, always, at the full moon, at midnight. And I have to be there to let them in. James thought of everything. If they met here, he said, we would always know what they were doing. But I can't do it any more. All those stairs ... you'll see. I'm crippled for days afterward. So, last time, I told them you were coming to take over: a new Handmaiden of the Star. God knows, I was an old enough one. Fantastic, of course, that they should have accepted you with so little enquiry. But there were reasons ... They think nothing of women. That helps. And being so powerful, so dreaded—it makes them over-confident. Besides, they don't know it all. You'll see. And, tonight, you will swear a dreadful oath to reveal nothing of what you see or hear. You will break it only to me. That is, if you are ready to help me?"

"I have to, don't I?"

"Have I been unfair to you? I suppose I have. Leaving you so little time, so little choice. But what else could I do? You'll understand better when you hear them. They're dangerous. Never for a minute forget that. Sometimes it's easy to forget, listening to them talk, on and on, about freedom, equality, the liberty Bonaparte is going to give them. Bonaparte! They're idealists, you see, most of them. That's what makes them so dangerous."

"But what do we have to do?"

"We listen. After she has opened the great door, the Handmaiden withdraws to her own cell; she is supposed to know no more of what goes on. But James was a clever man, Juana. He arranged it, at first, merely as a precaution. He built a secret opening, so that I could hear what went on in the main hall when he was away. Is your memory good?"

"Reasonably."

"It had better be. The fate of Portugal may depend on it—and England's too. If these madmen let the French into Portugal, give them control of the Tagus, how long do you think England could last? But it's getting late. No time for more now. Tonight you will do whatever I tell you, without question. Say nothing but what I tell you to say; try not even to think of what I have told you. If you can, try not to be afraid. Fear dulls the mind."

"I don't think I'm afraid. Not very."

"You'd be a fool if you weren't a little. I know I am when I go down there."

"Down?"

"Yes. Down the winding stair." She rose stiffly and moved over to the huge clothes-press at the side of the room. "Did you think me a sentimental fool to save my old dresses? Look! They make admirable cover." She pushed the hanging clothes aside to reveal the wooden back of the press. "There. Push on that knot in the wood."

CHAPTER 6

The back of the cupboard swung open under Juana's hand to reveal a door in the wall, bolted on their side. Obeying orders, she slid back the bolt and pushed open the door. A dark chasm gaped before her and a dank smell of earth and rock rose up to mingle with the spicy scent of the closet.

"Feel on the shelf high up on your right," said Mrs. Brett. "You'll find tinder-box and candles. You must never use the ones from my room. Someone would notice, sooner or later. That's it." If she saw Juana's hand shake as she lit the candle, she forbore to comment. "Luckily the air is quiet down there," she went on, "but I always take the tinder-box with me, just in case. We must get you a black gown, with pockets. For tonight, give it to me, I will carry it, and the candle. Now, follow me, and not a word till I give you leave."

At first the stairway was merely a dusty replica of the one by which Juana had reached her grandmother's rooms, but soon, when, she thought, they were level with the ground floor of the castle, they came to a second door, also bolted on their side.

"There." Mrs. Brett's voice echoed strangely as she closed it behind them. "Now we are clear of the castle. You can speak, but quietly."

Peering into the blackness ahead of them, Juana had, for the moment, nothing to say. They were in some vast chamber of the rock and, in front of them, another flight of steps, guarded on each side by a rope, led straight down into the dark.

"I'll go first." Again Mrs. Brett's voice echoed hollow in the huge cavern. "It's quite easy. The steps are regular, you'll find, once you've got the feel of them. They built well, the Moors."

"The Moors?"

"Yes. This stairway is as old as the oldest part of the castle. It leads down to the little harbour below us; the one the sardine boats use. That's the way the others come. By water. They can't get in till we have opened the gate for them. James took no chances when he made this into their

73

meeting chamber." And then: "Seventy-five, seventy-six—eighty steps in this flight. You must remember to count them for yourself next time. There, it's flat now for a little way. They cut through the rock here." She held up the candle to show Juana the entrance to a dark tunnel, then bent her head slightly and entered it.

Following, Juana felt the skirts of her cloak brush against the damp walls, then caught her breath in a near shriek as something moved suddenly beside her.

"Good girl." Mrs. Brett's voice was reassuring. "It's only bats. I should have warned you. There: we're out again. Seventy-five steps this time."

The dark journey seemed endless, but at last they reached a short flight that ended at a locked and bolted door. "Here." Mrs. Brett handed Juana a huge key. "You must open it. You'll be alone next time. I could see they did not much like the idea of two of us, so I promised it would only be this once. Besides—I may not have the strength to come."

"I can't think how you have managed so long." Juana turned the key in the heavy lock.

"I managed because I had to. You will do the same. There: this is the council chamber. Light the candles, child." She moved forward, the tiny flame of her candle merely emphasising the vast blackness of the cavern. Following, Juana saw a long table, with heavy brass candelabra set at intervals down it.

"The acolytes change them after the meeting." Mrs. Brett handed Juana a taper.

"Does my voice sound as odd as yours?" Juana began lighting the big candles. There were forty-nine of them, seven in each candlestick, but when she had lit them all they merely served to emphasise the huge darkness of the cavern.

"You noticed? Yes—it's one of the great advantages of this as a meeting place. Something about the size of it makes voices unrecognisable. You could meet your own father down here, masked, and not know him. Now light the braziers, child."

These stood in a rough outer circle round the huge table. They, too, were ready to be lit, and when Juana put her taper to the first one, if flared up at once.

"They use resin, I think." Mrs. Brett stood huddled over the first brazier as Juana lighted the others. It was deathly cold down here, and Juana could hear water dripping somewhere.

No wonder Mrs. Brett was always unwell at the full of the moon; the miracle was that she had survived at all.

"There's a brazier in my cell too." The old lady might have read her thoughts. "James thought of everything. You'll see. This way, and don't let the taper go out."

Carrying it carefully, Juana followed her down a path cut through the rough rocks that surrounded the candlelit table. It led to another heavy wooden door in the rock wall. Unbolted, this revealed a small enclosed cavern furnished with another brazier and one chair.

Mrs. Brett sank on to this gratefully as Juana lit the brazier. "You'll have to sit on the ground tonight. Until they come. But, first, feel along the rock above the door and press where you find a rough place. There!"

As Juana obeyed, a section of what seemed virgin rock had slid aside, leaving an opening through which she could see the council table, with its candles burning steadily in the still cavern.

"Now press again." The rock slid together, silently. "James made that himself," Mrs. Brett went on. "You must never open it until you hear the big doors clang shut. Then you count ten, slowly, to give the acolytes time to get to their place at the foot of the table, blow out your candle, and open it. It can't be seen from the table, so long as the cell is dark, but you must keep watch every minute it's open, for fear anyone should leave his seat. By the rules of the Order, no one should, still less should they enter this room. I am unknown to them, as they are to me. But the way things are going now, anything might happen. So keep good watch, child. Ah!" The sombre note of a gong had sounded from somewhere outside. "There are the acolytes now. Follow me; do as I do."

She pulled the hood of her cloak close around her face, watched Juana do the same, picked up the candle and led the way back across the main cavern to a huge pair of doors that Juana had not noticed before. As she pushed back the heavy bolt, Juana could see that her thin old hands were shaking.

The bolt slid back and invisible hands pulled the big doors outwards. Juana could see nothing but the flare of two torches, and behind them, blackness. But she could hear the sound of the sea, very near, crashing and roaring against the cliffs, and smell salt in the cold air.

Beside her, Mrs. Brett spoke, her voice resonant, unrecognisable: "Who comes here?"

"The Sons of the Star." A man's voice from behind the right-hand torch.

"And why do you come?"

"That we may gain wisdom, knowledge, power, and peace."

Mrs. Brett moved backward and to one side. "Enter, Sons of the Star, and may your hearts' desire be granted."

The two torch-bearers advanced into the big cavern and Juana saw that they were robed like black monks, their cowls pulled so well forward that nothing could be seen of their faces.

"Is the council chamber prepared?" As the leader asked the question, the other shot the bolt in the big doors.

"Search and see." Mrs. Brett took Juana by the hand to lead her back to the table, where they stood side by side, motionless, clearly revealed in the light of the seven candelabra, watching the two black-robed figures search the cavern. They were very thorough about it. When one of them turned the key on the inside of the door that led up to the castle, and removed it, Juana felt a pang of pure terror, and, at the same moment, felt her grandmother's hand reassuringly on hers.

Now the two men had gone into the little cell, holding their torches high to search every corner of it. And again, admitting terror, Juana saw the leader remove the key from the lock before he returned to join them by the table.

"All is prepared." Like Mrs. Brett's, his voice echoed unrecognisably. "And yet all is not ready. Since you are two, who should be one, wait here, unworthy, to answer the question of the Star. And remember that to move or speak without leave in the presence of the Star is instant death."

"We will remember." Mrs. Brett's hand was soothing on Juana's, but it was impossible to tell whether she had expected this.

"Then all is prepared. Open the gates, and let the Sons of the Star come in." As he spoke, he put one foot on a stool, one on the table, and reached high with his torch to set light to a huge lantern, shaped like a seven-pointed star, that hung above the table.

The other man moved away down the hall, his torch casting strange shadows as he went, and unbolted and threw open the doors.

Juana heard the sound of the sea again and the scrape of feet on stone, then a procession of robed and cowled figures entered the cavern two by two and moved slowly towards the table. The acolyte who had opened the door remained by it, while the other moved forward from the table to meet the procession. The right-hand man of the first pair stopped and spoke. "Son of the Star, is our council chamber ready?"

"Not yet, most excellent Star." And suddenly Juana was aware that the acolyte was almost as terrified as she. It was not a discovery likely to make her feel any better herself.

"And why is it not ready?" The colloquial Portuguese told her that this was not part of the rehearsed formula, but an improvisation.

"Most excellent Star, there are two here, where should be one. Unworthy though they be, I have detained them here to meet the question of the Star."

"You have done well, my son." Juana thought the acolyte drooped with relief. "Let the intruders stand forward and explain themselves. One unworthy female under our sacred roof is too many; two are an insult to the Star."

"An insult, however, for which the Star should have been prepared." Mrs. Brett took a step forward, and Juana did the same. "I explained at the last meeting that I could no longer carry on my duties and must arrange a substitute. And here she is. An unworthy female, perhaps, but prepared to go to some trouble to make your meetings possible. For the same reward, of course, as I have received all the years, and the same promise of immunity."

"How like a female to speak of rewards. To serve the Star is a privilege, woman, and one of which none of your sex is worthy."

Juana felt her grandmother stiffen beside her, and was afraid, for a moment, of what she might say. But after a slight pause she spoke mildly enough. "A promise is a promise, most excellent Star, and this is an old one. I had thought the Sons of the Star prided themselves on their long memories."

"We do. As those who cross us find to their cost. But we waste precious time on you, woman. Tell me, Sons of the Star, is she right in what she claims? Did she make such a request at our last meeting, from which I was, unavoidably, absent?" And, it annoys him, thought Juana, to have to admit to being less than omniscient.

There was a murmur among the robed figures and then one stepped forward. "Yes, oh Star. The female did, in fact, make such a request, and it was granted."

"And I was not informed! But we'll not discuss that now. Woman, by what right do you suggest this substitution?"

"By the right of age and infirmity."

"And this, your substitute, do you vouch for her as you would for yourself? Your life for her life, if she fail or betray us?"

"I do."

"And you?" He turned his cowled head towards Juana. "Do you realise what you are undertaking?"

"I think so." Her voice shook a little, but she hoped that the strange acoustics of the place masked it.

"You promise that once a month, at the full of the moon, in sickness and in health, maimed or halt, at whatever cost to yourself, you will be here to throw open the gates of the Star?"

"I promise." She wished she was back in England.

"And having opened the gates, you will retire to your own cell, as befits one of the inferior sex, and take no cognisance, not even in thought, of what goes on in this chamber?"

"I promise." Her voice was steadier this time, perhaps because she knew it was a lie.

"And when all is finished, and the acolytes let you forth again, you will close all behind them, and return to your own place, and speak not a word of what you have seen or done?"

"I promise."

"Not to your nearest and dearest, not to your mother or your lover, neither under torture nor under fear of your life."

"I promise." And, how unreasonable, she thought, her irritation at this elaborate mumbo-jumbo suddenly rising in a flood to give her unexpected courage.

She needed it at once. "And if you fail us in any point of this," he went on, "do you devote yourself to the vengeance of the Star, which is more horrible than the vengeance of ordinary men, because slower and more subtle?"

"I do."

"To be no longer even a woman—miserable creation of the left hand of God—but a thing, a death in life, mindless, speechless, an example to others. Out of your own mouth, do you condemn yourself to this, should you betray us?"

She could not help it: she hesitated for a moment. Then: "I do."

"It is well. Remember, woman, that the arm of the Star can stretch round the globe, the memory of the Star is like the memory of God, and the vengeance of the Star is more bitter than death."

"I will remember." And, it's blasphemy, she thought, and, really rather absurd: the arm of the Star, indeed. But she was glad, just the same, that it seemed to be over.

The speaker had turned away from her to summon the acolytes. "It is well. I am satisfied. Let the council chamber be freed from the presence of these inferior creations of God."

But as the acolytes moved forward to lead them away, another voice spoke up from the crowd of hooded figures, who had spread out into a loose semi-circle to watch and listen. "Most excellent Star, should we not know who the woman is?"

The simple, practical question seemed to take them all aback, and, surprisingly, it was Mrs. Brett who answered it. "I may be merely an inferior creature," she said, "but I have been guardian of the gates for more than fifty years, and I have never heard such a question asked in the house of the Star. Do you ask each other to throw off your cowls and show your faces? Do you, when a new member is initiated, ask him his name, or do you let two of his brothers vouch for him? Most excellent Star, I claim that this suggestion is an affront to the secrecy of the Star."

"Yes—well"—the man they called the Star hesitated for the first time—"that's rather another thing, you know." And then, recapturing his dignity, "The word of even one of the Sons of the Star is like the word of God, but you are merely a woman."

"Just so. And therefore, I am sure, after I made my request at the last meeting that that night's Star made his own enquiries, where enquiries should be made. To him I appeal."

"She's right, most excellent Star"—how maddening it was not to be able to recognise voices—"enquiries have been made, and have proved satisfactory on every point."

And that was a surprising thing, thought Juana.

"Made by you?" This was another voice.

"No, by last month's Star. As you know, he is not here tonight."

"But you vouch for him and for her?" The leader obviously felt it was time he got the meeting under control. "Your life for their life, your blood for their blood, your death for their death?"

"I do."

"Very well, Brother of the Ragged Staff. You will give your symbol to the junior acolyte, in token of this. And now, we have lost too much time. Remove these talking women, and let us to business."

Listening to the key grinding in the lock on the other side of the cell door, Juana looked apprehensively round at the high roof and damp-smeared walls of the cell. Suppose the door was not unlocked, how long would they last?

"We can talk now, until we open the panel." Mrs. Brett settled on the chair with a sigh of relief. "I'm sorry about all that. I hope it didn't frighten you too much. I didn't expect that last month's Star would have left already. Tonight's has always been more difficult."

"You know him? Who is he?" They were speaking in whispers.

"The less you know, child, the better."

"But when I'm on my own?" She could not help a shudder at the thought. "How shall I tell you who says what?"

"They all have their symbols, received when they were admitted as Sons of the Star. One on the front of the cowl, its replica in the pocket, to be handed in as identification when necessary. You heard."

"Yes, I see. But will I be able to tell them from here?"

"You will have to. And you'll find you can. The symbols are picked out in some kind of strange paint that catches the light. But it's another reason why I have known, for some time, that I should have to give up. I have been finding it increasingly difficult to tell them apart. Ah!"—once again the leaden sound of the gong had echoed through the wall. "They are about to close the great doors. Count ten, child, slowly, then blow out the candle and open the panel. And not a sound till it's closed again."

" . . . Eight, nine, ten." When Juana blew out the candle, the darkness in the cell was absolute and it took her what seemed an age to feel her way back to the door and fumble for the rough place in the rock above it. But at last the panel slid back and she found herself looking straight at the council table and the cowled figures seated round it, all clearly illuminated by the star-shaped lamp. The leader was speaking: " . . . The news is bad, Brothers. The day of Portugal's liberation has been postponed again. The Tsar of Russia has refused to ratify d'Oubril's treaty with the French. Instead, he and the Prussians are conspiring against Napoleon, and the French army at Bayonne—the one our friend Junot was to have brought to our help—has been ordered to Germany."

"Is this certain?" The speaker rose to his feet and Juana

80

saw how the light of the central lamp caught the silver lion on his cowl.

"Most certain, Brother of the Lion. I have it here, in Junot's own hand. The messenger reached me only today."

"It's always the same: fine promises and no performance." This speaker had a silver hand on his cowl. "I vote, most excellent Star, that we leave waiting on the French and take action on our own account. The whole country fears us; the army is away on the coast; the Prince Regent is at Mafra. We have our agents there, and at Sintra and Queluz with his wife and the old Queen. Let us strike now, fast and hard. With the House of Braganza extinct, who will be more able to take over the country than the Sons of the Star?"

"You are ill-informed, Brother of the Silver Hand. The Prince Regent returned to Belem today. But I have more news for you; there is a plot against him afoot among the English—may they rot in the hell they deserve."

"The English plotting against Dom John?" If Juana had not been so cold, and so frightened, she would have found something rather ridiculous about the way each speaker in turn bobbed to his feet so that the light caught his silver identifying emblem. Only the acolytes, standing submissively to right and left of the Star, had none.

"Yes. Lord St. Vincent is an impatient man. He does not know yet, that the French have marched away from Bayonne. He still expects an invasion and has been trying to persuade Dom John that he and his family should sail for the Brazils, and safety. Our brother at Mafra has done his best to persuade the Prince Regent to go, but unfortunately without success, since his sloth is even greater than his cowardice."

"Unfortunately?"

"You do not think, Brother of the Silver Hand. Why murder the Braganzas if we can persuade them to disgrace themselves in the eyes of their people? The assassin's is but a clumsy weapon, at the best of times. Murders make martyrs. You, of all people, should know that."

"But if they refuse to go?" This was the Brother of the Lion.

"St. Vincent proposes to kidnap them. He plans a great review of the British fleet. Dom John and as many of his family as possible will be lured aboard the *Hibernia* and carried off to the Brazils. Nothing could be better for our purpose. There will be a few days of complete confusion. We alone will be ready. Those of the royal family who remain in Portugal must be disposed of, at once, with the exception of

81

one of the Princes—it doesn't much matter which. The Prince Regent will be disgraced by his flight, and his wife dead—there must be no bungling there, lest she bring down the Spanish about our ears—and then, what more natural than that the Sons of the Star should come forward to bring order out of chaos and rule in the name of the young Prince? The murders, of course, will have been no affair of ours; merely accidental results of the confused state of the country. We will be the law-givers, the restorers of order: I doubt if we shall even need the Prince as figurehead for long."

Juana was shuddering so much that her teeth chattered. She had a moment's wild, irrational fear that the noise they made might be heard in the council chamber.

But the conspirators were busy now with practical details of their atrocious plan. The Brother of the Lion was to dispose of the Regent's estranged wife, Carlota Joaquina, at her *quinta* of Ramalhao at Sintra. The Brother of the Silver Hand would deal with the old mad Queen at Queluz. Others were told off to look after other members of the royal family who might not be involved in the proposed kidnapping.

"You will be ready, day and night." The leader summed it up.

"And the signal?" asked a brother who had not spoken before and who had his back to Juana so that she could not see his symbol.

"The signal will be the kidnapping. We will be ready. No one else will. And now—the night draws on—we must be in our places by morning. Who knows, our chance may come tomorrow?" He raised his hands as if in blessing. "Sons of the Star, we meet only to part; we separate that we may come together; we pledge ourselves, one and all, to work without fear and without fail for the greater glory of the Star. What is the penalty for failure?"

"Death." The voices echoed strangely.

"And the doom of treachery?"

"The death in life that is worse than death."

"So be it. And now, brothers, may the Star speed you on your way, and make you worthy of its light."

The two acolytes rose, as if this was their signal, and turned towards the big doors, and as they did so, Juana touched the rough stone with a shaking hand and the panel slid into place.

"Good," whispered Mrs. Brett. "Now, light the candle, quickly."

But this was more than Juana could do. Working in the

dark, her shaking hands were incapable of striking the light she needed. She felt panic rising in her and at the same moment her grandmother's firm, cold hand took the tinder-box from her. "Never mind, you have done admirably." And then, as the candle flickered into life under her steady hands, "Sit down here by me, as if you'd been asleep most of the time. Your head in my lap. That's it."

It was horrible to be able to hear nothing, now, from the big cavern. "Suppose they don't let us out?" whispered Juana.

"There will be no one to admit them to their next meeting."

Juana shuddered. "But they may be running the country in a month's time."

"I doubt that. Ah!" The key grated in the lock on the other side of the door and it swung open to reveal the two acolytes. Behind them, the big cavern was empty and dark. Juana watched, shivering, as the two men went silently to work in the little cell, pushing the faintly smouldering brazier aside, preparing another one, and changing the guttering candle. Then, without a word said, they left the cell and moved, side by side, across the cavern and out through the big doors. Once more, Juana heard the sea roaring below, before the doors shut it out and Mrs. Brett drove the big bolt home.

Going back, the climb seemed endless, even to Juana. Mrs. Brett looked ghastly: her breath laboured, her hands clutched like claws at the guide rope by the stairs. Juana helped her where she could, but much of the time the stairway was too narrow. Once, Mrs. Brett swayed in front of her, and she wondered, for an endless moment, whether she would be able to catch her, or whether they would fall together to certain death in the cavern below.

But at last they reached the door that meant they were entering the castle itself. "Silently now." Mrs. Brett spoke with difficulty.

The stairway was wider here, and Juana could help her up it and at last out through the clothes-press and into her own room.

"Help me to bed, child. We'll talk in the morning."

"But, Grandmother, shouldn't we do something?"

"There's nothing we can do tonight, since we've no messenger. Pray, if you like. And hope Mr. Varlow comes early. At least he's never failed me." She fell back with a sigh of exhaustion on the big bed. "Sleep well, Juana. You've earned it."

But not even her own exhaustion could bring sleep to Juana. She lay wide-eyed in the darkness, suffering again the events of the day. Next time she must go alone down the winding stair, counting the steps—did she remember how many? Next time she would be alone to face the Sons of the Star. But would there be a next time? Suppose their atrocious plan of murder and usurpation had already succeeded. If there had been any doubt in her mind, before, about whether she could really play the terrifying role for which her grandmother—and Gair Varlow—had chosen her, now she knew she had no choice. In England, politics had not concerned her much. She had hated Napoleon, because everyone else did, and been a Tory, because her father was a Whig. But this was not politics, it was murder.

Shivering, but not with cold, she thought: this was what Gair Varlow wanted me for. This was why he brought me to Forland House and wooed me among the roses. For this. For murder, for conspiracy, for possible death. There had been a moment, back in Saint Roque, when she had begun to understand something of this and had wanted, bitterly, passionately, to walk out of the great church doors, back down the stinking lanes, back to the ship, and England. Why had she not gone?

Perhaps because to do so would have been to let him see how he had hurt her, and there was savage comfort in concealing that. She would show him that she could play his game as well as he, and with as little feeling. For he had made no bones about it. He meant to go on using her. Tomorrow he would arrive, "Ostensibly to call on you," he had said. "You won't mind?" he had asked. Mind? She found she was biting the sheet, made herself lie still and slept at last, heavily.

Manuela was peering anxiously down at her. "Mrs. Brett is asking for you, menina. She said to let you sleep through dinner, but it's late now. Past one o'clock." They kept Portuguese hours at the castle and dined at eleven.

"How is she this morning?" Juana was out of bed with the words.

"As usual." It was hard to tell just what this implied.

In fact, Juana was amazed to find her grandmother up and dressed. She remarked on it as soon as they were alone: "I had hoped you would rest in bed today, ma'am."

"Impossible. Lock the outer door, Juana." And then, when Juana had made sure that there was no one within earshot, "Don't you realise after last night, the danger of this business? Nothing must be unusual today. And—I have to see Mr. Varlow."

"Could not I?"

"Alone? A young lady? Have you forgotten what life here is like? And there is no one in the castle we can trust. Never forget that, Juana."

"But surely I could give him a letter?"

"At a pinch, yes. But we avoid writing if we can. The Sons of the Star are everywhere. You take your life in your hand if you write."

"But, Grandmother, are they really so powerful?" Juana had had a great deal of time, in the sleepless night, to think about this. "They seemed—somehow—absurd. All that question and answer business! It was like boys at school. And —really—to let you watch them all these years and never even notice—"

"Don't be misled by that," the old woman interrupted her. "In fact, it's the measure of their power. It would simply not occur to them that I might be any kind of a threat. You heard what they think of women. They just think of one as negligible, a female, a thing. But they are none the less dangerous for that. For God's sake, Juana, don't fall into their own error of over-confidence. That way lies danger— no, the certainty of a horrible death." She rose stiffly to her feet, walked, limping, over to the anteroom door, then turned back to face Juana. "It seemed so simple, risking your life, before I had seen you again. After all, what is one life, compared with the safety of a whole country? Now, I feel different. For my sake, Juana, be careful."

"Thank you, Grandmother." It was heart-warming. "I'll be careful."

A timid knock summoned Juana to the outer door where she found Estella looking both nervous and shocked: "There's a young gentleman come to call, *menina,* asking for you. A Senhor Varlow." She pronounced it oddly.

"What's this?" Mrs. Brett's voice, loud and bullying from the inner room. "A young gentleman daring to ask for my granddaughter?"

"He's an English gentleman," Estella volunteered timidly.

"I'm sorry, ma'am." Juana took her cue. "I met him at Forland House. I suppose he doesn't know our Portuguese customs."

"Then it's time he learned about them. Bring him here, Estella, and I will teach him to come paying calls on unmarried young ladies."

So the interview Juana had dreaded began with a magnificent scolding, delivered in full voice by the old lady, who clearly intended everyone in the castle to know how she felt about Gair Varlow. Since Estella heard every word of it, there was no doubt that the story would be all over the castle by supper-time. At last Mrs. Brett drew breath and spoke more mildly: "And what have you to say for yourself, young man?"

"I must plead ignorance, ma'am. And beg your forgiveness, and Miss Brett's. I had the good fortune to meet her at Forland House, to hear her sing. When I heard she had come to Portugal, I could not believe in my good luck. I wished to lose no time in . . . in paying my respects, to her and her family." He was every inch the love-lorn suitor, fumbling for words, even, Juana could have sworn, blushing a little. Watching the consummate performance, she thought it would be easy to hate him.

Luckily he and Mrs. Brett were now keeping up a conversation of splendid banalities about the news of the day. After about five minutes of this, Mrs. Brett drooped a little in her big upright chair. "You will forgive me, Mr. Varlow, I know. I am a little tired today. I do not normally entertain strangers. Estella!"

"Yes, ma'am?" Estella emerged from her retirement in the antechamber.

"Mr. Varlow wishes to meet the family. Will you fetch Elvira, please, to introduce him—and warn my sons to expect a guest. Wake them, if necessary." And then, in quite a different tone, as soon as the outer door was closed behind Estella. "Juana, the door. Don't lock it: stand by it. Mr. Varlow, come closer."

So Juana, leaning against the outer door, heard only a phrase here and there of their quick, low-voiced conversation. She gathered that the review of the fleet to which St. Vincent proposed to invite the Prince Regent was planned for the following week. "I'll warn Strangford," Varlow said. "He'll take care of it. Though, frankly, I doubt if even St. Vincent would be mad enough to put such a plan into execution. It sounds like an after-dinner project to me."

"Yes." Mrs. Brett was pleased with him. "That's what I thought."

On duty at the door, Juana thought she heard a noise outside, and opened it a crack. Nothing. She closed it again, in time to hear Gair Varlow say: "No; it may take some time to find another messenger I can trust. In the meanwhile,

I am afraid my courtship of Miss Brett will have to be fairly assiduous."

"Yes," agreed the old lady. "And not just once a month, after the full moon, either. That would be too obvious."

Sick with anger—at herself, at him—Juana was grateful that she could keep her face turned away from the other two. But now she did hear voices on the stair. "They're coming, ma'am." She joined them in time for Elvira's knock on the outer door.

Elvira seemed less odd this morning, and was talking in fairly coherent prose. She greeted Gair Varlow quite normally and led the way back across the courtyard to the family's part of the castle, where they found Miguel deep in talk with a priest Juana had not met before and did not much like now. Father Ignatius was short and stout, with a sharp and sliding eye. He apologised, at length, and with a humility that failed to ring true, for being absent on the "propitious occasion" of her return.

"Nothing but my duty would have called me away," he wound up with a flourish, and Juana found herself thinking: what duty? Had he, perhaps, been one of the cowled Sons of the Star? How maddening it was that acoustics of the cavern took the individuality out of voices. From now on, she must suspect everyone.

Turning away from him, a little too abruptly, she could not help being amused to find Gair Varlow already deep in talk with Miguel about Pombal's expulsion of the Jesuits. It was a subject on which Miguel would fulminate for hours, and she listened with a mixture of irritation and awe as Gair kept him going with a well-timed and brilliantly uncommittal word here and there.

Prospero joined them a few minutes later, explaining, with apologies, that he had been absorbed in a knotty point for the preface to his edition of Camoens. "It's a question of what really happened to King Sebastian," he explained, shaking Gair absentmindedly by the hand. "You know the story?"

"Of the King who disappeared after being defeated by the Moors? Yes, indeed. That was during Camoens' lifetime, was it not? Is it true that many Portuguese still believe that he is waiting, like King Arthur, in some limbo, and will return one day to save his country in its hour of need?"

Prospero shrugged. "Our peasants will believe anything. Sebastianism always revives when there's trouble. I expect if you asked Iago or Tomas—our footmen—they would tell you they confidently expect him to appear at the eleventh hour and rout the French."

"Fantastic! But apropos of the *Lusiads,* sir, have you met my principal, Lord Strangford, who translated them?"

Prospero had not, and would like to, he said, although he made it clear that he had his doubts about Strangford's translation of the famous Portuguese poem. "There are several points I should like to discuss with him."

"I am sure he would be most grateful for any help you can give him with a view to a future edition. With your permission, I will hope to arrange a meeting next time Lord Strangford comes to Sintra. Perhaps you would all honor us with a visit?" He finished the glass of wine and the little sweet cake Elvira had offered him and rose to take his leave. "You will bring your charming niece?" Once again, the note was absolutely right, and once again Juana found it intolerable.

But, "A very personable young man," was Prospero's verdict, after Gair had gone.

"Right-thinking, too, for an Englishman," said Miguel. "Really not at all an unsuitable young man, my dear Juana, if he has any means."

"He has nothing." It came out more angrily than Juana had intended, and once again she was uncomfortably aware of Father Ignatius' sharp eye upon her.

Elvira burst into song:

"How shall I your true love know
From another one?
By his cockle-hat and staff,
And his sandal shoon."

CHAPTER 7

After that dramatic beginning, it was odd to find life in the castle settling down into a humdrum, domestic routine. Juana often found it hard to believe, as the monotonous rhythm of her days established itself, that down below, deep in the heart of the cliff, lay the cavern where, in a month's time—no, less than three weeks now—she must play, alone, her part of danger.

They rose early at the castle to take advantage of the cool morning hours. Juana breakfasted on rolls and coffee with her uncles and aunt, then visited her grandmother (if she was well enough) before riding out for an hour or two on her mule, Rosinante. She had objected, furiously, at first, to being accompanied by one of the servants, but Mrs. Brett had been firm: "I'm sorry, child. You're in Portugal now."

So Tomas or Iago ran ahead with his lead-tipped staff while Rosinante ambled up and down among the orange groves and grape vines of the Pleasant Valley, and Juana tried to work out where, underneath, the secret cavern must lie. Her grandmother had told her that it was far enough from the Castle on the Rock so that the connection between them need not be obvious to the Sons of the Star who came by boat to a concealed entrance in the cliffs. But when Juana had asked if she knew where that was, Mrs. Brett had shaken her head: "Don't even wonder, child. It's not safe."

Though it was mid-September by now, the hills towards Sintra were still bleached brown, waiting for the autumn rains. To enter the Pleasant Valley was like entering a different world. Here, as at Sintra, the Moorish method of irrigation was still practised, making the fullest use of every drop of water from the little stream that ran down the valley. Here grapes were ripening on their vines, trained up poles in the tidy Portuguese fashion, and Juana pulled up Rosinante from time to time to pick a few of the ripest and eat them, hot and sweet and tasting of sunshine. There were small green oranges already, shining among dark leaves, and she spent a whole peaceful morning watching the men dig out the earth from around their roots, water them, and put it back.

As Maria had prophesied, the sun and air were doing her good, and so was the blessed freedom, in Portuguese, from her stammer. She felt more adventurous every day and rode a little farther down the path by the valley stream. Soon she had passed the limits of her childhood explorations with Pedro and Roberto. They had never gone beyond the flat table of rock, about halfway down the valley with the olive press and the big tanks where the grapes were brought at harvest time and trampled all night by barefoot *gallegos* who worked their way, thus, from vineyard to vineyard. Down to this pressing floor, the path was really a road, wide enough for the lumbering oxcarts to take away the casks of must or oil when the pressing was over. Beyond it, there were only the labourers' paths among the vines. The sides of the valley grew steeper, and the cultivated area smaller, hemmed in by a wilderness of tangling myrtle and cistus and creeping oak, which thinned out, higher up, to show the granite bones of the valley.

Juana's private ambition was to follow the stream all the way down to the sea. The odd thing about the Pleasant Valley, and the secret of its fertility, was that in it you were unaware of the nearby Atlantic. It ran almost parallel with the line of the cliffs, and its stream turned sharply to the right at the bottom to vanish in a tangle of undergrowth. But surely where water went, she could go too?

So day after day she tried the paths that fanned out downwards from the central plateau, only to find that each one petered out where the vines ended. She had not told Iago, who usually accompanied her, about her plan. Was it that it seemed rather a childish one? Or was there more to it? She did not remember being forbidden to come down here when she was a child, but the fact remained that she and her cousins had never done so.

She had almost overlooked the path that ran by the stream itself, because its entrance was masked by an untidy thicket of evergreen oaks. When she did notice it, one hot, still September morning, and turned Rosinante's head down it, Iago came running towards her from the plateau, where he had paused to talk to the men who were cleaning out the wine troughs. "Not that way, senhora," he shouted before he had reached her. "You can't get through."

"Yes I can. Look! The path is much better this side of the thicket. I believe it will take me down by the stream."

"It will take you farther than that." He was shaking with fright. "It will take you straight to Hell!"

"Iago! What in the world do you mean?"

"Don't you remember? Surely you must have been told about the Jaws of Death when you were a child? It's not safe down there." He seized Rosinante's reins to turn her in the narrow path and lead her back out of the shadow of the oaks into the hot sunshine of the plateau. He was white and sweating with terror, and she forbore to question him until he had led the mule some little way back up the road above the pressing floor. At last she pulled Rosinante to a halt in the shade of a huge bay tree. "Now, Iago, explain."

He crossed himself and looked about him nervously. "Don't make me, senhora."

"If you don't, I shall go right back there." She made as if to turn Rosinante.

"No, no, not that! I'll tell you—but you've really not heard of the Jaws of Death?"

"No. I know we did not go down there as children, but that was just because it was too far."

"I suppose your grandmother did not want you told. I've only been here a few years, but everyone on the place knows about the Jaws of Death. It's death to go down there. You know about the *bruchas*?" Again he crossed himself.

"The Portuguese witches? Of course. Maria used to tell us stories of them when we were children. But that's all they are, stories."

"Not here," he said. "Maybe in England, they are just stories. It's different here. My cousin Batista said the same as you. He'd been to school; at the *Necessidades* in Lisbon; his mother had ambitions for him; he was going to become Pope, was Batista, or a Cardinal anyway. Well—he came here, one year, to help with the vintage. He said there should be a short way to the sea, down there—" He looked around nervously. "We told him, all of us. We warned him, but he would go. He set out, one hot morning, very like this one, only it was October; we were busy treading the grapes. It was darkening up for a storm. We were working against time. God forgive me, I forgot all about him for a while, but when the lightning came, I knew. It was the *bruchas*. We found him, five days later, down in the cove where the sardine boats land. There wasn't a scratch on him, not a thing to show how he died. But I'll never forget his face. He'd seen the *bruchas*. It's death to see them . . ."

The *bruchas*, Juana wondered, or the Sons of the Star? She shivered. Much of the time, these peaceful sun-drenched days, she contrived to forget about the cavern in the cliff, and the dark assignation she must keep there at the end of the month, but Iago's terror was infectious. She was glad to be back in the upper valley where labourers, here and there among the vines, shouted cheerfully to each other as they worked.

Iago must have talked. Mrs. Brett sent for Juana that evening. "You've been exploring. You're not to. I told you that you must not even think about the entrance to the cavern. I meant it, Juana."

"I'm sorry, ma'am. I didn't think. I only wanted to find a way to the sea."

"You can't afford not to think. I can't do without you, Juana. Iago may be a superstitious fool, but he's right about the Jaws of Death. To go down there is to sign one's death warrant."

"So there is an entrance—"

"I said don't think about it." The old lady was white with anger. "Are you tired of living, Juana?"

"I'm a little bored with it." The answer surprised Juana herself. But it was true enough. What was there to do in this castle where hordes of half-trained servants made it not only unnecessary but impossible to lift a finger for oneself.

"Ungrateful!"

"I'm sorry." She meant it. "But you must see there's no one here for me to talk to." It was extraordinary. Back in England she had longed for just this solitude that was weighing so heavily on her now.

Surprisingly, Mrs. Brett laughed. "Mr. Varlow was quite right," she said. "He told me that a few weeks of sunshine would make a new creature of you. I just didn't expect it to happen so fast."

"What else did he say?"

"That you had character, if not—" she stopped.

"If not looks. Don't spare my feelings, Grandmother. If I am to work with Mr. Varlow—and it seems I must—the fewer illusions there are between us, the better." Illusions! Something inside her still shivered in useless anguish at memory of those days of sundrenched, delusive happiness back at Forland House. Never again. "There's something we ought to think about. If Mr. Varlow must really pretend to court me, how am I to receive his attentions?"

"What do you suggest?" Her grandmother's tone showed surprised respect.

Juana's first instinct was to say that she would treat her suitor with disdain, but wiser councils prevailed. "I think I shall play hot and cold. Too young to know my own mind? That kind of thing? It won't do to be too discouraging. Only—one thing I must insist on—you will explain to him what I am doing."

"Insist?" It was not a word often used to Mrs. Brett. She took it well. "Portugal is certainly doing you good, child. Very well. Since you insist, I'll make a chance to explain. And in the meantime, no more adventuring down the Pleasant Valley."

Had the family been discussing her explorations? Her Uncle Miguel asked her, over breakfast next morning, whether she would oblige him by taking her ride that day up to the Cork Convent, the curious eyrie high up on the ridge, where a group of Franciscan monks lived, piously uncomfortable, in cork-lined cells. "I have a letter to be delivered to the Prior there," he explained. "Some business about my Little Brothers of Saint Antony."

"Of course I'll go." Juana had pleasant memories of childhood excursions to this high point, and of being made much of by the little group of monks who lived there. "But I won't be back in time for dinner, surely?"

"No indeed. It would hurt the Fathers' feelings if you did not dine there. Outside, that is. Unaccompanied females are not allowed in their cloisters. But on a day like today—"

"I shall enjoy it."

She was grateful to Miguel. It was good to get away from the castle, and the Pleasant Valley, and even, she admitted to herself, from her family. From Prospero and Miguel who moved so silently about the castle and in whose voices she was always searching for echoes of the Sons of the Star. No doubt it was merely her imagination that made her test their words and phrases for hints of a knowledge that matched her own. And Elvira—how mad was Elvira?

It had rained a little in the night and the air on the ridge road was fragrant with scents of lavender and thyme and a whole botany of flowering heathers. Juana's spirits rose at the idea of a day's outing, and she was glad, too, that it was Tomas, not Iago, who had accompanied her. When they turned off the Sintra road on to the track that led up the higher ridge running down to Cabo Roca, he stopped to wait for her. "This is better than the Pleasant Valley, senhora?"

"No *bruchas* here?"

He crossed himself. "Don't speak about them!"

The monks gave them a royal reception. They had been late starting because Miguel had thought of a last-minute postscript to his letter. It was well past noon when they climbed the last steep path to the monastery and the Fathers had already eaten, but they insisted that Juana sit down on the little stretch of level, sweet-smelling turf outside their curious abode while they prepared a meal for her. It took a long time coming, and appalled her, when it did, with its high-flavoured cabbage and strong, saffron-coloured rice. Still, the dessert was delicious, and Juana forgot a slight anxiety about how time was going on as she quenched a raging thirst with peaches and nectarines.

But the sun was sinking towards the Atlantic, and a hint of mist shrouded the distant view of Cape Espichel. She rose to her feet to thank the Prior for his hospitality and say good-bye. She had forgotten how long it would take. He made a speech. She made a speech, amazed to hear herself doing so. Imagine, in England, making a speech.

Tomas was beginning to look anxious when they finally got away. "We must lose no time, senhora, if we are not to be benighted."

"No." She dismissed the thought that it might be wise to ask for a couple of lay brothers to accompany them with torches. By what she had seen of the way they did things at the Cork Convent, it would be full dark by the time they were ready. Better to go on and lose no time. A pity, of course, that there was no moon. But at least it meant that there were almost two weeks to go until the next meeting in the cavern below the castle.

By the time they reached the Sintra road the colour was ebbing fast from the hills. "We're late." Tomas was having difficulty keeping up the pace she set.

"I'm afraid so. Take my bridle; Rosinante will help you along."

"Thank you." He looked over his shoulder nervously. "I wish you'd not gone down the valley yesterday."

"Don't be absurd, Tomas." But his obvious fright was infectious. She found herself looking ahead at a dark little wood of ilexes, and wishing the road did not go through it.

94

Tomas had seen it too. His grip on Rosinante's bridle tightened and the mule slowed down.

"Don't, Tomas!" It came out sharper than she meant. She must not let him see that she had caught his fear. "Gently," she went on. "Give poor Rosinante a chance."

They were into the shadow of the ilexes now and suddenly Rosinante stopped dead. "See what you've done." Juana kicked the mule, but she refused to budge, setting her ears back and gazing mutinously ahead. "Give her a pull, Tomas. We don't want to stay here all night." She was fighting panic now, but managed not to show it.

"What do you think she sees, senhora? The *bruchas*?" Turned back towards her, his face showed white in the shadows as he pulled unavailingly at the mule's bridle.

"You know better than that. Pull harder."

At last, reluctantly, Rosinante moved forward into the darker shadow of the wood, with Tomas still walking close beside on the pretext of encouraging her. What did he really fear, Juana wondered, the *bruchas*, or, like her, illogically, horribly, the Sons of the Star?

Absurd, of course. They were halfway through the little wood now and she could see light ahead. Ridiculous to have been so frightened. Ridiculous? There was movement in the wood around her. Muffled figures emerged from the bushes. She had time for one scream before something heavy and stifling was thrown over her head and she was dragged struggling from the mule's back. Behind her, the sound of scuffling told her that the same thing must be happening to Tomas.

And all the time, worst of all, not a word was said. Struggling and stifling under the heavy weight of the blanket, she had no idea how many men surrounded her. She tried to speak, but the blanket was held too tight around her face; she tried to stop in her tracks, but inexorable hands forced her along—back, she thought, down the road towards Sintra.

The blanket stank of horse and she thought with irrational rage what a sordid way this was to die, thought, illogically, of Gair Varlow, and heard, suddenly, the sound of a horse ridden hard towards them.

One horseman. Coming to her help? Gair Varlow? Mere self-delusion to think so. No doubt this was the leader of her attackers. Besides, what could one man do?

But her captors had stopped, were whispering together, unintelligible through the thick folds of blanket. The horseman sounded very near now, slowing down, no doubt to enter the wood. Then he was upon them. "What's going on here?" A strange voice, speaking Portuguese. "Let her go!" The sound of blows, a scuffle, a curse ... She was pushed violently to the ground and lay for a moment, dazed, before she realised she was free and managed to throw off the stifling folds of the horse blanket.

Heather pricked sharply through her light riding habit. She was lying by the road just outside the little wood. Near her, Tomas lay prone, swathed in another blanket, muttering prayers under his breath. Sitting up, she looked back along the road. A commotion in the thick growth of cistus and myrtle below it showed where her attackers had fled. Now a solitary horseman appeared from behind an outcrop of rock and rode back towards her. She had never seen him before. Brown skin, dark curling hair cut short, an air of command that turned to solicitude as he jumped down from his horse, threw the reins carelessly on its neck, and bent over her. "Useless to follow them further," he said in Portuguese. "An army could hide in that scrub. But you're not hurt, cousin?"

"I don't think so." She took the hand he held out and rose shakily to her feet. "Thanks to you." His hand firm on hers was hot, very slightly damp, and infinitely reassuring. She looked at him, puzzled. "Cousin?"

"You must be Juana Brett." And as she nodded, wordlessly, he raised her hand to kiss it. "I'm your cousin, Vasco de Mascarenhas. Is it too much to hope that you have heard of me?"

"Of course I have." She had indeed. He was the wild one of her mother's family. There was a long story, she knew. Her head was beginning to ache and it was hard to think straight.

"You're hurt! I'm a brute to keep you standing here." He took her arm solicitously to lead her back into the shadow of the wood, and she was grateful for the support. "Thank God, I got here in time," he went on. "I told the old lady she should never have let you ride so far alone."

"I had Tomas."

"Much good he was! Get up, you!" He stirred Tomas with his foot. "Stop snivelling and catch your mistress's mule." And then, to Juana, as Tomas rose trembling to his feet: "But what happened? Who were they?"

"I've no idea." It was the safe answer. "You've been at the Castle on the Rock? Seen my grandmother?"

96

"Yes. I've been abroad—on family business—I'll tell you about it. When I got back and heard you had come home I came at once. My father loved your mother. It was hopeless, of course. It's all a long time ago. I'd do anything for you, Juana Brett. Thank God I came when I did. They were not even anxious about you back at the castle. What are they thinking of to let you ramble about the countryside like this?" She could feel the warmth of his supporting arm through her thin habit. "Thank God, it was no worse. You're sure you're not hurt?"

"Not the least in the world. But very greatful." She detached herself gently from his supporting arm as Tomas returned leading Rosinante. "Well done, Tomas. They didn't hurt you?"

"Cowards never get hurt," interrupted the stranger. But he was not a stranger, he was her cousin Vasco. "And you, cousin," he went on, "are you strong enough to ride?" He took consent for granted, scooping her up in strong arms as if she weighed nothing and setting her in the saddle. "Of course you are. We're not a family of weaklings."

She smiled down at the dark, strong-boned face. "Certainly not, cousin, if you make so little of me."

"Diana," he said. And then, "You will have to forgive me for not being as tall as you."

Disconcertingly, he had read her thoughts. "You saved my life," she said and, oddly, remembered saying very much the same thing, once, to Gair Varlow.

"Nothing in mine has ever given me so much happiness." He whistled to his horse. "I'm only sorry I could not bring your attackers to justice. You've no idea who they were?" He had asked it before.

"How should I? They never said a word." In retrospect, this was more disturbing than ever. Could they have feared being recognised?

"It's very strange," he said. "I had thought the days of brigands were past. Or at least here, so near Lisbon. In the Alentejo it's different. I suppose they meant to hold you to ransom."

"Horrible." Either way it was horrible. But why should the Sons of the Star attack her?

"Don't think about it. You're safe now. I'm here. And they'll be really anxious at the castle by now. Serve them right, mind you. But let's hurry, Cousin Juana." He made the name a caress.

Did he know how little she liked re-entering the little wood? He rode very close to her, his hand over hers on Rosinante's bridle. "There," he said, as they emerged on the other side. "Open country all the way now. Look, cousin, the first star is out. Wish, Juana, and your wish will be granted."

The sickle moon had risen, and there was indeed one star showing in the velvet sky above it. "I don't know what to wish for," Juana said, and knew it the truth.

"Wish for happiness, cousin."

CHAPTER 8

At the castle, Vasco de Mascarenhas had a short way with question and exclamation alike.

"Miss Brett has had a most alarming experience." He was lifting her gently from her saddle as Prospero and Miguel appeared on the steps below the family's apartments. "She needs rest, quiet—" His haughty Roman gaze took in the crowd of inquisitive servants in the courtyard. "No!" This to Maria who had pushed forward to kiss Juana's hands and asked hysterically what had happened to her. " 'Quiet,' I said. Where shall I take you, cousin?" His arm was warm and comforting round her waist.

"My mother is waiting in the Ladies' Parlour." Prospero came across the centre of the courtyard to meet them. "She wishes to know what happened. You've very late, Juana. We've been anxious about you."

"I'm delighted to hear it," said Vasco. "But my cousin is not well enough, just now, to answer questions. I will tell you what you need to know. Tell Mrs. Brett I will be with her as soon as I have seen my cousin to her room."

Juana was near to laughter at her uncle's appalled expression. Imagine carrying such a message to old Mrs. Brett. "Thank you, cousin." She disengaged herself from his supporting arm. "But I'm not a case for the smelling bottle yet. Aunt Elvira!" Her aunt had appeared behind her brothers. "I'm so glad to see you." There were tears in her eyes as she hurried across the courtyard to embrace her. "I've had such a fright! But is Grandmother really up and waiting?"

"She is indeed." Miguel's tone was reproachful. "We've been worried to death about you, Juana. Thank God my prayers were not unavailing."

"You had better thank Senhor de Mascarenhas. You've met each other?" It was odd, and oddly comforting, to have the situation dwindle into a social one.

"Just now." Stiff bows from Prospero and Miguel suggested that they were not best pleased with her choice of rescuer. "But what happened, Juana? What possessed you to stay out so late?"

"All in good time." Once again, Vasco took charge of the situation. "Come, cousin. If you really feel strong enough—" Did his tone, perhaps, suggest that a little female weakness would not come amiss?

But it was pleasant, for once, to be treated as in need of support. She was glad to let Vasco bear the brunt of her grandmother's cross-examination. "Undoubtedly brigands." He summed it up. "I expect they thought you good for a considerable ransom, ma'am." He treated Mrs. Brett with the frank familiarity of one man speaking to another and Juana was amused to see that her formidable grandmother seemed to like it.

"Yes," said Mrs. Brett. I owe you thanks on many counts, sir."

"Yes indeed," put in Miguel, "but I still don't understand how you came to be so late in starting back, Juana. You must have realised that you were likely to be benighted."

"It's not so easy to get away from the reverend Fathers," said Juana. "And, if you remember, Uncle, we were late in starting out." And, suddenly, horribly, remembered how he had kept her waiting in the courtyard while he added the postscript to his letter. What had it said? "Keep her with you as long as possible?" Absurd. Why in the name of sanity should she suspect her uncle of having anything to do with what had happened to her?

"You didn't recognise them of course?" Prospero's question distracted her from this unpleasant line of thought.

"Or any distinguishing features?" Father Ignatius had been sitting inconspicuously, as was his wont, in a corner of the room, and his sudden question startled her.

"No, how should I? I was wrapped in a stinking horse blanket all the time, and they said nothing—that was the most unnerving thing about them somehow. Not until they heard Vasco"—angrily she found herself colouring at the unexpected use of his Christian name—"my cousin coming. And then they spoke in whispers. No, I wouldn't recognise them again if they were to enter the room this minute."

"Which, thank God, they won't," said Miguel. "A miraculous escape, my child. We must say a special prayer of thanksgiving for you in chapel tomorrow. I hope it will serve to turn your thoughts in a proper direction."

"It makes me very grateful to my cousin."

"Yes indeed." Mrs. Brett leaned forward in her big chair. "We owe you a debt beyond measure, sir. But it's growing late. You will stay with us awhile, and give us an opportunity to show our gratitude?"

Juana listened to Vasco's courteous acceptance with a mixture of surprise and pleasure. The Bretts kept themselves to themselves. Visitors as opposed to hangers-on like Father Ignatius were a rare event at the castle. It was something that had puzzled her before she learned about the Sons of the Star. At all events, she was delighted that an exception was being made for her new-found cousin. She would be glad of a chance to get to know him better, gladder still of his protective company, just now, in the castle.

Because—she faced it at last, alone in her room—the attack on her had cast a new and terrifying light on her position. Before, she had wondered about her uncles, about Father Ignatius even; had listened to their voices, searching in vain for some intonation, some echo of a phrase used down in the big cavern. Now, she must wonder, not only if one or more of them belonged to the Sons of the Star, but if they had perhaps, horribly, organised the attack on her. With her special knowledge, it was almost impossible to believe in Vasco's theory of brigands and ransom. Did she even think he believed it himself? And had not there been something odd about the eager way her family had seized on it as the obvious explanation?

Most significant of all, nothing was said, next day, about the attack on her, but Vasco stayed close by her, and she was grateful. She might decide not to suspect the Sons of the Star, but she could not stop being afraid. She hardly felt safe even in the castle, remembering childhood stories of hidden doors and secret passages. How could she be sure that the only entrance to the winding stair was in her grandmother's room? There might be others, bolted on the far side. Alone for a moment in any room, she found herself listening for footsteps behind the panelling, waiting for some section of wall to swing open and reveal her enemies.

And when she was not alone, the equally horrible alternative was always before her. Suppose her attackers had not been sent by the Sons of the Star at all? Suppose they had been hired by someone in her own family? Or actually been some of her family? Only Vasco's company was really safe, and how long was he staying?

By siesta next day she had had all she could bear of these imaginings. She climbed the stairs to her grandmother's room and amazed Manuela by insisting on seeing her.

101

"But she's resting, *menina*."

"I can't help it. Will you announce me, Manuela, or must I do it myself?" She was surprised at her own firmness, but it worked. Manuela opened the farther door and ushered her in, excusing herself to the old lady as she did so.

Mrs. Brett was lying flat on her back, staring at flies on the ceiling. She did not move. "Very well, Manuela. You may go. See that we are not disturbed." And then still without turning her head. "You're in a panic, I suppose?"

"I'd be a fool not to be. I'm going to send for Gair Varlow. I thought I should tell you first."

"Send for Varlow? Absurd." She sat up in bed, an eldritch figure in dimity nightgown and wrapepr. What use could he be?"

"He could find out, I should think, or at least try to, whether it was the Sons of the Star who attacked me. If it was, I'm not going to the next meeting. It would be suicide."

"The Sons of the Star? Ridiculous." She sounded really angry. "I never imagined you such a fool, Juana. Do you think, if it had been the Sons of the Star, they would have let you go for one man? They would not have dared to fail."

She had thought this herself. "But then, who?"

"Brigands, of course, as your cousin said. You've forgotten what Portugal is like, Juana. Anything's possible here. And we are known for a rich family . . . richer, I think, than we really are. It would have cost me a pretty penny to get you back."

"So they may try again?"

"Oh, I doubt that. They will have had a good fright . . . No doubt they had a boat somewhere along the shore. They are probably clear down to the Algarve by now, planning something quite different. Or—who knows—they may even have been pirates. It does happen. A quick dash on shore and some expensive white slaves for the Turk's harems. You owe your cousin a great deal, Juana. What do you think of him, by the way?"

"I like him. Did his father really love my mother?"

"He told you that? Yes, I believe so. It was quite impossible, of course. For two members of a family in such disgrace to marry would have been suicide. And there were other reasons. You know his story?"

"Vasco's? I remember he was always spoken of as—I don't know—wild?"

The old lady laughed. "It's one way of putting it. Elvira, I

102

suppose. She always did mince her words. Your cousin Vasco is the bastard son of a bastard father. Or that's what they say."

"How do you mean?"

"Why, that it was the safe thing to be when Pombal was killing off the Mascarenhas family root and branch. Your cousin called on me yesterday to tell me he was hopeful of proving his legitimacy, and his father's before him, and to ask whether I would allow him to visit you in the meantime. I liked him for it. You know, of course, that the bar sinister is not taken so seriously here as in England. I hope you're not going to make a mountain of it."

"Of course not. Besides, I'm too grateful . . ."

"I should think so. But for him, you might be on your way to Algiers by now. You ought to be entertaining him, instead of keeping me awake with your imaginary terrors."

"You're sure they are imaginary? That it could not have been the Sons of the Star?" She could not bring herself to mention her other suspicions.

"As sure as one can be of anything. In fact, I wouldn't be in your attackers' shoes just now. If they have any sense, they are well away, in the Algarve or farther. The Sons of the Star do not tolerate interference with those they protect. Trust me, you don't need to fear another attack."

It was a sinister kind of comfort, but Juana did abandon the idea of sending for Gair Varlow. For one thing, it would be impossibly difficult to talk to him with Vasco there. And common sense combined with her grandmother to convince her that it could not have been the Sons of the Star who had attacked her. It would be time enough to tell Gair Varlow about the episode when he came at the end of the month to hear her report on the next meeting. There was something, indeed, rather satisfactory about the idea of working the story, casually, into the conversation as something not worth his notice.

Besides, it was easy to shake off her terrors in Vasco's entertaining company. Here, at last, was a real companion for her rides, and, best of all, someone to talk to. They spent all their time together, walking, riding, playing chess, and, endlessly, talking. His father and her mother had been first cousins and, he told her, before the Tavora plot brought disaster on the whole family, a match had been planned between them. "My father was older, of course. When Pombal struck, his parents saved his life, and their own, by a quick flight to Spain. But he never forgot the little cousin whose cradle he had rocked. After King Joseph's death, and Pombal's fall from power, he came back, as soon as he dared; but too late. Your mother was married. Do you know what he did?"

"No?" Juana was fascinated. No one had ever troubled to tell her about her mother's family.

"The most romantic thing. He married her best friend—a connection of theirs who had been in the convent with her. It was not a very happy marriage, I'm afraid." He said it so dispassionately that she was surprised to remember he was talking about his own parents. And then remembered, too, with a kind of horror, what her grandmother had told her. "The bastard son of a bastard father." How brave to speak thus. "They got permission to go abroad quite soon," he went on. "I don't think my father could bear to see your mother married to someone else. But our mothers always kept in touch. I found a packet of letters, after mine died. You'd be surprised how much I know about you, cousin. And all of it good. I've still got your mother's last letter, written quite a short while before she died. I'll show it you sometime. It will make you cry. It almost made me. I've thought about you all my life, Juana Brett. When I heard your father had carried you off to England, and married again, I wanted to put on my armour and ride to your rescue." He laughed. "A boy's dream. What could I do? I grew up in France, you know. Our countries were at war. I was helpless."

"In France?" She was amazed. "Vasco! Tell me all about it."

It was a story of such romance and danger as made it easy to forget her own troubles. He had been a boy still when the French revolution broke out, but a boy with eyes to see and a heart to remember its horrors. From time to time he would break off: "It's too bad; it's not for a woman's ears."

He spoke little of his father, but she gained, somehow, the impression that he had broken his wife's heart by throwing in his lot with the most murderous of the Jacobins. It was his death, she suspected, that had freed Vasco to return to Portugal. "And how glad I am that I did." The velvet brown eyes held hers for a moment. Then, briskly, "My man's arrived at last from Lisbon with my spare horse. Tomas has found you a sidesaddle. We're going to have a real ride today—to the Cork Convent." It was almost an order.

How had he known that she dreaded re-entering that dark

little wood? "Must we?" She had breakfasted, as usual, in her riding habit, so there was no excuse for delay.

"Yes. We Mascarenhas always remount after a fall." As he put her up into her saddle, she thought how bravely, considering his circumstances, he used the family name. "I see your grandmother told you about me?" Disconcertingly, he must have read her thoughts. "I'm glad of it," he went on as he caught up with her outside the castle gate. "It's not a subject one would normally discuss with a young lady, but our circumstances are not normal. Besides, you are no ordinary young lady, cousin."

She was not altogether sure that this was a compliment. "I'm quite an ordinary English one."

"I doubt that. Besides, you are to be Portuguese now, or so I hope with all my heart."

"Why, thank you." But something in his tone had disconcerted her and she turned the conversation to indifferent subjects for a while. At last, with a shudder: "I find I am quite a good enough Portuguese not to like re-entering that wood." They could see it now, lying dark across the road ahead. "Do you think the *bruchas* are waiting for me, cousin?" She wished she was sure her pretended fear was not real.

"No, nor the bandits either. But I'm sure you will feel better when you have ridden through and proved it to yourself. And to your man," he added, seeing Tomas, who had been running ahead, hesitate at sight of the wood and turn back towards them.

"Let him keep beside us." Juana was afraid he would try and force Tomas to go through the wood first.

"Your wish is my command, cousin."

In the little wood a late bird sang. Juana did not even flinch when some animal, startled by the noise they made, crashed through the undergrowth and away from them. "Thank you"—she turned impulsively to Vasco as they emerged once more into the sunshine—"I'm almost more grateful for what you have done today than for saving me in the first place."

"No *bruchas*?" he said. "I'm proud of you, Juana."

Once again, she had an uncomfortable feeling that things were moving a little fast for her. "Look at that stretch of grass," she said. "Will you trust me at a gallop, cousin?"

"I'd trust you with my life."

"Flatterer!" She turned away from him to call to Tomas.

"Sit down and wait for us here. We'll be back. You don't actually want to go up to the Cork Convent, do you cousin?"

"Not if you don't. I'd infinitely rather stay out here on the hills with you." But she had urged her horse to a gallop and was already well ahead of him.

"That was wonderful!" Stopping at last for breath, Juana pulled off her plumed riding hat to let the sea breeze cool her cheeks. "Almost as good as flying."

"Like a *brucha*?"

She laughed. "Ghosts and cobwebs. They're all blown away." They stopped below an outcrop of rock and now she strained her eyes upward against the bright sun. "Can you see that white flower, cousin? It looks like an orchis, but surely it's too late in the year for them?"

"You'd like to know?" He was off his horse in a flash. "Here, hold the reins for me."

"You mustn't. It's not safe! Not in riding boots!"

He was on his way up already, climbing like a cat, like a squirrel, his heavy boots striking sparks from the hard rock. She watched, breath held, while he reached the clump of flowers, picked them, then returned, one-handed, down the cliff.

"For my cousin!" His colour was high and his breath quick as he bent to brush the flowers with his lips before handing them to her.

"They're beautiful!" In fact, the delicate flowers of the white cyclamen had suffered a good deal in transit. "But you shouldn't have done it." She smiled at him over them. "I'd never have forgiven myself."

"Your wish is my command." He had said it before.

"Then I must be careful what I wish."

Back at the castle, they were dismounting in the courtyard when Iago brought Juana a parcel. "They said you should have it at once, senhora."

"Who, Iago?"

"I don't know." He looked frightened. "Two of them. Dressed as friars. But they weren't friars. They didn't bless me."

"*Jesus Maria!*" Juana had removed an outer layer of coarse sailcloth to reveal a bloodstained note.

"Don't!" Vasco snatched the parcel from her and it fell open to reveal four bloody human ears. "Horrible! Take them away, you!" He thrust the parcel on Iago and took Juana's arm to lead her indoors.

"But what does it say?" She controlled nausea.

"The note?" He opened it, fastidiously avoiding the blood-stains, and read: " 'Thus perish all who molest those the Star protects. Fear not. And speak not.' " He looked at her. "Good advice, cousin. But I'm glad to know you are so powerfully protected. I was afraid for you—" He looked quickly round the empty courtyard. "Of them."

"So was I. But it's horrible, cousin. The men who attacked me. They must be . . ."

"Dead. You have nothing more to fear. Selfishly, I could almost regret it. It means I lose my excuse to act as your shadow. My man brought me a summons from Lisbon that I had meant to ignore, but now I fear I must leave you for a while."

"Oh?" She felt an odd mixture of disappointment and relief. "You must go at once?"

"Soon. There's a man in Lisbon who may have evidence of my parents' marriage. I'm sure you understand, cousin, how important it is to me, now, to remove the blot from my name. But you're badly shaken; I've no right to keep you here talking. Besides, I must find that man of yours—what's his name? Iago—before he starts a panic among the servants."

"Too late, I should think. But I'd be grateful if you'd try. How do they expect me to say nothing?"

"The parcel must be common knowledge, but if you'll be rulled by me you'll not speak of the note."

"But Iago saw it."

He looked disconcerted. "So he did. In that case, we must think of some harmless message. 'May all your enemies perish thus'? I'll dispose of the actual note. And, if you'll allow me, I'll tell your family as much as they need to know—which is as little as possible."

So he did not trust them either. "Thank you."

"You're looking worse and worse. May I see you to your room? You'll be better out of the way until the first excitement is over."

It was good to lean on his strong arm and feel the warmth of his hand under her elbow. It was good to be looked after, protected. It was perhaps a little absurd to have him help her up the stairway to her room as if she could not have managed it by herself, but it was pleasant just the same.

CHAPTER 9

Vasco left next day. He did not ask if he might come back, he said he would. "As soon as I can." He held Juana's hand for a long moment, before turning away to pay his respectful farewells to her aunt and uncles. He had already been honoured by a summons to Mrs. Brett's own rooms to take his leave of her.

"She saw him alone," Manuela told Juana.

"She says he's no fool," said Estella.

" 'And my poor fool is dead,' " said Elvira. " 'At his head a grass green turf, At his feet a stone.' We shall all be dull now Senhor de Mascarenhas has left us."

They were indeed. Juana, who had thought herself relieved at his going, was surprised to find how much she missed his cheerful company. Riding with him, learning it was best to let him beat her at chess, listening to his stories of life in Paris, it had been easy to forget how time was ebbing away towards the full moon and the Sons of the Star.

An invitation from Lord Strangford provided a welcome distraction. He was giving a farewell party for Lord St. Vincent at his country house in Sintra. "The crisis is over," Mrs. Brett summed it up, "for the moment. We'll all go, I think. Your Mr. Varlow will doubtless be there, Juana. I doubt you'll find him dull company after your cousin."

Juana sighed. Could her grandmother really have forgotten that the party was a few days before the full moon? At such a time, she was hardly likely to find Gair Varlow's company dull.

"Don't stoop child!" It was the day of the party and Juana had been helping her grandmother down the steep stairs from her room. The old lady's voice was sharp as she went on. "There's nothing shameful about being tall!"

"No?" Juana thought how Daisy and Teresa used to tease her.

"No. Have some pride, can't you? They used to twit you with it, I collect, those stepsisters of yours?" The old lady could be disconcertingly sharp at times.

"A little. It was my fault, I'm sure, for minding so much."

Looking back, she saw, with surprise, that this was true. Daisy and Teresa had teased each other too.

Mrs. Brett had stopped in the shade of the cloister. "Have you ever wondered what made your aunt the poor thing she is?"

"Of course."

"I'll tell you. It was her brothers who began it. She was never brilliant, you understand, but a good, sweet girl whose only aim in life was to please. Her kind brothers, my Prospero and my Miguel, discovered that by teasing they could make her blush. From the blush to tears was an easy step ... They were driving her crazy without knowing what they were doing. I should have stopped them, of course, but with no husband I found them hard to handle. In the end, in despair, I sent Elvira to stay with my relatives in England. I thought she would be happy there. She was miserable. By the time I understood, it was too late. She came home the poor thing she is. Do you understand what I am trying to tell you, Juana?"

"I think so." She straightened her shoulders.

"Exactly. And now"—she moved forward into the sunshine—"let us go to this party."

As Lord Strangford came forward to greet them it struck Juana for the first time that the party must inevitably be conducted in English. Sweat prickled in the palms of her hands, as she tried to chart a course without "t's" or "d's" through the hazard of the introductions. Lord Strangford was surprisingly young, auburn-haired and blue-eyed and bubbling with Irish charm. She found she did not like him. Lord St. Vincent, on the other hand, grizzled and tanned by years at sea, struck her as the kind of father one would have liked to have had. What a fine quarter-deck sanity he would have brought to one's miseries.

Misery? Lord Strangford had given one arm to her grandmother and the other to her and was leading them into the cool, tiled saloon where wine and sweetmeats were being served. "I'm delighted to meet you at last, Miss Brett. My Mr. Varlow says you are the new Catalini. Perhaps, later on, you will give us a song?"

She had not sung in public since that night at Forland House. Could she? In English? She simply did not know. "I'll d—d—" Idiot not to have foreseen the hazards of the phrase, "do my best."

Mrs. Brett interrupted her. "My grand-daughter will be

109

delighted to sing for you. Those *modinhas*, perhaps, Juana, that you were singing to your cousin the other day? As a student of the Portuguese arts, Lord Strangford would be interested, I am sure. They are charming, don't you find, my lord, the melancholy Brazilian folk songs?"

"Miss Brett!" Gair Varlow appeared, every inch the lover, at her elbow. "Let me give you a glass of this carcavelhos wine and congratulate you on your Portuguese glow. You were made for sunshine, I can see."

"I was so pale and pitiful in England?" She loathed this charade.

"Never pitiful, Miss Brett. A snowdrop, perhaps . . ."

"Drooping on its stalk?" At least, since he was as tall as herself, she could hold herself up and look him in the eye.

He had been moving them, little by little, so that she was in a corner while he faced her with his back to the room. Now, bending towards her with a lover's eagerness, he said, very low: "Miss Brett, I hate it quite as much as you do." Then went on, louder: "Or a lily, perhaps, the fleur de lis, queen of flowers? But now, a flower of the sun: the sunflower, the marigold . . ."

"A poppy, maybe?" Suddenly it was simply a game the two of them could play. A game like chess?

"The rose, Miss Brett. The rose of England. And, now, before you sing for us, let me show you Lord Strangford's garden."

This was daring. No Portuguese young lady would think of strolling alone with a young man. Did she care? She thought not. Gair Varlow had taken her arm to steer her back to where her grandmother and Lord Strangford were discussing the poetry of Mr. Pope.

He seized his chance when Mrs. Brett paused after quoting her favourite passage from *The Rape of the Lock*. "My Lord—Mrs. Brett—may I have your permission to take Miss Brett for a turn on the terrace before she sings for us?"

"Outside?" Mrs. Brett could be very much the great lady when she chose. "Alone?"

"This is an English party, ma'am," intervened Lord Strangford. "Surely English customs can prevail? As for Mr. Varlow, I'd trust him with my own daughter."

"If you had one," said Mrs. Brett. "But it's true, I've lived so long in Portugal I tend to forget our healthy English customs. So, run along, child, before I remember where we are."

110

"Lord, she's clever." Gair Varlow waited to speak until they were well out of earshot of the house. "Do you see what she's doing?" He lapsed into Portuguese. "She's establishing that we can be alone together. I was wondering how she would work it. You can't very well report to me with your Aunt Elvira listening. Frankly, I'm never quite sure just how mad she really is."

"I know what you mean. There's something north-north-west about it."

"Precisely. 'When the wind is southerly, she knows a hawk from a handsaw.' " And then, turning to face her in a paved space between well-trimmed myrtle hedges. "I'm sorry you find this so disagreeable."

Now she found she could laugh about it. "It must be quite as bad for you, Mr. Varlow. We'll just have to make the best of it until you discover another messenger. What hopes have you?"

"Not many. Things have reached such a point here that no one can be trusted. What with Dom John's party and his wife's; the Catholics and the madmen who believe the French talk about liberty and equality . . ." He moved a little nearer to her and took a quick look up and down the deserted terrace. "Not to mention the Sons of the Star. I hear you've had a demonstration of their kind of vengeance. I can't tell you how sorry I am you had such an unpleasant experience, but I hope it has taught you to take them seriously."

"Seriously! If it were not for my cousin, I doubt if I'd be in a position to take anything seriously now. But how did you come to hear?" She was oddly disappointed at having her story forestalled.

"Of course I heard. Lord Strangford was bound to, since it concerned an Englishwoman, and you must give me credit, Miss Brett, for some concern for you."

"Thank you."

"This cousin of yours who rescued you. Tell me about him. Is he to be trusted, do you think?"

"Trusted? He saved my life."

"Yes, but who is he? I've managed, so far, to find out nothing about him."

"I suppose not. He grew up in France, you see, and has only just came back."

"France? I don't much like the sound of that."

She laughed. "Oh, Mr. Varlow! How tedious it must be to trust no one. My poor cousin! I suppose I had better explain

111

to you. He has quite other things to think of than your all-important politics." It made her angry to find herself blushing as she explained Vasco's circumstances to Gair. "He's gone to Lisbon now," she concluded, "to find someone he hopes can prove his parents' marriage."

"And then?"

"He says he'll come back. I hope he does. I'm bored to death out there at the castle. It's just as well I've not had to count on you for company, Mr. Varlow. I thought you were to pay me constant court?" Why had the fact of Vasco made it so much easier to deal with Gair?

"I'm sorry. And you're right. I do owe you an apology. But you must see that so long as St. Vincent's been here there's remained a chance that he might put that mad kidnapping plan of his into execution. But the crisis is over now, thank God. I shall be free to play my part again. So long as Lord Strangford continues at Sintra it will be the most natural thing in the world for a love-lorn swain to ride constantly to the Castle on the Rock."

"I shall look forward to it." Her mocking note was just right. "And you'll be riding over?"

"Why, yes."

"Then I shall persuade my grandmother to let me ride out with you as I did with my cousin." She turned away to pick a sweet-scented sprig of jasmine.

"You will be thought a very unusual young lady by the Portuguese."

"I don't care. You know how they treat their own young women? Shut up, almost as if in a harem; allowed to giggle in the shadows when there are visitors, but not to appear. It's no wonder if they have not a thought in their heads, save of food and dress."

"And religion."

"Yes, but what does it mean to them? They play with religion as children do with their dolls. Oh—I'm not being fair, I suppose, but I'd forgotten what it's like. Or maybe I never knew. I was a child when I left here, with a child's freedom."

"Miss Brett, I'm sorry."

"No need to be. Don't think I'm not glad I came. My grandmother needs me. It's the first time in my life that anyone has." They had reached the end of the paved walk, and she bent for a minute to gaze down into the tumbling stream it led to, then turned to face him. "It's time we went back. But,

112

first, since we must see so much of each other, promise me that you will never feel in the slightest degree responsible for me."

"But how can I help it?"

"That's your problem." She turned away and walked swiftly back towards the house.

The party was in full swing now, the rooms crowded with people and echoing with a babble of talk in two languages. Juana paused in the doorway, her eyes dazzled from the bright sunshine, and Gair Varlow paused beside her. "It's such a small thing to beg." His voice was the lover's again, and he spoke as if he had been begging thus all the time. "The flower you are going to throw away would be my most treasured possession. I should wear it next my heart." And he laid a hand on the blue superfine that covered that improbable organ.

"Your heart, Mr. Varlow? Have you one?"

"I had. Till I met you." This with a languishing glance that irritated more than it amused her.

Did he recognise this? At all events, he was suddenly the perfect secretary again. "Miss Brett, the Princess is here. May I have your permission to ask leave to present you?"

It seemed very complicated. "If you wish," she said. And then, puzzled. "But where?"

"The Princess? Over there, talking to Lord Strangford."

"Good gracious." Dom John's wife, the Spanish Princess Carlota Joaquina was one of the ugliest women Juana had ever seen. Short and thick-set, she had bad teeth, bloodshot eyes, and coarse frizzy hair. And as if that was not enough, she had chosen to attend Lord Strangford's party in a man's green hunting jacket and a green cloth petticoat short enough to show her stocky ankles.

"It's a great honour that she should choose to come." Gair's voice held a warning. "She is a neighbour of Lord Strangford's, you know. She lives mostly at her *quinta* of Ramalhao here in Sintra and has come in, like a neighbour, incognito. You'll excuse me? I must pay my respects and ask her permission to present you."

"Must I?"

"I think so." And then, reverting to the lover's voice, "But, first, must I beg again, on my knees perhaps?"

"For goodness sake, don't," She twisted the sprig of jasmine between her fingers. "It's beginning to droop already, poor thing." She watched with irritation as he made a busi-

113

ness of tucking it in his buttonhole, then bowed and turned away.

"Juana!" The furious voice made her spill the drink she held.

"Pedro! You made me jump." She had minded, a little, that neither Pedro nor Roberto had visited the Castle on the Rock since she had arrived, and now held out her hand in warm greeting. "It's good to see you."

"I wish I could say the same to you. What in the world are you doing here?"

"I came with my grandmother."

"Mrs. Brett? She's here?"

"Don't look so cross, Pedro. I know Portuguese young ladies don't go out much, but do try to remember I'm not really Portuguese." Then, aware that this merely made him angrier: "And after all, this is an English party."

"So much the worse." They were talking low, in Portuguese.

"Oh, Pedro! It's all over now. The French army is halfway across Europe and we can all breathe again. Anyway, what are you doing here?" Anything to change the conversation.

"I'm in attendance, of course. You don't think I'd have come here of my own accord?"

She laughed angrily. "And I deluded myself that you had come to see me! But of course, if you think I ought to be mewed up in the castle, like a nun . . ."

"A nun! That is not at all what you made me think of when I saw you flirting with that hanger-on of Lord Strangford's. Yes, I saw you come in from the garden with him, and give him the flower you were carrying! I'm glad to see that at least you have the grace to blush."

"If I am, it's with anger. What right have you—" She stopped. "We must not quarrel here. You're in attendance, you said?"

"On the Princess, my mistress."

"But I thought—"

"A lot of nonsense, just like a woman. You would say"— he lowered his voice—"that because you met me last time in the train of the Prince Regent I must serve him. In fact, Roberto serves Dom John and I his wife. Unfortunately"— lower than ever—"they are not, at the moment, on good terms."

She could not help a smile for the understatement. Everyone knew that Carlota Joaquina had recently tried to per-

114

suade her father, the King of Spain, to help her get her husband declared unfit to rule, so that she could take his place. Everyone knew, too, that, having failed, she had been reduced to a kind of voluntary retirement at her *quinta* of Ramalhao. "Yes," she said now, "I did hear something of the kind."

"Quite so. But they know their duty to the country. They must keep in touch, must meet for ceremonial occasions. They find it convenient to have Roberto and me to act as messengers between them. He serves the Prince; I serve the Princess. We both serve Portugal."

"Most creditable." It seemed a long time since they had played Blind Man's Buff in the courtyard of the Castle on the Rock.

"Where is our grandmother?" He was hardly paying attention to her. "It is not suitable that you should be talking alone, even with me."

"She was with Lord Strangford." And then, at his impatient exclamation, "After all, he is our host. And a very charming one." She knew it would enrage him.

It did. "That popinjay! I warn you, Juana, steer clear of him. It's bad enough to be giving flowers to his servant. But Strangford! A liar and a loose fish: writes improper letters to Lord Rosslyn and then boasts about them. I tell you, I don't like to see you in his house."

"Or be here yourself? But how well informed you are, Pedro." A curious, horrid idea had been growing in her mind as they talked. It was what he had said about women that started it—something about her talking nonsense, like a woman. It had sounded disconcertingly like the kind of thing the Sons of the Star said. Could he be one of them?

"Well informed?" He took her up on it. "Nonsense. Everyone knows that. The trouble about you English is that you have no sense. You think you are above comment."

"I'm glad that at least you admit I am English."

This was too much. He held out his arm, ceremonious courtesy masking rage. "Let me take you to our grandmother."

"But Mr. Varlow wants to present me to the Princess."

"Varlow! Nonsense! I will present you, cousin, if that is your wish."

"I never said it was." But she submitted to the presentation with a good grace and was surprised to find herself liking the ugly, forthright woman, who plunged at once into a series of

115

the most personal questions. Juana was a stranger in Portugal like herself. Was she happy? Was she homesick? And then, suddenly, "Hullo! What's happening?" She looked past Juana with the easy rudeness of the great.

Turning, Juana saw that a young naval officer had come dustily into the room and was making the quickest way manners allowed towards Lord St. Vincent.

"Despatches," said Carlota Joaquina. "They must be important ones. Come along, child. You're English. You have a right to know."

Lord St. Vincent had glanced quickly over his letter and now held up a hand for silence. Since most eyes had been upon him already, there was an instant hush in the room, so that Juana could hear the shrilling of crickets outside.

"Bad news, I'm afraid." St. Vincent spoke across the crowd to Strangford. "I'm sorry to break up your party, but Fox is dead."

"God rest his soul." The Princess's strident voice rose above a little hurricane of exclamation and comment. And then, to Juana: "He was one of your Whigs, was he not? Will this mean a change of government, do you think? The Admiral looks sick enough."

"Yes," Juana said. "I think everyone loved Mr. Fox." She was thinking about Gair Varlow. He was Fox's man. What would happen to him now?

Looking round, she could see that the same kind of question was in the minds of all the English. They were not only mourning the death of a great man, they were wondering, every one of them, how it would affect them personally. The party broke up almost at once, with a mixture of condolences and thanks for Lord Strangford, who had already declared his intention of riding back to Lisbon that night. Of course, Gair Varlow would go with him, and Juana was afraid, for a moment, that in the general confusion he would not manage even to say good-bye.

But he came hurrying up as Pedro was helping Mrs. Brett into her carriage. "Mrs. Brett! Miss Brett! This terrible news has made us all forget our manners." His hand was reassuring on Juana's as he helped her mount the steep carriage step.

She had entered from the far side so as not to inconvenience her grandmother and now was able to bend towards Gair and ask, "But Mr. Fox's death—may it not change things?"

"Miss Brett, nothing can change me!" His hand touched her sprig of jasmine, wilting in his buttonhole; his tone was a lover's; his look, for her alone, before he turned and left them, held a promise.

"Insufferable!" Pedro was leaning in at the other carriage window. "What are you thinking of, ma'am, to let that puppy dangle after Juana?"

Mrs. Brett had sunk with a sigh of exhaustion into her corner, but her eyes and voice were sharp as she answered. "I've never objected to the company you keep, Pedro. I hope I'm old enough to choose my own. It's lonely for Juana at the castle. I don't notice that you or your brother have put yourselves out to come and entertain her. As for Mr. Varlow, I've had some enquiries made. He is of perfectly good family, but penniless. Quite impossible, in fact, as a husband for Juana, but if he wants to make a fool of himself over her, it's his own affair. I won't have you interfering. Is that understood?" She closed her eyes. "Tell the coachman to drive on."

CHAPTER 10

The Castle on the Rock had never seemed so dreary as on the day after Lord Strangford's party. The weather had changed in the night, and Juana woke to a darkened room and the sound of rain lashing against the windows. She had forgotten how violent these autumn storms could be, swelling streams to torrents, turning paths to streams. No one would ride out from Lisbon today, or, very likely, for many days to come. If Gair Varlow should feel that his work here was ended with Fox's death, and decide to sail with Lord St. Vincent, he might not even be able to come out and say good-bye.

Was she imagining things? His last words had certainly been reassuring enough. "Nothing can change me," he had said, miming the abject lover but intending her to understand that she could count on him, whatever happened. Doubtless he had meant it at the time. But, if he were suddenly to be summoned home? She was beyond illusions about him. He would obey orders.

She shivered and jumped out of bed, to feel the floor chilly under her bare feet. A pool of water lay by the window she had left open, and as she went to close it, lightning tore the sky open, closely followed by its crack of thunder. Rain soaked her nightdress and the window struggled in her hands as she fought to pull it shut. Far below, the Atlantic had been lashed into a fury of whitecaps. Surely Lord St. Vincent would never sail today?

Hurrying along the rain-swept cloister, she found Elvira already seated at the breakfast table. " 'Great nature weeps,' " was her greeting. " 'Weep men and beasts therefore.' The whole ocean would not be tears enough for Mr. Fox." She poured coffee with a shaking hand. "I met him once. At the Duchess of Devonshire's. He was a great man. The world is different this morning."

"Yes"—Prospero had entered the room as she spoke—"it's wet. You won't get your ride today, Juana. What will you do with yourself?"

She had been wondering this herself, but put a cheerful

face on it. "All kinds of things, Uncle. I might begin by exploring the castle. Do you know there are whole bits of it I don't in the least remember?"

"And all of them full of rats and bats and cobwebs. I'd spare my pretty new dresses, if I were you. Come to me in the library instead. I need a secretary today. You write a better hand than mine, and I promised Lord Strangford I'd send him copies of several passages from Camoens where my reading differs from his. He said he would send his Mr. Varlow out for them—the one who made such sheep's eyes at you yesterday, Juana. I didn't think my boy Pedro liked it much."

"No?" Nothing would induce her to discuss Gair—or Vasco either—with her uncle. She turned with relief as the door opened. "Good morning, Uncle Miguel."

"Bless you, my child." It was always hard to decide just how seriously Uncle Miguel expected his blessings to be taken.

"Coffee, Miguel?" asked Elvira, and then, in the same perfectly everyday tone, " 'Upon such sacrifices, The heavens themselves throw incense.' "

Prospero kept Juana busy most of the day, and in fact she was glad enough to abandon her half-formulated plan of exploring the uninhabited parts of the castle. If there really were other secret entrances besides the one in her grandmother's room, was she sure she wanted to find them?

When the failing light released her at last from Prospero's dull verse, she found her aunt sitting in the Ladies' Parlour, stitching away at her embroidery.

"What are you making?" Juana moved a branch of candles nearer.

"Thank you." Elvira bit off her thread and held up the canvas so that Juana could see the exquisitely fine needlepoint. "You're an observant child. I don't often work on these. They're a set of chair covers." She laughed. "They were to be part of my trousseau. English flowers, you see. One on each. But I'd only got to the primrose when he changed his mind. I thought I'd never go on with them."

"I'm sorry. I had no idea . . ."

"You thought I'd always been old and sad and a little mad? Why not? It's hard for the young to believe in old age: merciful, really, that they can't. But, Juana, I'm anxious about you. What are you going to do here, all alone? You can't spend all your time roaming about the valley, or working for your uncles, either. Mother's busy just keeping alive. Oh, she'll use you, as she has the rest of us, but that's all. I can't help you. I'm—what you see. You must make a plan for yourself, child, if you don't want to get like me."

"A plan?"

"Yes. What do you want to be? No need to tell me—" Had she seen Juana's instinctive recoil? "Just think about it. Men learn how to be the kind of person they want. They go to school, have tutors ... We have to teach ourselves. We make ourselves what we are." She looked up from her work, her eyes unusually bright. "I made myself 'poor Elvira.' It's an easy part ... What's yours to be? Remember, no one here is going to help you." They had been talking Portuguese, now she switched to English. "You might begin with that stammer. There's something rather 'poor Juana' about that, don't you think? You could begin by saying, 'I'll do my best.' Quickly!"

"I'll d—" She stuck. "It's no use. I can't."

"So you want to spend the rest of your life here in Portugal?"

"I'm not sure." She was surprised at herself.

"That's what I thought. You'd better do some thinking, too. If you want to go back to England, you must learn to speak properly. You'll never do what you don't try. Practise on me, any time you like. My English is so rusty, a little stammering will give me time. Anyway, who cares what a mad old spinster thinks?"

"Talking English?" Miguel had come in unnoticed, on slippered feet. His voice was disapproving.

"Talking? Were we really talking? Did I speak, and did she answer? Shall I talk, and will she listen? No, no, Miguel"— Elvira rolled up her embroidery and rose—"it's quite impossible. I am silence, you know, and nobody heeds me. 'Good night, ladies, good night, sweet ladies ...' " She drifted from the room.

"Poor creature. You don't mind her too much, Juana?"

"Of course not. But what's wrong with speaking English?"

"Has no one explained? We think it best, with things as they are, always to speak in a language that the servants can understand."

"In case they are spying on us? To make it easier? Uncle, that's horrible."

"Life is horrible. Have you not understood that yet, child? I was hoping you might have. That your disability might have

120

taught you something of the truth." He came closer, to stand over her. "Have you not thought, Juana, that the answer for you lies in the service of God? Who knows but that He put the impediment into your speech to give you time to remember Him. Just think how happy you would be in a Silent Order."

"I? Uncle, are you mad?" She felt as if, running in the dark, she had come to the edge of a cliff.

"No, child, just sane with a greater wisdom than you are ready for. But foolish, too, in my generation. I had meant to wait longer before I spoke. Forget it for now, child, but remember when His time is ripe."

"If you mean ripe for my entering a nunnery, I can tell you this minute, Uncle, it never will be."

"Never is a long time. Remember, Juana, that we are all dust before the breath of the Lord. Why should the dust rise up and say, 'I will be thus,' or 'I will not be so'?"

A little shiver ran down her spine. Why let him frighten her? She jumped to her feet. "I must get ready for supper."

The storm blew itself out in the night and Juana woke to brilliant light and Maria's eager voice at her door, "Have you seen them, senhora?"

"Seen what?"

"The English ships." She moved over to the seaward window. "Look! You can see them from here. They must have come out with the tide."

"They're going!" Juana joined her at the window and watched the six graceful line-of-battle ships beating up the coast, *Hibernia* in the lead. "They're really going." She had not realised what a sense of security those six ships had given her until now, when she saw them sailing away. So far, she could always change her mind, beg Gair Varlow to arrange a passage home for her. Not that she would, of course, but at least it had been possible. Now, they were gone, and she was alone here. And, there was worse. Fox's death might well mean a change of government in England. What more likely, if so, than that Gair Varlow would be recalled. He might be out there now, going home with St. Vincent.

Maria was looking at her anxiously. "What's the matter, *menina*? Does it make you sad to see them go?"

"A little. It's nothing." She managed a laugh. "Iago would say a ghost had walked over my grave."

"Oh, that Iago! You mustn't listen to him. He's from the

Alentejo, you know, and superstitious like all of them down there. If I listened to half the stories he tells, I'd never have a quiet moment in this castle. He thinks it's a trysting place for the *bruchas*. They meet here at the full moon, he says, and Satan comes to them, out there on the cliff." She crossed herself. "It's all nonsense, of course."

"Of course." Not nonsense, but the Sons of the Star. If only the full moon was safely past ... All the time, as Juana lived her quiet life in the castle, a kind of metronome was ticking away at the back of her mind, numbering off the days to the full moon, when she must go down the winding stair alone. Not many more now.

Far out to sea, the *Hibernia* had changed course to round Cabo Roca. Soon she would be out of sight. Suppose Gair Varlow was on her. She would suppose no such thing. "I'm hungry, Maria! Fasten my dress for me?"

She escaped from breakfast as soon as she could and ran down to the stables to tell Iago to saddle Rosinante.

"We can't go down the valley today. The stream's in flood this morning, and the paths not much better." No doubt he was glad of this excuse to keep her away from the Jaws of Death.

"Yes, I thought it would be. We'll ride, instead, a little way along the Sintra road. That's on the ridge and should have drained off pretty well by now. We might even get a glimpse of the English ships." It made as good a pretext as any to cover her urgent need to get away from the castle, where, somehow, however lonely, she was never alone. Besides, the dark little wood on the Sintra road must be faced alone sometimes, and Vasco was right, the sooner the better.

She rode slowly, deep in thought. Her dreams had been disturbed by echoes of what Elvira had said to her. Waking, she had tried in vain to dismiss it as a madwoman's ramblings. But there had been nothing mad about Elvira when she had spoken of her mother: "She'll use you, as she has the rest of us." What, exactly, had she meant? Was she suggesting that old Mrs. Brett actually wanted her sons to live the lives of drones?

Yesterday, Juana had rejected this idea. Of course her grandmother was fond of her—was not just using her. Out here, today, with St. Vincent's ships silhouetted against the sky, she admitted doubt. If her grandmother really cared about her, would she have withdrawn, as she had done since Lord Strangford's party, and shut herself up in her own rooms, with Manuela and Estella, when the moon was almost full and she must know what this meant, in terror, for Juana?

The loneliness was the worst. If only there was someone she could discuss it with, someone to argue away her terror of going down that long dark stair alone. Someone? But who? If Vasco had stayed, would she have told him?

St. Vincent's ships were dwindling towards the horizon now. In a few days, some of them might be in sight of England. And—I'm homesick, she thought, that's really what's the matter with me. Memories crowded in on her: coal fires, the clank of milking pails, the smell of an English stable. Most surprising of all, out here on this hot, fragrant hillside, she admitted to herself that she missed Daisy and Teresa. At least, they had been company.

In a minute, she would be in tears. She kicked Rosinante into her shambling trot, then pulled her up again with a sharp little stab of terror at sight of a single horseman emerging from the dark wood on the hill below her.

Iago had seen him too. "Let's turn back, senhora. It might be one of them—the bandits." He was shaking with fright.

"Don't be silly, Iago." She was angry with him for echoing her own illogical terror. "They'd never dare in broad daylight like this. Besides—" She hesitated, not liking to speak of that horrible, bloodstained package.

"There were only four ears, senhora. I counted. And it was six men attacked you, Senhor de Mascarenhas said. The others may have come for vengeance. Let's go back, quickly."

"Nonsense. Don't you see he's waving to us? It's Senhor Varlow." She hoped he could not see that she was shivering with relief. "We'll go to meet him; but keep close to me, Iago." After all, the proprieties thus observed, they could safely talk in English. If she stammered, Gair Varlow would just have to bear it. So: "Good morning," she began when he approached.

But, "*Bom dia*," Gair answered, his warning glance at Iago reminding her unpleasantly of what her Uncle Miguel had said about speaking Portuguese so that the servants could understand.

She took the cue, just the same, and answered in Portuguese. "I was afraid you might have sailed with Lord St. Vincent." She spoke impulsively and was furious when he thanked her, with an eye on Iago, in flowery terms for her concern. "I've been wishing I'd sailed with them." Saying it

123

deliberately to shake him, she was delighted at how well she succeeded.

"You want to go back? Already? Miss Brett, this is terrible news." Now he really meant it.

"Yes," she said. "I'm homesick. Isn't it comic? I never thought I'd find myself missing England, but I do just the same. I was thinking, before we met, that I would ask my grandmother's leave to return." Had she been? She was not sure.

"Do you want to kill her?" He was serious enough now.

"Oh, I think she'd manage to survive." Poor man, he could not, with Iago running a few paces behind them, refer to the Sons of the Star. She watched with wry satisfaction as he searched for an answer.

It seemed odd enough when it came. He swore, picturesquely, in Portuguese: "*Corpo de deus*, I've dropped my riding glove. When I saw you, I expect. Here, you"—he raised his voice to summon Iago, who had kept behind them but comfortably within earshot—"there's a testoon for you if you find my glove. I must have dropped it back there by the little wood. It's the fellow of this one." He held out his left hand in its leather gauntlet. "My sister gave them to me," he added, as if in explanation, to Juana.

"Oh, in that case, you mustn't lose it. Run quickly, Iago, and we'll wait here for you."

The offered bribe had been just right. Iago looked doubtful for a moment, then started for the wood. Gair plunged at once into a lover's speech of self-congratulation on having her, at last, to himself, spun it out until Iago was well out of earshot, and then "You aren't serious, I hope?"

"I'm not sure. You don't know what its like here, for a woman. Even my aunt warned me, yesterday, of what I'd become if I stayed."

"I don't remember that you were exactly happy in England." And then, forestalling her answer, "But, frankly, it's not a question of your happiness. Nor even of your grandmother's life or death. Though I think you should face it that a few more trips down that winding stair in the cold winter months will kill her. I don't know how you will feel about having that on your conscience. That's your affair. What concerns me is the problem of finding a substitute. It was not easy for Mrs. Brett to persuade the Sons of the Star to let you take her place. Even if I could find someone to take yours—which is doubtful—there's still the problem of getting

124

their permission. It's a sore point with many of them, this dependence on a female. You must have gathered what they think of women."

"Yes. I didn't much like it."

"Exactly. That's what I'm trying to explain to you. Don't you see? You think Portugal no place for a woman. Just imagine what it would be like with the Sons of the Star in power. Women would not just be inferior, they'd be chattels."

"But do you seriously think there is a chance of their succeeding?"

"A chance? There's a strong likelihood. That was a well-designed plan they made at their last meeting. They were quite right, you know. Lord St. Vincent is an impatient old fire-eater. He had gone so far as to confide in Strangford that he was tempted to abduct Dom John if he wouldn't listen to reason. It was madness, of course. It would have had the worst possible effect. But he meant it just the same. The *coup* the Sons of the Star planned, put into effect in the chaos after the court left, would in all probability have succeeded. You might be living, now, under their authority—their tyranny. Face facts, Miss Brett. If you propose to fail us, don't flatter yourself that what you do doesn't matter. It will probably be the most important action of your life. This is your chance to affect the course of history. Throw it away, if you must, but at least have no illusions about what you are doing. Oh, I don't even know that I blame you. The whole thing's been impossibly hard on you. I wish I could have explained to you in England. It would have been much better, I can see now, if you had been consulted before you were brought here. But, think a little, in the frame of mind you were in, when first we met, you would have agreed?"

"Yes." She could not blame him for reminding her of how he had saved her life. "You're right. I was in despair." How long ago it seemed, that moonlight night, and how extraordinarily childish her behaviour. "It's true," she went on. "I owe you a great deal, Mr. Varlow. But for you, I might be dead."

"I doubt that. I think, even if I had not been there, you'd have thought twice about that river. You're no coward."

"But I am. Don't you see? That's just it. I'm terrified of going down that stair alone. And the full moon's two days off." It was an extraordinary relief to have said it.

"Of course you're afraid." His answer surprised her. "You'd be a fool not to be. Frankly, I'm relieved that you

125

are. Because I'm afraid for you. If anything happened to you, I'd never forgive myself."

"That would be the greatest comfort to me, of course."

"Miss Brett!" He looked over his shoulder. "Your man's coming back. Try to understand ... to see that I had no alternative. It's not just Portugal that's at stake, remember, it's England too. If Portugal falls to the French, how long do you think England can stand alone? Imagine if Napoleon had the Tagus to collect his armada in as the Spaniards did. That's what we're fighting for, you and I, the safety of England. Be afraid, you've every right to be, and I hope it will be your best protection, but for God's sake, and England's, don't fail us."

"But how do I know you won't fail me? Suppose the Government falls, now Fox is dead?"

"I'll suppose no such thing. The Tories are in even worse case than the Whigs. But surely you did not seriously believe that I would leave you without a word and go off with St. Vincent?"

She was ashamed now. "I was afraid of it. I've been so lonely. It's hard to think straight."

"I know. The loneliness is the worst of all." It was what she had thought herself. "I promise myself, sometimes," he went on, "that when this job is done, I'll retire, go into Parliament perhaps, live like other people."

"You mean, you feel it too?"

"Of course. I've not been able to talk freely, not even to my sister, since I started this work. Oh, she knows that I am a Government agent of some kind. She thinks I have something to do with trade. It makes her very angry when I have to behave so unpredictably, and I don't blame her, but I can't explain. And, even out here, Strangford's technically my superior, but I can't talk to him. He's charming, of course, but the less he knows, the better."

"You mean even he doesn't know—" Iago was very near now.

"No. He just thinks me remarkably well informed. You're the only one"—he raised his voice, and filled it with passion—"whose opinion I care for. Miss Brett, I beg of you; have some pity on me and say you won't go back to England."

"I'll think it over." But they both knew she had yielded.

CHAPTER 11

They found Roberto at the castle, and Juana had a moment of near panic. If Pedro had objected to her merely talking to Gair at Strangford's party, what would Roberto do when he found him riding with her?

But he greeted them as if it was the most natural thing in the world. "I came to break it to you, Juana, that St. Vincent has gone, but I find that Mr. Varlow has been before me. I'm not the only one, it seems, who is ready to get himself muddy for your sake."

Could he actually approve of Gair's apparent courtship? "You're both in a great hurry to bring me bad news," she said. "I was telling Mr. Varlow that I saw St. Vincent's ships go. It made me so homesick I was tempted to book passage on the next packet."

"You've changed your mind, I hope."

"Oh yes. Mr. Varlow persuaded me that Portugal can't do without me."

"I don't like it." Gair was as surprised as she when Roberto made a pretext to leave them alone together out on the seaward terrace with the castle walls looming above them, and the roar of the Atlantic below. "It's not natural," he went on. "He should be furious that I am paying court to you."

"Yes, it's true. I expected trouble when I saw him, and now look at us!"

"Exactly. It's unnatural, and, in my trade, one must learn that what is unnatural is almost always dangerous."

"*Our* trade," she said. "Still, while it lasts, we had better make the most of it. I have been wanting to ask you what I should do if I ever need to get in touch with you urgently."

"Ah." He was pleased with her. "That's why I persuaded Lord Strangford to be impressed by your uncle's translations of Camoens, which, between ourselves, are worth a special place in the *Dunciad*. If you ever need me in a hurry, send a messenger to Lord Strangford, asking for your transcriptions back. It doesn't matter what pretext you give, just ask for them. I will come at once."

"If you can."

127

"Miss Brett, you must trust me. I involved you in this. I will take care of you." He took her hand, and her heart gave a great, infuriating jump. "There's someone watching us from the castle," he explained, "from the right-hand turret. We've been talking altogether too seriously." He raised her hand to his lips and kissed it with passion, turning a little so as to get his back to the castle. "There's no one deaf in your household is there?"

"Deaf? No, I don't think so." She sounded as surprised as she felt.

"They might be able to read our lips," he explained. "We'd best assume they can. Turn sideways a little and they won't be able to see."

"But that's my window! In the right-hand turret?" She did as she was told. "Are you sure?"

"Quite sure. But of course it may be entirely innocent. Your maid, perhaps?"

"Maria? It's siesta. I'm sure she's fast asleep in her own quarters."

"Probably. But her husband's one of them."

"Tomas! How do you know?"

"We know quite a few of the lower members. I won't tell you how. The less you know, the safer you will be. Could you pick me a bunch of flowers, do you think?"

"Flowers? Here?" On this high terrace, exposed to wind and salt from the furious Atlantic below, there was nothing but a few blasted-looking aloes and a forlorn row of geraniums in pots sheltered by the containing wall.

He laughed. "I'm sorry. I'm not much of a conspirator after all. But, think, what would you be doing if I was really courting you?"

"Making a fool of myself!" And then, changing her tone. "I'm sorry, Mr. Varlow. I'm afraid I must be a disappointment to you, but you must remember that I've hardly had your experience in this kind of affair."

"It's I who should be sorry. But here comes your cousin."

She thought it a relief to him and was hardly surprised.

Roberto had come to say good-bye and ask if Gair was riding to Lisbon. "We could ride together as far as Queluz. Company will make the road seem shorter."

Gair accepted with enthusiasm, finely modulating into regret at leaving Juana. The whole performance irritated her enough so that she could take the parting with equanimity. Only after the two of them had ridden out the castle gate

128

and down the long slope of the hill did she face the certainty that Gair would not be back before the night of the meeting. There were so many things she should have asked him, and one that she should have told him. Tomas was a member of the Sons of the Star, he had said. And Tomas had been with her when she was attacked. What did it mean? Or did it mean anything? She was angry with herself now for having wasted their time together. She would not let it happen again. Or would she? Had he not, perhaps, been parrying her questions, avoiding the discussion she wanted? For fear she would lose her nerve again? Very likely, and not cheering.

Mrs. Brett sent for her next day for the first time since Lord Stangford's party. "She's a little better," said Manuela, "but weak still. You won't let her tire herself, will you? She insists on seeing you alone. She won't even have us in the antechamber."

"I'll try not to tire her. But it's hard . . ."

"She tires herself." Estella was waiting for them in the anteroom. "There's nothing anyone can do to stop her. But she'll make herself worse if she doesn't see you, *menina*."

"She's really ill?" Here was a new and terrifying thought. Had she let herself believe too easily in Elvira's theory of a selfish old woman caring for no one but herself?

"We thought she was dying," said Manuela.

"Only she wouldn't," said Estella.

"We wanted to send for the doctor."

"And the priest."

"But she lost her temper and called us a couple of meddling old busybodies."

"So then we thought she would probably live."

"You will see for yourself," concluded Manuela, opening the door of the inner room.

Juana did see. Her grandmother seemed to have aged ten years since the day of the party. If she had seemed withered before, now she was desiccated, ready to blow away, down into the darkness. Only her eyes still glittered with intelligence in the wreck of her face. "Those two have been frightening you, child. Don't let them. I won't fail you. I'm stronger than they think. But, before we talk, make sure the anteroom is empty, and leave the door open."

"Oh, Grandmother, I'm sorry." It was an apology for her own suspicions. How could she have let Elvira convince her so easily? Guiltily, she almost felt as if it was her fault that

129

Mrs. Brett had been ill; as if she had ill-wished her. But that was to think like Iago. Was there something about Portugal that made one superstitious?

"Don't be sorry. It's a waste of time. Unless you are sorry that I have to go on living. It's no pleasure. But I mean to, so long as I must. Those old women out there wanted to send for the doctor, who'd probably have bled and killed me, and the priest, who'd have made all right with extreme unction. I'm not ready for that yet. There's too much to think about. We have to decide what you're to do if I die. I wish I could have seen Mr. Varlow yesterday, but it would have seemed too odd. Specially with Roberto here. What did *he* want, by the way?"

"I don't know. Mr. Varlow said he didn't like it. He was so friendly. You remember what Pedro was like at the party?"

"Yes. That *is* odd. They've always hunted in couples, those two. Don't trust them, Juana."

"Who can I trust?"

"Me. Your Cousin Vasco, of course. Gair Varlow. Yourself. Maria, I think, in small matters, but remember that her husband—" She was tiring, and paused here for breath.

"—Is one of them. Mr. Varlow told me."

"Yes. Tomas—and who else here in the castle? You'd think it would be easy enough to find out, but I never have. Someone, I'm sure." She pulled herself up among her pillows. "I've sent for my lawyer from Lisbon—Senhor Gonçalves. He's coming tomorrow. I've no choice now. I'll have to leave the castle to you. They won't like it, the rest of them, but I can't help that."

"Grandmother, no!"

"But I must. Don't you see? If I should die—I don't mean to, but if I should"—she was looking past Juana, as if she could see death in the corner of the room, waiting—"you've got to be able to carry on. I shall say, in my will, that as my heir you are to move into my room. It would seem so odd otherwise, and of course you'll have to, because of the stair. You won't fail me, Juana; not now? You've been wishing you were back in England, haven't you?"

"Yes." Useless to prevaricate.

"Well then, think. At least, now, there is England to be homesick for. I don't know what it means to you. Freedom, perhaps? Being able to say what you think, wherever you are? It's true, you know: even for us Catholics. No looking over one's shoulder there. We're working for a great future,

130

you and I, for England and Portugal. For all the little freedoms of living ... For them, surely, no sacrifice is too great. And, after all, inheriting the castle is not such a sacrifice."

"But it's not fair to Pedro and Roberto."

"I can't help that. When did they ever think of anything but themselves? You could marry one of them, if you really feel badly about it."

"Never! Besides, they wouldn't have me."

"Not even for the castle?" Juana had a curious feeling that the old woman was pleased with her answer. "Well, it's their loss."

"Thank you."

"No compliment, child. I meant the castle, not you. As to marrying: I doubt if they will. Poor things, they try so hard to be good Portuguese, but when it comes to the women! I've seen their faces. They're ambitious, Juana, your cousins, but they're not stupid. It would be a mistake to think that. But they have neither of them ever cared a rap for me. Or for the castle. You at least had the grace to be homesick for it, when you were in England. And to come when I sent for you. I don't see why you shouldn't have it. Frankly, I'm beyond caring much. It will be a relief to have it settled. When I am dead, it will be your problem. Best tell Mr. Varlow you're an heiress, hadn't you?"

"No!" Intolerable to think that if Gair Varlow knew, he might well start pretending that his pretence courtship was real. "Promise me, ma'am, that you won't tell him. If you don't promise, I won't go on."

"Very well. I won't tell him. Oddly enough, I still believe in love matches. And Gair Varlow's not the man for one of those. Nor the man for you. Use him, child, as he uses you, but don't hope for more. Unless you're prepared to take second best; to let him marry you for the castle—which I rather think he would, don't you?—and hope that love would come later?"

"I'd rather die."

"No need for melodrama. We've enough of that as it is. The moon is full tomorrow. Sit down quietly there, by the bed, Juana, and tell me, in order, everything you must do."

Senhor Gonçalves, the lawyer, arrived from Lisbon next day, a neat man in dusty black with a huge bag and an expression of perpetual disapproval. This was more pro-

131

nounced than ever when he joined the family after his long session with Mrs. Brett, and Juana thought he had a very sharp look for her when he was introduced. No doubt he disapproved intensely of Mrs. Brett's new will. She hardly blamed him. She did not much like it herself.

He had no intention of being questioned about what he had been doing, but drank his glass of wine and talked about the news from France and the prospects for the grape harvest, then rose firmly to take his leave.

"Can I persuade you to take the Guincho road, senhor?" Prospero, too, had risen. "I promised I'd take advantage of the full moon to visit friends there this evening."

But Gonçalves pleaded business in Sintra and left alone, followed by Prospero: "I'll be late back, don't wait up for me."

Miguel withdrew to his own rooms immediately after supper, explaining that he had urgent business to attend to in connection with his Little Brothers of Saint Antony. Elvira burst into rhymed couplets and followed him. Watching her go, Juana thought how odd it was that they should separate thus on this night of all nights. Was Miguel really writing letters in his room? And Prospero supping with friends in Guincho? And where was Father Ignatius, who had not appeared all day? Were they all, secretly, separately or together, dressing in the black robes of the Sons of the Star, ready to go out, when the house was quiet, down by some secret way to the council chamber? The great gate of the castle was closed and locked at night, but she could remember from her childhood that there had been two or three ways at least that a determined person could climb in and out. And yet it was fantastically hard to imagine either her uncles or the priest doing so. Very likely it was all coincidence, all imagination . . .

The session with the lawyer must have been an exhausting one. Juana found Mrs. Brett looking so worn out, so drained of strength that she forgot her own terror in concern for her, and dressed as fast as she could in the new black dress with its all-concealing hood and deep pockets. But when it came to the fastenings, her shaking hands failed her.

"Come here, child." Her grandmother had noticed. "I'll do it. There; now the hood, the key in your pocket, and you're ready. But it's early yet. Sit down, for a while, and rest."

"No." Juana bent to kiss the withered cheek, and felt it cold with exhaustion. She must let the old lady rest. "I think

132

I'll go now, ma'am. I'd rather feel I have all the time in the world and need not hurry down those steps."

"Sensible." Mrs. Brett was at once approving and relieved. "Good luck, Juana. I wish I could come with you." She was hardly capable of walking across the room. "But, thank God, I don't have to." She sank back among her pillows and was already breathing heavily towards sleep as Juana felt for the secret panel at the back of the cupboard.

Why did the knowledge that her grandmother was already asleep make the dark journey down the winding stair seem so much worse? After all, waking or sleeping, she could not help Juana once the secret door was shut behind her. Feeling for the candle and tinder-box, Juana fought panic for a few endless moments in the darkness. What was to stop her going back through the doorway, back from this dank darkness to warmth, and light, and the familiar, reassuring scent of burnt lavender?

And have her grandmother try to go in her place? She took a deep, steadying breath, found the candle at last, and managed to light it at the second try. Its flame flickered for a moment, then burnt steadily, showing the stair plunging down into blackness. Her breath was coming too fast again. She leaned against the rough wood of the door and made herself count slowly to a hundred. Just as well she had come early. But now there was no excuse for further delay. If she did not start down, quickly, now, this minute, she never would.

At least there was no chance of mistaking the way. There was no choice at any point as the steep stairs plunged down, and down again, and sideways, into the heavy darkness. There was something steadying about the need to count the steps as she descended, and, mercifully, she had remembered about the bats. Reaching the bottom door at last she felt in her pocket for the big key, but paused a minute before she fitted it in the lock. So far, her only terror had been of the darkness. As long as this door was locked and bolted on her side, no one could reach the winding stair except through her grandmother's room.

Was she sure that the same was true of the other side? Might there not be more ways into the council chamber than the big door that it was her task to unlock? It seemed unlikely, but how could she be certain? She set her teeth, pushed back the bolt, and unlocked the door. Silence greeted her, and a breath of the air of the cavern, perceptibly colder

133

and damper than that on the stairs, reminding her that the Atlantic was not far off.

How long had it taken her to grope her cautious way down the stair? She made herself move forward at once into the darkness, and light the candles on the council table from her own. Then she felt in her right-hand pocket for a taper and moved round lighting the braziers the acolytes had left ready a month ago. There was something wonderfully comforting about the way the resin caught and flared up at once. Now the flickering shadows on the cavern roof were warm red, instead of cold candlelight. But the warmth of the braziers merely served to accentuate the deathly chill of the council chamber. She pulled her hood more closely round her and looked about for the path to the cell door.

It felt much safer in there, with the brazier lit and the secret spy-hole opened—to make sure she could—and closed again. She sat down on the heavy wooden chair where, last time, her grandmother had sat, and resigned herself to the possibility of a long wait. Then she stood up, reluctantly. Why not make a fuller investigation of the council chamber while she had the chance?

It was rough going, since the rock was only smoothed away round the table itself and on the paths that led to the three doorways, and she wished that she had a lantern instead of the precariously flickering candle. She tried blowing it out, in the hope that she would be able to see her way by the light of the candles on the big central table, but found at once that this would not do, and had to lose what seemed a great deal of time feeling her way back to the central table and relighting her candle from one of the candelabras. Another time, she would carry the tinder-box in her pocket.

Her candle relit, she made her way back down the path to the cell and started off round the cave wall in the opposite direction to the one she had taken before. This way, the going was rougher still, and she had to put down her candle, from time to time, while she climbed over one of the ribs of rock that ran out from the cavern wall. It was damp, too, and she wondered if she was nearing the source of the water drip that seemed to echo her own quick heartbeat. Thinking of this, she took a careless step, slipped on the damp rock, and fell.

For a moment, aching all over, she thought she had broken a bone and gave way to pure, shaking fright. Then, slowly and carefully, she picked herself up, put her full weight on the foot that hurt most and decided that it was

134

merely wrenched. And, mercifully, the candle was still burning on the rock where she had put it.

How long had all this taken? New terror seized her. Any minute now the gong might sound, summoning her to open the big door. What would the acolytes think if she took too long to obey the summons? Already, as she thought this, she was working her way down a channel in the rock to the central table. She had just reached it, and settled, with a sigh of relief, on one of the heavy wooden chairs, when the gong did indeed sound, louder than she had remembered, echoing strangely in that strangely echoing place.

No time to wonder if her fall had left its mark on her black dress. But unlikely that it would be visible by candle-light. She pulled her hood closely round her face, picked up the candle, and made herself walk without limping towards the door. Nothing she did tonight must be in the least odd; nothing must need explaining.

Shooting back the bolt, she saw that her hands were shaking, and remembered without comfort that her grandmother's had done so too. As before, the doors were pulled outwards as soon as the bolt was free, and she could see the flare of two torches outside, and hear, behind them, the sullen roar of the Atlantic.

"Who comes here?" she asked, her voice unrecognisable even to herself.

"The Sons of the Star."

"And why do you come?"

"That we may gain wisdom, knowledge, power and peace."

She moved aside to let them in: "Enter, Sons of the Star, and may your hearts' desire be granted." What nonsense it all is, she thought with a comforting little rush of reason. And tried to decide whether the acolytes who had now moved forward into the cavern were the same ones as last time. She rather thought not.

"Is the council chamber ready?" asked the leader.

"Search and see," said Juana, her question answered. He had got his words wrong: he should have said "prepared." They must be new.

This was confirmed by the length of time they took to investigate the big cave and then Juana's own cell. One good thing, they were not likely to notice that the candles on the big central table had already burned down some distance. She should have thought of that when she first lit them.

"All is prepared." The two acolytes returned to the central table. This was where the routine would be different tonight.

"Are you ready to go to your own place, Handmaiden of the Star?" The two of them stood, now, one on either side of her, nearer than she liked.

"I am ready." She kept her voice steady with an effort, and it echoed back, unrecognisable from the high roof.

"Then come."

She walked, not limping, though it hurt horribly, down the path to the cell door and listened, cold all over, as they locked it on her.

It seemed an age till the gong sounded for the second time. This was the worst moment of all. She counted ten, then waited, unable to bring herself to open the panel. Until she did so, she was what they thought her, the Handmaiden of the Star. Opening it, she declared herself their enemy. Suppose, this first time, they were keeping watch on her?

Thinking merely made it worse. She gritted her teeth, blew out the candle and felt for the secret spring. As the panel slid open, she saw that everything was as it had been last time. The Sons of the Star were seated round their table, the two acolytes stood behind the chair of the leader, and, as before, he was speaking. "Strangford persuaded St. Vincent not to abduct the Prince Regent," he said. "He knows Portugal too well, understands too much, is dangerously well-informed. Before we turn to our new plans, Brothers, I put it to you that Lord Strangford is our enemy. What say you, Sons of the Star?"

He turned to the robed figure on his right, who spoke one word: "Death."

His neighbour said the same, and so on about halfway round the table, until it came to the turn of a man who had his back to Juana. He rose to his feet, still with his back to her so that she could not set the emblem on his cowl. "Most excellent Star," he said, "with all respect, I submit that it is not Strangford who is our enemy, but the Englishman who keeps him informed. Strangford is nothing, a poetaster, a braggart. It is the other we must fear."

"And who is he?"

Gair, of course. Juana thought, with cold terror, that if she had yielded to temptation and left the panel shut, she would not have heard this.

The man with his back to her was speaking again. "I do not know—yet. One among Strangford's following, I am sure, but as to which—"

"Then we must kill them all," said the leader. And once

again the one word, "death," echoed round the table, and again the same man broke the chain.

"Most excellent Star, first let us find out our real enemy, the man behind Strangford. He must be killed at once, I agree, but for the rest of the Englishmen, why not let them live until we are ready to strike? Kill them now, they will be replaced, maybe by men who understand the situation better."

"You counsel well, Brother of the Broken Cross. It shall be as you suggest. You will find out, before our next meeting, the name of the man who is keeping Strangford informed. And having found him, deal with him. We pass his sentence now."

This time, the word "death" was unanimous.

Juana shivered convulsively, but this was no time to be thinking of the threat to Gair; she must concentrate on the general discussion that now broke out. The Brother of the Ragged Staff had recent news from Paris and confirmed that all hope of aid from France was, for the time being, at an end. "Napoleon and his armies have marched east," he said. "They may be at Berlin by now, for all I know."

As at the previous meeting, there were two schools of thought. Many of the members wanted to strike at once, now the English ships were gone, to dispose of the older members of the royal family and govern in the name of one of the Princes. "It hardly matters which," said the Brother of the Silver Hand, "since the oldest is only nine."

The Brother of the Broken Cross had an objection to this plan. "What of Spain?" he asked. "I myself have been employed by Carlota Joaquina to carry her letters to her parents there. So far, they have made no move to help her, but if we rise, be sure they will take advantage of the country's confusion and attack. We all know what kind of a state the army is in. Without a French force to support us we'd not have a chance against Spain. It is liberty we want, not bondage to our oldest enemy."

There was a murmur of agreement round the table, and in the end the meeting broke up without a decision.

"We must wait, Brothers," the leader summed up, "wait and hope. In the meantime, as you know, our Brother of the Crescent Moon follows Napoleon to urge our cause. He will not fail us. It is merely to wait a little, and make ready, while we wait. You all know your tasks." He raised his hands: "Sons of the Star, we meet only to part ..." It was the beginning of the final invocation. Juana's hands were so cold that she could hardly manage the spring of the secret panel. She had to make three tries before she contrived to relight her candle. Idiot! She had not thought to replenish the brazier—something Mrs. Brett had done the time before—and it was almost out. How in the world could she explain this if the acolytes should notice, as they were almost bound to do? She let herself slump down on the chair, put her head on the rough table and was, she hoped, convincingly asleep when the key grated in the lock. Pretending to wake as the acolytes entered the cell, she was aware, for the first time, of a new terror. The others were all gone now, she was alone down here with two men who thought nothing of murder. Her hood had slipped back a little from her face as she pretended to wake, and she pulled it forward again with a trembling hand.

"Fear nothing, Servant of the Star." In this small cell, voices were less distorted and she thought there was something familiar about this acolyte's. But how could one be sure? At all events, his words were encouraging. "No need to be scared of us," he went on, reassuringly colloquial. "Though I don't say I blame you. I was scared myself back in there."

She bowed her acknowledgement, unwilling to speak, here where he might recognise her voice.

"This work should be done in silence," the other acolyte spoke reprovingly as they went to work preparing a new brazier and changing the candle. Then: "The candlestick is cold, woman. Why is that?"

It was the question she had dreaded, and prepared for. "It went out while I was asleep. I had to relight it." She spoke through her hood, her voice muffled and, she hoped, unrecognisable.

"Women sleep while men—"

"Talk." His companion surprised Juana by his intervention. "All is finished here, Brother."

At last, Juana bolted the big door behind them and turned with a sigh of relief to the long climb up the winding stair. Her foot was hurting again, and the stairs seemed endless. But it had not really gone off too badly. And all the danger, all the terror and pain were trivial compared with the discovered threat to Gair. She must warn him at once. But how? Her grandmother was still fast asleep. There was nothing she could do till morning.

CHAPTER 12

"But suppose he doesn't come for days!" Juana was relieved to see that her grandmother looked a little better this morning. "Shouldn't I send to ask for my Camoens transcriptions back? You remember we agreed I could summon him that way in a crisis?"

"Don't be absurd, child. He'll come. Today if he can. At the worst, tomorrow. Panic never helped anyone."

Panic? But it was true; she had been close to it. Bad enough to be afraid for herself; this terror for Gair was something beyond reason. "They know so much," she tried to explain it. "They're bound to find him out."

"I'm glad, at least, it has made you realise how dangerous they are. But you do Gair Varlow less than justice. You've not been here long enough to see the picture he has managed to create of himself. If they think Strangford—what did you say?—a nothing and a poetaster, they must have dismissed Gair Varlow as even less worth their notice. It's all over Lisbon that he only got his appointment here through the influence of his sister's husband, who was tired of having his brother-in-law hanging on his sleeve." She managed an exhausted pretence at a laugh. "No need to look so angry. It's an admirable cover. And Mr. Varlow's not the man I think him if it doesn't turn out that there is also a likely candidate among Lord Strangford's suite for the part of secret service agent."

"But if there is, he'll be killed!"

"If there is, he'll be expendable."

For a moment, Juana came near to hating her grandmother. How could she shrug off a man's life like that? Was it perhaps this streak of ruthlessness in her that had made such disasters of her children's lives?

"It's time you went out for your ride." Mrs. Brett interrupted her thoughts. "Nothing must seem out of the way this morning. Besides, I'd like you to go down the Pleasant Valley and see how they are getting on with the preparations for the grape harvest. It should be starting any time now."

"Yes, ma'am." But this was another blow. She had meant to ride part of the way towards Sintra in the hope of meeting Gair. Had her grandmother guessed?

Her next words suggested that she had: "I'll see to it that Mr. Varlow stays for dinner, if he should come while you are out. He'll have to, as I don't propose to get up today. Don't look so anxious, child. He'll manage to see you alone. It's his business."

And that was curiously cold comfort, Juana thought, as she hurried across the courtyard to the stables, eager to get this unwelcome errand done.

Iago was whistling through his teeth as he greased the wheels of the family carriage. He greeted her with his usual elaborate respect, but went on to explain that Tomas would have to accompany her this morning as he had orders to prepare the carriage. "The Senhor Miguel has unexpected business in Lisbon."

Juana looked about her. "But where is Tomas?"

"That's the difficulty, senhora. I don't know. I haven't seen him this morning."

"You mean he hasn't come to work?" Tomas lived in the little huddle of peasant houses between the castle and the Pleasant Valley.

"No. And no message either. I suppose Maria didn't say anything?"

"Maria slept in the castle last night. She mostly does, now she's waiting on me. But what's to do, Iago? Mrs. Brett wants me to ride down the Pleasant Valley and let her know how the preparations for the vintage are coming on."

Iago dropped his tools at once. This put an entirely different complexion on Juana's morning ride. Mrs. Brett's slightest wish had priority over the needs of any other inhabitant of the castle. "In that case, I'll call Jaime. He will have to take the Senhor Miguel to Lisbon. I'll be with you directly, senhora."

Naturally, this was not the case. Juana had to wait, controlling impatience as best she might, while Iago finished getting the carriage ready, since Jaime could not be expected to demean himself with such a task. Then Miguel appeared, and the whole thing had to be explained all over again to him.

"That's not like Tomas," he said. "Have you sent to see what's the matter, Juana?"

"Who could I send?" Impatience was beginning to boil up in her. "I'll go myself on my way down to the valley. I wish I'd known you were going into Lisbon, Uncle. I'd have had some more of Uncle Prospero's translation copied out ready

140

for Lord Strangford." Here had been the perfect opportunity to send to Gair and she had not even known about it.

"I'm sorry, child. I didn't know myself till Father Ignatius got back this morning with the message. It's my little Brothers of Saint Antony." He did not explain further. "I can wait a few minutes now, if you wish."

"Thank you, Uncle, but it's no use. It would take too long." She had suddenly realised that she could hardly send for the Camoens without making at least a pretence of consulting Prospero. Besides, was Miguel a safe messenger? Why did he have to go so urgently into Lisbon this morning? "Anyway, I'd need to discuss it with Uncle Prospero, and I don't suppose he's down yet."

"Down? Oh—of course, you breakfasted with the old lady. You wouldn't know. Prospero didn't get back last night. He sent to say he would stay at Guincho. You're ready at last, Jaime? Good. Enjoy your ride, child, and may God watch over you."

"Thank you, Uncle." She hated Miguel's blessings. But at last Iago had finished harnessing the four shaggy mules to the old carriage and had picked up his long, metal-tipped cane, ready to accompany her.

Tomas' mother looked even older than Mrs. Brett, though Juana knew she could hardly be half her age. Toothless, skinny, and almost bald under her voluminous black draperies, she was busy preparing *bacalhao* for her grandchildren's dinner. No, she told Juana, she had not seen Tomas since the night before. "I expect he's out with the sardine boats." It sounded like an excuse she had used many times before.

"Without asking leave at the castle?"

"I know nothing about that." The old woman's eyes swivelled to look past Juana. "Tomas never tells me anything about his work. It's none of my business. Perhaps that wife of his would know something. She who's too good to live here with her husband and children."

The hatred in her voice shook Juana. It had not occurred to her before to what an extent she had taken Maria away from her family. It ought to have. "I'm sorry—" she began.

"No need. We do better without her." And the old woman turned away to her cooking with a rudeness that amazed Juana.

"You mustn't mind her." Iago felt it incumbent on him to apologise. "She's always been a queer one." He crossed

141

himself. "I wouldn't want to meet her, out on the cliff, on All Saints' Eve."

"Nonsense, Iago. She's not a *brucha*, she's a poor old woman with too much to do. I must see to it that Maria gets home more often."

"I wouldn't, senhora." Iago's respectful voice held a warning. "I don't think anyone would thank you for that."

What exactly did he mean? She thought he wanted her to question him, but thought, too, that she would rather not know any more about Maria's private affairs. "We'd best be getting down the valley." She kicked Rosinante into a reluctant amble and started down the long sloping track that led to the pressing floor, with Iago running a few paces behind. She had not been down here since the bad weather and saw that, as usual, her grandmother had been right. The few days of sunshine after the rain had brought the grapes on immensely. They would be ready for the harvest any time now.

"The grapes are nearly ripe, Iago." She turned back to speak to him. "I hope Senhor Macarao is here today."

"He's always here when he's needed. I expect we'll find he had work for Tomas. He's a skilled man with the vines, Tomas, the best there is." But he sounded puzzled, just the same, as if he was trying to explain Tomas' disappearance to himself.

"Of course. That will be it." She greeted the suggestion with what struck her as disproportionate relief. "Why didn't we think of it sooner?" As she spoke, she came out from the shade of a thicket of ilex and myrtle to her first view of the pressing floor. "Good gracious, what can be the matter?" It was not nearly time yet for the mid-day break, yet all the men who should have been working among the vines up and down the valley were gathered in a gesticulating mob in the open space round the pressing floor.

"I don't know, senhora"—Iago caught up with her and pulled Rosinante to a halt—"but I don't like the look of it. Let me go first." He broke into a trot, while Juana urged Rosinante forward again to follow him.

The crowd parted at sight of her, and Senhor Macarao came forward. Normally a rotund, jovial little man, shining with good living, he looked sallow today under his tan. "Don't come any farther, senhora." It was a measure of his disturbed state that he omitted the usual elaborate greetings as he seized Rosinante's bridle.

"What's the matter?" She could see now that most of the

men were crowded round something that lay on the pressing floor.

"It's poor Tomas, senhora. He has met with an accident."

"An accident? You mean—"

"He's dead, I'm afraid. He must have got up early to come out and work on the vines—he was always a good worker, was Tomas."

"But what happened to him?"

He shrugged. "Who knows? A fall, perhaps. A seizure of some kind? We've only just found him, and now, with your permission, senhora, we must get him home, fetch the priest to him. Poor Tomas"—he crossed himself—"dead without the last rites of the church."

"God rest his soul. Can I help in any way, senhor?"

"If you'll be so good as to break the news to Mrs. Brett?" He obviously wanted to be rid of her. Hardly surprising, perhaps? And yet there seemed something odd about the whole business. It was true that Tomas was an expert worker with the vines, but equally true that he was bone idle and used his position in the castle to escape all the work he could. Would he really have got up early to come down here? And—something else. "You've only just found him?"

"Yes." He had not meant to tell her this. "His body was down at the bottom of the valley. He must have gone down there for something, tripped . . . fallen? He might have lain there for days if my dog hadn't found him."

The bottom of the valley. Down towards the Jaws of Death; the place Iago thought was haunted. The way to the Cavern of the Star? She was cold in the hot sunlight. "I'd like to see him, senhor."

"See him? You?"

"Yes. Some member of the family must. I'm here. I think it my duty." She felt sick at the very thought. "He was our servant," she finished, as if that settled it.

They had laid Tomas' body on an improvised stretcher of poles. Juana fell on her knees on the hot stone of the pressing floor to say a prayer beside it. The face was covered. There was no sign of any injury. She could not ask to see more. She did not want to.

"Very well, senhor"—she rose to her feet—"take him to his house. I will tell Mrs. Brett, and send Father Ignatius." She stood back and watched as the men lifted the improvised bier and started the slow march up the valley. "Iago!" He had been in the thick of the group, no doubt asking questions of his own. "We'll go this way and get there ahead of them." She turned Rosinante up one of the paths that led between the rows of vines.

They were soon out of earshot of the others and as the path widened towards the head of the valley Iago caught up to trot beside her. He was white and shaking. "The *bruchas* got him, senhora. I told you how it would be if you went down there. There wasn't a mark on him. But his face! I'll never forget it. He saw his death coming and knew there was no escape. But why did he go down there, senhora, that's what I want to know?"

So did Juana. Or rather she was afraid she did know. But there was no time to think about it now. They were almost back to the little group of houses. "I must tell his mother, Iago."

"Yes, senhora." It was her job, and they both knew it.

The old woman took the news with a stoicism that Juana found at once impressive and unsympathetic. "It's the will of God." She went on spooning food into the mouths of her grandchildren.

"Don't worry about anything. We'll look after you. I'll send Maria down right away, and Father Ignatius." In face of the old woman's calm, Juana felt she was babbling absurdly.

"Send the priest, by all means. As to Maria—" The old woman spat on the floor.

"I'll talk to my grandmother." Juana felt it cowardly, could think of nothing else to say, and was grateful to escape from the hot little room, with its tragedy and its smells of food and child, into the less oppressive heat of the sun.

It was still early when they got back to the castle, and Juana went first to the chapel, where Father Ignatius could usually be found at this time of day. "I'll go at once." He was almost as plump as Senhor Macarao, but pale with it, and flabby. Even today, Juana could not bring herself to like him, or to be grateful for his words of sympathy.

"I must go and tell my grandmother." She cut short his expressions of regret that she had been exposed to such an unpleasant experience.

"Of course. And Maria?"

"Yes. I'll send her down. They'll need her."

"Yes." He, too, looked doubtful.

Mrs. Brett's reaction and Maria's were equally predictable. Mrs. Brett was playing cribbage with Estella. "Dead?" She

144

discarded. "And just before the vintage! Oh well, we'll manage, I expect. You to play, Estella." And then, looking up from her cards, "Don't stand there gawping, child. Run along and tell Maria." She might have been talking about the weather.

It was almost a relief when Maria, also predictably, went into hysterics. At least it was a human reaction. "What am I to do?" she asked at last, through hiccups and sobs.

"I told his mother you'd go down there."

"And what did she say?"

"She wasn't best pleased. But you'll have to go, Maria."

"Yes. But I won't stay. She's taken my children from me, as she took my husband. She can rear them. You won't turn me off, *menina?*"

"Of course not. If you really want to stay." Indeed, it had already struck her that this was probably the only way that Maria could support a family of four. "Tomas has no other relatives, has he?"

"Not here." Maria had taken her point. "He's from the Alentejo, like Iago. I expect his mother will want me to go back there. But I won't. Not if you'll keep me."

"Of course I will. Come back when you can, Maria. Don't worry about anything."

Absurd advice. She might as well tell herself not to worry. If only there was someone she could talk to ... But it was no good going back to Mrs. Brett's rooms. She had made it perfectly clear that she did not want to discuss Tomas' death. Besides, her callous attitude to it was intolerable. Juana picked up the volume of Shakespeare she had found in the castle library and went down to the seaward terrace, where, defying the hot sun, she made herself recite the last speech she had learned: "Oh, what a rogue and peasant slave am I ..."

It had a curiously calming effect, particularly as today she really thought she was stammering a little less. Was this, perhaps, because half her mind was elsewhere all the time, busy with Tomas' death and her fears for Gair Varlow?

The bell rang for dinner, and still there was no sign of Gair. Since Miguel was in Lisbon, and neither Prospero nor Father Ignatius had returned, Juana and Elvira were alone. Usually, on these occasions, Juana had thought Elvira tended to be more rational than usual, but today she was white and distraught, pushing the food about on her plate, eating hardly anything, and muttering to herself:

145

> *"He is dead and gone, lady,*
> *He is dead and gone."*

Her maid, standing, as usual, behind her chair, tried in vain to get her to eat.

"Take it away." Elvira pushed back her chair and stood up. "You are Beelzebub, tempting me, but I'll not eat and I'll not drink; I'll not talk and I'll not think . . . We are all mortal, Juana. Never forget that."

"No, Aunt." Juana had found it equally difficult to eat, and now gave up pretending. "Jaime, would you serve fruit and sweetmeats with our coffee on the loggia?" Perhaps alone with her out there, she would be able to persuade Elvira to eat something.

"Certainly, senhora." Jaime was always quick to take a hint, and soon appeared on the terrace with a tray loaded with their own fruit and some of the little sweet cakes of flour, egg, and honey that Elvira usually ate for breakfast. "You'll ring if you need me?"

"Yes, thank you, Jaime." She could rely on him to keep the other servants out of the way.

It was cooler here, in the shade of the vine, but Juana wished the loggia did not look out toward the Pleasant Valley. At least they could not see the peasants' houses, where, by now, Tomas' body must be lying in brief state. She poured coffee and handed it to her aunt, then helped herself to two of the little cakes and pushed the plate a little nearer to Elvira. "I couldn't eat in there," she said.

"You must eat." Elvira sounded perfectly normal now. "It doesn't matter about me, but you must eat, Juana." She absent-mindedly helped herself to a bunch of grapes. Then, looking around to make sure that Jaime had closed the door of the Ladies' Parlour securely behind him, she leaned towards Juana: "Tomas was a spy. I'm glad he's dead. He watched outside rooms; he listened at doors; he lurked on the stairs. Juana! You must go back to England, quickly, before it's too late. It's not safe for you here. You should never have come. The old woman will swallow you up, as she's swallowed the rest of us. 'Will you walk into my parlour,' said the spider to the fly—' Go home, Juana. Make any excuse; make none. Just go."

"I wish I could." For a moment, she was horribly tempted.

" 'Stand not upon the order of your going,' " said Elvira, "but go, Juana, quickly, before it's too late. There's someone coming, and I must go. Only remember I told you so." She picked up a handful of the little cakes and moved towards the castle door as it opened and Jaime ushered Gair Varlow out into the loggia. She dropped a low curtsey. " 'Welcome lords and ladies all To my bower and to my hall.' You may go, Jaime." And, as the door closed behind him, "And so must I. To bed, to sleep, perhaps to die. Only, go back to England, Juana!"

"Poor thing." Gair said it mechanically as he looked quickly and carefully about him. "Are we really alone? It's too good to be true." It was the conspirator speaking, not the lover.

"We'd better make the most of it. My Uncle Prospero may return any moment. Miguel has gone to Lisbon."

"I know. I met him on the way. But what's the matter? It's not just your crazy aunt, is it?"

"I'm not sure she is crazy at all." There was no time for that. "Tomas is dead." Incredible that in the shock of this discovery she had almost forgotten her anxiety about Gair.

"Tomas?"

"You know! The servant. The one you said was a member —"

"Hush!" He went to the parapet and looked over. But the drop was impossibly steep. No one could be listening there. "How did he die?"

"They found him this morning among the bushes down near the Jaws of Death. Iago says there wasn't a mark on him, but his face was terrified, as if he saw his death coming. Of course Iago thinks it's the *bruchas.*"

"And a very safe thing to think. I only wish you could do so too. But, since you can't, for God's sake think it an accident."

"How can I? He was one of the acolytes last night. I didn't realise at the time, but I thought there was something familiar about his voice. He spoke, you see, when he came into the little cell: voices aren't so distorted there. And I answered him. Suppose he recognised me?"

"If he did, we must simply be thankful he was killed."

"It's horrible!" She turned on him. "My grandmother didn't care either. And there's his mother, down there, and his children! I don't care if he was a spy; he didn't deserve to be dead. It's bad enough if they killed him, but if he was killed because he recognised me . . ." How could she explain how much worse it made it?

147

"Don't think about it. Besides, we've so little time. What happened at the meeting?"

It was the distraction she needed. "It was horrible. They almost decided to kill Lord Strangford. Then someone—the Brother of the Broken Cross—said that was foolish: they should merely kill the man behind Strangford. He meant you."

"But he didn't know?"

"No. He has been told to find out, and kill you. Just like that. And, there's worse. If he doesn't, I think they'll kill them all, Strangford's people."

"They're quite capable of it. We must see that they find someone."

"That's what my grandmother said. That you'd have someone ready. Someone who didn't matter." She could not keep the disgust out of her voice.

"A scapegoat. Well, of course. But don't look at me like that. Your grandmother may be quite ruthless but I'm not. Frankly, I don't even think it's good policy. Of course we've got our scapegoat ready. I'll tell you his name. He's that Mr. Brougham who came out with Rosslyn. He's off, just now, feeling very important and touring the north of the country getting in touch with some of our more expendable agents. When he returns, we'll let them find out he's the man—and pack him back to England before they have time to strike."

"You're sure?"

"Of course. He won't know anything about it. That's the beauty of it. He thinks he's a secret agent, so he'll take all the proper precautions. And by the time they are on to him, he'll be safe in England. Their arm is long, but not as long as that, thank God. But tell me, what else was discussed?"

She told him, as quickly and clearly as she could, about the argument over when to strike. At last he nodded his approval. "I knew you had a clear mind. So the upshot of it is, they will await the result of yet another appeal to Napoleon."

"Yes."

"And who is the messenger?"

"The Brother of the Crescent Moon. He's there already, I think."

"I see."

He had been standing close to her, leaning down so that they could speak quietly. Now he dropped suddenly on one knee. "Only say you'll be mine."

148

The door swung open and Prospero advanced on them. "I'm afraid I intrude. Surely not a proposal in form?"

"Good gracious no." Juana knew she was blushing and thought angrily that it would serve Gair Varlow right if she accepted him on the spot. "You must know, Uncle, that Mr. Varlow is never serious."

CHAPTER 13

The mysterious death of Tomas cast a cloud over the grape harvest. Juana remembered this as the gayest of occasions, with the *gallegos* singing as they trod out the cold must, and the castle servants making constant excuses to go down to the Pleasant Valley and join in the festivities. This year the singing sounded forced; men kept looking over their shoulders towards the bottom of the valley, and the grapes down there never got picked at all.

"It's no use trying to make them." Senhor Macarao had come up to the castle to report to Mrs. Brett.

"No, indeed." She was up and dressed, sitting in her straight-backed chair to receive him. "They'd probably run for it."

"That's what I thought. They're nervous enough as it is. As if poor Tomas' death wasn't bad enough, they're saying today that they heard the Enchanted Mooress ring her bell last night."

"Who says that?" Mrs. Brett's voice was sharp.

"I'd forgotten about the Mooress and her bell." Juana dropped her embroidery and leaned forward to join in the conversation. "Do they really think they heard that?"

Macarao shrugged. "They'll believe anything when they're panicky like this."

"But who says so?" Mrs. Brett asked her question again, impatiently.

"Why, all of them. The moon's coming up for the full, and they worked all night. We got behind because of the funeral and, frankly, I think they'll all be glad to be finished here and away. They say the bell rang, off and on, for hours. Of course they've no sense of time, those peasants. It means nothing."

"You didn't hear it?"

"No." He seemed puzzled at her insistence. "Of course not. An imaginary Mooress, ringing an imaginary bell on a bit of cliff that's supposed to have fallen into the sea centuries ago! To warn that the crusaders are coming!" His tone suggested that she was showing signs of senility at last. "I certainly did

150

not hear it." And then, "As a matter of fact, I wasn't there. I had to go into Lisbon last night to arrange for more casks. It's a good year after all."

"I'm glad to hear it. Even without the grapes from the bottom of the valley. Very well, Senhor Macarao, that will be all." She waited until he had bowed his way out. "You didn't do that very well, Juana. Forgotten about the Mooress indeed! How could you, with Iago talking about her all the time?"

"I'm sorry. Do you think Macarao noticed?"

"Probably not. Being from the Algarve, he's still treated as a foreigner here, even after all these years. He probably knows nothing about the signal. Did you hear it?"

"No."

"Nor did I. But we might well not have, with the wind from the sea to drown it. Don't get your hopes up, though, till we're sure."

"I'll try not to. Where do they ring it, ma'am?" The sound of what was supposedly the Enchanted Mooress's bell was the signal to the Sons of the Star that their next meeting had been cancelled.

"Anywhere on the ridge. Three nights before the meeting is due, to give time for the word to be passed along. Ring for Manuela, child. She'll probably know about it by now."

Manuela did. "The Mooress's bell? Yes indeed. They all heard it in the servants' wing. Father Ignatius said a special prayer about it this morning. You'd have known, Juana, if you'd been there." This, with a hint of reproach, to Juana, who disliked Father Ignatius so much that she avoided morning prayers when she could.

"Juana breakfasted with me this morning." Mrs. Brett's tone made it a reproof. "Fetch Jaime, Manuela. The servants are bound to be in as much of a panic as the men in the vineyards. We must think of something to occupy them. Just the same," she went on, as the door closed behind Manuela, "one has to admit that their superstition has its uses. It's never occurred to anyone to go out and investigate the bell when they hear it ringing."

"Never?"

"Not for years? It's supposed to be death to see the Mooress."

"And?"

"It is, of course."

Juana shuddered. Once again, she found her grandmother's

151

calm acceptance of murder almost as bad as murder itself. "Grandmother—"

"Yes?"

"About Tomas: you don't know anything?"

"What should I know? Except that we must arrange for a pension for his old witch of a mother. I meant to talk to Macarao about it, but his story of the Mooress's bell put it clean out of my head. Ride down the valley this morning, Juana, and tell him to come up again after the siesta. Take Iago and see if you can talk some of the nonsense out of him. He's bound to be spreading panic in the servants' hall." She looked up. "Come in, Jaime. Did you hear the bell?"

"I'm an old man, senhora. I sleep deeply." Was he hedging? "Luis heard it. He's asked leave to go into Lisbon today and say a mass for his dead mother. He promised it her on her deathbed and then did nothing about it. He thinks the Mooress is after him."

Mrs. Brett laughed. "How absurd they are. A ghostly Mooress pursuing a Christian for breach of faith. How is he doing, Jaime?" Luis was the new footman who had replaced Tomas.

"I'm pleased with him." This, from Jaime, was high praise.

"Very well. Let him go to Lisbon this evening and say as many masses as he likes. He need not be back till tomorrow." And, when Jaime had bowed and left them, "That should take care of getting the news of the cancellation spread about."

"You think Luis is one of them?"

"Very likely. He turned up promptly enough after Tomas' death. Don't look so scared, child. The best thing you can do is assume that everyone belongs. That way, you'll always be safe. But at least you've got a month's respite."

"Yes, thank God."

The month seemed to go like a flash. Juana had hardly done savouring the reprive from one meeting when the moon was rounding to the full again and she must begin to prepare herself for the next. But at least there was one piece of good news. Her grandmother gave it to her on a wet November morning when a week of steady rain had turned the far hills green and brought brilliant pink and white lilies into blossom in the Pleasant Valley. "Have you worked out the date for the meeting after next?" Mrs. Brett asked.

"No." One at a time seemed quite enough.

"Then I've good news for you. It's December twenty-fifth. They never meet on a holy day. You'll have another free month. They'll announce it at this meeting—no need for the enchanted Mooress and her bell." And then, at a soft tapping on the outer door, "See who's there, Juana."

It was Manuela, looking at once frightened and important. "I'm sorry to intrude, but Senhor de Mascarenhas is here. He's brought a horse."

"A horse?" Mrs. Brett leaned forward in the big bed.

"A lady's horse. He says it's a present for Juana. If you approve, of course."

"A very expensive present. Do you know anything about this, Juana?"

"Of course not." She had heard nothing of her cousin since he had left in September and had never decided whether she was relieved or disappointed.

"I beg your pardon." The old lady's apology came as a surprise to Juana. "Normally, of course, a young lady could not possibly accept such a present . . ."

"No." It was what Juana had expected and she was surprised that her grandmother seemed to find the matter even open to question.

"But in the special circumstances," Mrs. Brett went on. "I don't really know . . ." She came to a decision. "I think I had best get up and see this lavish young man. Go down, Juana, and tell him I am coming."

"And about the horse?" She could not help thinking how pleasant it would be to have one.

"Say as many pretty things as you like, but nothing definite. Tell him I'm thinking it over. It's true."

Vasco was waiting in the courtyard, where his servant held the reins of an elegant Arab mare equipped with a beautifully made sidesaddle. Juana could not help giving her an admiring glance as she greeted her cousin.

"You like her?" She had forgotten that glowing, concentrated look of his. "I couldn't bear the thought of a Diana like you forced to bear with that old curmudgeon of a mule. Besides, on Sheba you could show a clean pair of heels to any number of bandits. I shall feel much happier about you, out here on the cliffs, if I know you are riding her."

"It's wonderfully good of you—"

"It's wonderfully selfish," he interrupted before she was able to voice her doubts. "What greater pleasure could I have, cousin, than in giving pleasure to you?"

153

This was going a little fast for her. "My grandmother wants to see you," she said. "She is considering whether I ought to accept such a splendid present."

She had never seen him angry before. But there was no mistaking the dark flush that coloured his brown skin. "Your grandmother—" He stopped, changed his tone entirely. "I beg your pardon, cousin. I nearly said something I should have regretted. But surely this is a matter between you and me, as cousins, as Mascarenhas—"

"You've proved it?" Something in the confident way he had used the name encouraged her to ask the question.

"To my own satisfaction. But—here's the rub—to get legal proof I need one more witness—a man who was actually present at my parents' marriage. He's in the Spanish army now, in the contingent that is fighting for Napoleon in Europe. I have come to say goodbye to you, cousin."

"Oh." Now she was almost sure she was sorry to see him go. And yet there was something a little disconcerting about the way he seemed, as soon as he arrived, to take charge of her.

"Say you will miss me a little? Will think of me sometimes? Will be good to Sheba for my sake?"

"Will you be gone for long?" She found herself trying to pull the conversation back into safer channels.

"Impossible to tell. But not a minute longer than I must. I've been chasing all over Portugal after my witnesses. You must understand, cousin, that since I met you it has become more imperative than ever that I prove my birth as good as yours. But I've no right even to say that to you now. Only—don't forget me, Juana, when I'm gone."

"Of course not." She felt a little breathless, even, oddly, a little frightened. "How could I"—she made an effort at a lighter note—"if my grandmother lets me keep your beautiful Sheba." And she moved a little away from him to fondle the glossy brown nose.

"She'll let you." It came out curiously definite as he came to stand very close beside her and join in fondling the handsome mare. "She's fit for a Queen," he said.

To Juana's relieved surprise, Mrs. Brett did agree to her keeping the horse, but as a loan. "Between cousins, there can be no objection to that."

"I shall consider it a gift." Vasco rose. "May I write to you, sometimes, cousin, to tell you how I speed in my search?"

"I don't know—" with a doubtful glance at her grandmother. But Mrs. Brett was talking to Prospero and apparently had not heard the request.

"I don't expect you to answer," Vasco went on. "That would be asking too much, I know. Besides, I shall be moving as fast as I can—it's doubtful if letters would reach me. I shall write, cousin, and hope that you have too much heart to burn my poor letters unread. Be good to Sheba; think of me sometimes. I shall return as soon as I have a clear name to—" He stopped, caught her unresisting hand, kissed it, and took his leave.

Sheba was a delight. It was impossible not to feel kindly towards Vasco—and anyway, why should she not?—when her rides had turned from penance to pleasure. She rode further and further afield, making Iago or Luis ride Rosinante so that they would not get too far behind. It was an odd thing, she thought; no one knew that her grandmother had made her her heir, but they all treated her with a new respect these days. It did not occur to her that this might result from a change in herself.

November 26th came round at last and Juana found herself not quite so frightened as she had feared to be. After all, she had gone down the winding stair alone before. Practice makes anything easier. She refused to let herself think about Tomas, and went down the long stairs with a good heart and a steady hand. She had decided not to try and explore the big cavern: it was altogether too risky. Instead, she sat by the brazier in her little cell, recited the speech she had just learned—"The quality of mercy is not strained"—and waited for the gong to sound.

Mrs. Brett had confirmed her theory that the acolytes were different each time, so today she had a comfortable sense of being the experienced member of the trio. She thought the others went about their duties even more nervously than the last pair, and wondered if they knew about Tomas. But then they had, all three of them, plenty to be nervous about.

In fact, the meeting went fast and smoothly. As Gair had predicted, the Brother of the Broken Cross reported that he had found the English secret agent. A Mr. Brougham, he had left for England before any action could be taken. "He will doubtless return," said the leader. "We will wait till then. There is no great urgency about it. Our Brother of the Crescent Moon sends word that he was unable to see Napoleon before he left for Prussia. He only caught up with him in Berlin, after his victory at Jena, and, so far, Napoleon has continued too busy to see him." There was an angry murmur from the hooded figures round the table. "It's natural enough," the leader explained, "with a conquered country to be disposed of. And, I have good news for you, Brothers. On the twenty-first of this month, Napoleon issued a decree, dated from Berlin, declaring a total blockade of England. Since he was too busy to see our Brother, the Emperor sent him advance information of this, as a proof of his good faith. Our Brother of the Golden Eagle has ridden day and night to bring us the news. He is here tonight, ready to answer your questions."

"Good news." The Brother of the Silver Hand rose to his feet. "With England hamstrung by a total blockade, we can do what we like here. I move that we wait only long enough for the blockade to take effect, then strike, swift and hard."

"But what about Spain?" Predictably, this was the Brother of the Broken Cross. "We will still need at least the promise of support from France before we can move in safety. Tell me, Brother of the Golden Eagle, which way will Napoleon turn next?"

"Eastward," The Brother of the Golden Eagle spoke with a strong German accent. "He has an account to settle with Russia. He means to bring the Tsar to his knees before he returns to Paris."

"So still we must wait!"

"Not for too long, I hope," interposed the leader. "Do not forget that we are powerfully represented at Napoleon's court. Our Brother of the Crescent Moon will lose no opportunity to press our case with the Emperor. When the time is ripe, he promises to return, in person, to bring us the news, and join in our great enterprise. In the meanwhile"—he looked round the circle of hooded figures—"has anyone else a question for our Brother from Germany? Then it remains but to announce that since the full moon, next month, falls on Christmas Day, there will be no meeting."

"What if there is news from our Brother of the Crescent?" asked the Brother of the Broken Cross.

"If the matter is urgent, I will summon a special meeting. You all know the signal, Brothers? For three days running a madman will appear in the cloisters of Saint Geronimo, crying that he has been chased by the *escolares* and their wolves. And now: Sons of the Star, we meet only to part—"

It was the signal for Juana to close her spy-hole. Only

later, climbing wearily up the winding stair, did she remember that no one had mentioned the death of Tomas. She remarked on this to Gair. "Surely, if they killed him, something would have been said? Or"—she had been thinking about it a great deal—"do you know, I have been to three of their meetings now, and I'm more and more convinced that they are not real."

"What do you mean?"

"Why, that it's all—I don't know—a parade, somehow; make-believe. A few of them—three really: the leader and the Brothers of the Broken Cross and the Silver Hand— pretend, for the benefit of the others, to discuss what they have already decided in private. Do you think I'm mad to suggest it?"

"On the contrary, I think you're very acute. It's something I'd wondered myself, from your grandmother's reports. The discussion goes so smoothly and so fast. It's as if there were a secret committee that really made the decisions."

"Yes. And another thing: when the leader says his last bit about parting to meet again he gabbles it off as if the whole business bored him. What do you think it means, Gair?" She coloured. What in the world had made her use his Christian name?

"I've no idea." Had he not even noticed? "But I must think of some way to find out. At least, Napoleon's eastward march has given us time. I'm sure they'll risk no action until there's a French army at Bayonne to back them up." He rose to his feet. "We've been out here long enough alone. Rely on me to let you know if a madman appears at the Geronimos', but I don't expect it." And then, opening the door to usher her back from the loggia into the Ladies' Parlour, "I hope you enjoy Mr. Scott's poem." A new copy of *The Lay of the Last Minstrel* had been his pretext for calling.

He had just left when Estella came running across the central courtyard to summon Juana to her grandmother. Juana had never seen plump Estella run before, and even on this comparatively cool day of late November it had reduced her to a trembling, hard-breathing state of near-collapse. "You must go to Mrs. Brett directly." She could hardly get the words out. "This instant. I've never seen her so angry. Don't waste a minute."

"But what's the matter?"

"I don't know." Her breath was steadying. "Something in her letters from England. Go quick, Juana, and see if you can soothe her. It can't be good for her to be in a state like this. I was afraid she'd do herself an injury."

"Then you'd better let my niece go and find out what is the matter." Juana would never get used to the way her uncles crept about the castle in carpet slippers. This time it was Prospero who had come quietly in behind Estella while she was talking. "We don't want poor Mother to do herself an injury."

"No indeed." Juana brushed past him and ran in her turn across the sunny centre of the courtyard. She found her grandmother prowling furiously about her room, a letter crumpled in her hand. "It's intolerable!" She almost shouted at Juana. "Why did you take so long? Not that it matters. There's nothing we can do. He took good care of that. The fool! The idiot! I thought Prospero and Miguel were enough to bear, but this passes everything. Here! Read this! You might as well."

Her father? She took his letter, then felt a qualm of doubt. "Should I?"

"Why not? You might as well know what a poor worm you have for a father. It's that woman of course. She dictated it. You can read her in every crawling line. Go on, child, read it. And tell me what in the world we are going to do with them."

What could it mean? Juana banished her scruples, smoothed out the crumpled letter, and began to read. "Oh dear!" Her grandmother was right; it was a pitiful letter. But she could be sorry for her father having to write it, with his wife's scorn for spur. He had speculated, it seemed, on the chances of peace with France, and had lost heavily when Lauderdale returned to report failure. "I don't quite understand—" Juana turned to the second page of the closely written letter.

"You don't need to. Any more than your father does. I could have told him that if he speculated, he was bound to be unlucky. He's that kind of man. But to use the house as security! That passes everything."

"They've lost it!" Juana had reached the heart of the matter. She had always thought she hated that house, now, suddenly, she was not so sure. "They're coming here?" She could not believe what she was reading.

"Yes! On the next packet. No time to put them off. There must be an accumulation of debt that Reginald does not dare mention."

158

Juana thought this all too likely. She finished the letter quickly. "Oh, the poor things!" There was something extraordinarily pitiful about the little messages her father put in as from Daisy and Teresa. "So looking forward to seeing Portugal," indeed. She remembered how they had condoled with her on her exile to that barbarous country.

" 'Poor things!' That's all very fine, but what about us? What are we going to do with them? Reginald and his wife are one thing: I suppose if my son has to run for it to escape the debtors' prison, I must take him in, and his wife too, though I know I'll detest her. But why I should be saddled with her two daughters! A couple of strapping English wenches with not a thought in their heads—everything you have told me about them has made me dislike them more. And Protestants, too, I suppose?"

"I'm afraid so." Juana's conscience was pricking her horribly. Talking about Daisy and Teresa to her grandmother it had been dangerously easy to turn them into figures of what she now saw to have been rather cruel fun. Poor Daisy, poor Teresa ... "They're not so bad, really." She tried, now, to undo some of the damage she had done. But how could she have dreamed that they would ever come here? "It was a good deal my fault, I'm sure, that we didn't get on."

Her grandmother snorted. "Changed your tune, haven't you?"

"Yes. I'm ashamed of myself. You see—I find I'm glad they're coming. I'm looking forward to seeing them."

"It's more than I am. Well, in that case, you can be responsible for them. Everything. The arrangements for meeting them ... their rooms ... I don't want to hear anything more about it. And still less do I want to see them when they get here. They'll be here for Christmas, probably."

"I suppose they will." Once again, Juana was amazed at her own reaction. Had the prospect of Christmas in the Castle on the Rock been so dismal? "Don't worry, Grandmother. I'll look after everything. If you don't think Aunt Elvira will mind?"

"She'd better not. If you have any trouble with anyone, refer them to me. Once. That will be enough. I refuse to be bothered with this affair. I suppose you've thought how you will get away from those stepsisters of yours when it comes time to go down the winding stair again?"

"I'll manage."

"You'll not tell them."

"Of course not. But, Grandmother, one other thing." It was hard to say it, but she must. "They'll need money."

"Money? Why?"

"If father's in debt?"

"That's his problem. I didn't ask him to come—or to bring his embarrassments with him. Food they shall have, and shelter. That's all."

"I see. Well then, I need some money. You asked *me* to come. Remember? We haven't talked about money before. I didn't like to. And I brought a little with me. Father was always generous with what he had. But it's almost all gone now. You know how it is. The servants expect their vails. One can't be mean, as a Brett. And then there's charity . . ." She reached into the pocket of her dress and brought out the purse she had netted herself—how long ago it seemed—in England before she came away. "That's all I've got left." She emptied a few small coins on the table beside her grandmother. "If you want me to take over the housekeeping from Aunt Elvira—and that's what it comes down to, isn't it?— you'll have to pay me."

For a moment, she was afraid she had gone too far. Then, surprisingly, Mrs. Brett laughed. "You sound just like your grandfather," she said. "Poor James. I'd be a pleasanter person if he'd lived. As it is, don't expect me to play the sweet old lady. Not even for you, and I'm fond of you. Still less for your family. As to your allowance, you should have spoken up for it sooner. I'm an old woman. Why should I be expected to do all the thinking? Of course you must have one. And back-dated, too, to when you got here. Send Senhor Macarao to me this evening and I'll give him my orders. What you do with it is your own affair. Just don't tell me." Did she see this as an easy way out of the problem of her son and his family?

When she learned the size of the allowance she was to get, Juana thought this must be the case. "But that's too much, Grandmother." She wished at once that she had not spoken. Too much, perhaps, for her, but not for all her family.

"Nonsense. You're my heir, remember? And that reminds me, I think I'd better announce that. Arrange a Christmas party to welcome your family. It's time your cousins came to see us, Pedro and Roberto. I'll have an unpleasant surprise for them."

Juana sighed and took her leave. Was it all an illusion that old age brought wisdom, benevolence, and so forth? Had her

160

grandmother always been the tartar she seemed now, or was she getting worse with the years?

She was glad to find Elvira alone in the Ladies' Parlour, working at her set of embroidered chair-covers. It was always a good sign when she got these out. It meant that she was at her most rational. Now she looked up and smiled her sweet, vague smile at Juana. "Did you manage to calm poor Mother down?"

"A little." She loved her aunt for not asking what was the matter, and hurried to tell her. "My family are coming out from England. Poor Father's in debt. Grandmother's not at all pleased."

"I don't suppose she is." Elvira set a few stitches in her pattern. "But I don't know what else she expected, when she refused to give him an allowance."

"Nothing?"

"Didn't you know?"

"I wasn't sure." Her stepmother had hinted at this often enough, but one never knew how much to believe of what Cynthia Brett said.

"Nothing," Elvira said. "She said if he wouldn't stay here, he could do without her help. But she gives Miguel and Prospero allowances. Your father was always my favourite. I suppose he's lived on what your mother left him. And that wasn't much, I can tell you. Poor Reginald, I shall be glad to see him."

"Aunt Elvira, Grandmother says I'm to make the arrangements for them. Do you mind?"

"Mind? Why should I mind, child? I am the wind that blows where it pleases; I am the moon that waxes and changes—Prospero! I didn't hear you coming."

"Why should you?" Prospero closed the door quietly behind him. "How's poor Mother, Juana? What's upset her so?"

CHAPTER 14

Gair Varlow learned of the Brett family's impending arrival in a letter from his sister. "Those dull Bretts have done a midnight flit," Vanessa wrote. "Just ahead of their creditors, by all reports. Will you be pleased to see them in Portugal, I wonder?"

He was very far from pleased. Their presence at the Castle on the Rock would further complicate a situation that was bad enough already. But at least Vanessa's letter had come in the diplomatic bag and by fast cutter. The first packet the Bretts could have caught would not arrive for another day or so. There was time to confer with Juana. He asked leave of Lord Strangford and rode out to the Castle on the Rock that same afternoon. It was a clear December day, with a brisk wind from the sea turning the wings of the windmills along the shore and blowing lateen sails about like butterflies on the Tagus. But Gair hardly noticed them, or the spring flowers that were beginning to come up already, now the rains were over.

He had too much to think about. Juana had done admirably so far, but he had been well aware of the strain it had been on her. Sometimes he thought he had been mad to involve her; often his conscience told him he had been wicked. The murder of his messenger, the attack on Juana herself, and worst of all, the death of Tomas had been a series of threats he could neither ignore nor entirely understand. Impossible to tell how close to Juana the danger was, but no use to try and pretend it did not exist. Sometimes, in the dark hours of early morning, he thought he should persuade her to go back to England. But how could he? Too much depended on her.

And now her family's arrival must inevitably mean a new burden for her. Only her father spoke Portuguese. She would have to interpret for the others, would have to speak English with them, would stammer ... What would this do to her? He did not like to think.

His pretext for calling was, of course, Vanessa's letter, and the chance that Mrs. Brett might not yet have heard of her son's imminent arrival. But Juana's first words, when Jaime ushered him into the Ladies' Parlour, settled that. "You find us all at sixes and sevens." She sounded surprisingly cheerful. "My family are arriving any day now and we are having such a spring cleaning of apartments for them! I didn't know there was so much dust in the whole of Portugal! And as for spiders! Do you know, Mr. Varlow, we found toads as big as dinner plates in one of the cellars? If you'd only got here a little sooner, I could have showed you. Would you like to see the rooms I'm getting ready for them? Not the toads—my family."

"Yes, indeed." No hope of talking to her here, with Elvira stitching away at her embroidery, and her uncles liable to appear, soft-footed, when least wanted.

"Such a battle, too, to settle where to put them." Juana led the way down from the parlour to the central courtyard. "You'd think in a vast place like this, it would be no problem. But Uncle Miguel didn't want them in rooms off the cloisters, because he and Father Ignatius like to say their prayers there, and when I suggested putting them in the old wing, Uncle Prospero nearly had a fit. My grandmother won't have them anywhere near her, and I don't much want them looking out on the terrace. So in the end"—she opened a door leading off a corner of the cloisters—"they're in the haunted wing, poor things. But you're not to say so. I've sworn the whole household to secrecy. If you tell Daisy and Teresa and start them having hysterics on me, I'll never speak to you again. What are you going to do about them by the way?"

It was what he had been wondering himself, but that did not make her question any less disconcerting. "Do?"

She laughed. "No need to pretend with me. You know perfectly well you were courting Daisy with your left hand and Teresa with your right, back at Forland House. And now look at you! All's well"—she had seen his anxious glance up and down the range of empty rooms—"the servants are at their dinner. I've got the only key." She held it up. "I want to be friends with Daisy and Teresa," she went on. "It's important to me. Besides, it will make things so much easier. So what are you going to do? They'll be furious if they think you've really changed!"

He almost said, "But I have." This was no time for that. "What do you advise?" How odd to be asking her.

"I've been thinking about it ever since we heard they were coming, and I believe I've got the answer. There's something

163

I've been meaning to tell you." She paused, and he found himself glad to see her at a loss for a word. It was curiously disconcerting to have her take the lead as she had been doing.

"Yes?" He moved over to the window to look out at the Pleasant Valley.

"It's about my grandmother. She's not a bit well, you know. And she's worried about what will happen if she dies. About the stair—because it goes down from her room. And everything." It was difficult to say it. "She sent for her lawyer a while ago and changed her will. She's going to announce it at Christmas dinner." She hesitated, watching him.

"Announce what?"

"That she's made me her heir. Only"—in a rush—"she doesn't know this, but I must tell *you*. I shan't keep it; not a moment longer than I have to. It wouldn't be right. I shall share it with the others. It won't come to much that way, because of course Pedro must have the castle, as the eldest. But, for the time being—do you see—it provides an admirable pretext for you to court me." This came out in a rush as she moved away into the next room, muttering something incomprehensible about toads and cobwebs.

He let her go, too angry to speak. She had been afraid that if he thought she was her grandmother's heir he would start courting her in earnest. Well? He stood there a minute, looking at himself with dislike. She might have been right. The unwelcome bit of self-knowledge did nothing to improve his temper. But the silence was drawing out too long. He followed her into the next room. "You think I'll make a convincing fortune-hunter?" He could not help it, nor his tone.

"I expect you'll manage. I'm sorry if you don't like it, but you've told me often enough that no sacrifice is too great. This will be their sitting room." She changed the subject ruthlessly. "I think it will do admirably when we've found some furniture for it. I'm trying to make them as independent as possible."

"Is it as bad as that?" He followed her lead into this safer topic.

"Just about. I'm afraid I'm the only one who's pleased to see them. But I am." She made it almost an ultimatum.

"I'm glad," he said peaceably. "I hadn't thought how dull it must be for you here."

"No. Why should you have?"

He rode back to Lisbon in a thoroughly bad temper.

The packet arrived a few days later and Gair debated with himself whether to go aboard, pay his respects to the Bretts, and, incidentally, try to establish the new relationship with Daisy and Teresa. But the sight of the carriage from the Castle on the Rock standing in Black Horse Square made up his mind for him. Almost certainly, Juana would have come in person to meet her family. He would leave her a free field for the first encounter. After all, she seemed almost disconcertingly competent, these days, to handle her own affairs.

Lord Strangford had just had official news of Napoleon's Berlin Decrees and his staff were unusually busy as a result. Gair felt he could not possibly ask leave to go and find out how things were settling down at the Castle on the Rock. It made him oddly restless and he wished more than ever that it had been possible to find a safe messenger to go between him and Juana. But they had agreed that the risk was too great.

He was accordingly delighted, two days before Christmas, to receive a note from Mrs. Brett inviting him to a small Christmas party, "To celebrate my son's arrival from England." No word of Juana, or of anything else that mattered. The note was entirely formal and gave no hint even as to whether Juana might have suggested the invitation. He found he badly wanted to know.

Christmas Day was fine, with larks singing above the ridge road, and the scent of gorse heavy in the air. Gair had been late in starting and rode hard. Dinner was to be at three o'clock, Mrs. Brett had said. It was not an occasion for which one was late. Coming up the last long slope towards the Castle on the Rock, he recognised two horsemen ahead of him as Pedro and Roberto Brett-Alvidrar. He had not met either of them since that curious occasion in the autumn when Roberto had seemed actually to be encouraging his suit to Juana. Now, grateful for this chance to see how they would receive him, he spurred on his horse to catch them.

"You are coming to our Christmas dinner?" Pedro's question, after the formal greetings were over, came out curiously neutral.

"Yes. Mrs. Brett was so kind . . ."

"To meet the new arrivals." The sneer in Roberto's voice was not directed at Gair. "So much the better. An outsider should make a difficult family occasion go more easily."

"Hardly an outsider," said Pedro, but his brother did not seem to hear, and changed the subject to politics. He wanted

165

to know, disconcertingly, how likely Gair thought a change of government in England. It was a question that had exercised Gair a good deal since Fox's death. If the Tory party should return to power before he had had a chance to make his mark ,he might be condemned to a life of obscurity. It did not bear thinking about. Nor did the idea that came, unbidden, along with it, that he was risking Juana's life to advance his own career.

Juana received them in the seldom-used grand saloon. "Pedro! Roberto!" As tall as they, she let them kiss her brown cheek in turn, and Gair, watching, felt a queer little pang of envy.

"And me?" Was it getting too easy to play the lover's part? She laughed. "No, no, Mr. Varlow. Not you! I have two old friends for you. Daisy! Teresa! See who's here!"

The two girls had been busy arranging a great bowl of sweet-smelling rosemary, bay, and whole branches with oranges, nearly golden, hanging among dark green leaves. Now they came forward, smiling, hand-in-hand, their pink and gold prettiness like light in the dark room. And yet, Gair found his eyes moving instinctively back to Juana. She's worth ten of them, he thought. And, lord, how she's changed since I last saw them all together.

But there was no time for thinking. Daisy and Teresa were laughing up at him, greeting him with the special warmth due to an old flame. This was indescribably difficult. His eyes went to Juana in automatic appeal, and she came to his rescue. "And here are my cousins," she said. "Pedro, Roberto; my sisters, Daisy and Teresa."

But, somehow, Pedro had already got hold of Daisy's hand, and Roberto of Teresa's. "Welcome to Portugal," said Pedro, and "Welcome," echoed Roberto, his tone in extraordinary contrast to the sneer he had used earlier in speaking of the new arrivals. The two pairs of eyes met and held. Teresa was blushing; Pedro had forgotten to let go of Daisy's hand. Gair had always laughed at the notion of love at first sight. Now he could only laugh at himself. Once again his eyes were drawn to Juana, who was watching the two couples with a look of surprised delight that delighted him.

The tableau held for a long moment, then broke up as Prospero and Miguel appeared, closely followed by Elvira, with Reginald and Cynthia Brett. "Grandmother will meet us in the dining room," Juana explained, carrying off the flurry of necessary introductions with an ease that amazed Gair. It

166

was all done in English, without a stammer, but with a curious precision of speech, as if she were saying a part in a play. It seemed an age since Forland House. Whatever happens, it's done her good to be here, he thought, and then— am I making excuses for myself?

Mrs. Brett was waiting for them enthroned at the centre of the long dining table. "You're welcome, all of you. I'm too old to get up and greet you severally. Juana will act hostess for me." Gair thought he saw a quick exchange of glances between Pedro and Roberto. "We are talking English today," Mrs. Brett went on, "in honour of our guests. You have all met?" She made no further effort at introductions, but sat impassively in her big chair and watched the little bustle they made as they found their places.

It had been an awkward enough group to arrange, Gair thought, as he found his own unwelcome place beside Cynthia Brett, who in turn was on old Mrs. Brett's left. Her husband was on his mother's right, with Elvira beyond him, and Prospero beyond her again at the end of the table, facing down to Miguel at the other end, beyond Gair himself. On the other side, Juana was sitting across from her grandmother, with Pedro and Roberto on either side of her, Daisy and Teresa beyond them, and Manuela and Estella tucked rather awkwardly in on the corners beside Prospero and Miguel.

Gair was just thinking, with an odd little twinge of relief, that Father Ignatius had been left out of this family party, when he came hurrying into the room, murmured an apology to Mrs. Brett, took his place between Elvira and Prospero, and folded his hands to say grace.

The food and wine were excellent, but it was very far from being a lively party. Doing his duty as best he might by Cynthia Brett, Gair wondered who had arranged the seating. Juana, probably, though her grandmother must have insisted on Juana's own position. Old Mrs. Brett was eating hardly anything and speaking not at all, so that Cynthia Brett fell entirely to him to entertain.

"What do you hear from dear Lady Forland?" she asked in her piercing voice as Jaime removed her soup plate. "I was so sorry not to be able to call on her before I left, but it was all done in such ridiculous haste. You will make her my apologies when you write, Mr. Varlow?"

"Of course." He was afraid she was glad to find him here, had already, in all probability, seized on him as a rescuer for one of her daughters. He looked across the table and caught

167

Juana's eye. She was marooned between her two cousins, who were both absorbed in their other neighbours. Daisy's colour was becomingly high; Teresa was sparkling across her champagne glass at Roberto.

"I told Juana she should put you next to the girls, as an old friend." Cynthia's strident voice brought him back to his duty. "No reason why you should be saddled with an old woman like me."

Paying the necessary compliment, he hoped to turn the conversation to less personal channels by asking her how she liked Portugal. Juana's reproachful eye, from the other side of the table, warned him that this was a mistake.

But it was too late, Cynthia was launched. "Like it!" Her voice rose higher still. "My dear Mr. Varlow, I am not touched in the head. How could I like it? Dirt, and grease, and absolutely no conversation! Don't ask me how I like Portugal; tell me instead how you endure it. Is there any society in Lisbon? What am I going to do with my poor girls?"

The whole table was listening to her now, her daughters obviously in agony. "Mamma!" said Teresa, who was sitting across the table from her. "Don't!"

Cynthia drained her wine glass and Gair realised, with horror, that she had been fortifying herself already for this occasion. She took no notice of her daughter. "The wine's not bad," she told him, loudly confidential, "but the food! What's this, pray?" She helped herself to the dish Jaime was impassively holding out to her.

"It's chicken, senhora." Jaime's English was as fluent as her own.

She bridled. "My good man, I was hardly speaking to you." And, turning to Gair as if Jaime did not exist, "You see what I mean? A barbarous country. Intolerable. I don't know how I shall stand it."

"That's quite enough." Mrs. Brett leaned forward from the other side of Cynthia. "We will now imitate the English and discuss the weather." She leaned back again to speak to Jaime, who was now behind her chair. "What was that you were saying this morning, Jaime, about it's being earthquake weather?"

Gair knew that in fact autumn, not winter, was the time when the danger of earthquakes was greatest, but Jaime took his cue, and the whole table was soon discussing the chances

168

of another shock as bad as the one that had destroyed so much of Lisbon fifty years before.

This led, logically, to King Joseph's great minister, Pombal, who had rebuilt the city, but here, Gair soon saw, was dangerous ground again. Everyone began to talk at once. "He was a son of Satan," said Father Ignatius. "He did a great deal for Portugal," said Prospero. "He was not fit to live," said Miguel.

Pedro and Roberto had embarked furiously on what was obviously an old argument, talking across Juana, who had gone very white. Across the table, her father was contentedly drinking his wine, unconcerned with the argument that raged round him. If he remembered how his first wife's family had suffered at Pombal's hands, he gave no sign of it.

Half the party had lapsed into Portuguese in the excitement of the argument, and Gair was uncomfortably aware of the servants behind their chairs, drinking in every word. He glanced at Mrs. Brett, hoping that she might intervene once more to steer the talk into safer channels, but she had withdrawn into herself, like an old tortoise, and was taking no notice of what went on around her.

Pedro's defence of Pombal was growing more and more impassioned. "At least he kept order," he said, "and stood up to the English. We could do with a man like him now."

"A man?" Roberto leaned forward so that for a moment Gair could not see Juana. "A tyrant, you mean. Think what he did . . ."

As he went on to speak of the executions following the Tavora plot, he leaned back again, and Gair saw Juana's face. In a moment she was going to explode. She might say anything. She must be stopped. His brain was paralysed. He could think of nothing he could reasonably interject into this dangerous talk. "Broken on the wheel," Roberto was saying. "Even to think was dangerous."

"And now it's so safe?" Juana began, and suddenly all the other voices were silent, and Gair knew, as if he could read her thoughts, that in a moment she would speak of the Sons of the Star, and their kind of tyranny. And still he could think of nothing to say. But behind him, Jaime dropped a bowl of fruit, and, at the same moment, Elvira spoke for the first time that day: " 'The robin redbreast and the nightingale Never sing well in cages.' " And then, everyday again: "I thought we were to speak English."

"Oh, I'm sorry." It was the break in tension they had

169

needed. Juana leaned forward to apologise to her stepmother in English. "I forgot."

"It makes no difference to me," said Cynthia Brett. "I don't understand a word of these Portuguese politics, in Portuguese or in English. Who is this man Pombal anyway?"

For a moment, Gair was afraid it would all begin over again, but now Miguel leaned forward. "The best thing that can be said for him is that he's dead. And had best be, too, as a subject. Reginald, since this is an English party, I'll take wine with you."

The little formality, unpractised in Portugal, changed the course of the conversation. They had all had time to think. Jaime and the other servants had finished picking up the dropped fruit and were busy serving dessert. Teresa was explaining the custom of taking wine to Roberto, who thought nothing of it, and Daisy and Pedro had their heads close together, talking in low voices about hunting. Between the two couples, Juana sat as if changed to stone, listening with horror to what she had nearly said.

Mrs. Brett pulled herself upright and looked round the table. "If you all have your dessert . . ." she said. "Jaime, fill up the glasses, and leave us."

He must have expected this unusual command. He and the other servants went about their business as calmly as if this happened every day. Only Reginald protested. "You'd best leave the bottles on the table, Jaime, if you're going."

His mother looked at him coldly. "Yes," she said, "perhaps it would be as well, Jaime." This meant a further delay while Jaime opened new bottles of the sweet carcavelhos wine they were drinking with their dessert. By now a heavy silence had fallen on the party, and all eyes were fixed on Mrs. Brett. "Thank you, Jaime." She nodded to him as he bowed his way out behind the other servants. "Now, here we are"—she looked round the table—"the family."

"And Mr. Varlow," said Miguel.

"I invited Mr. Varlow." That settled that. "I also wished Father Ignatius to be here, as the keeper of our consciences. So, now we are alone, I want you all to drink a toast with me. To my heir: to Juana."

There was a little, shocked silence, and then Prospero rose to his feet. "To my dear niece," he said. "Juana."

Joining in the toast, Gair looked round with amazement. He would never have thought they would take it so well.

170

Even Pedro and Roberto contrived to look pleased as they turned to drink Juana's health where she sat between them, her colour high, her hands clasped together on the damask tablecloth.

Then, inevitably, brutally: "Speech!" said Miguel.

Juana stood up and looked round at them. "You're all so kind," she said in English. There were tears in her eyes. "I d—d—" Her hands writhed together on the table and she looked across it at Gair. "I can't think how to thank you." It came out in a rush. "Just ... thank you. And thank you, ma'am. I'll t—t—I'll try to do what's right." Was it an apology or a promise or a bit of both?

She sat down amid a little buzz of affectionate congratulation. Gair could hardly believe his ears. He simply had not thought this family capable of such good behaviour. Then he caught old Mrs. Brett's eye. Almost imperceptibly, she shook her head. So she did not believe in it, the old cynic. Well, did he?

Besides him, Cynthia Brett emptied her glass and leaned forward. "The dark horse, eh?" Her words ran together. "And we thought you were being so self-sacrificing when you insisted on coming over to look after your poor old grandmother. Risking your life in Portugal! Well, now look at us all." Her bright, muddled glance swept round the table. "Let us eat, drink, and be merry," she said, "for tomorrow Napoleon will be here."

"Nonsense," said old Mrs. Brett, and as if it had been a cue, they all started talking at once.

CHAPTER 15

"Try again, Juana. You can do it, I'm sure." Daisy sounded brisk as a governess. "Keep your hands still, head up, and off you go."

The retaining wall of the terrace was warm under Juana's elbows as she gazed out across the cliffs to the wild Atlantic that had been lashed to fury for three days by a spring gale. You could not see the waves break below, but you could hear their thunder and see the spray tossing, from time to time, as high as the cliff. Now, at last, with evening, the March sun was shining and the three girls had come out on to the terrace for Juana's elocution lesson.

It had been a great success, she thought, asking Daisy and Teresa to help her try and master her stammer. This way, they could bully her to some advantage, and, this way, she did not mind it. Who had changed the most, she asked herself, looking affectionately at Daisy and Teresa, she or they? It was hard to remember the bad old days back in England when their teasing used to bring on her stammer. Of course, they were happy now. It showed all over them, and she smiled to herself, thinking of Pedro and Roberto's constant visits. And then, of course, her own position was so different. As heir to the castle, she came next, now, to her grandmother in the curious Portuguese hierarchy of respect.

She thought this horribly hard on Pedro and Roberto, but Gair Varlow inevitably pleaded patience. She had only to wait, he said, and, sooner or later, the Sons of the Star must commit themselves, must strike—and be destroyed. But their January and February meetings had been curiously inconclusive. It was more and more obvious that whatever the rank and file might feel, the leaders proposed to wait for active support from Napoleon before they struck. And Napoleon was far off in Eastern Europe, where he and the Russians had fought, at Eylau, one of the bloodiest and most inconclusive battles in human memory. This news had been reported at the February meeting in the great cavern, but the messenger had had few words of encouragement for his Brothers of the Star. "The French call it a victory," he said, "but the

Russians sang *Te Deum* for it. Till he has conquered them, Napoleon will have no time or thoughts to spare for us."

"Juana, what are you dreaming about?" Daisy's impatient voice brought her back to the present, to the roar of the sea below and the warm sun on the terrace. She shivered a little, just the same, as if the chill of the dark cell were still in her bones.

"I'm sorry," she said. "I was thinking about something else."

"Mr. Varlow perhaps?"

"Good gracious, no. I only think about him when the weather is bad. Today's much too fine. But, come, let's to work. I know it by heart, I think." She fixed her eyes on the distant, dimly seen promontory of Cape Espichel and began:

> *"Oh that this too, too solid flesh would melt*
> *Thaw and resolve itself into a d—d—"*

She held her hands ramrod still against her sides and struggled with the word for an agonising few seconds, then gave up. "It's no good. I can't do it. Not today." Had thinking about the cavern made her worse? "Let's do some Portuguese instead."

"But you're much better, you know." Teresa was sitting in the sun at the far end of the terrace. "You got through the 'Too, too,' bit with no trouble at all. And how about 'Let's do some Portuguese'? We'll cure you yet, Juana, just see if we don't."

"Or she'll cure herself." Elvira emerged from the shadowed entrance to the castle. "Your grandmother is asking for you, Juana."

Mrs. Brett had not come downstairs since the Christmas party, but Juana thought that this was as much because she wished to avoid her unwelcome guests as on account of ill health. "There you are at last," she said impatiently. "I suppose you were amusing yourself as usual with those baby-doll stepsisters of yours. I've been sending all over the castle for you."

"I'm sorry, ma'am. We were out on the terrace, working on my stammer." It was always a relief to get back into Portuguese.

"English!" It came out as a snort. "Why do you bother? Your duty lies here. You're the only one of the family I can

173

trust." She moved restlessly among her pillows. "Can I trust you?"

"I hope so." Not for the first time, Juana was tempted to tell her grandmother how she planned to share the estate, but restrained herself. The smallest check to her wishes these days was apt to make the old lady ill with anger. The risk was too great.

"So do I. But I wish I knew what Pedro and Roberto were up to. They were here yesterday?" It was not really a question. She was always well informed about what went on in the castle. Manuela and Estella saw to that.

"Yes. Most of the day. To say good-bye for a while. Pedro is going to Madrid on an errand for the Princess, and Roberto to Mafra with the Prince Regent. We shall miss them."

"Dancing attendance! I never heard of anything so absurd in my life. On two pink and white English dolls with not a penny to bless themselves with."

"But they're not fools, Grandmother, Daisy and Teresa. You know what the Portuguese girls are like. Can you wonder that Roberto and Pedro prefer my sisters?"

"Stepsisters. They're no kin of mine, thank God. What I would like to know is just what those two boys are planning. It's not natural, I tell you: not for them to take being disinherited so calmly." She kept coming back to this, and Juana, who was equally puzzled by her cousins' behaviour, could never think what to say. Sometimes she wondered whether Pedro and Roberto could possibly have divined her own intention to share with them. But it seemed extraordinarily unlikely. Besides, would they be content merely to share?

"Stop dreaming, Juana and pay attention! I sent for you because I've had bad news. I don't know what we are going to do."

"Why? What's the matter?"

"The English mail's in. Senhor Macarao brought it out with him from Lisbon. I think the Whig Government's really going to fall at last. They've raised the Irish question again. No good ever came of that. God knows they have been shaky enough since Mr. Fox died, but I think this is the end."

"You mean the Tories—"

"Are bound to get in. And then what will happen to Mr. Varlow?"

174

"He'll lose his place?"

"Probably. It's happened before, of course. One gets used to it. But I'm too old now for changes."

Too old, too, Juana found herself thinking, to spare a thought for what this change must mean to her. She had taken on this dangerous assignment in the first place as much for Gair Varlow as for her grandmother. And, these days, Mrs. Brett was more and more the invalid, less and less the ally. Without Gair Varlow ... with a stranger ... It did not bear thinking of.

"You can't stop, you know." The old woman could still read her thoughts. "They'd kill you."

"How many of them know who I am, do you think?"

"Too many for safety." She pulled her shawl around her with hands that got more like claws every day. "Oh, well, you never know your luck. Maybe the new man will be someone more eligible than Mr. Varlow. And that reminds me, what do you hear from your cousin?"

"He's still searching among the wounded from Eylau." Juana made herself speak quietly, but felt sick with suppressed anger. More and more, these days, her grandmother struck her as heartless, inhuman, hardly a person any more. "He refuses to give up hope, he says." She made herself go on talking.

"He's a man, that one. Worth ten of the Englishman. I wish he'd come back." Dried-up hands plucked restlessly at the fringe of her shawl. "I'm worried for you, Juana. Suppose I die ... Suppose Mr. Varlow goes ... Write and tell your cousin I want him to come back, name or no name. No—if you don't want to do that"—had she seen Juana's instinctive recoil?—"write for my signature."

"But I don't know where he is, ma'am. He gives no address." As so often, when it was a question of Vasco, she did not know whether she was glad or sorry. But her grandmother's reaction surprised her. "It's all too difficult—" Tears spilled out of the dark-circled eyes. "It's gone on too long. I don't know what to do. I can't even remember any more. How long is it till the meeting, Juana?"

"Only six days."

"That's good. No need to send for Mr. Varlow. We can count on his coming out afterwards to hear your report. You must ask him then what chance he thinks there is of his being replaced."

"Yes." Juana's nails bit into the palms of her hands. It was all very well for her grandmother to be glad the meeting was so soon. She did not have to go down the winding stair.

The meeting on March 23rd began like all the others. When Juana opened the secret window of her cell, the hooded figures were in their places round the table, under the huge star whose light cast long shadows behind them on the rocky floor. As usual, the leader was speaking: "... a new member. Is it the will of you all that he be introduced now?"

"It is." The words buzzed round the table.

"Then let him be admitted." The acolytes went back to reopen the big doors, but Juana was staring at the leader. Surely, tonight, for the first time, he was someone new? She thought he was both shorter and more squarely built than the man who had occupied the chair of the Star at the previous meetings.

It was only as the acolytes returned, leading a third gowned figure between them that she remembered she should have shut the secret panel the minute they moved away from the table. Lucky for her that they had gone straight to the big door and back again. Otherwise ... It did not bear thinking of. She was so shaken by her own carelessness that she missed the beginning of the ritual by which the new member was initiated as one of the Sons of the Star. When she began to notice again, he was kneeling on the bare rock across the council table from the leader, with the seat between them vacant. The two acolytes stood on either side of him, holding a rope that tied his hands and seemed also to go round his neck. His head was entirely covered by a black cloth which reminded her suddenly of the blanket the brigands had thrown over her head. She found that even in the cold cell her hands were sweating in sympathy as he repeated the horrible oaths by which he was sworn in as a Son of the Star.

At last it was over. The two acolytes removed the covering from his head, revealing him as already wearing a hood like the others. The two members who sat on either side of the vacant chair came forward as his sponsors. One of them attached his emblem, a silver serpent, to his hood, the other took the ends of the rope from the acolytes.

"Unbind his hands," said the leader, "but leave the noose about his neck to remind him of the death in life that will be his if he should betray the oaths he has taken." And then, as the new member took his seat directly opposite him, "You,

176

Brother of the Silver Serpent, will be silent tonight, in token of your submission to the rules of the Brotherhood. Next month, you will be one of us and free to speak as the equal of anyone here. And now, Brothers, to business. I am come from Poland to bring you hope, and a message from Napoleon himself. As soon as he has disposed of the Russian threat, he means to turn his attention once more to the west. Then, Brothers our hour will come."

"How soon?" asked the Brother of the Silver Hand.

"Who can tell, Brother? But it should not be long now, since the Russians are embroiled with the Turks as well as the French."

A vigorous discussion followed. The Brother of the Lion reported the fall of the Ministry of All the Talents in England and the Brother of the Silver Hand argued that they should strike at once, without waiting for French support. As usual the question of Spain was raised at this point and the upshot of it all was that the new leader agreed, rather reluctantly, to return to Poland and press their cause with Napoleon.

"He didn't much like it," Juana told her grandmother next day. "Do they often change leaders, ma'am?"

"Oh, yes." Mrs. Brett seemed to be thinking about something else. "They do change from time to time. It makes no difference. Have you thought how you are going to contrive to see Mr. Varlow alone, child?"

"I expect I'll manage somehow. Daisy and Teresa are only too helpful." She disliked the coy way they made excuses to leave her alone with Gair, but had to admit its usefulness.

But this time, Gair did not come. Seven slow days dragged by with not a word from him. "This is intolerable," Mrs. Brett said at last. "There's been no message even? You're sure?"

"Of course I'm sure." Anxious and restless herself, it was hard to endure her grandmother's nervously repeated questions. "Shall I send for him?"

"I don't know. What do *you* think? I'm tired, Juana. You must decide. Send me Manuela; tell her I must rest . . ." Her voice trailed off. She was almost asleep already.

Juana had never felt so lonely. Up to now, her grandmother had been the leader in their strange partnership. She had taken the decisions; Juana's part had been to obey. Today, unmistakably, she had abdicated: "You must decide."

Daisy and Teresa were laughing together in the cloisters at the foot of Mrs. Brett's staircase. "There you are, Juana. We've been looking all over for you. Luis is back from Lisbon with the mail. There's a letter for you. Nobody writes to us." But Teresa's bright glance as she said this suggested that she was sufficiently contented with her lot.

A letter from Gair? "Where is it?"

"And who's it from?" Daisy was in one of her teasing moods. "Tell true, Juana, who would you have it from? Mr. Varlow who neglects us so, or that mysterious cousin of yours? We long to meet him, Teresa and I. Is he really as handsome as Maria says? To listen to her, he's Adonis himself. He's a worker of miracles, too; that we do know. How else did he persuade the old lady to let you keep the mare? *And* receive his letters! Mamma says she was never so shocked in her life." Her voice was tolerant. With the advent of Pedro and Roberto, Cynthia Brett had been quietly relegated to the background of her daughters' lives.

Juana often felt sorry for her, but just now she had other things to think of. "But my letter?" She made it casual. To show eagerness would merely encourage Daisy to prolong the torment.

"First guess who it's from!" Daisy produced the letter from her pocket and held it up tantalisingly out of reach. Then she had a better idea and darted out into the centre of the courtyard to hold it over the pool where the goldfish swam. "Guess quick, Juana, or I'll drop it in."

"That's enough!" Juana was surprised at her own anger. "Stop playing the fool, Daisy, and give me my letter."

"Temper!" But Daisy sounded subdued as she handed over the letter. "I'm sorry, Juana, I didn't mean—"

"Of course not." The letter was from Vasco. She knew his handwriting by now. It was dated, as the last one had been, from Eylau. He had still not found his vital witness. "These delays are breaking my heart," he wrote. "But not my spirit, cousin. Think of me sometimes, here in the frozen north. I think of you constantly." It was phrases like this that made it a relief to be unable to answer him. Or was it? Did not her helpless silence seem, somehow, to be suggesting acquiescence? In each of his letters he wrote more like a lover, less like a cousin. She was not sure how she felt about this, was sure only that he was going altogether too fast for her. Sometimes she even found herself wishing her grandmother had not let her accept Sheba or receive his letters.

178

"How is the gallant cousin?" Daisy's voice was a reminder of everything she disliked about the business.

"Cold," said Juana. "It's still freezing up there, he says, and the snow deep on the ground. Those poor soldiers."

"Yes, poor things." Daisy's sympathy was perfunctory. Her imagination did not extend much beyond her own affairs. "But when is he coming back, Juana? Does he say?"

"No." If the monosyllable was intended as a rebuke, Daisy did not notice.

"Still pursuing his quest?" she asked. "I do think it's the most romantic thing. Like Tristram, or something out of Mrs. Radcliffe."

Juana could not help laughing. "I'm afraid he doesn't find it very romantic," she said. "He is going from one stinking sickbed to another, he says."

"Oh," Daisy wrinkled her pretty nose in distaste. "How horrid."

When Gair Varlow finally arrived next day, Juana did not try to conceal her relief. "I began to think you were never coming."

"I'm sorry." He answered the reproach in her voice. "I've been hoping for news from England."

"There's none yet?"

"Nothing certain. Except that the Ministry of All the Talents has fallen. That's sure enough, I'm afraid."

"They seemed to think the Tories were bound to get in." When they were alone, "they" invariably meant that Sons of the Star.

"I'm afraid they are almost certainly right."

"What will happen to you?"

"I don't know."

She could see he hated to have to admit it. "If you go, I go too," she said. "Tell them that. You got me out here. I won't do it for anyone else."

"But your grandmother?"

"Doesn't care. Not about me. Not about anything, I sometimes think. Gair, sometimes I don't trust her. It's horrible. I don't understand it. Of course, she's so old." She was making excuses for her. She knew, too, what he was going to say next. "And don't read me a lecture about patriotism, either! I hope I'm a good Englishwoman, and hate Napoleon and all that kind of thing, but there are limits, and I've just about reached them! It begins to seem as if it would go on forever. And now, this week, waiting for you; wondering if you'd

179

never come, if you'd been sent home already ... It was the last straw, don't you see? Tell the people you work for that I won't go on; not if they send you home." And then, furiously, "Gair! You're not even listening!"

"I'm sorry." He had been on the defensive ever since he had arrived. "I truly am. Only—I was trying to think what I should tell you."

"The truth, perhaps? It would make a change."

"Truth can be dangerous. It's you I'm thinking of; I beg you to believe that. The less you know, the less danger you are in."

"I'm not so sure of that. Sometimes ignorance is more dangerous than anything. Oh! Here they come!" Daisy and Teresa had been riding when Gair arrived, so that they had been able to achieve this *tête-à-tête* on the seaward terrace, but now she heard the girls' voices as they came out through the castle. "What is it you have to tell me? Quick!"

"Just this. I have reason to hope that whatever happens I won't be recalled. I'll let you know as soon as it's certain." He turned away from her to greet Daisy and Teresa as they emerged into the sunshine. "Miss Daisy! Miss Teresa! I was beginning to think you would never come."

They were still in their riding habits, their cheeks flushed and their golden curls becomingly ruffled from their morning ride. Daisy laughed. "You missed us, Mr. Varlow? Has Juana been telling you she's had another letter from her handsome cousin? Your nose is quite out of joint, I can tell you. We're all Portuguese here now. You English might as well go home to your fog and fox-hunting. There's no future for you here."

"I hope you are wrong," he said.

CHAPTER 16

At the April meeting of the Sons of the Star, the new Brother of the Silver Serpent spoke for the first time. His theme was caution. "How do we know we can trust the French?" he asked, citing the example of Holland where what had at first seemed liberation had soon showed itself in its true colours as tyranny. "Surely, Brothers, we do not wish to exchange the comparatively mild rule of Dom John for that of one of Napoleon's brothers. I say: Let us act alone, or not at all."

"I was impressed with him," Juana told Gair two days later. "He seemed to me to talk sense."

"Did he convince the others?"

"He shook them, I think. At least, nothing was decided, though the Brother of the Silver Hand made one of his inflammatory speeches, calling for action at once. But I think they are waiting for the leader who was here last time—the one who has gone back to Napoleon. I think he's the real master. The meeting seemed different when he ran it. While he's away, I think, they're merely marking time. They've actually cancelled the May and June meetings, thank God."

"Have they?"

"Yes. They agreed not to meet until July, unless there's an emergency. I can't tell you what a relief it is."

"I'm glad. And I've good news for you too. I've heard at last from Canning, the new Foreign Minister. Nothing's to be changed. It's what I hoped. Strangford stays too. But it's time we joined the others." They had managed a few minutes alone at the edge of the seaward terrace, defying the north wind that rattled the stiff leaves of the aloes and blew her short hair about her face.

"I'd forgotten the *nordado*." She turned beside him to walk back to Daisy and Teresa, who were sitting in the sun, sheltered by the retaining wall of the terrace.

"It blows all summer, they say," he joined her in this innocuous topic.

"Straight from England."

"You're never homesick, Juana?" Daisy came forward to

meet them. "Myself, I don't care if I never see England again. They can keep it all: fog, mud, roast beef . . ."

"Even Almack's." Teresa looked up from her sewing. "You can't really want to go back, Juana?"

"I d—d—I'm not sure." Sometimes she did not understand herself. But then, it was all very well for Daisy and Teresa, up here in the sunshine with the sea wind blowing. They knew nothing of the dark cavern that lay deep in the heart of the cliff. Speaking still only the most rudimentary Portuguese, they were happily unaware of the currents of suspicion Juana felt seething beneath the placid surface of life at the castle. No need for them to be listening always for some word or phrase that might betray a familiar household figure as one of the Sons of the Star. "I'm sorry?" She realised, belatedly, that Daisy had said something to her.

"Moonstruck!" Daisy laughed. And that was nearer the mark than she knew. "Confess, Juana, you were miles away. In Poland, perhaps?"

"Poland?" Juana regretted it the minute she had spoken.

"Isn't that where Eylau is? And a certain cousin, who talks of coming back, and never does? But at least he writes to you. Has he named the day yet? For his return, I mean," she added innocently.

"Of course not. It's no affair of mine." She was annoyed with Daisy for raising the subject in front of Gair Varlow, angrier still because she was afraid her anger showed.

Life at the castle was not, somehow, quite so pleasant now as it had been in the first flush of family reunion after Christmas. Cynthia Brett hated the heat and grumbled about it endlessly. Elvira hardly spoke at all, and, when she did, confined herself, disconcertingly, to octosyllabic couplets. Pedro and Roberto were still away—Pedro presumably waiting on the Spanish court's pleasure at Madrid, and Roberto in attendance on Dom John at Mafra. Missing them, Daisy and Teresa had slid back a little into the old sport of baiting their stepsister, and the question of Gair and Vasco was an all-too-obvious subject.

It was almost a relief to Juana when Gair rode out to the castle one breathless May morning to pay a formal call of leave-taking. "I could not go, even for so short a time, without saying good-bye to *you*." This, with a languishing air, to Juana, was for the benefit of the family group he had found assembled in the comparative coolness of the Ladies' Parlour.

"You're going back to England?" Her heart plummeted. Had he been recalled after all?

"For two weeks only." Quickly, to reassure her. "My sister is not well," he went on. "Lord Strangford has kindly given me permission to pay her a visit."

"Lady Forland?" Cynthia Brett pounced on it, and the conversation became general. Only, taking his leave, Gair lingered for a lover's moment beside Juana. "Even the two weeks Lord Strangford allows me will seem too long," he said, making it a promise.

"He's gone to see Canning, of course," said Mrs. Brett when Juana told her about it. "Two weeks, he said? I expect he arranged it as soon as he heard the May and June meetings were cancelled. Even allowing for the journey, he should be back in ample time for the next one."

"But suppose they hold an emergency one?"

"We'll just have to cross that bridge when we come to it."

But hot May dragged into hotter June and nothing of any kind happened at the castle except that Cynthia Brett kept more and more to her own rooms and looked, Juana though, increasingly ill when she did appear. Anxious about her, she finally asked Daisy what was the matter. "Is there anything we ought to be doing for her?"

"Nothing. Don't pry, Juana!" And then, "I'm sorry. It's the heat . . . it's making us all nervy. I can't sleep, can you? As to Mother, she's homesick, of course. It's nothing . . ."

Juana was not so sure. Her father, who had seemed at first to settle back contentedly enough into the quiet routine of life at the castle, now looked hag-ridden as never before. Juana longed to ask him what was the matter, but could not quite bring herself to do so.

But at least her grandmother seemed better these days, though she still kept to her own rooms. "Nothing would induce me to act hostess to that woman."

"I wish you'd send them home, ma'am." Juana had been waiting for a chance to say it.

"Your family? You've changed your tune, haven't you?"

"Not the girls. I don't think they'd want to go. Just my father and stepmother. I don't think she's at all well. And besides, now Napoleon has taken Danzig, anything may happen. Seriously, ma'am, don't you think we've rather too many English in the castle for comfort?"

"Nonsense! You're beginning to sound like your cousins! You'll be calling yourself Brett-Mascarenhas yet. And not a bad name, either," she added surprisingly. "What's the news of him, by the way?"

"Vasco? None, since he wrote from Eylau."

"I wish he'd come back." Fretfully. "I wish you could have written him. He'd take care of you."

"I don't need taking care of, ma'am."

Was it true? Life seemed to stand still. There was no immediate sense of threat, and none of safety. And there was no news. Almost, sometimes, Juana found herself reduced to regretting the cancelled meetings of the Sons of the Star. However terrifying, at least she could count on learning the latest news from them. She greeted Pedro with real pleasure when he rode into the castle courtyard one stifling July morning. "Pedro! It's good to see you. Are you straight back from Spain? How was your journey?"

"As you'd expect. Dust, and filthy inns, and, in Madrid, the usual interminable delays. But I'm back at last. How are your sisters, Juana? Not too tired of life in the castle, I hope? I have a message for them—and for you too—from my mistress, the Princess. She is giving an entertainment next week at Ramalhao and hopes you will be able to come."

"The three of us? But, Pedro—"

"And Elvira, of course. That goes without saying. I hope you're not turning Portuguese, Juana? Do you intend to shut yourself up in a darkened room until you marry?" He had dismounted and thrown his reins to a servant, but turned to dip his wrists in the shady pool below the fountain in the centre of the courtyard.

Juana followed him into the shadow of the trellised vine. "I don't understand you, Pedro. When we met that time at Lord Strangford's party, you scolded me for being there. What's made you change your tune?"

He looked up at her from the edge of the pool where he had seated himself, his eyes bright in his shadowed face. "That was an English party. This is a Portuguese one. And your sisters will like to meet the Princess, surely? It's practically a royal command, you know."

"I suppose so. I'll have to consult my grandmother."

"Tell her Lord Strangford will be there, and his people, if that makes her any happier. Or you—" Again she was aware of his eyes, curiously bright in the shadow. "Seriously, Juana, I don't think this the moment for anyone with the slightest English taint to be stand-offish with the Portuguese royal family. Not if you want to stay here."

She almost said, "But I don't." Instead, "Yes, I see what you mean. I'll certainly talk to my grandmother. But are my uncles not invited?"

"No. This is a party for the young in heart, the Princess says. It is to help us forget the news from the north."

"Is there anything new?"

"Nothing worse than the fall of Danzig. But at least Napoleon is still looking eastward. So long as he is occupied with the Russians, we should be safe."

"And in Spain?"

"Godoy remains all powerful. 'The Prince of the Peace!'" He stood up. "I had best not talk of him. Where will I find your sisters, Juana?"

"An entertainment at Ramalhao?" Old Mrs. Brett looked even more doubtful than Juana had expected. "I don't know about that."

"Lord Strangford is to be there. And his people, Pedro said. You know Mr. Varlow sent word he was back but too busy to come out. It would be a chance . . ."

"Yes, I see . . ." Doubtfully.

"'And Pedro thinks it would be wise to go."

"There is that. Fetch me a glass of my cordial, Juana. I'm tired today. Too tired to think. You must do what you think best. But, of course, if you go, Elvira must go too."

Elvira did not want to go. "Nor should you, Juana. Nor your sisters. By all one hears, Ramalhao is no place for young girls."

"But Pedro will be there, and Lord Strangford's household."

"Meaning Mr. Varlow?" Elvira was disconcertingly acute today. And of course she was quite right. Juana did badly want to see Gair. His verbal message, sent by Senhor Macarao, whom he had met in Lisbon, had been merely maddening. He was back, he longed to see her, but could not for the moment be spared. It might mean anything. It might even mean that he was being replaced after all and had to train his successor. And here she was, starved for news, desperate for some kind of certainty. And the Princess's party was to be held on the twelfth of July, only a week before the next meeting of the Sons of the Star. Absurdly, perhaps illogically, Juana felt she must see Gair before that.

Elvira was looking beyond her from the sunlit loggia to the shadowed doorway of the house. "'By the pricking of my thumbs, something wicked this way comes.' Don't go, Juana. I smell trouble. 'Double, double, toil and trouble.'" She dropped her embroidery and scurried away to the far end of the loggia.

"What set her off?" Prospero came out of the house on silent feet. "I thought she was better."

"She is, mostly. She doesn't want to go to the Princess's party."

"Not go? Nonsense. Of course you must go. I only wish Miguel and I were invited, but my boys will be there to take care of you."

"Roberto too?"

"I believe so."

"Oh well, in that case ..." Juana had heard enough about Carlota Joaquina's parties to feel relieved that she and her stepsisters would each have a man to look after them.

So it was disconcerting to arrive at the party, just as the sun was setting, and be presented, at once, with a domino and mask. "The Princess's orders," explained Carlota Joaquina's *camareira mor*, a winkled old woman in rusty black. "All her guests are to remain masked until supper-time."

"Delicious!" Daisy was already wrapping herself in the all-concealing domino.

"Don't look so anxious, Juana." Teresa adjusted her mask at the glass. "They'll contrive to find us, masked or no." She turned to the old woman. *"Os Ingleses,"* she began in halting Portuguese, and then, giving it up, in English: "Have they come yet? Milord Strangford?"

"Nao entendo." The woman looked puzzled.

"Os Ingleses!" Teresa raised her voice. "Are they here yet? Oh, Juana, translate! You're the one who wants to know, after all."

"I don't! But of course she did. She turned to the *camarei-ra mor* and asked the question in Portuguese.

"Milord Strangford?" The old woman shook her head. "We sent no invitation to him."

"What does she say?" Teresa was satisfied now with the set of her mask and eager to be out where the music was playing.

"That Lord Strangford wasn't asked."

"Oh, poor Juana! But never mind; Pedro and Roberto will find you a cavalier!"

"Aunt Elvira!" Juana turned impulsively to her aunt, hoping for support. Every instinct urged her to leave at once.

But Elvira had been stranger than usual all day. Now she broke disconcertingly into Camoens' lament for his beloved: "'*Minha alma gentilha . . .*'"

The *camareira mor* took her arm. "Don't trouble yourself about the old one," she said to Juana. "I will see she is well cared for. Do you go down and amuse yourselves. I was told to tell you that the air in the courtyard is sweet."

"What does she say?" Daisy turned from the glass.

"She advises us to go down to the courtyard. Apparently she was told to do so."

"Pedro, of course. No need to look so grave, Juana. Anyone would think you were our chaperone, instead of the youngest of us."

In the courtyard, water splashed as background to the melancholy music of a group of guitarists. A singer was whispering the words of a *modinha:*

> "*Love is so sweet*
> *Love is so bitter . . .*"

The light was beginning to fail, but the moon was not up yet. Masked figures moved to and fro among the shadows of vine and colonnade, some of them already in pairs, others still on the hunt.

As the three girls hesitated at the top of the shallow steps, two masked figures advanced from the shadows to greet them. Watching each of them take a hand of one of her companions, Juana realised what an unmistakable tall figure she herself must present.

"Quick!" Pedro's voice. "The fireworks are about to begin." He had Daisy's arm and offered his other one to Juana. "The bottom of the long walk is the best place to see them."

Roberto and Teresa had moved off already, but Daisy hung back. "Should we not find a cavalier for Juana?"

"No names! It's the Princess's order that we should all be incognito until we unmask at supper. Come, it's nearly dark."

Making their way out of the courtyard and down one of the long, jasmine-scented alleyways that were laid out between orange and lemon groves, they found themselves part of a crowd of masked figures all moving in the same direction. "What a squeeze," said Daisy. "I had no idea it would be such a large party."

"Nor I." If she had known, Juana thought, she would most certainly not have come. Passionately now, she wished she had followed instinct and gone home when she discovered Lord Strangford had not been invited. And to make matters worse, all Pedro's attention was centered on Daisy, and her own position as the spare third was awkward in the extreme. The alley was really wide enough for two, but she dared not let go Pedro's arm, for fear of losing him in the crowd. So she scraped along, half beside, half behind the other two, and was grateful for her domino as a protection against spiky leaves and branches. Ahead of them she could see that the alley opened on to a wider space lit by coloured lanterns, and she was just congratulating herself that they must catch up with Roberto and Teresa there when they met a noisy group of masks and she was torn suddenly from Pedro's arm and swept back the way she had come.

"A prize! A prize!" One of the masks seized her arm. "No cavalier is allowed two ladies tonight. A lawful prize!"

"No! Let me go!" Struggling with him, she saw with horror that Pedro and Daisy had gone on down the alley to join the crowd at the end. They must have thought she had left them willingly. "Let me go, I say!"

"A spirited filly!" Like her, he spoke in Portuguese.

At least he did not know her. Instinctively, she stooped a little to conceal her betraying height. "Please let me go. I want to rejoin my friends."

"I *am* your friend." He tightened his grip on her arm. "Come with me, my pretty, and I will show you just how good a friend I can be." He pulled her back into a dark side alley. Short of screaming and precipitating just the kind of scene she must avoid, there was no way she could stop him. "But I want to see the fireworks!" If she could not save herself by force, she must do so by guile.

"Fireworks! I'll show you something better than fireworks." His slurring speech warned her that, unusually for a Portuguese, he was considerably the worse for drink. No use reasoning with him. She must wait and watch for her chance to escape.

He pulled her down on to a rustic seat in a vine-covered arbour. "Now, my pretty, it's time to unmask!" But his hand went, not to her mask, but to her muslin gown, where the domino had fallen open.

"No!" As she struggled, the first rockets roared and hissed into the sky. It was her chance. His grip slackened, she pulled away and was off, in a flash down the nearest alley. He came after her, swearing, but she found a turning among heavy-

188

scented jasmines, took it, then plunged into the bushes to stand, face hidden by her domino, hardly breathing as he blundered by. Another shower of fireworks terrified her with the chance of being seen, but must merely have confused him. She heard him carry on down the path, but stayed there, statue-still, for a few more minutes, just in case . . .

More fireworks. They would have been beautiful in other circumstances. At least they lit up the garden enough to show her that this path led back towards the house. Nothing mattered now but to get back there and find the *camareira mor* and Elvira. She must just hope that Daisy and Teresa were safe with her cousins, while blaming herself bitterly for having come to such a party. Not only herself. How could her family have let her? They must have known.

Everyone was watching the fireworks, which roared and sparkled and flashed above her as she made her way unmolested back to the house. Pausing in the darkness of the archway that led into the courtyard, she saw one tall mask standing alone. Waiting for someone? Tall. Wild illogical hope boiled up in her, and as she entertained it, sceptically, he called, low and cautious: "Juana?"

"Gair! Thank God." She hurried forward into the lamplit courtyard.

"I'm sorry if I have kept you waiting." Something very odd about his tone.

"Kept me waiting? What in the world do you mean? But, oh Gair, I'm glad to see you."

"You surely expected me, since you asked me to come." Again that disconcerting note.

"Asked you to come? What do you mean? I thought you were coming, it's true. Pedro said all Lord Strangford's people would be here."

"Lord Strangford at a party like this! I was appalled when I got your note, but there was no time to stop you. How could you do such a crazy thing?" He took her arm. "We can't talk here. Come out into the garden and for God's sake keep your mask on."

"Gair! You're hurting me."

"I'm sorry." They were out among the rose beds of the formal garden. "I've been worried to death about you. I was in Lisbon when I got your note." He led her to a seat in the centre of the garden where they could not be overheard. "I got here as fast as I could. But how could you be so stupid, Juana? This kind of party is well enough if you're escorted—

the hostess's name gives a kind of sanction—but to come on your own . . ."

"I did nothing of the kind. My sisters are here, and Aunt Elvira, and my cousins."

"I hope they are taking better care of your sisters than they have of you."

"It wasn't Pedro's fault. We were separated in the crowd."

"Exactly." It gave him a kind of savage satisfaction. "And then?"

"It's no concern of yours." Anger rose in her to match his. "But why do you keep talking as if I had asked you to come?"

"Because you did."

"Nonsense. Now you're the one who is crazy. We agreed, did we not, that I'd only write you in an emergency? Does this look like one?"

"By what you say, it might well have been. Yes—it's true—I was surprised; but life must be dull for you at the Castle on the Rock—"

"So you thought I was snatching at straws of entertainment?" The fact that this was partly true added fuel to her anger. "And would risk anything just to go to a party like this?"

"That's what you said, after all."

She stood up in one furious movement. "How many times do I have to tell you that I wrote you no note!"

"A forgery!" Anger bred by his anxiety for her had made him slow to take it in. "I should have guessed, I suppose. Forgive me, Juana. But, why? I don't like it: I don't understand it. But thank God it brought me here, and in time. I'm sorry I was so angry. You must understand: I was frightened sick for you."

"You were right to be." A burst of laughter nearby as a group of masks crossed the garden in pursuit of a couple of squealing girls gave point to her words. Suddenly, remembering her conspicuous height, she sat down again beside him. "I'm sorry too. Of course I didn't write, but I'm certainly glad you came. I was frightened. But what do you think it means?"

"I wish I knew. Trouble, I'm sure. I think I had best take you home at once."

"Gair, we can't do that. I can't leave Daisy and Teresa here."

"But your cousins will be looking after them. And your

190

aunt. No one will notice if you leave. You can plead head-ache, anything . . ."

"And go home alone with you at this time of night? Here, in Portugal? It would be bad enough in England . . . You're not thinking, Gair."

"I wonder if that's it," he said. "Who wants to compromise you, Juana?"

"No one. Why should they?"

"That's what I'd like to know." He stood up. "We'd best find your sisters. Then you can all go home together."

It was easier said than done. The fireworks were over now, and they had to search the long alleys by the glimmering light of paper lanterns hung here and there more for decoration than use. But then, as Juana pointed out, they would most easily recognise her sisters by ear, since they would be talking in English. "It's very odd that we have not heard either of them."

"Yes." He sounded anxious, and said again, "I don't like it, Juana."

"It's a pity." They returned at last to the rose garden. "It's such a beautiful evening. Shall we give up and just enjoy it?"

"We may have to. Moonlight and roses. What do they remind you of?"

"The night we met, of course. And the first lie you told me."

"Lie?"

"Don't you remember? You told me the river was shallow. I'd look a fool, you said, stuck in a foot of mud. Oh dear . . . do you ever wish you were back in England?"

"Often. And out of this whole business. I hope I may manage it, too, when this job is done."

"What do you mean?"

"I've been wanting a chance to tell you. I saw Canning when I was in England, the new man at the Foreign Office."

"We thought so. What did you think of him? What did he say?"

"That the Tories' coming to power would make no differ-ence to my work here. That they had confidence in me and would reward me well if I can bring it to a successful conclusion. It may mean a start for me in England at last."

"Under the Tories?"

"I don't see why not. The important thing, for the mo-ment, is to defeat Napoleon, and, frankly, I'm beginning to think the Tories are the men to do it. They mean business.

191

And I liked what I saw of Canning. He's a man one can trust. But you can see why I am so anxious that nothing should go wrong here."

"I can indeed!" Angrily. "What in the world made me imagine you were anxious about *me*, I wonder?"

"But of course I was. Juana. Be fair . . ."

"Why should I? Oh! What's that?" A flourish of trumpets had sounded from the house.

"The signal for supper. And for unmasking."

"So what do we do?"

"There's nothing we can do, but eat supper and unmask— and watch out, all the time, for traps."

"What kind of traps?"

"I wish to God I knew."

It was a curiously motley crowd that gathered in the big frescoed dining room and spread out on to a wide terrace and into the other public rooms. Members of the nobility had spent the evening assiduously courting tradesmen's daughters from Lisbon, picked, apparently, for their looks. Now, with the unmasking, the occasion became perceptibly stiffer. The few girls of good family who were present, and the Princess's *acafatas,* or ladies in waiting, looked sideways at their cavaliers from behind their fans; talk flowed with difficulty and food provided a welcome alternative.

Princess Carlotta Joaquina greeted Juana effusively. "There you are, child. Eat well, and get ready to delight us."

"To—?" Juana looked her puzzlement, uncertain how to address this resplendently ugly Princess.

"You've not told her!" The Princess turned towards the door of the room where Pedro had just appeared, with Daisy, flushed and sparkling, on his arm.

"My apologies, Your Highness. We were separated in the crowd before I could tell her the honour that was in store for her."

"You're to sing for us, child," the Princess explained. "You'll not refuse my guests the pleasure?" And then, in a lower voice. "You can see they are a mixed lot, and likely to hang heavy in hand now they are unmasked. You'll not refuse me your help?"

"I shall be delighted." What else could she say? "But what . . . ?"

"Oh, that's all arranged for. Your cousin has told me you know the marriage scene from *The Groom Deceived*. It's a favourite opera of mine. I've had my musicians learn their part; my music master sings the priest; it's only to find a husband for you. He need not sing, you know. Perhaps your cousin?"

Juana disliked the whole idea intensely. In the scene the Princess referred to, the heroine of the opera tricked her sister's lover into marriage with the help of a conniving priest, who performed the actual ceremony on stage. She tried in vain to think of an excuse, but before she could voice her reluctance Pedro had produced an objection of his own. "I'm not tall enough to act as foil for my cousin," he said. "Senhor Varlow's the man, if he'll do it."

The Princess clapped her hands. "Of course," she said. "You'll oblige me in this, senhor, as well as in gracing my party?" It was, Juana realised, her way of reminding Gair that he had not, in fact, been invited.

"I shall be honoured." There was nothing else he could say. And then to Juana, as the Princess moved away to give her orders for the setting up of the stage, "Is it very bad?"

"I don't like it."

"Better with me—"

"Yes." She had to turn away at a summons from the *camareira mor,* who led her off to a private apartment where the complete outfit of a peasant bride was laid out ready for her.

"We were sure you would agree." And indeed as an elderly waiting woman helped her into the bride's tight bodice and full skirt, she realised that it would have been quite impossible to escape this performance. She would just have to make the best of it.

"It suits you." The *camareira mor* herself adjusted the flowing veil and handed her a tight bouquet of carnations. "Look!" She led her over to a long glass.

"The skirt is too short!" Juana protested.

"That's how they wear them, senhora. And you have as neat an ankle as you could wish. It's only a play, after all."

"Yes." She could hear the musicians tuning up in the next room. "The Princess's music master: does he sing well?"

Why did this question seem to disconcert the *camareira mor?* "Oh, he's bound to, or she'd not have given him the part. Yes?"

One of the Princess's Negro pages had bounced into the room. "Her Highness and her guests are ready." He made great eyes of admiration at Juana.

No time at least for stage-fright. Juana gave one last

downward twitch to the full, short skirts, and followed the *camareira mor*.

"Where are we going?"

"To the terrace. You'll see." She led the way out on to one end of the big terrace which had been built up into a small stage and curtained off from the rest. Gair was waiting for them there, in the plush breeches and black jacket of a peasant's best dress, with beside him a short, stout man in the robes and cowl of a friar.

"Excellent. You're ready!" The "friar" came forward to greet her in an odd falsetto voice, his face invisible in the shadow of his cowl. "You know your part, senhora? Yours is easy, senhor. You are the butt of the piece, and must merely say 'yes,' or 'no,' as the situation requires."

"That should be easy enough." Gair still looked anything but happy.

"Good. Off you go. We two begin. Your cue is, 'Where's the happy man?'" He took Juana's hand and drew her across to the centre of the little stage, then hurried down to the curtain to speak through it to the leader of the small orchestra. "The overture's a short one," he reminded Juana as he returned.

"I remember." Something familiar about his voice? She wished she could see his face.

The orchestra played for a few minutes, then the curtains were drawn back by two of the Princess's Negro pages while six more filed on to the sides of the stage with lamps in their hands. So illuminated, Juana could hardly see the audience below her on the terrace. Somewhere, in the valley, a nightingale was singing. She remembered Forland House, had a moment of complete panic, thinking that even in Portuguese she might find herself stammering, took a deep breath, heard her cue and began to sing.

She and the friar were conspiring to deceive the unlucky bridegroom, who thought he was marrying her well-dowered older sister. In their first duet they made their plans, congratulated themselves on their ingenuity, and wondered whether the groom would recognise her through the veil. The Portuguese composer was largely indebted to the opening scene of *Figaro*, but the music was none the worse for that, Juana thought, as she began to lose herself in it.

The "friar's" voice was something of a disappointment, and he did not seem to know his part very well. Once or twice, she had to whisper him his cue, and, in helping him, forgot to be nervous for herself. When the duet came to its winding, inconclusive close, a roar of applause from the terrace confirmed her knowledge that she was in good voice.

Now the "friar" had some comic business arranging a little altar in the centre of the stage and searching his deep pockets for his Bible. At last he was ready. " 'Are you veiled, oh veiled completely? Veiled completely as you can?' " He came across to pull the veil down over Juana's face, his own cowl concealing everything but a very bright pair of eyes. " 'Then we're ready for the wedding,' " he sang. " 'Where oh where's the happy man?' "

Juana had the impression that Gair had been talking to someone off stage, protesting perhaps? Invisible hands seemed to push him on, so that he appeared looking quite as absurd as the scene required.

She had forgotten just how exactly the scene that followed was based on the wedding service. In England, she thought, it would be considered sacrilegious. Odd that the devout Portuguese did not seem to mind it.

She did not much like it herself. If only she had refused to go beyond the first duet. But how could she? This seemed to be an evening plagued with second thoughts. Someone must have been coaching Gair off stage. He produced the ring from his breastpocket and held it out to the "friar," who was now rather chanting than singing in his high voice as he asked whether anyone knew any impediment to the marriage.

"I do!" The voice came from somewhere below the terrace, in the garden itself. "I forbid the banns." The speaker pushed forward through the audience, who made way for him, whispering and laughing, convinced that this was part of the show. Only the three of them, who knew it was not, stood as if paralysed while he pushed the guitarist aside, climbed lightly on to the improvised stage and moved forward between Juana and Gair.

"Unless you want to marry this man, cousin?" Vasco. The pages' lamps showed him booted from riding, travel-stained, pale with fatigue. He spoke low, so that his words could not be heard by the audience.

"Vasco!"

"And in time, thank God." He turned on Gair. "As for you, sir, only blood—" He became aware of the pages watching goggle-eyed. "Draw the curtains, for God's sake." Then, catching the arm of the "friar" as he moved away towards the back of the stage: "Stay, you, and let's be sure." He pushed the cowl violently back from the man's face.

"Father Ignatius!" Juana gasped.

"It was a jest, senhora, merely a jest." He struggled in Vasco's brutal grasp. "I would have seen to it that the marriage was not complete."

"Would you? I wonder." Still holding him in an iron grasp, Vasco turned back to Gair: "And now, sir! As head of this lady's family, I await your explanation and your humble apology."

"Do you?" Gair said coolly. "It seems to me that I might well ask you the same thing. You seem to know a good deal more about this affair than I do. And as for you—" He turned fiercely on Father Ignatius.

"It was a joke, I tell you, merely a joke." The friar had given up struggling and stood limply by Vasco, his face sallow in the lamplight.

"Whose joke, I wonder?"

Gair and Vasco were still exchanging savage glances and Juana hurried to intervene: "Gair, Vasco," she turned from one to the other. "There's not time for this now. Listen!" Behind the drawn curtains they could hear a growing buzz of sound from the audience. "What are we going to do?"

"She's right." Now Gair took command. "What's between you and me, senhor, can be settled at leisure. For the moment, we have Miss Brett to consider. We must think how to keep this quiet. We'll have to improvise, patch it up as best we may. We must finish the scene."

"But how?" Juana asked.

"When the curtain is drawn, you"—to Vasco—"will make an apology, as if you were part of the performance, saying your doubts are satisfied. Then you"—his tone to Father Ignatius was even sharper—"will finish the scene as quickly as possible, making quite sure that there is no possibility of the marriage being valid." He forestalled Juana's protest. "No, Juana, we must go through with it. Listen!" The buzz of the audience was growing into a roar.

"You're right." Juana turned to Father Ignatius. "When Senhor de Mascarenhas has made his apology and withdrawn his objection, you will begin at 'Now the knot is tied precisely, Now the knot is tightly tied.' That leaves out the entire ceremony," she explained.

"Good." Vasco shouted an order to the pages, the curtains were drawn back and he moved forward to sing a brilliantly

196

improvised recitative in which he suggested that he had mistaken the bride for her sister. Father Ignatius then picked up the plot where Juana had ordered and, miraculously, the opera flowed on to its conclusion and a wild outburst of applause.

Juana had to come forward over and over again to receive the crowd's ovation and a shower of carnations and rose petals. Standing at the front of the improvised stage, bowing and smiling, she heard Vasco's tight whisper behind her. "Tomorrow; at first light," he said.

"No!" She turned, gestured to the pages to draw the curtains, and moved back between Vasco and Gair. "You're wrong, cousin. Mr. Varlow knew no more about it than I did. The last thing he wants is actually to marry me. Courtship is one thing, but he has a career to think of, a fortune to make."

"It's true, I'm afraid"—Gair's tone was rueful—"I cannot afford to think of marriage for many years to come."

"Not even to an heiress, senhor?"

"She wouldn't be an heiress long if she married me," Gair said. And then, "Of course! That's it. You have your cousins to thank for this, Juana. Where's the friar?"

But Father Ignatius had vanished.

CHAPTER 17

"What do we do now?" Juana looked from Gair to Vasco. Beyond the curtains, they could hear the stir as the audience broke up. It would not be long before they were interrupted.

"Nothing," said Gair. "Anything we do must merely make a bad situation worse. The audience seem to have noticed nothing beyond a brief interruption in the opera. We must leave it like that."

"He's right, cousin." But Vasco looked at Gair with dislike before turning his velvet brown gaze full on Juana. "We have your reputation to think of. All other considerations must give way to that. As to your cousins, leave them to me."

"No!" His tone frightened her. "I'm sure Father Ignatius was telling the truth. It was only—I'm sure it was just a joke that went too far. Please, let's say no more about it? Vasco? Gair? Promise?" She was thinking of Daisy and Teresa.

"Of course," said Gair. "It's merely common sense."

Vasco seized her hand and pressed it to his lips. "Asked like that," he said, "I could deny you nothing."

"Then that's settled," said Gair. "But we certainly owe *you* a debt of thanks, senhor. Your arrival was a timely one for us." His tone held more dislike than gratitude.

"Yes, thank God." He did not explain how he had learned of the plot. Instead, with the full power of his extraordinary brown eyes on Juana, "You have not asked if I have succeeded in my quest, cousin."

"It's hardly my affair." Here was the chance she badly wanted to put herself at arm's length from his again.

"Don't say that, I beg, since I so much hope to make it so." Ignoring Gair, he spoke as if they were alone on the stage. "As you know, I have been halfway across Europe looking for a vital witness to my parents' marriage."

"Have you so?" To Juana's relief, Gair interrupted what Vasco had been trying to turn into a *tête-à-tête*. "Then perhaps you can tell us the news from Poland?"

"It's as bad as can be. Napoleon defeated the Russians at Friedland at the beginning of June. I'm amazed that the news hasn't reached here sooner, but it's all of a piece with the way things are run here in Portugal."

"Yes? And what now?" The two men had forgotten Juana.

"Peace. Napoleon and Tsar Alexander met at Tilsit—or, to be precise, on a barge on the Nieman. They embraced like brothers and made up all their differences—at the expense of the rest of the world. Prussia hardly exists any more, and England is to be destroyed." He turned back to Juana. "I don't think you quite understand the full implications of your cousins' plot against you. At this point, marriage to an Englishman might well mean loss of property—maybe of liberty as well. England is doomed, cousin. We can only hope that Portugal will manage to survive the storm."

"You think Napoleon invincible then?" Gair's tone was dry.

In a moment they would be quarrelling again. "But did you find your witness, cousin?" Juana asked, to lower the tension, and thought, with irritation, as she did so, that they would both think it just like a woman to descend thus from the historic to the personal.

"Yes. I'll tell you about it—" But not now, said his look. "Here comes the Princess. Follow my lead, cousin."

Carlota Joaquina greeted Vasco warmly, as an old friend. "So it was you who took such liberties with my opera, Senhor de Mascarenhas!"

"I hope you agree that I improved it, Your Highness."

To Juana's relief the party broke up soon afterwards without their having encountered Pedro or Roberto. Gair and Vasco, who had both stayed close at her side, escorted her to the carriage, where they found Teresa already waiting. Roberto, she said crossly, had had to leave early to go back to Mafra.

Vasco handed Juana up into the carriage. "Remember"—his voice was low so that Teresa could not hear—"least said, soonest mended." Behind him, a look from Gair confirmed the warning.

But she had something of her own to say. "You won't—?" She looked from one man to the other, still anxious that they might quarrel after she had left.

"Fail to call on you tomorrow." Gair finished her sentence on a note of reassurance. "Rest well, Miss Brett. It's almost morning already."

Vasco bent to kiss her hand. "I too shall look forward to visiting you tomorrow, cousin." He stepped back, as Pedro and Daisy appeared behind him.

Juana held her breath at the unlucky meeting, but nothing happened. The three men greeted each other as casual acquaintances; Pedro handed Daisy up into the carriage and turned quickly away. It was safely over.

"So that's the handsome cousin, is it?" Teresa leaned forward to stare out at Vasco as the coachman whipped up his mules.

"Vasco de Mascarenhas?" Daisy too gazed back to where Gair and Vasco could still be seen by the fitful light of the pages' torches. "I wish I had got a better look at him. You might have warned me, Teresa. And as for you, Juana, I never saw such a dark horse. All that talk about not wanting to stay, and you end up with two cavaliers to our one. And they're both calling tomorrow. It's more than Pedro can. He's off on another of the Princess's errands."

"And Robert's gone back to Mafra." But Teresa's grumble was merely superficial. Listening as they compared notes about the party, Juana was aware of a kind of subdued glow about them. If Pedro and Roberto had not actually proposed tonight, they must have done the next best thing.

For her part, she was delighted to hear her stepsisters complain, in proprietorial tones, that Pedro and Roberto would both be away for some time. She did not at all want to meet them, and only hoped that Father Ignatius would keep away too. She had done her best to convince Gair and Vasco that it had all been nothing but a joke. Could she convince herself?

Manuela interrupted her breakfast next morning with an urgent summons from Mrs. Brett. Prepared to be cross-examined about the party, Juana was taken aback by her grandmother's abrupt greeting.

"You were right," she began without preamble. "I owe you an apology. We must start arranging, at once, for your family to go back to England."

"Why, what's the matter, ma'am?"

"Here; read this." She handed Juana a note from Gair. "It was meant for you, of course."

Juana's heart sank as she read the careful message. Gair much regretted being unable to call today, but official business made it impossible. The news of Tilsit was out, and there was worse than the mere fact of peace between France and Russia. Napoleon had celebrated his victory by demanding that Portugal come down finally on his side against England. Under threat of war, he insisted that Portugal close her ports to British shipping, arrest all English residents and confiscate their property. "This news is not public yet," Gair ended, "and of course nothing will happen at once, but I know you will want to be thinking what is best to do for your family."

"It's bad." Juana finished reading.

"As bad as possible."

"You think the Portuguese will yield to Napoleon's demands?"

"I'll be surprised if they don't. There will be some time, of course, as Mr. Varlow says, but not too much for all we have to do. Write a note to Senhor Gonçalves, child, telling him to come at once and advise me. If only you were Portuguese, how much simpler everything would be. I'm English, nothing will change that, but if I could hand the castle over to you . . ."

"But I'm English too. It will have to be Pedro and Roberto." She had wondered last night whether to tell her grandmother about their plot against her. Now she knew she never would. Mercifully, Mrs. Brett seemed better today.

"You're no more English than they are. Not really. But there's time to think about that. The first thing is your family. Frankly, I'll be glad to be rid of them, however much it costs. Did you know your stepmother drinks?"

"Oh?" Suddenly a whole series of unconnected episodes fell into place. "The poor thing. I hadn't realised. She didn't, though, before she came here. I'm sure of that."

"Well, let's hope she stops when she gets back. Ride down the Pleasant Valley this morning, Juana, and find Senhor Macarao for me. If I'm to pay off your father's debts, I may have to sell some land. We'll need him as well as Senhor Gonçalves."

"I suppose so. But the girls, ma'am, Daisy and Teresa. What if they don't want to go?"

"You think they won't?"

"I'm sure they won't." Daisy and Teresa, this morning, had been shining with happiness.

"Can you tell me one good reason why I should keep them here? They're no kin of mine, nor of yours, come to that. Their place is with their mother."

"In the state she's in?"

"That's not my affair. Haven't we enough hangers-on in the castle already?"

"Too many. I agree with you there. But Daisy and Teresa are my stepsisters—and my friends." And then, seeing how

201

little effect this had, "Besides, I think they are going to be your grand-daughters, ma'am." She was frightened as she said it. Her grandmother did seem much stronger this morning, but it was always bad for her to fly into a rage. Still, she had to know . . . She waited for the explosion.

It did not come. "So that's it. Something happened last night?"

"I think so. Nothing definite, I think, but enough . . ."

"Without consulting me. But it's in character. You see how right I was to wash my hands of my precious grandsons. Well, if they want to saddle themselves with a couple of overblown English roses, just when it will do them most harm, it's their own affair. In fact, I suppose their positions with Dom John and his wife will carry it off for them. But you will marry to please me, Juana."

"I hope I shall marry to please us both, ma'am."

Emerging from the cloisters into the brilliant sunshine of the courtyard, Juana saw Vasco ride in at the castle gate and greeted him with unaffected pleasure: "Cousin, how glad I am to see you. I have to do an errand for my grandmother down to the Pleasant Valley. Will you come with me?" She could never forget Tomas' death, nor the shadow of the Sons of the Star that hung about the lower valley. Vasco would be a much more reassuring companion than Iago or Luis.

"There is nothing I would like better." He put such feeling into the words that Juana felt a momentary qualm. In the morning's emergency, she had let herself forget the problem he presented. Well, it was too late now. And indeed the ride should give her a chance to get on to the kind of friendly cousin-to-cousin basis with him that she wanted.

Iago appeared with Sheba saddled and his long staff in his hand ready to accompany her.

"Here!" Vasco threw him his horse's reins, picked up Juana as if she weighed nothing, and set her lightly in the saddle. "No need to ask if Sheba is happy here." His arm stayed round her waist a moment longer than was necessary. "How often, this long winter, I have envied her."

"I can't tell you how grateful I have been to you for her, cousin." She made it matter-of-fact.

"It makes me very happy." He took his reins from Iago. "We'll not need your man."

"No?" She was not sure about this.

202

"No." He vaulted into the saddle. "You," to Iago. "Show my man where he may put my lead horse."

"Senhora?" Iago stood obstinately where he was, prepared to take orders only from her, and Juana thought she heard Vasco mutter a curse under his breath.

"Do as you are bid, Iago." There was no need to make an issue of this. "My cousin will take care of me."

"You are well served," Vasco said, as they rode out the big gate and round the side of the castle.

She thought it cost him an effort to say it. He had not at all liked having Iago appeal from him to her. "Yes," she said, to make it easier for him. "They're fond of me, I think."

"They'd be worse than brutes otherwise." Once again, his voice was charged with more feeling than she was ready for. She was glad that they were busy for a while guiding their horses down the rough track that led to the peasants' houses at the head of the Pleasant Valley.

The labourers, who began work in the cool of the dawn, were already at home for their midday meal, and Juana rode slowly through the little group of houses, exchanging greetings with the family parties who sat, each in the shade of their own vine or fig tree, eating *bacalhau* and vegetables and drinking the valley's light red wine.

"They live well, your people." Vasco had ridden silently beside her until they were down into the valley itself. "It's no wonder they are grateful to you."

"Not to me, cousin. I merely do what my grandmother tells me. I wouldn't have the first idea of how to run an estate like this."

"Nor should a woman. I'm glad to hear it. There are more suitable occupations for the gentle sex."

Now, suddenly, she was irritated. "Don't be absurd, cousin. I came to Portugal to help my grandmother. I may not know much about running the estate, but at least I can do my best, and what I'm told."

"Quite right. That is a woman's place."

"Thank you!" Her spurt of irritation communicated itself to Sheba, who broke into an uneasy trot that made conversation impossible. They found Macarao peacefully eating black bread and garlic sausage under a fig tree by the pressing floor, but when he heard Mrs. Brett's summons he hurried to fetch his mule and ride away up the valley.

Juana made to follow him, but Vasco's hand on Sheba's reins held her back. "Stay a little, cousin. I've so much to say

203

to you, and we can't talk as we ride. Still less at the castle! Besides, you look tired out after your late night. Come and rest a while in the shade and let me tell you the story of my adventures in Europe."

It reminded her, pleasantly, of the happy times they had spent together in the autumn and his stories of life in republican France. And she was tired. The shade looked cool and inviting. She was glad to let him lift her down from the saddle, but stiffened as he held her a moment longer than was necessary. "It's impossible to get a quiet word with you at the castle," he began. And then, "What's the matter?" He must have felt her instinctive withdrawal. "Surely you know you're safe with me?"

"Of course." She had been surprised at her own reaction. "One of our men was killed down here," she explained as much to herself as to him. "I don't much like the place."

"All the more monstrous that your grandmother should send you down here with no better protection than a servant." As he spoke he was urging her gently but irresistibly across the dusty plateau to one of the vine-shaded benches where the women sat to watch the treading of the grapes. "It's all of a piece." He took out his silk handkerchief and dusted the bench for her. "Nobody takes the slightest care of you up at the castle. I don't know which is worse, to let a fortune-hunter like Senhor Varlow dangle after you, or to send you off to risk your reputation at the Princess's. I cannot bear to think what would have happened if I had not got there when I did."

"It was timely, cousin. I have been wanting a chance to thank you. And to ask how you came to arrive so luckily for me." She had wondered about that a good deal.

"By sheer good fortune. But let us not waste this precious moment talking about the past. It is the future I care about. I must have the right to protect you, cousin, as you should be protected, to care for you as you need caring for. I had meant to wait longer, to court you as a woman likes to be courted; but to come back and find you in such danger—it's more than a man can bear. Cousin, I have loved you since the first moment I saw you. It's for you, only for you, that I have worked so hard to clear my name. I can offer it you now, unsullied, my own: Mascarenhas. There may be more to come, but take me now, Juana, on trust, as the man I am, and I swear to you, you will never regret it." He lifted her hand which he had retained all this time, and covered it with kisses. "I have some influence, here in Portugal. Now my name is clear, I think I can say I have a great future. Think of wealth, Juana; think of power."

"As if I cared for that!"

Her thoughts had been racing as he spoke, had almost seemed to come full circle. Her first instinct had been resistance, refusal, but then a treacherous shiver at the continued pressure of his hand on hers had combined with a delicious sensation of relief at the idea of being looked after to counsel yielding. And then, again, something in his speech had made yielding impossible.

"Spoken like yourself!" He pulled her towards him and she realised how completely he had misunderstood her.

"No!" She held back. "I'm sorry; you don't understand. I meant to say that if I cared for you, nothing else would matter."

"But you do!" Sitting beside her, he was tall as she. "Your hand has told me so. See, it trembles when I touch it. You're mine, Juana, your body knows it, if your mind does not. I'll show you." His other arm was round her waist, pulling her to him. He was enormously strong; ruthlessly gentle. Half of her wanted to fight; half to yield. His lips found hers. She had never been kissed before. Reason rocked on its foundations. It was heaven. It was forgetting everything; it was losing oneself. His tongue forced itself between her lips; his body was hot against hers. It was nightmare. She was afraid even to pull away.

"I told you." When he freed her to speak, her lips felt bruised. She was shaking all over; and still part of her was grateful for the support of his arm round her waist.

"No," she said again. "I don't know you, cousin." And, saying it, realised how true it was.

The brown eyes that held her own so steadily were at once tender and, surely, condescending. "I've been too sudden for you, little one. Forgive me. My feelings overcame me. I've loved you so hard since first I saw you. But I promise you, I'll not touch you again till you give me leave. I shall wait, my love, until you come to me of your own accord, till you offer me those lips that are my heaven."

"But—"

"No more now." He touched her lips, very gently, with a hot finger. "Say nothing. Only remember I am all yours, and give me leave to prove it to you. I will ask you again,

205

menina, and again, if need be. But, believe me, I know your heart better than you do yourself."

For the moment, she was glad to leave it at that, though she knew herself cowardly to do so. She regretted it when they got back to the castle and she became aware of a subtle difference in his behaviour to her, and, equally, knew that the rest of the party were noticing it too. More than once, during dinner, she caught Daisy's or Teresa's bright speculative eye fixed on her. She thought she was glad when Vasco rose, soon after dinner, to take his leave. But he had one more thing to say to her. "Remember"—he bent low over her hand—"if the time should come when you need a Portuguese hand and heart, they are all yours."

After this, it was disconcerting to have Senhor Gonçalves urge on her the necessity of marrying a Portuguese without delay. At her grandmother's request, she had joined them in Mrs. Brett's rooms, where they had already been talking for more than an hour, and Mrs. Brett lay exhausted among her pillows. "He will explain it all to you, Juana, better than I can. Listen to him, child, for all our sakes."

And the lawyer, horribly embarrassed, had explained the urgency of her making what he called a suitable marriage. "Ideally, of course, a pure Portuguese. I have told Mrs. Brett that a marriage with one of the Brett-Alvidrars, though better than nothing, still has its aspects of hazard."

"It's impossible," said Juana. "My grandmother knows perfectly well that Pedro and Roberto love my stepsisters. But, senhor, surely you can persuade her that the answer is simply to change her will."

He looked, poor man, more harassed than ever. "But, senhora, I have tried; I've done everything. She says it's impossible. And I tell you, unless something is done soon, you will lose the Castle on the Rock. All of you. Your uncles, your aunt. Imagine! They've lived all their lives here. What will happen to them? Most particularly your aunt . . ."

"Yes." Elvira was always miserable when she had to leave the castle, even for a few hours. To have to leave it for good would probably kill her.

"Senhora!" The old lawyer had drawn her away from the bed towards the red-curtained window. "Forgive me; this is painful for both of us. But your grandmother seemed to think there might be a Portuguese gentleman—she seemed to have hopes—"

"I see." Of course she saw. "When you need a Portuguese

206

hand and heart," Vasco had said. What she could not understand was why her grandmother should favour the marriage. "I don't understand," she said now, looking past the lawyer to the bed where the old lady lay still as death, somewhere between sleeping and waking. "You're sure she won't change her will?"

"Yes. And, frankly, if she did, I'm not sure, in her condition, whether a new one would stand."

"Oh!" This was a new and frightening thought. "Senhor Gonçalves, how much time do you think I've got?"

"It's running out fast for all of us, senhora. I beg you to think hard of what I have said. In the meanwhile I have your grandmother's instructions to book passages on the packet for your parents and your stepsisters." The enquiring glance with which he said this showed her more clearly than anything else that now, at last, he had accepted her as the heir to the castle. In future he would not act without her consent as well as her grandmother's orders.

"Have they been consulted?" she asked now.

"I don't know."

"Then they must be. Will you come with me, senhor? She's asleep, I think. We won't disturb her."

As she had expected, Daisy and Teresa refused to go. "No one is going to arrest us."

"And we've no property to confiscate."

"You won't make us, Juana?"

"Quite heartless," said their mother. Juana and the lawyer had visited her in her own apartment where they had found her dozing stertorously in a chair. Her condition was all too obvious. Now she cried a little, noisily. "My own daughters," she said, "that I've loved and cherished. You must make them come home with us, Mr. Brett."

"Father!"

"Please!"

Reginald Brett looked even more miserable than usual. "I'm afraid my mother must decide, my dears," he said.

Senhor Gonçalves had taken in the whole deplorable scene. Now he cleared his throat apologetically. "Mrs. Brett is old and ill," he said. "I rather fancy that she will acquiesce in anything that the young senhora decides."

"Juana!" said the two girls in unison.

Juana had a long look of sympathy for her father. But, "Of course you must stay if you want to," she said. "I shall be glad of your company."

"So long as they understand the hazards," said the lawyer, rising to take his leave. "And you, Miss Brett, you will think hard of what I have said to you?"

"Of course." Send for Vasco? Marry him for her own safety? The idea was intolerable. But why? She had to emerge from her daydream to accept Daisy and Teresa's enthusiastic thanks. "Senhor Gonçalves said it was all your doing," said Daisy.

"You'll never know how grateful we are," said Teresa.

CHAPTER 18

Reginald and Cynthia Brett left the next week, and though Juana felt horribly sorry for her father, she had to admit that it was a relief to see them go. Life was bad enough at the castle without the constant scenes Cynthia Brett had made. Elvira had been stranger than ever since Carlota Joaquina's party and wandered forlornly from room to room, singing snatches from *The Groom Deceived*. She had given up any attempt at embroidery, and carried, instead, skeins of silk, which she wound and unwound endlessly. Prospero said he was revising his Camoens and spent most of his time shut up in the library, while Miguel was increasingly disturbed because Father Ignatius had not been seen since the day of the Princess's party. Since no one but Juana knew of the sinister part the friar had played in the opera, this seemed inexplicable, and Miguel, who depended on Father Ignatius for all the real work in connection with his Little Brothers of Saint Antony, took it more and more to heart.

Juana was worried about Father Ignatius too. At first, she had been glad when he did not put in an appearance. She had never liked him, and found his part in the plot against her unforgivable. But when he neither came nor sent any apology or explanation she found herself increasingly frightened for him. She could not help connecting his disappearance with the mysterious death of Tomas. Tomas, she had thought, had recognised her when he was serving as acolyte to the Sons of the Star. And Tomas had died that same night. Could there be a connection between Father Ignatius' involvement in the plot against her and his disappearance? She hoped she was imagining things, but longed passionately to see Gair and put her fears to him. She almost found herself looking forward to the July meeting of the Sons of the Star, because it must mean a visit from him for her report.

The meeting fell on the nineteenth, the very day that Reginald and Cynthia Brett left. It was easy enough to suggest an early night for all of them, since they had been up with the dawn to see off the travellers. It was easy, too, to plead anxiety for her grandmother and go to visit her on her way to her own room. Mrs. Brett had not left her bed since the news of Tilsit. Juana had hoped that with the departure of her father and stepmother the old lady might take on a new lease of life, might even begin to come downstairs again, but tonight she could only wonder whether she would ever summon up enough strength to leave her bed. She seemed to be reduced to an enormous pair of eyes. They followed Juana, disconcertingly, this way and that, as she put on her black dress and got ready to go down the winding stair.

When Juana was ready, a feeble hand summoned her over to the bed. "Child!" She spoke with difficulty, in a croaking whisper. "I'm sorry. Whatever happens, forgive me?"

"Of course." Juana put her warm hand on the dry claw that lay on the sheets. "There's nothing to forgive. Whatever happens, I'm glad I came." It was true, though she could not imagine why.

"God bless you!" But already the old eyes were hooded in sleep.

When Juana opened the secret panel she knew at once that the real leader was back. There was something electric in the air of the cavern, and the squat, strong figure under the star was unmistakable. The only surprising thing was that at the moment he seemed almost to be apologising for the cancellation of the last two meetings. "We were waiting," he explained, "until the situation in Poland was clearer. Now, at last, Brothers, we know where we stand. Napoleon has dealt with the Russians: they will not dare meddle in Europe again in our lifetime. Now he is ready to turn his eyes back to the west. Already, Portugal is shaking under his ultimatum. Brothers, our moment is at hand!"

"What, precisely, do you mean by that?" The Brother of the Silver Serpent was on his feet.

"That I have Napoleon's promise of armed assistance in our plan to take over the government of our suffering country." But Juana did not think he had much liked the question.

"And have you also his promise that he will withdraw his forces when Dom John has fallen?"

"Brother," said the leader, "I know you for a new member, and treat your questions therefore with more patience than I might otherwise show, but do not tempt me too far. I tell you of a powerful ally in our fight for freedom, and you can think of nothing but a series of miserable quibbles. When Portugal is free, we will be masters here, and no one else. No one, then, will stay in our country without our leave."

"But when do we act?" asked the Brother of the Silver Hand.

"Not for a little while yet, Brother. The French ultimatum does not expire until the first of September."

"But suppose Dom John yields at once and gets rid of the English?"

"He will not. I know it. We have ample time to concert our plans. Most important of all is to be sure that the army is on our side when the moment of action comes. I suggest that our new Brother of the Silver Serpent be deputed to visit General Gomez Freire at his headquarters on the coast and make sure that he is safe for us. Is it agreed, Brothers?"

"Agreed," went the murmur round the table.

"It is well. And now, Brothers, we have a painful duty to perform. A traitor to the Star awaits your verdict. Bring in the prisoner, my sons."

As the two acolytes moved away from the table, Juana remembered to close the secret panel. But how would she know when to open it again? She must open it. The traitor might be anyone. Gair? Vasco? She must know. She counted ten, as for the beginning of a meeting, then, very slowly, ten again. Her hand shook uncontrollably as she opened the panel.

The acolytes stood facing the council table with a hooded figure between them. As when the new member had been admitted at the March meeting, each of them held one end of a noose that lay lightly round their prisoner's neck.

There was a little, horrible pause. Then the leader spoke: "Brother of the Lion, you are brought here for judgement by your Brothers. I now proclaim you a traitor to your order, a betrayer of our trust, a conspirer with our enemies. What is the penalty, Brothers, for one who has done this?" He turned to the Brother on his right.

"Death."

Juana shuddered as the word went round the table. But the Brother of the Silver Serpent was on his feet. "What has he done?"

"Tell them, Brother of the Ragged Staff, since they wish to know."

"He has admitted it all, in the cells of the Star. Is it your wish that I read you his confession?"

"It's not true!" the hooded prisoner screamed. "I was forced—" But the leader had made a sign to the two acolytes who pulled suddenly on the rope round his neck and his

211

words ended in a horrible choking sound. He swayed and fell.

"The mercy of the Star is infinite," said the leader. "He died fast, who should have died slowly. Read his confession, Brother of the Ragged Staff."

"It was horrible," Juana told Gair next day. "They carried him away at the end of the meeting as if he'd been a thing—a sack of potatoes. And the 'confession' didn't seem to add up to much anyway. I thought the Brother of the Silver Serpent would ask more questions, but I suppose he thought it was too late, with the poor man dead."

"You didn't see who it was?"

"No. The acolytes were careful to keep his hood over his face as they carried him out. Gair, I'm frightened."

"I don't wonder. What happens if you are ill, Juana? If you really can't go down to let them in?"

"I don't know. I always assumed my grandmother would go, but now she's not strong enough. Why?"

"It's getting too dangerous. I don't want you to go down there again. Ask her if there is not some way out, some alternative arrangement."

"Gair, I can't. She's too ill; I can't worry her. Besides, if there had been one, she would have told me. And anyway, the nearer things come to a crisis, surely the more important it is that you know what they are doing. I'm terrified. I won't pretend I'm not. But I know I have to go."

"I suppose so." He sounded curiously unconvinced, and her heart warmed to him. Did he really think the risk to her more important than the job to be done?

He bent towards her, suddenly the suitor. "Here comes your cousin."

It was Vasco's first visit since the day he had proposed, and Juana was delighted to have Gair present. Vasco, on the other hand, looked far from pleased. "I took the liberty of this early call"—a look suggested that Gair's had been too early altogether—"to condole with you on your father's departure."

"Thank you." She let him kiss her hand and noticed how much better he did it than Gair. They made an odd contrast altogether, she thought, as she listened to their limping, unenthusiastic conversation about the news of the day. Even on this sweltering July morning, Gair was completely the elegant Englishman, contriving to look pale, cool, and composed in blue broadcloth and high cravat. Vasco, on the other hand, a head shorter and very much more solidly built, had a deep and glowing tan and wore his well-cut clothes with an almost republican casualness. His shirt was open at the neck, with a silk scarf loosely tied, and he laughed, catching her eye on him, took out a silk handkerchief to mop his forehead, and apologised for behaving "quite like one of the family."

"Of course, cousin." Gair was looking put out, she noticed with a little spurt of pleasure. "You'll both stay for dinner, gentlemen?"

Over coffee on the shady loggia, Vasco announced that he had taken a house at Sintra for the hot months. A quick look told Juana that this was done entirely for her sake, and indeed he rode over most days after that and she devoted immense ingenuity to avoiding being alone with him. To her relief, he seemed either not to notice or not to mind this. He was content, apparently, to sit on the loggia or terrace with her and her sisters, talking, or reading aloud to them in his fluent English as they sewed. It was extraordinarily domestic and peaceful, and occasionally Juana found herself actually wondering whether she could have imagined the scene in the Pleasant Valley. But, no. An occasional glance, a quick phrase, a pressure of the hand would remind her of what lay between them. "I shall wait," he had said, and here he was visibly, peacefully, lovingly waiting.

He never stayed long. He was deeply occupied, he explained once, with legal business in connection with proving his legitimacy. "You know why I am so eager to have it proved beyond any shadow of doubt." This, aside to her, one August morning was the nearest he came to a reference to the scene in the Pleasant Valley.

She was grateful for his restraint, but, she admitted to herself with a pang of surprise, a little frightened. There was something altogether too calm, too certain about him. Like her sisters, who hardly referred to Pedro and Roberto but looked content as two cream-fed cats, he seemed to be biding his time.

But then, everyone was doing that. Napoleon's ultimatum to the Portuguese was public knowledge by now, and so too was the fact that no answer had been sent to it. Dom John was still at Mafra; the army, under Gomez Freire, was on the coast. Nothing was said, nothing done as the hot August days ebbed away. Even the August meeting of the Sons of the Star was oddly inconclusive. Like everyone else, they

213

were biding their time, waiting on events. Afterwards, Juana thought that perhaps the curiously negative tone of the meeting was partly due to the absence of the new Brother of the Silver Serpent who had not returned from his mission to Gomez Freire. Was he the only one with the courage to stand up to the new leader? In his absence, the meeting seemed, more than usually, merely to reflect decisions that had been taken already by some more powerful inner circle.

Expecting Gair, Juana was taken aback when Senhor Gonçalves called next day and asked, not for old Mrs. Brett, but for her. When she joined him in the little room beyond the Ladies' Parlour which had somehow become her study, he came straight to the point. "Miss Brett, the French ultimatum expires in less than two weeks. On the first of September the French ambassador—and the Spanish one, since they have associated themselves with the French in this matter—will ask for their papers, and leave. After that, anything may happen ... I must ask whether you have come to a decision."

"What kind of a decision?" She was not going to make it easier for him.

"Why—about yourself ... the estate. Miss Brett, you must face facts." He seemed to be having a hard enough time in doing so himself. Now he went off on a new tack: "The French will invade, you know, when the ultimatum expires. Then, to be English will mean imprisonment, death maybe; loss of property ... Or look at it the other way: suppose Dom John gives in to the French demands. He may do so any day now. There's been no news from Mafra for a while. Today, tomorrow, any time may come his edict annexing English property to the state. Think of your family, if you won't think of yourself. I don't want to intrude on your private affairs, Miss Brett"—he hovered uncertainly between the Portuguese and the English form of address—"but we lawyers do tend to hear things. There's a certain cousin of yours—Senhor de Mascarenhas—Miss Brett"—suddenly he appeared to throw discretion to the winds—"I'll tell you everything. He came to see me yesterday. I've seldom been more impressed with a young man. It was all most proper; everything one could wish for. Since your father is in England, he said, he had come to me. Your uncles—well, we all know about them. And your grandmother, of course, is old and ill. He wants you to know, not only that he loves you, which I believe he has told you himself, but something about

214

his position. His claim is good, he proved it to me. He is de Mascarenhas, with all that implies. And as to fortune, I am empowered to tell you that his mother's estate has doubled under his management. He will be generosity itself, I am sure, in the question of settlements. He understands, you see, that you are an English young lady. There will be no difficulty about pin money or any of those curious English customs. And, don't you see: marry him and you are safe. No one can touch you."

"And the castle?"

He looked, surely, more embarrassed than ever. "The castle?"

"If I marry Senhor de Mascarenhas, who will the Castle on the Rock belong to? After my grandmother's death, that is?"

"But, senhora, how can you ask?"

"I am asking, senhor."

"Man and wife are one flesh," said the lawyer. "All they have is in common."

"Exactly. Senhor, I must think about this." What was the use of marrying to save the castle for her family, if by doing so she merely handed it over to Vasco? Besides, the more she was urged to it, the more doubtful, illogically, obstinately, perhaps, she felt about marriage with Vasco. She tried to explain something of her doubts to the lawyer: "You see, senhor, for me it is so much more than just marrying. It is accepting a whole way of life. It is becoming Portuguese."

"But that is precisely my point." He was holding on to patience with an effort.

"I know." She rose to her feet. "Senhor, I promise, I will think about it, hard, and send for you." She must get rid of him. Gair might arrive at any minute to hear her report on last night's meeting.

In fact, he did not appear till next morning, when he arrived just in time to accompany her on her morning ride. "We're all at sixes and sevens in Lisbon," he explained. "Dom John has sent a confidential note to Lord Strangford advising that he tell any Englishmen who can do so to sell up and go. It's bad, Juana. I think I ought to urge you to go."

"But what about you?"

"We'll stay till the last moment, of course. The navy will see that we get away. But we have diplomatic immunity. It's different for you."

"Don't forget that I'm half Portuguese."

"If you weren't, I'd put you on the next packet. But what happened at the meeting?"

"Nothing much. The leader had it all his own way; partly because the Brother of the Silver Serpent wasn't there, I think. He's still on the coast with Gomez Freire."

"I see. Well, it looks as if we still have a breathing space to decide what's best for you."

"But you must see, I have no choice. It's not just a question of your business now. You brought me here, it's true, but now I am here, I'm committed. While my grandmother lives, I must stay for her sake. And if she dies, there is the problem of the castle. Senhor Gonçalves was here yesterday. He wants me to marry a Portuguese." She had thought she did not intend to tell him this. "They're all thinking of the castle. They don't want to lose it. I don't blame them. If only my grandmother hadn't left it to me. And Senhor Gonçalves says that even if I could persuade her to change her will he doesn't think it would be valid."

"She's as bad as that?"

"I'm afraid so. And, Gair, it's so difficult. Do you mind if I talk to you about it? After all, you got me into this. And there's no one else I can discuss it with. The thing is, if I decide to marry, for their sake, for the castle—how can I be sure it would work? I mean—you remember I told you, back last winter, that I intend to give it back to Pedro and Roberto. But—if I was married when I inherited it, would I be able to? Wouldn't it go to my husband? Wouldn't he be able to stop me?"

"If he wanted to. Yes, I should think so. But, Juana, you mustn't think of sacrificing yourself like this. If it is a sacrifice?" A slight flush stained his cool, pale cheek.

"I don't know. I don't seem to be able to make up my mind about anything. It's all such a muddle. There are so many people to think about. How can I fail them all?"

"You should think of yourself. What do you owe them, after all? Your selfish uncles; your cousins who plotted to disgrace you—and, that reminds me, has there been any word from Father Ignatius?"

"No. I wish there had."

"I wish you were safe back in England. Juana—" He stopped. "There's someone coming up the hill. For God's sake, don't do anything without consulting me. I think it's your cousin Roberto. Juana—"

"He's coming fast," she warned. "I've not seen him since that night at the Princess's."

"Nor have I." Whatever he had been going to say, he gave it up as Roberto approached them at a rapid trot. "Be careful, Juana."

"Of course." But the greetings went off easily enough, although she thought Roberto seemed anxious, keyed up. "Teresa's very well," she told him. "She's missed you. We all have." She and Gair had turned to ride back to the castle with him but when they reached the gate Gair reined in his horse. "I must be getting back to Lisbon," he settled back with an effort into his part of suitor. "I begged the morning off, Miss Brett, because I felt I must warn you, but my orders were to return as soon as I could. You'll think of what I have said? I've been telling Miss Brett," he explained to Roberto, "about your master's advice to the English."

"Quite so." But Roberto looked puzzled. "Something very odd there," he said to Juana as they dismounted.

"What do you mean?"

"Why, that I was Dom John's messenger to Lord Strangford. I've just come from Lisbon. Mr. Varlow wasn't there. How does he know about Dom John's warning?"

"Goodness knows!" She made it casual, but felt a horrid little stab of doubt. Had Gair been lying to her? Was there no one she could trust?

"There's probably some simple explanation." Roberto dismissed it. "But it's not to talk about him that I've come. Juana, I must see you alone."

"Oh?" Be careful, Gair had said. She looked about her. "It's cool here in the cloisters."

"You don't trust me, and I don't blame you." He followed her into the shadowed cloister. "Juana, you must believe me; I had nothing to do with what happened at the Princess's. I've only just heard about it. Pedro told me; he wanted to know if I'd heard anything of Father Ignatius. I've never been so angry. I'd have fought him, Juana, if he wasn't my brother. I can't tell you how sorry I am. It won't happen again; nothing. I promise you. He may be my elder brother, but I'm the Prince's man. He won't dare try anything. I've come to ask if you will try to forgive him. And, please, believe I had nothing to do with it?"

"Roberto, I'm so glad." Impulsively, she held out both hands to him. "I minded so much. About you particularly." There were tears in her eyes.

"Bless you, Juana. You do believe me?"

"Of course. And, Roberto, don't be too angry with Pedro. Even at the time, I didn't altogether blame him. It isn't fair, what our grandmother has done." And suddenly, all at once, without further thought, she was telling him how she planned to hand the castle back to him and his brother. "We'll share, don't you see? There will be plenty for all of us. Only—don't tell anyone—not yet—it's all so difficult." Here at last was someone who could advise her, and she poured out the whole story of Senhor Gonçalves' pressure. "And I don't want to marry anyone." She had managed not to mention Vasco's name. "Why in the world are you laughing, Roberto?"

"Because I'm so happy, I think. I knew we could trust you, Ju." It was the first time he had used the childhood name. "And, thank God, I can do something for you in return. Tell your croaking lawyer I spoke to the Prince about you only yesterday. He signed the decree making you fully Portuguese at the same time as mine and Pedro's."

"Before you knew. Oh, Roberto, I'm going to cry."

"Don't. There comes Teresa."

CHAPTER 19

"Senhora! Senhora! Wake up!"

"What is it?" Juana pulled herself up from the depths of sleep. It was still dark. Estella was standing by her bed, a candle guttering in her shaking hand.

"It's your grandmother, senhora. Something's happened to her. We're frightened, Manuela and I. Come quick and tell us what to do."

"What's the matter?"

"We don't know. She was much better this evening—well, you saw her. She was talking of maybe getting up tomorrow. She said she would settle down early for the night. 'I feel like a real sleep,' she told us. 'I'll be better in the morning.' We were so pleased, Manuela and I. And now—" Tears choked her.

Juana took the candle from Estella's shaking hand. "But what happened?"

"We don't know. I was sleeping in the antechamber tonight —you know one of us always does. I slept well, but nobody could have come through the room without waking me. The outer door was locked anyway. She insists on that."

"I know." Juana restrained impatience. She must let the shaken creature tell it her own way. To try and hurry her would merely confuse her.

"I was waked by Mrs. Brett's bell. At least I think I was. That must have been it. But how it came to be so far from the bed—I suppose it must have fallen and rolled. She'd done herself harm, I'm afraid, trying to reach it."

"Harm? What do you mean?" They were out in the cloisters now, in the black darkness of a moonless night, and Juana had to shelter the wavering candle flame with her hand.

"She's got a terrible bruise coming on her face. And—she can't speak. We got her back into bed, Manuela and I, but she just lies there, and shakes, and cries. Senhora, I'm frightened."

"Well, no wonder," said Juana bracingly as she led the way up the winding stair to her grandmother's rooms. "I'm glad you came for me. You haven't waked anyone else?"

"Not yet." It was disturbing but understandable that it should not have occurred to Estella to wake one of the old lady's sons. What use would Prospero or Miguel be at a sickbed?

"Thank God, you've come." Manuela met them at the door of the bedroom. "She looks worse every minute. Should we send for the doctor?"

"At once." One look at the old lady had settled the question for Juana. Mrs. Brett was flat on her back, breathing stertorously, asleep or unconscious. The bruise was beginning to show horribly on one gaunt cheekbone, and all that side of her face seemed drawn down, out of focus. "Manuela, wake Jaime. Tell him Mrs. Brett's ill—no more than that, mind. She must have fallen and hurt herself trying to reach the bell, but we don't want a lot of talk about this in the castle. Tell Jaime to send one of the men to Sintra at once for the doctor. Iago had better go; he knows the road better than Luis. And, you, Estella, go and get some clothes on, then come back to me here so that I can do the same." She bent to feel the dried-up hand that lay loosely on the crimson quilt. "She's icy cold. More bedding, Estella, before you go."

Alone at last, Juana lit every candle in the room before she made herself go to the big closet and check on the fastening of the secret door. But the bolt was securely shot on her side. It was merely absurd to let herself imagine that someone—one of the Sons of the Star—had made his way up from the big cavern to attack the old lady. Besides, why in the world should they? The accident must have happened as she herself had suggested. There was the handbell, still lying where it had fallen, some way from the bed. It would be easy enough for the old woman, feeling herself worse all of a sudden, to knock it over when she tried to ring it. And then, trying to get out of bed in the dark, falling, no doubt, against the corner of her bedside table. It was a horrid enough picture as it was. No need to make it worse by imagining attackers who could come through a bolted door. But from now on, old Mrs. Brett must not sleep alone. She had insisted on it, so far, and only Juana had known the real reason.

In fact, it was easy enough to persuade the doctor that Mrs. Brett would be nursed more easily in a ground floor room on her own stairway. "I doubt if she'll notice the difference," he said. "Poor old thing. It's going to mean real nursing from now on. Someone with her all the time. Frankly, I can't hold out much hope of an improvement, but how long she will linger like this is another question."

"It settles everything," Juana told Gair next day. He had ridden out from Lisbon with the news that the French and Spanish ambassadors had left on the expiration of the French ultimatum. "Barring a miracle, it means war," he said. "I think you ought to go home, Juana."

"I wish I could." Suddenly, England was home. "But I can't." She explained what had happened. "I can't go now. They'd let her die out of sheer stupidity, those women. But it's not so bad as you think." She anticipated further protest by telling him about Roberto's visit. "I'm Portuguese now," she concluded. "They can't touch me. Or the castle."

"Thank God for that."

Seeing Gair's reaction, Juana found herself wondering what Vasco's would be. But there was something she had been wanting to ask Gair. "Tell me"—she found it hard to begin—"the last time you came—when we met Roberto—you said you had come straight from Lisbon, from Lord Strangford's, from Santa Martha ..." Absurd to beat about the bush so.

"Yes I did, didn't I?" He had been expecting this. "And I suppose your cousin Roberto gave me the lie direct after I had left. How was I to know he had been Dom John's messenger!"

"So you admit—"

"That I lied to you? I have to, don't I?" He was irritatingly cheerful about it. "What did you say to your cousin?"

"I laughed it off. What else could I do?"

"Quite right."

She found the bland approval infuriating. So you mean I can't believe a thing you tell me!"

"No, no." He was serious now. "Be reasonable, Juana. You must see that the less you know the better, for your own sake. I promise I will never lie to you on any subject that concerns you."

And with that, she had to be content. Besides, there were more urgent causes for anxiety. "Then tell me this: If it's war, you will have to go back to England?"

"Of course. That's why I want you safe out of the country first. You must see that I can't leave you here, involved with the Sons of the Star, with even your grandmother beyond helping you."

She shivered. "I can't say I very much like the idea myself. But I can't go now. How much time do you think there is?"

"God knows. Now Napoleon is back in Paris, I would expect things to move fast. But I think at least we can safely wait till after the next meeting. They will have the latest news."

Juana disliked establishing herself in Mrs. Brett's vacated room, but what else could she do? And it seemed reasonable enough to her family since it brought her so much closer to the invalid. Only she knew what sleepless nights she owed to the hidden door at the back of the closet. It was solidly bolted. She was sure that it could not be opened from the far side, but still she could not forget the livid bruise slowly fading on Mrs. Brett's cheek. She had convinced everyone else that it had been done by falling against a table. She could not quite convince herself. If only Mrs. Brett would recover enough to tell them what had happened ... But the doctor held out little hope of this.

She had arranged to take turns with Manuela, Estella, and Maria in the big, cool downstairs sickroom. On the night of the next meeting, it was Maria's turn and she asked her to summon Manuela rather than herself if she needed help. "I'm worn out, Maria. I must have a quiet night." If only she could. It was extraordinarily worse, she found, to go down the winding stair from an empty room.

The Sons of the Star were growing impatient. As soon as the leader had finished his opening speech, the Brother of the Hand was on his feet. "So the French and Spanish ambassadors have left together," he said. "Surely, Brothers, that means they will attack us together? Why do we wait for them? Why not strike now?"

"Let us first hear what our Brother of the Silver Serpent has to report from the army," said the leader.

"I think we must leave the army out of our calculations." The silver serpent gleamed on the speaker's hood. "Gomez Freire is loyal to the Crown. The best we can hope for is that, for lack of orders, which we should be able to compass, he will stay inactive on the coast while the blow is struck."

"And when will that be?" This was the Brother of the Broken Cross, backed up by a little mutter of approval from round the council table.

"Very soon." The leader was on his feet again. "There is talk once more at court, Brothers, of an evacuation to the Brazils. Then is our chance. We will be spared the necessity of destroying the royal family. If they flee, they destroy themselves. Who will want them back? We can begin our new era without the stain of royal blood. Brothers, you ask me to name the day we strike. I name it: the day the Prince Regent sails down the Tagus."

"Well, that's definite enough," said Gair next day. "And they accepted it?"

"After some argument, yes. The rest of the meeting was spent in arranging practical details. Gair, it's terrifying. They have it all planned down to the last 'elimination.' That's their word. It sounds so much better than 'murder,' doesn't it?"

"Don't worry," he said. "It won't happen. Now we have their date, we're safe."

"Are you sure?" There had been something not quite convincing about the way he said it.

"I hope so. The difficulty is to get the Portuguese to act. Well—you can see: the very people we apply to may in fact be members. Your grandmother never told you any names?"

"No, but she knew some."

"I know. She always promised that when it came to a crisis she'd tell me. Now she can't."

"No." It brought back, suddenly, all her doubts about the accident to the old lady, but before she could speak of them, Gair had gone off on a different tack.

"If we only had enough English soldiers," he said, "we could round up the leaders at their next meeting. To try and do it with Portuguese troops would be fatal: the news would be bound to get out. So—we have to wait for our navy to get here."

"They'll come?"

"Of course. You remember last year. The state the Portuguese fleet is in, they'll need British help to get Dom John safe to Brazil."

"You think he'll go?"

"Lord Strangford is urging him to. I think he's wrong, myself. I told Canning so when I was in England, but they'll none of them listen. I agree with the Sons of the Star. If the royal family flee when the country is in danger, why should they expect to come back? But I think that's what will happen, just the same."

"How soon?"

"God knows. Not immediately, that's certain. Dom John

still won't stir from Mafra; refuses to admit the danger. The army may be loyal, but it's had no orders, anyway I doubt if it's in a state to resist the French . . . It's all muddle, incompetence, inertia . . . It's unbelievable!"

"It makes you wonder—" she stopped, surprised at herself.

"Wonder what?"

"Whether the Sons of the Star are such a bad thing after all. At least they have a plan of action."

"Which amounts to handing the country over to the French. Don't forget their 'eliminations,' Juana. What's begun in blood will go on bloodily. And how many of your friends, do you think, are on their lists? But how's the old lady? How soon can you leave her? You do realise, don't you, that on the day Dom John sails, you must be safe out of the country?"

"I hope I can. Though where I'm to go . . ."

"Your father?"

"Is staying with his wife's family." Anything rather than that. Should she tell him of Vasco's proposal? But if she did decide to accept that strong, supportive arm, would even he be able to protect her from the Sons of the Star?

"Vanessa is expecting a child." Gair's *non sequitur* surprised her. "And her husband is not well," he went on. "She writes that she would be delighted to have you for an indefinite stay. I think you could do worse than to visit her until the crisis here is past. Then, when things have settled down, you can return if you want to."

"Doesn't that sound a little like Dom John? Running away, I mean."

"I don't care what it sounds like. I don't want you 'eliminated.' "

"Why, thank you!" She was more tempted than ever to tell him about Vasco's suit, even to ask his advice. After all, they were partners; she really ought to tell him. She was not sure whether to be glad or sorry that they were interrupted, at this point, by Daisy with the news that Vasco himself had just ridden into the courtyard.

"Then I'll take my leave," Gair stood up. "Your cousin is still settled at Sintra?" The question was casual, and in English, for Daisy's sake, but his eyes held both a warning and a question.

"I suppose so. We haven't seen him for a while."

"No," Daisy pursued it after Gair had left. "I was beginning to think you had tried Senhor de Mascarenhas too far,

224

Juana. Tell me, when are you going to make up your mind between those two?" And then, laughing, "Do you think it's safe to let them meet? We don't want them fighting it out in the castle courtyard."

"D—d—don't be absurd!" Irritation at the reminder of Gair's pseudo-courtship brought on her stammer and she was glad to be interrupted by Vasco himself.

He had been away, he told them, and had only just heard of Mrs. Brett's illness. "It's terrible news. Is there anything I can do?" He too spoke English out of consideration for Daisy.

"Nothing, thank you."

"The doctor holds out no hopes, he tells me."

"You've seen him?"

"Yes—he's my neighbour in Sintra. That's how I heard. I wish you had thought to send for me, cousin."

"But if you were away—"

"My people would have known where to find me. I don't think you quite understand how entirely my thoughts are devoted to you. My servants do. They know that any message from here must reach me, wherever I am. I'm afraid for you, Juana. Your grandmother's illness makes your position even more dangerous. I hope you don't rely too much on Dom John's declaring you Portuguese."

"Oh. You've heard about that?"

"Yes. I try to be informed of what concerns you. I know, for instance, that you are nursing the old lady yourself." His voice held disapproval.

"Of course I am." Who was his informant? But, of course, the doctor again . . .

"I wish you would help us to persuade her that she is overdoing it," Daisy said.

"That's why I came. It's not at all suitable, cousin. I am come to offer you the services of my old nurse—an excellent woman in a sickroom. She will take all responsibility off your hands."

"It's very good of you." What a genius he had for rubbing her up the wrong way. "But my grandmother would be miserable with a stranger looking after her. We are managing admirably as it is."

"You may be managing admirably for the old lady, but how about yourself? You're looking exhausted, cousin."

"Thank you for the compliment!" The fact that she knew it was true merely made it more irritating.

225

"Cousin!" His voice was reproachful. "Don't insist on taking me the wrong way. You must know how deeply I have your best interests at heart."

"She ought to by now," said Daisy. "But after all, you have neglected us for three whole weeks, senhor. We'd almost forgotten what you looked like, hadn't we, Juana?"

"D—d—d." Fatigue and the necessity of speaking English for Daisy's sake had brought on her stammer worse than ever. She made a new start: "I wish you wouldn't—"

"I won't," Daisy interrupted. "I'll do as I would be done by and leave you two to talk Portuguese in peace. Does that make you my friend for life, Senhor de Mascarenhas?"

"It does indeed." He rose to open the door of the Ladies' Parlour for her. Then, "Juana! Come out on to the loggia with me. I must talk to you. Please?" He took her hand in a firm grip that sent an involuntary shiver through her. "It's two months, almost to the day, since I last spoke." His tone might be pleading, but his arm was firm. The air on the loggia was cool; there had been a sprinkling of rain that morning and the sky was still overcast. "No one will come out here to disturb us." He led her to a seat screened by sweet-scented jasmine. "And the air will do you good," he added as an afterthought. "I don't like to see you looking so exhausted, Juana."

"I don't much like it myself." She could hardly explain that her sleepless night had been spent not at her grandmother's bedside but down below in the heart of the cliff.

"There are dark circles under your eyes." He lifted a hand and she shrank into herself, anticipating his touch. "Don't shrink from me, Juana. You know, in your heart, that you are mine. Admit it, my love, and make us both happy."

Admit it? Was it true? It would be wonderfully easy to let herself lean, just a little, towards him, to admit it without words. "I don't know—" It was an effort to make herself stay upright.

"You won't let yourself know. Why are you afraid, Juana? Afraid to love—afraid to live. You do know, really: you must know that all my happinesss lies in caring for you, serving you, protecting you. You look today like someone whose burden is too heavy to be borne. Share it with me, my love, or, better still, let me carry it for you. It's the man's place."

"I can't . . ." This was true. However much she might be tempted, she could not tell him about the Sons of the Star without Gair's permission.

226

"You mean, you won't!" She had forgotten that he could explode like this suddenly into anger. The hand that held hers closed on it like a vice.

"You're hurting me!"

"I'm sorry." He bent to kiss the hand he had hurt. "Forgive me." He was breathing hard, controlling himself with an effort. "You're driving me mad, Juana. You're trying me too far. Love like mine is too strong to be trifled with. But I'm a brute to frighten you when you're worn out. Think it over, my love, quietly, and write to me when you are ready. I shall be waiting at Sintra, counting the hours till I hear from you. Only, don't let them be too many. I need the right to protect you. Soon now, the country is going to be in chaos. Don't think that fop of an Englishman will protect you when the French invade. He'll be off, with the rest of them, whisked to safety on a ship of the line. I warn you, there will be plenty of informers to tell the French of this rich castle, and all its land, held by a couple of Englishwomen. What will they care for a document signed by Dom John? It will suit them to treat you as English, and English you will be. But—married to me: Mascarenhas twice over ... Juana, you and I are each other's fate. It was planned in our cradles ... fated long before that. Trust me, believe in me ... I can't tell you more now ... But there is a great—an unbelievable future awaiting us—" He looked past her, towards the castle. "There's somebody coming. Juana, write to me soon. You know you're mine." The hand that had held hers abandoned it to move upwards, touch her breast for a moment and send a pang of pure fire through her, then catch her other hand to pull her to her feet. "Mine," he said again. "Write soon."

Elvira had emerged from the doorway of the Ladies' Parlour. She looked about her vaguely. " 'I sent a letter to my love and on the way I dropped it Somebody'—Oh!" Miguel had followed her. "It's cold out here. What has happened to the sun? I want sunshine—" She moved carefully round Miguel and went back into the castle.

Miguel greeted Vasco warmly and urged him to stay to dinner, but he refused ."My cousin is worn out," he said. "I'll not tire her further."

When he had gone, Juana hoped her uncle would leave her alone to her chaotic thoughts, but instead: "Sit down a minute, child," he said. "I want to talk to you."

"Yes?"

"I consider myself responsible for you, now your father is

227

gone and my mother beyond caring. It's time you made up your mind, Juana."

"What do you mean?"

"Don't prevaricate, child. I'm not a fool. Senhor de Mascarenhas has asked you to marry him, has he not?"

"Yes."

"Today?"

"Yes."

"And what did you say? He did not look like a successful lover."

"I'm to write to him."

"Well, thank God for that. I was afraid you had been fool enough to refuse him outright. It's a good match, Juana; a better one, I think, than you understand. Your mother planned it for you in your cradle. You would not want to flout her dying wishes? Besides, there are the rest of us to be considered. When my mother made you her heir, she gave you a great responsibility. Now is the time to face it, Juana, and decide what you will do with it. The French are coming; make no mistake about that. And when they get here, your flimsy document of Dom John's is not going to be worth the paper it's written on. As I see it, you have three courses of action open to you."

"Oh?" She wished she could see any way of avoiding this.

"Yes. First, you marry Senhor de Mascarenhas, who adores you and is strong enough to protect both you and the castle. Second, you take that poor thing of an Englishman who has been dancing attendance on you all this time, hand over the castle to your cousins, and go back to England. I think you'd be mad to do it, but that's your affair."

"And the third thing I can do?"

"What I have always urged on you, Juana; what God intended for you. Give the castle to your cousins and take the veil yourself. That's where true happiness lies for you. I have already spoken to a friend of mine, the head of a convent in Lisbon. They will welcome you with open arms." He was standing over her now, black and oddly threatening.

"No!" She jumped to her feet. "Never that, Uncle. I tell you, I have no vocation. Nor, since we are talking so frankly, have I any idea of marrying Mr. Varlow. As to Senhor de Mascarenhas, I will tell you what I told him, that I am going to think it over."

"Don't take too long," he said.

228

September drifted into October. Juana woke each morning in her new turret room to see the castle islanded in autumn mist, so that it seemed more than ever a fairy place, cut off from the real world.

"Iago says this is Sebastian's weather." Maria was brushing Juana's hair by the open window.

"Sebastian?"

"You know, *menina*. The lost King who will come again when things are at the worst, and save us. Iago says he has slept for two hundred years on a secret island somewhere out there in the ocean. If the French really invade, he will sail up the Tagus with a fleet and drive them out."

"Surely you don't believe that, Maria?"

"I don't know, senhora. On a morning like this, anything seems possible. And they all believe it down in the valley. He'll come here first, you know."

"Here?"

"Don't you know the story? He never married, poor King Sebastian, but there was a Spanish lady, here, at the Castle on the Rock. She was the last person he visited before he sailed away to Morocco, and, they say, when he comes back, he will come here first to look for her. Who knows? Perhaps he will find her. Perhaps she is sleeping down there in the cliff somewhere, and will wake when his ship sails into the cove. One kiss and he will mount his horse and ride away to beat the French as they have never been beaten before. That's why no one's doing anything, don't you see? They're waiting . . ."

Juana sighed. What was the use of arguing? She was beginning to hope that Maria and Iago would make a match of it, and if this meant that Maria must share her future husband's superstitions, she felt she had best not interfere. Besides, she thought, running down the winding stair to her grandmother's rooms below, Maria's idea was not much more fantastic than the situation it explained. Almost a month had ebbed away since the French ultimatum had expired and the ambassadors had left, and, simply, nothing had happened. Dom John was still at Mafra and Carlota

Joaquina at Ramalhao; the old mad Queen wailed up and down the orange walks at Queluz and, according to Senhor Macarao, who went there most weeks, life in Lisbon went on as usual: "But the English are beginning to leave."

Was there a note of warning in his voice? There might well be. She seemed caught up in the general inertia. It was more than two weeks since Vasco had asked her to marry him and still she had decided nothing. When she tried to think about it, to think about Vasco, there was nothing but a strange blankness. When she was with him, it had been easy to imagine marrying him; now he was gone, it seemed quite fantastic. But she must decide soon, for all their sakes. Which meant, surely, that she must decide to marry him.

She put it off from day to day. There was always a good reason. After all, a French invasion had been threatened the year before and nothing had come of it. Might not Napoleon change his mind once again and march off in some quite different direction? The news of the British bombardment of Copenhagen and seizure of the Danish fleet, though it shocked her deeply, yet had its element of hope. It might rouse Napoleon to turn that way and give the unlucky Danes a lesson in neutrality. Surely she could wait for the news that a French army of invasion had actually started before making up her mind? Besides, she could not marry Vasco without telling him of her connection with the Sons of the Star, and she could not possibly do that without first warning Gair Varlow. It was a relief to have decided this, though she knew in her heart that once again she was merely making excuses.

The grape harvest had begun, and provided her with an admirable pretext for avoiding the anxious, questioning glances that haunted her in the castle. Since her grandmother's illness, she had found herself, inevitably, acting as Senhor Macarao's final authority, and spent much of her time down in the valley watching the great baskets of grapes brought in to the press. It was just part of the general madness of things that she was at the same time thinking of marrying Vasco, who would help with the estate, and almost in the same mental breath imagining herself fleeing to England as the French invaded. Who would run things then? She supposed Roberto or Pedro would have to come home, but they had not been to the castle since August. Even the news of their grandmother's illness had brought merely letters of apology and condolence. No doubt they were entirely occupied in

230

helping their royal master and mistress respectively to do nothing.

There was no sign of Gair either as the bright October days drew on and the *gallegos* down in the valley were once more at work treading the ice-cold must. Senhor Macarao, returning from Lisbon, reported that the English were now leaving in droves—"They are paying as much as much as £ 1200 for a family's passage."

Once again the remark held a warning, but she had her answer to herself ready now. She could do nothing till she had talked to Gair. He must be busy helping to arrange for the repatriation of the English; but he was bound to visit her on the day after the next meeting. The full moon was on October 16th. She would make up her mind on the seventeenth.

It meant making Vasco wait a whole month for his answer and something in her was frightened at this. At last, under pressure from Miguel, she wrote him a note of explanation and apology. Of course she could not give the true reasons for her delay, but there were plenty of false ones. Her grandmother was so ill . . . she herself was busy beyond thought directing the vintage ... she was thinking, deeply, about him ... she hoped he would forgive and understand her delay ...

Sending Iago off with the letter, she found herself wondering whether it might not bring Vasco back in person to plead his suit once more. If he came, if he touched her with those incendiary hands of his, would she forget everything, forget what she owed to Gair, forget her own doubts and yield to him?

She did not know whether she was glad or sorry when Iago returned to report that Senhor de Mascarenhas had been away from home, but that his servants had promised he would be sent the letter without delay. "They seemed to expect it, senhora."

Of course they did. But Vasco would expect a definite answer. Suddenly she remembered the moment, at their last meeting, when he had exploded into rage. She was glad she would not be there when he read her temporising letter.

She had grown almost used to going down the winding stair by now, but when she slid back the secret panel for the October meeting, she was at once conscious of a new tension in the air.

"... just returned from Bayonne," the leader was saying.

"Junot arrived there the day before I did, to take command of the French army. He had messages for me from Napoleon. We have the Emperor's promise, Brothers."

"His promise of what, exactly?" Juana was sure this was the Brother of the Silver Serpent even before she saw the emblem on his hood.

"That as soon as they have Portugal under control, they will hand over to us."

"And what must we do in exchange?"

"See to it that their entry to the country is unopposed. And that, evidently, is to our own advantage. Without bloodshed, with the royal family gone to Brazil, we have the ideal opportunity to give Portugal, at last, a democratic government."

There was an enthusiastic murmur round the table. But, "Without bloodshed?" asked the Brother of the Hand.

"With as little as possible," qualified the leader. "We all know that there are some enemies of Portugal who must be disposed of before we can begin to think of freedom. You know your duties, Brothers. On the day Dom John goes on board ship you strike, each your appointed victim. In the meantime, it is understood that we each, in our own way, do all we can to help in the French invasion. First, of course, we deny that it is happening. Napoleon himself intends to leave for Italy in order to throw dust in his enemies' eyes. We will make much of this. We will stress that last year the French threatened to come, and did not. Then, when the news of their invasion can no longer be denied, we insist that the French will have the mountains to cross ... the weather will be against them ... how can they get here before winter sets in? You, Brother of the Broken Cross, will keep Dom John at Mafra as long as you possibly can. When he does come to Lisbon, it must be simply to embark with the fleet."

"And his life will be spared?" The Brother of the Broken Cross rose to his feet. "He's a good enough man, in his way."

"If he leaves for Brazil, he is safe. The same goes for his wife and all their family. But if any of them stay behind, for whatever reason, whether by chance or by design, the Brother responsible for them knows his duty. We cannot let any squeamish scruples stand between Portugal and her day of freedom."

"Will there be free elections?" asked the Brother of the Broken Cross.

"As soon as the country is ready for them." It seemed a

232

doubtful enough promise to Juana, but the Brothers greeted it with a shout of approval. There was little further business. Questioned by the Brother of the Ragged Staff the leader said he did not know exactly how soon the French army planned to march. "Very likely we will have one more meeting, Brothers, here in secret, before we emerge into the light of day, masters of our country. And now, we meet only to part ..."

Juana slid the secret panel shut. One more meeting. It was more than time that she made up her mind. She would tell Gair everything when he came next day. Somehow, in doing so, she felt she would come to a decision.

She made an excuse, next morning, not to go down to the Pleasant Valley, where the vintage was almost finished. When Gair arrived, she would suggest they ride down there together. In the meantime, she sat with Daisy and Teresa in the Ladies' Parlour and pretended to learn a new speech from Shakspeare's plays: "If it were done when 'tis done ..." Daisy had suggested it: "If you can do that, with all its 't's and 'd's,' you can do anything."

But it was hard to concentrate today, knowing that Junot was with the French army ready to strike. Or might they not have marched already? It must have taken the leader some little time to get back from Bayonne. How did she know the French had not been close behind him?

Elvira drifted into the room. "I hear the sound of galloping hoofs. Danger threatens—"

"You'll never rhyme with that," said Teresa cheerfully.

"Someone is coming!" Daisy jumped up and ran to the window that overlooked the central courtyard. "It's Pedro and Roberto!"

"At last." Teresa joined her at the window. "But they're not coming up here."

"They're going to their father's rooms," Daisy said. "I wonder what that means."

"So do I." They exchanged a long glance.

Time ebbed and flowed and still there was no sign of the two young men. At last Daisy rose and left the room. Returning, "I've been round the cloisters," she said. "There's a terrible argument going on up in Uncle Prospero's rooms. You can hear them from the courtyard; all of them; shouting. What do you think it's about?"

"Us, I hope," said Teresa.

Juana hoped so too, but could not help being afraid they

233

were talking about her. Suppose Dom John had revoked his certificate of citizenship ... or, more likely, suppose the others had come round to Miguel and Vasco's way of thinking: had decided it was worthless. Any minute, they might appear and press her for a decision. And Gair had not come. She had not made up her mind.

"Here they come," said Daisy. "Is my hair tidy?" She joined Teresa at a big tarnished looking-glass.

"Miguel's with them," said Teresa. "I can hear his voice."

The four men entered the Ladies' Parlour and Roberto and Pedro went straight to Teresa and Daisy. Prospero looked red with anger, Juana saw, and Miguel even paler than usual. "What is it?" she asked.

"Bad news," Miguel told her. "Roberto has secret information that the French army of invasion has marched from Bayonne, with Junot at its head. The moment of decision has come, Juana. And God has sent you His warning. Do you remember the day the earth shook?"

"Yes, indeed." It had been a very small earthquake, but had panicked Manuela and Estella.

"That was the day Junot left the Tuileries to join the army. It is the writing on the wall. Portugal is doomed. There is nothing left but prayer."

"That's not what my sons think." Prospero had calmed down somewhat. "Juana! These ridiculous boys want to get married at once. What do you think of that?"

How odd it was to be consulted as if she were a power in the family. She was aware of Daisy and Teresa anxiously watching her. Prospero had spoken in Portuguese, but doubtless their lovers had explained the situation. "It seems a good idea to me," she said in English.

"We must," said Pedro. "I have to go to Spain tomorrow on my mistress's errand. I cannot leave things here like this."

"And God knows when I'll be able to get away from Mafra again," said Roberto.

"But if Dom John knows the French have marched?" Juana asked in Portuguese. "Won't he do something? Come to Queluz at least?"

"I don't know." Roberto too spoke in Portuguese, then translated quickly into English for Teresa. "He's keeping the news secret. For my sake you must say nothing about it. And it seems to make no difference to him. Only God knows what will become of us all."

"Yes," said Miguel, "so let us trust in God."

"But let us act for ourselves," said Pedro. "Daisy agrees."

"So does Teresa," said Roberto. "It will be a strange sort of wedding, my poor love, since I must ride back to Mafra this afternoon, but at least you will have the protection of my name." He turned to Juana. "Where is Father Ignatius?"

"Father—?" she looked at Pedro. "He never came back."

"If you really insist," Prospero seemed to have given in. "We must send to Sintra for a priest."

"Yes," said Miguel. "And, while you are sending—if this madness is towards—Juana, why not send for Senhor de Mascarenhas?"

"Send?" She was appalled at the suggestion.

"For your cousin. Pedro and Roberto are right, you know. I may not approve, but I understand. This is the way to safety for you Englishwomen. Junot is not a man to be trifled with, Juana. He's a man of the people, rough, determined. No use showing him a piece of paper and saying in your singer's voice, 'But I'm Portuguese.' He would kill himself laughing; kill you, very likely, and take the castle. And where does that leave the rest of us?"

Where indeed? Juana caught Roberto's eye fixed anxiously on her. She had made him promise to tell no one of her plan to share the estate with him and Pedro, and thought he had kept his word, but could well understand that he must think this the time to come out with it. And after all, why not? She no longer deluded herself that there was any hope of her grandmother's recovering. The old lady was dwindling from day to day. It could only be a question of weeks now. And Senhor Gonçalves had said, even before this illness, that he did not think a new will would stand, if she should decide to make one.

She looked round. They were her family. She could not really understand why she had not told them sooner. It would simplify everything. If she could sign a document, now, making over her rights in the castle to her cousins, the question of her marrying Vasco need not enter into it. Then she could decide about his suit freely, without reference to anything or anyone else. The castle would be safe, and she a free agent. "Uncle," she spoke to Miguel, who had kept his pale gaze fixed on her, "it's not like that. There's something I ought to tell you—should have told you sooner, perhaps." She had meant to consult Gair before she decided anything. It was too late now. She plunged into her explanation, in Portuguese, with a parenthetical apology for Daisy and Tere-

235

sa: "I can't d—d—I can't manage in English." Concluding, she turned from Miguel to Prospero: "So if we send for Senhor Gonçalves at once," she said, "I'm sure he can draw up some kind of document that will protect us all."

Miguel's voice drowned Pedro's and Roberto's as they translated rapidly for the girls' benefit: "Have you consulted Senhor de Mascarenhas about this?"

"No. Why should I? I shall tell him, of course, when I see him."

"I think you should tell him first," said Miguel.

"I would if I could." She wondered if this was true. "But he's away. I have not had an answer yet to the letter I wrote him. And you yourself say there is no time to be lost."

"Yes," said Prospero. "If you really mean this, Juana, I think we should act on it at once. I must say, it's a most generous . . ."

She missed the rest of his speech of thanks because Daisy and Teresa flung their arms round her neck to kiss and thank her. The little scene was interrupted by Jaime, announcing Gair Varlow.

"Goodness," said Daisy. "You'll need to tell him too, Juana."

"Yes," said Teresa, "but he was courting Juana before there was any question of the castle." She laughed and shook her blond curls. "What a dark horse you are, Juana."

Miguel had been giving quick orders to Jaime. "I'll write a note to Gonçalves," he said. "The priest from Sintra will get here first, but you had best delay your marriages until the lawyer arrives."

"Marriages?" Gair Varlow had followed Jaime into the crowded room. "Who am I to congratulate?" He could be relied on to speak English when Daisy and Teresa were present.

"Me," said Daisy.

"And me," said Teresa.

"Or rather, my brother and me," said Roberto. "Perhaps you will stay, Senhor Varlow, and honour us with your presence at our joint wedding?" And then, to Prospero, "As for the lawyer, we will wait as long as possible, but I must get back to Mafra tonight."

"And I to Ramalhao," said Pedro. "I leave for Spain tomorrow."

"You are indeed marrying in haste," said Gair.

"Not, I hope, to repent at leisure," broke in Teresa.

"No, indeed." Roberto's quelling look reminded the others that they must not speak of the French invasion.

"I wonder," Gair pursued the point. "Does this mean that there is some truth in the story I have heard that your master, Dom John, is about to sign a decree closing Portuguese ports to British ships?"

"You are well informed, senhor." Roberto looked relieved. This was a question he could answer. "Yes, I'm afraid it is true, the order will be signed any time now. That is partly why I am here today. It is the moment of decision for the few English who remain in this country. Fortunately my cousin Juana need no longer be considered as English, since my master has declared her Portuguese."

"You think it will hold?" Gair asked.

"For an individual, yes. For the owner of an immense property, I'm not sure. But, cousin"—he turned to Juana—"have I your permission to tell Senhor Varlow of your most generous offer?"

"Why not?" She realised, with bitter amusement, that Daisy and Teresa were all agog to see how Gair would take the discovery that she was not to be an heiress after all. How much more comic it would be if they knew he was not her suitor, that all the courtship of this long year had been nothing but an elaborate, intolerable charade. Still, at least, he had wooed her—pretended to woo her—for reasons of state, not for sordid considerations of money and land. It brought her up suddenly against the question of Vasco. Had she been foolish not to think that he might be courting her partly—wholly?, asked a voice at the back of her mind—for the castle? Had Gair's pretended courtship blinded her to the possibility of another one?

But she must get Gair alone to tell him the news of last night's meeting. For once, this proved easy enough. He had agreed to stay and witness the weddings, and since there was no chance of the priest arriving before dinner-time she was able to suggest, as she had planned, that he ride down the Pleasant Valley with her.

"The French army has marched," she told him as soon as they were out of earshot of the castle. "Under Junot. The Sons of the Star had the news last night; Roberto brought it this morning. Apparently Dom John knows, but means to keep it a secret. God knows why."

"I can imagine plenty of reasons," said Gair. "None of them to his credit. But, Juana, it makes me more anxious than ever about you. And this handing over the castle to your cousins: do you think that was wise?"

"Why not? It safeguards me better than anything, doesn't it?"

"I don't know. There's something special about the Castle on the Rock—something I've never quite understood. More, I've thought, than its connection with the Sons of the Star. Your grandmother said something one day— If only she could speak. Is there any hope?"

"None I'm afraid. It's only a question of time now. But, Gair, about the castle. Maria told me something odd the other day. She and Iago are very thick these days—I'm sure he must have told her. You know how superstitious he is. Anyway, she told me, quite seriously, that this was the last place the lost King Sebastian visited before he sailed for Morocco. She and Iago think he'll come here first when he returns to save Portugal. You know the story?"

"Of course, But why here?"

"There was—a lady, Maria says. He visited her last thing and will come to her when he returns. Maria thinks she is asleep somewhere in the caverns below the castle, waiting for him. He'll some sailing out of the mist, she says, and land in the cove down there. Really, when she was telling me, and staring out at the sea mist—you know what these October mornings are like—she almost had me convinced that we'd see a sixteenth-century galleon come sailing into the cove. Or would he have got himself a modern ship, do you think?"

"God knows what they expect. But it's no laughing matter, Juana. It's not only Maria and Iago who believe this foolishness."

"I know. Maria told me. They all believe it down in the valley."

"Yes, and elsewhere too. Up and down the country the peasants are waiting for Sebastian to come again and save them from the French. We've had reports from all over. It's not natural. Someone must have revived the old superstition for their own ends, but why? That's what we can't find out. But I had no idea there was a connection between Sebastian and the Castle on the Rock. That puts a new complexion on things. His mistress is supposed to be sleeping somewhere down in the caverns, you say?"

"That's what Maria says. Do you think there can be a connection with the Sons of the Star?"

"That's what I'm wondering. But what would it be? They've mentioned Sebastian?"

"No. There's nothing exactly superstitious about them. It's just a lot of ritual and mumbo-jumbo."

"Don't underestimate them, Juana. It's too dangerous. And, of course, they'd use Sebastianism if it suited their book. Which it well might, if only to keep the country quiet while the French take over. If the Portuguese are waiting for a supernatural saviour . . . And he's to come here to the castle first? I don't like that. Have you thought what might happen when the British squadron arrives as, please God, it will any day now? Suppose the peasants think it's Sebastian to the rescue? Anything might happen. Juana, if Dom John closes the ports, this week's Falmouth packet will be the last one. I think you must be on it. Lord Strangford will get you a passage."

"But Gair, the next meeting? It may be vital."

"Your safety is more so. And, besides, I've thought of that. We're of a height, you and I. Remember Viola and Sebastian. And you say voices aren't recognisable in the cavern. What's to stop me dressing in your robes and acting, that once, as Handmaiden of the Star? You can show me the way down before you go, and teach me the words."

"Gair, you'd do that for me?"

"Of course. After all, you've done it for me all this time."

"Not at all. I've done it for my grandmother. And that's the difficulty, Gair. I don't see how I can leave her now, sick as she is."

"Nonsense. Your stepsisters can look after her. After all, they're marrying into the family."

"Yes, that's true." Was she making excuses again? "When does the packet sail?"

"Tomorrow or the next day. You must decide quickly, Juana. I will have to make the arrangements at once. Believe me, it's the only thing to do."

"Gair, it's too soon. I can't."

"Why not? You admit that your stepsisters can look after the old lady. You've given up your inheritance here, and I respect you for it. You've often said you were homesick for England. Now's your chance to go home. You must see, Juana, that when the Sons of the Star find themselves betrayed they are going to look everywhere for the traitor. I tell you, it's not safe for you to stay."

"But if they are destroyed?"

"You're not thinking. What chance have we of destroying them all? With luck, and a detachment of Royal Marines, we may be able to deal with their headquarters here before the French arrive, but that still leaves the branches in the rest of the country. And, remember, the French will protect them."

"Yes. They think the French are going to hand over the government to them."

"They won't, of course." It was time to turn back up the Pleasant Valley. "But either way you are in danger. If it's a question of what to do when you get back to England, Vanessa will be really glad to have you. I had another letter from her by the packet. Forland's obviously very far from well ... and there's the child on the way ... She wants you to name your own terms—"

"I shan't be entirely penniless, you know, if I decide to go. I'm not touched in the head. I shall take an income from the estate here. That's one of the things the lawyer will have to arrange."

"You'll hardly get that when the French take over."

"You keep talking as if they are bound to."

"I'm afraid they are. It's not like you to refuse to face facts, Juana. The best we can hope for now is that the royal family get safe away to Brazil to act as a rallying point for the future."

"And that, it seems, the Sons of the Star intend to allow. It's even what they want."

"Yes. Don't you see, it's possible that our best plan would be to let the Sons of the Star continue ... to let them find out just how hollow Napoleon's promises are. Who knows? In a year's time, they themselves might provide the backbone of the revolt."

"You mean, there may not be a detachment of Marines at their next meeting?"

"Nothing's decided yet. We don't even know when the British squadron will get here. That's why you must leave on the packet, Juana."

They were back where they had started from. "But I can't. There's someone I have to see first."

He pounced on it. "Now we are coming to it. Who do you have to see that is more important than liberty, than life perhaps?"

She was in for it now. "It's my cousin Vasco. He has asked me to marry him and is waiting for my answer. I wanted to

240

talk to you about it, Gair, because of the Sons of the Star. You see, I would have to tell him . . ."

"Vasco de Mascarenhas?" This white calm masked seething rage. "Now I know you are out of your mind. You can't possibly be thinking of marrying him! A bastard who has spent a fortune on forged documents to prove his legitimacy? And a fortune, mind you, of most suspicious origin. I wanted to spare you this, Juana, since he's a member of your family, even if on the wrong side of the blanket. It never in my wildest dreams occurred to me that you could be such a fool as to let him pull the wool over your eyes. Naturally, I had him investigated as soon as I saw how he was dangling after you—and a very unconvincing job he made of it, I may say. You don't for a minute deceive yourself, do you, that it is for your *beaux yeux* he has been courting you? If only there were time, I would be glad for you to have one more meeting with him, so you could see how he changes his tune once he knows you are giving away the castle. Frankly, Juana, it's the first time I have ever thought you stupid, but I suppose there are none so blind as those who will not see."

"Thank you! I suppose you think I should be an expert, by now, in pseudo-courtships." She dug her heels into Sheba's side. "Tell your sister she can keep her charity," she threw back at him over her shoulder. "I shall stay in Portugal with my family."

"Juana—" He thundered up beside her as she rode through the cluster of peasant houses. "Listen to me. I'm sorry: I've been a fool; I lost my temper; I've done it all wrong. Juana, please—"

She was crying, and would not let him see it. She forced Sheba to the edge of the road so that, sitting sidesaddle, she could keep her back to him. If Vasco had been there just then, she would have accepted him.

In fact, he rode into the castle courtyard a little later, with the friar from Sintra, and sent Jaime to Juana with the request that she see him at once, alone.

Juana had never felt so completely at a loss. Jaime had delivered the message to her in the Ladies' Parlour where the entire party had assembled before moving into the dining room. "I've put him in your study, senhora." Jaime evidently expected her to see Vasco.

"But it's dinner-time." She was making excuses again.

"Dinner can wait," said Miguel. "You owe it to Senhor de Mascarenhas at least to see him, Juana."

241

She knew it was true, but still hedged. "Surely, after dinner
..."

"Don't see him at all," said Gair Varlow. "Remember
what I said to you, Juana."

"I certainly do." She had not spoken to him since they had
returned to the castle. "Tell my cousin I will see him at once,
Jaime. And ask the cook to hold back dinner." She managed
to get out of the room on her wave of anger, without
meeting Gair's eyes.

Since the room she now used as her study was merely
down two steps and along a short passage from the Ladies'
Parlour, she had little time to compose her thoughts for the
meeting with Vasco. "Cousin, I'm glad to see you." She heard
Jaime close the heavy door behind her and noticed with a
little stab, surely, of fear, how completely it cut off the sound
of voices from the room beyond.

"Juana!" For once, Vasco was formally dressed in dark
coat and foaming lace cravat. "He's dressed for his wedding," she thought, as he made a long business of kissing her
hand. As always, his touch sent a thrill of fire through her. A
bastard, Gair had said. That was not important, but something else was. A bastard who had spent a fortune on forged
papers. Why should Gair have made that up?

"Juana," Vasco said again. "Have you nothing to say to
me?" He still had her hand and led her to the seat behind her
desk. Seating her, he stood over her, his hand on her shoulder.

It was disconcerting to have lost the advantage of height.
She looked up at him. "Cousin, I'm sorry I've taken so
long—"

"You're driving me mad," he interrupted her. "But no
matter, so long as the answer is right at last. That friar told
me he is to marry your sisters this afternoon. What could be
more suitable than that you and I should join them? Juana!"

She was still hearing Gair's voice: "A fortune, mind you,
of most suspicious origin." What had Gair to gain by lying to
her? "I don't know—" She looked up at Vasco pleadingly. "I
don't really know you, cousin."

"Not know me!" For a moment she had been afraid that
he would explode, as he had done once before, into rage, but
his tone was quiet. "It's true, of course," he surprised her by
saying. "I know that in England you go a different way about
marriage. But this is Portugal, Juana, and time is short. Your
cousins are marrying your sisters, this afternoon, to give

242

them the protection of a Portuguese name. Let me do the same for you, my love, and I promise you, that's all I will ask. I too will ride away, when evening comes, as they must, and wait for the day when you will send for me and make me the happiest of men. Juana! Say yes, or, better still, say nothing, let me take your answer from your lips."

Somehow, despite herself, she managed to turn her head away. "But the castle——" she said.

"The castle?"

"I have to tell you, before we decide anything. I'm giving it to my cousins."

"Oh, that." He shrugged. "There'll be time enough to think of that when you are safe from the French. Marry me today, Juana, and leave the burden of all this decision to me. I tell you, my darling, I know much better than you, what is right for you."

"Do you?" She longed to be convinced.

"Of course I do." Now, at last, he swept her into his embrace. She was drowning, suffocating, helpless in his arms.

Then, suddenly, without decision, without thought even, she had pulled away, was across the room from him, breathing hard, staring at him. "You're just hurting me," she said. "It's not true. Not a word of it." And left him.

CHAPTER 21

"You refused him, thank God." Vasco had left at once, the strange weddings were over, and Gair and Juana were alone on the seaward terrace.

"Yes. But not because of your tale-bearing." A lie? She supposed so. If Gair had not alerted her, would she have recognised the brute force Vasco had tried to disguise as passion? But then, turn it the other way out: had Gair's warning perhaps made her unnecessarily suspicious? Had she misunderstood Vasco as hopelessly as, once before, she had Gair himself? Who was she to think she could tell real from pretended passion? Had she sent away the only man who really loved her? At the time, her reaction had been automatic. She had been stifling, frightened ... But had she been right?

Gair had turned away to gaze out across the cliff to the tossing white sea beyond. "I'm sorry." When he turned back to her, a flush along his cheekbones betrayed how hard her remark had hit him. "You think me a poor creature, don't you?"

"I think you what you are: a secret agent."

"A spy. But thank you for using the kinder phrase. It's more than I deserve. Juana, I've learned a great deal this last year. I know now that what I have done to you is unforgivable."

"Oh?" Now it was her turn to lean her elbows on the terrace wall and gaze blindly out to sea.

"I brought you here, last year, for my own ends. You've served them admirably. Your country owes you a great deal, Juana; both your countries. But I never thought what was going to happen to you. You do see now, don't you, that if the French take Lisbon, it's not safe for you to be here?"

"Yes."

"Even if you had married that cousin of yours, you'd not have been safe. Only Mrs. Brett knows how many people are aware of the connection between the castle and the Sons of the Star, and she can't tell us. Juana, please, let me arrange your passage on tomorrow's packet."

"So I can go back to England to act as companion to Lady

Forland? Penniless, because, as you yourself have pointed out, I shan't be able to draw my income from here. It's not an inspiring prospect, is it?"

"That's what I'm saying. That's why I can't forgive myself. I've used you, Juana, and done you nothing but harm."

Now, surprisingly, she was sorry for him. "Oh, no," she said, "it's not so bad as that. I've enjoyed my year here; I've learned a great deal. I've changed. Being a spy is a very educational occupation. I'll make an admirable companion for your sister—I shan't even stammer, much, thanks to what I've learned this year."

He glowed with relief. "You'll really go to Vanessa? I may arrange your passage on the packet? Thank God."

"Poor Mr. Varlow, have I weighed so heavily on your mind?" She picked up a stone from the terrace walk and threw it with all her strength out towards where foam rose high as the cliff. "And, no, I'm afraid you can't be quit of me so easily as that. You see, I can't leave Portugal until I have signed the papers handing over the castle to my cousins. It's no use getting me passage on the packet until I have seen Senhor Gonçalves." For though the priest had arrived, there was still no sign of the lawyer.

"Or some other lawyer?"

"I doubt if that would do. Gonçalves holds my grandmother's will."

"But it's not safe for you to stay."

"You're staying, aren't you?"

"For the time being. But the British squadron will arrive any day now. They will take Lord Strangford's household off."

"Well, then, if Senhor Gonçalves doesn't arrive in time, the squadron will just have to take me too. I'm sorry if it's awkward for you, but you must see it's your responsibility. If you hadn't brought me here, my grandmother would never have changed her will: the problem would not have arisen. Since it has, I look on it as your affair."

"But at least you'll come?"

"I don't see that I'll have any alternative. Thanks to you, I've infuriated my cousin. He'll be no support. Who else could I turn to?"

"Not your uncles, that's certain. Nor, probably, your other cousins. But, Juana, about Mascarenhas: please, believe me, believe I acted for the best."

"Whose best, I wonder? But it's time we went in."

245

"Not quite yet." He stood between her and the entrance to the castle, pale and quiet, an extraordinary contrast to Vasco de Mascarenhas. "Juana, listen to me for a few minutes more. I told you I had heard from Vanessa. It's true, what I said, that she'd be delighted to have you with her, on any terms. But there was more. Forland must be very ill. He's—setting his house in order. He's promised her one of his boroughs—for me."

"You mean—a seat in Parliament?"

"Yes. At last. It's what I've always wanted. But when Forland first married Vanessa he would do nothing for me. Well, why should he? But now, everything's changed. Vanessa says she thinks someone must have spoken to him: one of the new Government. He told her to write me, to say the seat was mine when it fell vacant—which should be soon—and with no strings."

"No strings? You mean, to vote as you please?"

"Yes. It's the most extraordinary thing anyone has ever done for me. A safe seat, given to me—a Whig—without obligation, by a Tory. And the odd thing is—I've said this to no one—but I think, in fact, I shall vote Tory, at least until this war is over. But that's not what I wanted to say to you." He had seen her quick, anxious glance back at the castle. "Juana, do you realise what this means? I've my foot on the ladder at last. Give me a seat in the House and I promise you, sooner or later, I'll be my own man, on my feet, hiding from no one, beholden to no one. No more 'tale-bearing' then, Juana."

"I'm sorry." She wished she had not said it.

"Don't be. I'd do more than carry tales if it would help to save you from Vasco de Mascarenhas. Juana, I beg of you, most earnestly, don't change your mind; don't think of trusting him."

"He's my cousin." She was angry all over again.

"And I'm nothing. I'm the man who has made such a botch of your life for you. But, Juana, at last I begin to think I may have a future. If I have, will you share it with me?"

She looked at him for a moment in silence, then swallowed a bitter mouthful of rage and spoke: "Do you think things are as bad as that, Mr. Varlow? That, once more, the only way to keep me in line is to offer marriage? Not that you even did so at Forland House, did you? A hint was enough then, was it not? Well, I tell you, I don't fool so easily these days. Had you not best go down on your knees and make me

a proposal in form? God knows you've had enough practice!"
And then, furious with herself, with him, with everything:
"Don't waste your time here, Mr. Varlow. Had you not
better get back to your spying?"

"But, Juana—"

"Don't." She was tempted to leave him there and then, but
thought better of it. "We have to go on working together till
this is over. Please don't make it any more difficult for me
than it already is. Let us pretend that the last few minutes
never happened. So—how shall I let you know if Senhor
Gonçalves arrives and I am free to leave on the packet?"

"Simply write me and ask for a passage. There can be no
harm in that. But, Juana, please—"

"No." She moved towards the castle door. "Time enough
when my passage is arranged to show you the way down the
winding stair. But, do you know, I have the strangest feeling
that Senhor Gonçalves is not going to appear."

The slow days were to prove her right. An apologetic note
from the lawyer arrived two days later. He had been out of
town on urgent business; had only just received their summons; was still unable to come for a few days. His messenger
brought news, as well as his note. The last Falmouth packet
had sailed that day.

So that was that. Juana had said nothing to her family
about going back to England. It would be impossibly difficult
to explain the decision without reference to the Sons of the
Star. Much easier to say nothing until the moment came to
leave. Now, apparently, she was committed to waiting for the
British squadron. There was nothing to be said, nothing to be
done. Gair Varlow must know that the packet had sailed
without her. It was up to him now.

A few days later came the news that Dom John had signed
the decree closing Portuguese ports to British shipping. Still,
incredibly, the fact that the French army of invasion had
actually marched had not been made public. Nor had there
been any word from Pedro or Roberto, who had ridden
away, reluctantly, on their wedding night.

"Pedro's in Spain, of course," said Daisy.

"And Roberto warned me he wouldn't write, because it
was not safe," explained Teresa.

They were taking their strange marriages admirably, Juana
thought, liking them better than ever. It encouraged her to
suggest that they begin to help both with the care of Mrs.

247

Brett and the running of the estate. "You never know," she said vaguely.

"Of course we'll help," said Daisy.

"We didn't like to seem pushing," said Teresa.

Old Mrs. Brett was beyond noticing who sat with her now, and Manuela and Estella were hardly up to the responsibility. It was a relief to install sensible Daisy and calm Teresa in the sickroom in their stead. The doctor came every few days and said, always, the same thing: "It's only a matter of time."

Juana felt guilty because she did not feel more. She and her grandmother had been partners; she owed her a great deal; she ought to mind, and found she did not. She did her best to make up for it by devoted attention, until Daisy and Teresa protested, insisting that they do their share.

They were right, she thought. They must begin to learn her duties in the castle. And, soon, she must warn them that she would be leaving—she hoped she would be leaving—when the British squadron arrived.

But nothing happened. She now sent a man into Lisbon every day for news. And there was no news. Trade was at a standstill; the English had all gone save Lord Strangford's people; Lisbon was full of rumours, and nothing else. Dom John remained at Mafra, and the army on the coast as if the only enemy was to be expected from there. Even the Portuguese fleet, in Lisbon harbour, shared the general inertia. When the French ultimatum had been received, back in August, they had taken on stores for a possible voyage to the Brazils. They had done nothing since.

"Half their provisions must be mouldy by now," said Daisy. Since she and Teresa had become Portuguese by marriage they had begun to take a lively interest in the news.

"I'm glad I shan't have to make the voyage," said Teresa.

"You don't think Roberto might have to go with Dom John?" Juana had wondered about this.

"He said he wouldn't," said Teresa.

Juana was both surprised and relieved. It had been a strange enough business, that double wedding, and seemed stranger still in retrospect. "I wish Senhor Gonçalves would come," she said now. It was two weeks since the lawyer had been sent for and still he sent merely apologies. The trouble was, Juana thought, that without referring to her danger from the Sons of the Star it was impossible to make him see how urgent her business was. Quite understandably, he delayed in Lisbon, seeing to the selling up of estates for his many other English clients. Like everyone else, he must assume that she was committed to life at the Castle on the Rock. That there was no hurry . . .

More and more, she wished that she had not parted from Gair Varlow in anger. However enraged by his proposal, she should not have let herself forget that he was, simply, her only hope. Not that she need be frightened of the Sons of the Star yet. There was no reason, so far, for them to suspect her. But she was frightened, just the same. She made a point of never leaving the castle alone and preferred to have company even on the terrace or loggia. It was impossible not to remember what had happened to Tomas—and what about Father Ignatius? No word had ever come from the priest and in her heart she was convinced that he had been the Brother of the Lion who had been so ruthlessly executed at the July meeting of the Sons of the Star. If they did discover how she had been betraying them, she would be lucky to suffer so quick a punishment.

Last thing every night, she checked on the inside bolt at the entrance to the winding stair simply for the reassurance of seeing it strong and solid on her side of the door. At least, in this room, she knew where the secret entrance was. She did not much like being alone anywhere else in the castle. If only Gair Varlow would come, pooh-pooh her terrors, and tell her when the British squadron was expected. Impossible, she found, to go on being angry with him. No doubt his proposal had been kindly meant. It had been, obviously, his way of making amends for the danger in which he had involved her. She wished, now, that she had not lost her temper.

But what was the use of wishing? He did not come. Nobody came. There had been no word from Vasco since he had ridden out of the castle courtyard two weeks before— "In a flaming rage," Daisy had reported. "I'd keep away from him for a while, Juana."

There was no need. He kept away from them. "I feel like a Princess in a fairy story," Daisy said, surprisingly, one sultry evening. "You know, in a magic castle where nothing ever happens."

"I do know." Juana fought a yawn. "But by the news from Lisbon the whole country's in the same state."

"Waiting for Sebastian?" asked Teresa. "Maria was telling me about him this morning."

"The lost Prince?" Daisy laughed. "He's as likely to save us

249

as Dom John. Why don't you go to bed, Juana? You look exhausted."

"I am tired." But Juana still delayed, ashamed to admit, even to herself, that she did not much like the lonely walk down the cloisters.

"I'll see you to your stair." Had Daisy noticed her hesitation? "And we can look in on the old lady as we go. I'm to take over from Maria first thing in the morning."

In the sickroom, all was quiet. "She's hardly moved," said Maria. "It can't be long now, God rest her soul."

"No." Juana stood for a minute by the bed. It was hard to believe that last year this frail husk of a woman had been the dominant creature who had led her, for the first time, down the winding stair. She shivered, thinking that the stair must go down past the wall of this room somewhere. "Take good care of her, Maria," she said. "Call me if you need me."

CHAPTER 22

"Maria?" Juana woke with a start. The room was lighted: Mrs. Brett must be worse. "I'll come at once." She sat up in bed, was suddenly, horribly aware of hooded figures all round her, of movement behind her, felt a sharp blow on the side of her head and plunged into unconsciousness.

When she next woke, it was broad daylight. What an incredibly vivid dream. She reached out for the glass of water that always stood by her bed. It was not there. This was not her room. Not a dream: reality. Terror filled her to overflowing. If she started to scream, she would not be able to stop. She put her hand to her mouth and bit it hard. She was not bound. She was lying in a luxurious bed whose heavy scarlet curtains cut off her view of all but a thin slice of what appeared to be an equally ornate bedroom. What in the world?

She sat up to look about her and at once a woman's figure appeared from behind the bed curtains. A complete stranger, this old, old woman, brown and wrinkled and beyond age as only a Portuguese peasant woman can become. She smiled broadly—could it be affectionately?—at Juana. "At last," she said. "You are better, senhora?"

Better? Remembering, Juana put a tentative hand to the side of her head, and winced.

The old woman clucked her sympathy: "A terrible bruise," she said. "Let me bathe it for you, my Princess." She bustled away behind the bed curtains, to return in a moment with a cloth wrung out in spirits of lavender with which she very gently soothed away the pain. "You are better?" she asked again, with real anxiety.

"But what's happened? Where am I?" Juana's thoughts had been scurrying in so many directions at once that she could hardly get the words out. But, surely, her first terror, of the Sons of the Star, must be unfounded? It was all fantastic, incredible: dream—or nightmare?

"In my master's house, of course," answered the old woman. "And safe, thank God and his strong arm. Who else would have dared attack those wicked ones—even for you, my Princess?" She lowered her voice on the "wicked ones."

251

"The Sons—"

"Hush! It's not safe; even here. If they could carry you off from your room at the castle, senhora, they can do anything. That's why you are to stay here, safely locked in, till my master returns."

"Your master?"

"Senhor de Mascarenhas. Your cousin, senhora, who adores you. 'Look after her,' he told me, 'like the Princess she is. Tell her I will return to sup with her this evening. Tell her she is my Queen.' Those were his words, senhora. He should be home soon. Do you think you are strong enough to get up and dress?"

"He saved me?" She was still trying to sort things out.

"From a whole gang of masked ruffians. I don't need to name them ... He's wounded, of course, but nothing to signify; not my master. He had affairs to attend to, or he'd have stayed himself till you woke. He'll be back without fail, he told me, for dinner. You'll be able to join him, senhora?"

"I don't see why not. I don't understand anything." Juana pushed back the bedclothes. She was still in the cambric nightgown she had put on the night before. The night before?

"How long have I been unconscious?" she asked.

"I don't know, senhora. He brought you home this morning. They must have carried you off last night. Thank God, he was there to save you."

"Yes." It was extraordinary, fantastic ... "But I've no clothes."

"There are clothes here, senhora. Clothes for a Queen. Let me help you."

Juana was glad of her support. The ground shook under her for a moment, then steadied. "There." She stood by herself and looked about the room. It was furnished with immense luxury in the old-fashioned Portuguese style of cut velvet and flounces. The huge door, she saw, was bolted securely on the inside.

The old woman followed her eyes. "It's locked on the outside too," she said. "Just for safety's sake. My master took the key."

The clothes that hung in a huge closet struck Juana as oddly old-fashioned. And yet the stiff silks and brocades seemed quite new and unworn. "Whose are they?" she asked as the old woman helped her into a stiff, dark taffeta.

"Yours for as long as you need them, senhora." It was

hardly an answer, but Juana had more important things to think of.

"My poor family," she said. "They'll be mad with worry. Or did Senhor de Mascarenhas send to them?"

"I'm sure he has done everything that is necessary." Once again it was not quite an answer.

Juana moved over to the room's one window, an ornate gothic affair of stone and small, leaded panes. It looked far down into a courtyard, sunless now as the afternoon drew on. "I slept a long time," she said.

"Yes, thank God. You'll be none the worse, my Princess."

"Why do you keep calling me that?" It was beginning to irritate her.

The old woman looked confused. "He will explain everything," she said. "He knows what's best for us all. I was his nurse, you know, and his father's before him."

"His father's! Then you must have known my mother?"

"Indeed I did." Suddenly there were tears in the pale old eyes. "She was my Princess first. But they took her away from me, that terrible time of the Plot, and gave her to the holy sisters to rear, and I never saw her again. Oh, how I cried. For a while I thought I would never stop. They took me away to France—oh, *Jesus Maria*, what wickedness!—but there was my poor mistress, and my Seb—the young master. Oh, senhora, a Prince among men! How lucky you are!"

"What do you mean?"

She looked, surely, frightened. "I'm talking too much, because of being so glad you're here. I've asked and asked when I was going to see you, and 'soon,' he always answered, 'she will come soon.' But you must rest, my jewel, you're looking exhausted, and it's all my fault. He will be angry if I've tired you." It was evident that in her life there was only one "he," her master.

Juana was glad to subside on to a flounced velvet *chaise longue*. She closed her eyes for a minute, then opened them to watch the old woman tidying the big bed. "We're locked in together?" she asked.

"Yes. He said it would be safer."

"But in his house? This is his house—at Sintra?" She had never seen it but knew it to be somewhere high up on the outskirts of the royal village.

"Yes, of course. But we've so few servants. Not enough to protect you from Them."

"I see." What use would a locked door be against the Sons

253

of the Star? There was something very strange about the whole situation. She was beginning to be frightened again. But that was absurd. Or—was it? Why were Daisy and Teresa not here already, and a detachment of men from the Pleasant Valley? "Why don't my sisters come?" she asked.

"What sisters, senhora? You have no sisters. Nor any kin save my master. Oh, but this is a happy day, to see the two of you united at last."

"United?" Now she knew she was frightened.

"I'm talking too much. He will explain." And then, with obvious relief: "I hear horses now. Let me brush your hair again, senhora. If only it was not so short—more like a boy than—" She stopped, and was very busy for a few minutes fluffing out Juana's short hair and adjusting the set of stiff taffeta sleeves and skirt. "He never liked to be kept waiting did my Seb—my master."

"What did you call him?"

"I? The master? What should I call him, but that?" And then, aware of Juana's unbelief, "Oh, some childish nickname I should have forgotten long since. Don't tell him: he'd be angry, now he's a great man."

A great man? Her cousin Vasco? "A bastard who has spent a fortune on forged documents to prove his legitimacy." Gair's remembered voice. "A fortune . . . of most suspicious origin." "Don't trust him," Gair had said. She bit her lips to stop them trembling. Where was Gair now?

A key rattled in the lock on the other side of the door.

"Here he is," said the old woman, and Juana had, for a moment, a strange feeling that she was frightened too. She moved quickly to the door on which a hand was now gently knocking.

"May I come in?" Vasco's voice.

The old woman looked at Juana, her hand on the bolt. What would happen if she were to say no? "Of course," she said.

In fact, there was something very reassuring about Vasco, his usual self, casual in open-necked shirt and breeches, hot from riding, shining from a quick wash, hurrying across the room to take her hand. "Cousin, you're none the worse?"

"Nothing but a slight headache. I owe you a world of thanks, it seems. It's the second time you've saved me, cousin."

"Thank God I was able to." His lips were hot on her hand. His other arm was bandaged. "You're hurt! What hap-

254

pened? I don't understand anything. And where are my family?"

"There's so much to explain. And, Juana, this is no place for us to talk. Your bedroom!" His glance lingered for a moment on the huge four-poster. "Will you not come down and sup with me?"

"With pleasure!" Had she actually been afraid this luxurious room was a prison? She was glad to let him take her hand and lead her down a graceful flight of stairs to the room directly below, where a cold meal lay ready on a long table. Glancing out of the window, she saw that this room, like hers, looked down through leaded panes on to the central courtyard of the house. They were still well above ground level.

Vasco was holding her chair for her. "I'm going to wait on you myself," he said, interpreting her puzzled glance. "After what happened last night, I trust no one, not even my own servants."

"Is it as bad as that?"

"I'm afraid so."

"But what did happen?" At last she could ask the question.

"How much do you remember?"

"Very little. Only waking, with Them all around me—then the blow on my head, and nothing more till I woke again, thank God, upstairs."

"Them? But you know who?"

"The Sons of the Star, surely, though I can't think why." How much should she tell him? She took a cautious bite of cold chicken and rice, found it made her feel better, and ventured a sip of wine.

He must have sensed her hesitation. "Juana, you must trust me. Our only safety, now, lies in absolute honesty with each other."

"What do you mean? And, Vasco, have you sent to tell my family I am safe?"

"Not yet. That's what I am trying to explain. We are in danger, you and I, grave danger. For the moment, we dare trust no one, tell no one you are here."

"But my family will be desperate with worry."

"Yes. But why? Because you are missing, or because you are not dead, as the Sons of the Star intended? How do you know which of your family you can trust? Have you never noticed that they tend to separate on the nights of the meetings?"

"The meetings? You know about them?"

"Who doesn't? Nobody dares speak of them, but that's different. You haven't answered my question."

"About my family? Yes, it's true; we often do all seem to separate on the night of the full moon, but there could be so many reasons for that. I can't believe they would conspire against me."

"No? You're not facing facts. What about the party at Ramalhao? You'd be mad to trust them, any of them, after that. They'll stop at nothing to get the castle from you."

"But I've already said I'd give it to them."

"There's more to it than that. It's not only your family you have to fear, is it?" He refilled their wine glasses. "You're hedging with me, and in a way I respect you for it. Shall I make it easier for you and tell you that I have known, all year, that you were the Handmaiden of the Star?"

"You've known? Good God, but how?"

"For the best of reasons. Because I told your grandmother to send for you."

"You?" Now her confusion was complete.

"Who else?"

"But why?"

"Because I need you, Juana. Portugal needs you."

"Portugal?" What lunacy was this? Impossible, surely, that he and Gair had been working together all the time.

"It's incredible that you should not know. But you don't, do you?"

"I certainly don't know what you are talking about." Every instinct told her to play for time.

"It was safest not to tell you. Our inheritance is a great danger, Juana, as well as a great responsibility."

"You mean because of the Tavora plot? As Mascarenhas? I don't understand . . ."

"No, no." Impatiently. "Our story goes back much further than that. Do you know what my second name is?"

"Your second name?" Could he be mad?

"It's Sebastian, Juana, after our famous ancestor. And you are named for his wife. Surely you must know the story of the lost Prince Sebastian?"

"Yes, of course, But you can't mean— He was never married."

"Yes he was. Just before he sailed for Morocco, he married the lady he loved, the lady of the rock, our Spanish ancestress, the first Juana. She bore his son after the fatal battle, after his death. The times were dangerous, but her secret was well kept. When Prince Henry died and the House of Aviz was thought to be extinct, her son was only a year old; she did not dare try to claim the throne for him. All through the sixty years of Spanish occupation she lived quietly at the Castle on the Rock with her son and her grandchildren. The restoration of the House of Braganza killed her. She was a great lady, Juana, from everything I can find out about her, but her son was unworthy of her, and of his father. He made no effort to claim his inheritance or even to prove the validity of his mother's marriage. It has been left to me to do that. It has taken me years, but I have done it at last. Juana, you and I are the only surviving descendents of King Sebastian, his legitimate heirs. Your grandfather was older than mine. Since we claim through female descent you are rightful Queen of Portugal." Suddenly he was kneeling on the floor at her feet, kissing her hands. Then, just as quickly, he was standing over her, his colour high. "I can get you this crown, Juana. You know the people believe that Sebastian will return in Portugal's hour of need? Well, he will return. I, Sebastian, will return. Then you will see an end to the inertia that has gripped the country under the miserable Braganzas. I tell you, the army will follow me to a man; we will drive the French from our gates; Portugal will be itself again. Only first, Juana, to avoid any possibility of conflict, you and I must be married. You must see that."

She did indeed. She was not sure how much of the fantastic story she believed. She was not even sure how much of it he believed himself, but one thing stood out brutally clear. Because of his own illegitimacy ("forged documents," Gair had said) he needed her beside him to back his incredible claim. It all began to make a terrifying kind of sense. The old woman's odd talk ... the clothes hanging ready in the closet ... Vasco had carried her off. His elaborate courtesy, that dramatic kissing of hands merely masked the fact that she was entirely in his power. And there was so dangerously much that she did not understand. She took a deep breath. "You have amazed me, cousin. I don't know what to say." She must have time to think.

"I don't wonder. It's a tremendous prospect, is it not? Queen of Portugal. Think of all the good you can do, Juana. Think how this country needs you. Your grandmother wanted it for you: remember that. She knew. That's why she sent for you. If she could speak now she would tell you to take up your destiny and be a Queen. It's fate, you see, that our family should have come back, quite by chance, to the Castle on the Rock. As its owner—as my wife—I tell you, Juana, we can't fail. It's our duty, don't you see, to save the country."

"You overwhelm me, cousin." The more he told her, the less she trusted him. Now, at last, she understood why there had always been something strange about his love-making. Nothing he had ever said to her had been quite true. She would be mad to believe him now. She would be madder still to let him see that she did not. "It's too much for me," she said. "You must give me time to take it in." Dared she ask some of the questions that boiled in her brain? "But my grandmother knew, you say?" That should be safe enough.

"Of course. I told you. That's why she sent for you. Oh, she was glad enough to give up acting as Handmaiden—she was absurdly too old for that: I don't know how she had managed to keep it up so long—all those stairs, and the cold down there. Ridiculous at her age."

"So you're a member, and I never knew." Had he intended to betray it? She managed, she hoped, to sound as if she was simply impressed by his cleverness. But once again her brain was racing. Twice he was supposed to have rescued her from the Sons of the Star. And he was one of them. No wonder he had found it so easy. She looked at the bandage on his left arm and wondered if there was any wound underneath it. Dangerous even to think of that. The more she learned, the more aware she was of her own danger. And there was something else. Something more frightening still. If her grandmother had been conspiring with Vasco all the time, had she told him about the secret panel? About Gair?

She thought not. She hoped not. But how to find out? "How in the world did you manage to meet my grandmother?" She asked in tones of simple admiration. "Without my ever having any idea."

"Oh, that was easy enough." She did not think he much liked the question. "But there will be time for explanations later. Just now, you are in grave danger; you must give me the right to protect you."

"You mean from the Sons of the Star? But, if you're a member?"

"Don't you see?" He did not enjoy having his logic questioned. "There's a division in the ranks. That's where the danger lies. The better part of the members are heart and

258

soul for me, for Sebastian, but there are still some madmen who think the French will bring Portugal freedom. They are the ones we have to fear."

"I see." She was trembling at once with terror and with relief. Her grandmother had not betrayed her all the way. Vasco did not know about the secret panel. He had no idea that she had listened to the meetings and therefore knew that Sebastian's name had never even been mentioned. He thought of her merely as the Handmaiden of the Star, a woman, beneath serious consideration. He must continue to do so. "A Queen," she said. "It's like a dream, cousin." A nightmare.

"So you agree? You'll marry me, my Queen?"

Something very odd about his tone. She had never thought so fast, remembered so much. Was she beginning to understand? He did not want to marry her. Did not want to marry at all? No time to think it out further; she must use this instinctive knowledge for all it was worth. "Vasco!" She stopped. "Sebastian, my King, of course I'll marry you." She seized his hand, kissed it with passion, and thought she felt him recoil. "But—a royal marriage? Not a hole and corner one like my stepsisters'. Surely you and I should wait and be married as a King and Queen should, in the Cathedral?"

Would it work? With his reluctance on her side? "The *Se* at Lisbon?" He considered it. "You're right in a way. Publicly, before the world."

"Yes." Dared she? "There must seem nothing doubtful about this marriage, cousin."

"I believe you're right. He did not like the implication, but he took it. And had taken, too, she thought, the bait of her sudden capitulation. "It would not be long to wait," he went on thoughtfully, and now she was sure of the relief in his voice. "I meet my friends tonight, my Queen. I can tell them I have your promise?"

"Of course." His friends. The inner circle of the Sons of the Star?

"I told them I would be married." He was still considering it. "The friar waits below. It could be a marriage only, for now, my Queen. The true marriage could take place, when we are victorious, in the Cathedral."

What a fool he must think her? "I told them I would be married." He might as well have admitted that he had been responsible for the whole plot against her. Well, the more foolish he thought her, the better her chance of escape. But her line now must be not so much folly as ambition. She rose

259

to her feet, every inch, she hoped, a Queen. "No, cousin," she said, "it is the King I marry, not the man. You have forgotten, I think, how recently I refused you." Much better she remind him of this than that he remember, later, and begin to wonder. "As a man, I like you well enough, but this side of marriage. As a King, I know you my master. Only, give me time—a little time—so I may learn to love you as I should. In the meanwhile, you have my promise." She turned, swept from the room, and resisted a fierce temptation to make a run for it, down the stairs—hopeless, of course. Instead, she walked, as stately as possible, up to the room above; her prison. She knew that now.

He was following her, but at least she had the initiative. "I'm exhausted, cousin." She turned at the door to face him. "I will bid you good night. But first I must thank you again for rescuing me." At all costs she must not let him see that she knew he had in fact been her kidnapper.

"Thank God I was able to. But we must continue to take every possible precaution. You will not mind if I lock you in for the night? Old Luisa will take good care of you. My men are on guard in the courtyard below, but I do not dare trust even my friends, who are coming here tonight. I will feel safer if I know your door is both locked and bolted."

"Your meeting is here?"

"Why, yes. We meet without any melodrama; we are simply a group of friends, gathered for a hand of cards. In the morning I hope to be able to tell you it has been a profitable one."

"Yes." If only, by some miracle, she could hear what he said to them. "And in the morning we will send word to my family that I am safe?"

"I hope so."

She was beginning to be able to tell when he was lying to her. He had no intention of letting anyone know where she was. Would he tell his accomplices that they were already married? Very likely. "I would like to meet your friends," she said.

"Impossible!" And then, reasonably, "We have your reputation to think of, my Queen." He had stayed, all this time, on the threshold of her room. Now he looked past her. "Luisa, your mistress is tired."

In some ways it was actually a relief to hear the key grate in the lock on the other side of the door and watch Luisa shoot the bolt. She might be a prisoner but at least, for the moment, she was safe. And at last she had time to think. Lying in the great four-poster bed ("Fit for a Queen," Luisa had said as she retired to her own pallet) she sorted out the day's terrifying discoveries. She was sure, now, that Vasco was the real leader of the Sons of the Star, the one whose return from abroad had meant such a change in the tone of the meetings. He might, or might not, be a little mad, but it would be lunacy to underestimate him. His claim to the throne might be, as she suspected, the merest fabrication, but that did not make him any less dangerous. When she thought how he had kept the Sons of the Star in hand, meeting after meeting, delaying action until he had built up his own claim, she could not help a kind of appalled respect for him.

And meanwhile, as she and Gair had suspected, his inner circle of friends had been meeting here at Sintra, making the real plans. How was she to find out what they were? And, more important still, how escape and warn Gair Varlow?

How right he had been to urge her not to trust Vasco. She remembered, with a thrill of terror, the second time Vasco had proposed to her. It had been touch and go, helpless in his arms, whether she yielded and told him what she knew about the Sons of the Star. To have done so, she saw now, would have been to sign her own death warrant—and Gair's. From now on, she must watch every word, every breath, every look. Still more, she must watch for a chance of escape.

For it was obvious that Vasco intended to keep her a prisoner until the time came to strike. It would be done with the greatest courtesy, but it would be done quite ruthlessly. Luisa was at once gaoler and chaperone. She would not be allowed to leave the room save in Vasco's company. He had told her that the courtyard below was full of his servants. Protecting her, or guarding her? What chance had she of escaping from this high room, with its one window overlooking the court?

Her hope must lie, fantastically, in the next meeting of the Sons of the Star. They would need their Handmaiden to let them in. She must persuade Vasco of this, and, first, she must persuade him that she was both negligible and committed to his cause. Thank God, she thought, she had managed a good beginning.

She woke next morning to the sound of rain, and wondered who had taken charge of the preparations for the olive harvest down in the Pleasant Valley. What could her family be thinking about her disappearance? And—more important

261

than anything—had Gair heard about it? He, at least, could be relied on to draw some of the right conclusions. But he was so busy in Lisbon, it might be days before he visited the Castle on the Rock, and in the meantime, with her grandmother beyond helping her, there was no reason why anyone should let him know of her disappearance.

It brought her back to the question that had been plaguing her. How, in fact, had she been kidnapped? She forced herself, reluctantly, to remember that terrifying moment of midnight awakening. She had been looking towards the big closet that hid the entrance to the winding stair. Its door had been shut; she was sure of that now. And the light had come from the other side of the room, the blow on her head from behind her.

The answer was obvious. There must be another secret entrance to the room; one about which her grandmother had not chosen to tell her. It explained so much. That was how Vasco had managed to keep in touch with the old lady. No wonder he had not much liked it when she raised the question. And now, horribly, she remembered the night of Mrs. Brett's "attack." Vasco must have visited her that night, must have lost his temper for some reason and struck her. An old lady—his ally. It cast a terrifying light on Juana's own position.

She made herself present a cheerful morning face to old Luisa, who woke, grumbling, to unlock the bedroom door for a girl with cans of hot water. "I hope you slept at least." The old woman locked the door again behind the girl and approached the bed.

"Like a log." Surprisingly, it was true, and her head felt wonderfully clearer for it. "But did not you?"

"No!" The old woman gestured angrily to the pallet which had been placed by the huge ornamental fireplace, a rarity in Portugal. "I might have known no good would come of those foreign contractions. This house was built by an Englishman," she explained, as she fetched a heavy brocade dress for Juana's inspection. "He would have those fireplaces in all the main rooms. This one must connect with the one in the room below—they kept me awake till God knows when with their talk, talk, talk."

"They?"

"The master and his friends. He entertains them in the dining room below—they play some gambling game with cards—and talk! I thought I'd go crazy."

"You mean you could actually hear what they said?" Juana was washing her face vigorously at the heavily ornamented handbasin and put the question casually over her shoulder. Fantastic, maddening, to have had such a chance and missed it.

"I could have if I'd wanted to. What I wanted to do was sleep. I'll have my bed moved before next week."

"They come regularly?"

"Once a week. He's a devil for the cards, the master."

So the chance might return, if only she could make use of it. And if there was time. "When shall I see my cousin?" She was to play the adoring female and this question was surely in order.

"Over dinner. The master has been out for hours. But he said he would come to you at once when he returned."

There was nothing to be gained by trying to persuade old Luisa to let her out of the room. She must keep up the pretence that all the precautions were for her own safety. No doubt the old woman really believed they were.

When they met, she made herself greet Vasco with a warmth from which, she thought, he just perceptibly shrank, then with an even greater effort made herself wait to question him until they were seated at table. Once more they were alone. "We can talk more freely this way." He made sure the door was firmly shut. "And it's safer for you."

"Does that mean you don't think it safe yet to let my family know I am here?" She made the question as casual as possible. "They must be horribly anxious."

"Yes, but why? It's true, they have messengers out scouring the country for news of you. One came here last night. I think I must pay a call of condolence on the Castle on the Rock today."

He was enjoying it, Juana thought. He liked the sensation of power. He would be an appallingly dangerous ruler for any country. "You really think I can't trust them?"

"I'm sure you can't. You must let me be wise for you, Juana. You must be patient. It won't be for long, I promise you. Our day is at hand."

"You had good news last night?"

"Yes. Everything is going as I wish. The news of the French invasion is out at last, but Dom John still believes he can appease them with soft words. He is thinking of signing a decree confiscating British property."

263

"But, good God, the Castle on the Rock!" She had never signed the paper making it over to Pedro and Roberto.

He laughed. "You understimate me, my Queen. I too had thought of that. We need it, you and I, for sentimental reasons. It will be our country home, favoured above even Queluz or Sintra or that dreary priest-hole at Mafra." And then, casually, "There's something I forgot to tell you. Your grandmother died yesterday."

"Oh, no!" For lack of proper nursing? Because she missed her? Or for some more sinister reason? She would never know. And Vasco, who had almost certainly been the ultimate cause of her death, had hardly bothered to mention it.

"Yes, I'm afraid so." He sounded uninterested. "They're all at sixes and sevens at the castle, by what I hear, with the owner dead and the heir vanished, but it won't be long, I imagine, before they see the advantage in it. With you gone, your uncles can waive their claim and your cousins inherit. With the power of Dom John behind them, they should do well enough—they'll take care of our castle until we are ready to reclaim it from them."

"You think of everything, cousin." She was afraid he did, horribly afraid now that old Mrs. Brett had not died a natural death. She herself must unwittingly have prolonged the old lady's life by moving her downstairs, away from her own room with its two secret entrances. This was a new, grim reminder of Vasco's power as leader of the Sons of the Star. When he had needed to, he had been able to strike old Mrs. Brett, even protected as she was by a nurse in the room all the time.

"I have to think of everything." He expanded under her praise. "Napoleon is not the only great strategist in Europe, cousin. He will discover that when he and I measure swords at last."

He was a little mad, she thought, but that did not make him any less dangerous. "But if the French are really coming?" Was that too intelligent a question? "What's going to happen?" She amended it. "I think I'm frightened, cousin."

"No need to be. Not with me beside you. My friends, by the way, all sent you their loyal wishes and congratulations."

So he had told them they were married. "You must thank them for me," she said. "But will you be meeting again?" This, above all, she needed to find out.

"Oh yes. Once at least. There's plenty of time still. Junot has a long way to go before we need deal with him. Believe me, we'll be ready when the time comes. But first we have to set our own house in order. That's why I beg you to be patient for a little while, my Queen. We cannot make our final dispositions till the next meeting of the Sons of the Star. Until then, I must beg you to stay in asylum here. That will be the moment of declaration."

"I see. But, Vasco, about the meeting: who is going to open the doors if I'm not there?"

"What?" Here, quite obviously, was something he had not thought of.

"I'm sure you have some splendid plan about that," she hurried on. "But, Vasco, couldn't I do it? I should like to—it would be fitting somehow. To do it for you ... I'm sure you could arrange it." She must not for a minute suggest that she had realised about the second entrance to her grandmother's room.

"I'll think about it," he said, and with that she had to be content.

CHAPTER 23

> *"Now the clouds no more are grey,*
> *Now our cares are flown away,*
> *Evermore our hearts are gay."*

Juana stood as close to the window and sang as loud as she dared. She knew it for a forlorn hope, but surely there was just a chance that Gair might penetrate into the central courtyard of the *quinta*, and recognise the words he had composed for her back at Forland House?

She was clutching at straws, after a week of captivity that was exacerbated by having to pretend she was being guarded for her own sake. Two days before, Vasco had told her that Dom John had signed the decree confiscating British property and ordering the arrest of any British subjects who still remained in Portugal. "So you see how fortunate it is that you are safe here, my Queen."

She had thought it best not to remind him of the Portuguese citizenship Dom John had conferred on her. Nor did she dare ask how the decree would affect Lord Strangford and his people. She was quite horribly afraid that at some point in her strange association with Vasco old Mrs. Brett might have let something slip about her relationship with Gair. She simply dared not speak of him.

To her relief, she had not seen much of Vasco, who had been busy making his final dispositions for what he called his day of glory. When they did meet, she asked as many casual questions as she dared, but learned little about his plans. It was not, she thought, that he suspected her motives in questioning him, but simply that he considered the subject unsuitable for a woman. Each time they met, she was more aware of this attitude of his. To him, women were a necessary evil, only a little superior to the beasts of the field. How could she ever have thought of marrying him?

But the more freely he showed this contempt of her, the better. It meant that he had dismissed her as negligible, and there lay her best chance of escape. Today she had been his prisoner a week, which must mean that the inner circle of the Sons of the Star would be meeting in the room below hers tonight. At all costs she must contrive to listen at that tell-tale chimney. She had made plan after plan for getting rid of old Luisa, but none of them satisfied her. The trouble was that it must all seem to be an accident. If Vasco realised she was plotting against him, she was lost.

When he was out, her meals were served to her in her own room, but tonight he came knocking on her door a little before his normal supper hour. As usual, the formalities were observed. He bowed, and kissed her hand, and hoped he would have the pleasure of her company at supper, and she smirked—she was afraid—and said she would be delighted to join him.

He was in an expansive mood, and she soon learned why. "The English are packing up." He poured her a glass of wine. "I thought that last edict of Dom John's would be too much even for Lord Strangford to stomach. He's asked for his passports. The Arms of England are down already from his house, I hear, and he's waiting to leave. So that's one less enemy for me to deal with. Not that I'm afraid of any of them, but I don't want to shed your countrymen's blood if I can avoid it, my Queen. England is our oldest ally, and once I am established on the throne, I intend to make my peace with her—on my own terms. It will be easier if I have not had to deal with her Minister here."

"Yes." No doubt, in his vocabulary, "deal with" meant "kill." She must be very careful. It was unlike him to talk to her so freely. Was there anything behind it?

"I met that Englishman who used always to be hanging round the Castle on the Rock," Vasco went on. "He was riding back from there—been saying good-bye, he said. He asked me if I'd heard any news of you." He was watching her closely.

"Mr. Varlow?" She managed to make it light. "I'm surprised he's still interested, now it must seem obvious I'll never own the Castle on the Rock."

"So that was it? I thought so. A fortune-hunter, pure and simple." He sounded relieved.

"Oh, yes. He was after my sisters until my father lost his money." It was near enough the truth to sound convincing. "But how will the English get away?" Surely this was a natural question to ask?

He laughed. "That must be what Strangford is wondering. It's one thing to ask for one's passports, but quite another to go. There's been no packet for weeks now. If he tries to go overland he'll fall into the hands of the French or the Spanish. And the only foreign ships in the Tagus are a party of Russian warships—he'll hardly want to go aboard them, with Napoleon and the Tsar on such good terms. No, he must feel a pretty fool, just now, must Lord Strangford. I tell you, cousin, the cards are playing themselves into my hands. Two weeks, three at the most, and you will be a Queen."

"It's hard to believe." But she did believe him, with a chill of terror. She was sure, now, that this unwonted flow of talk masked a deep excitement. There was something infinitely more important that he had not told her. At all costs she must get rid of Luisa and contrive to listen to the meeting tonight. None of the plans she had made was perfect. Which one should she try? She yawned, gracefully, behind her hand. "I'm tired tonight, cousin. Will you excuse me if I leave you? You must have much to think about." She had nearly referred to the meeting, but restrained herself in time. Fatal to suggest she was clever enough to have remembered this was the day for it.

He was on his feet in an instant. "I'm afraid you find your confinement fatiguing, cousin. But I promise you, it won't be long now. In the meantime, let me give you a last glass of wine to help you sleep."

She almost said no, restrained herself in the nick of time, and watched, with fascination, in the big looking-glass above the fireplace, as he shook in three drops from a vial taken from his pocket. He must intend her to sleep through the meeting. It was, she thought, extraordinarily obliging of him to provide her with the weapon she needed. She yawned again. "It's good of you, cousin. It's true, I have been sleeping badly. Will you bring it upstairs for me, and I'll drink your health, last thing, when I am in bed?"

He was glad to be rid of her. "Of course."

Later, handing the glass to Luisa, she had a moment's qualm. Suppose it was poison, not merely a soporific? But that was impossible: Vasco needed her. It was the only strength of her position. "You drink it, Luisa," she said. "My cousin would pour it for me and I didn't want to hurt his feelings."

"Of course not, my Princess." Luisa approved of these sentiments. "It's the best carcavelhos," she said with obvious pleasure. "You're sure you don't want it?"

"Quite sure." She settled back in the luxurious bed. Please God it worked, and quickly.

Half an hour later, Luisa was stretched, fully dressed but snoring, on her pallet. Juana blew out the lamp and tiptoed over to the big, ornamental chimneypiece where the pallet had stood before Luisa had it moved.

At first, she was afraid it had all been for nothing. With her head close to the fireplace she could hear only a confused murmur of voices, a roar of laughter, the clink of glasses. But Luisa had told her she could have understood what was said if she had troubled to listen. She pulled a cushion over to the fireplace and sat down with her head as near the opening as she could get it. Time passed. The noise from below grew louder and more confused. Suddenly she realised what was going on. They were bidding for the bank at faro. Were all their plans made then? Was this to be purely a convivial meeting? It was hard to believe. She got up to stretch her aching limbs and make sure that Luisa was still deep asleep. She was beginning to feel tired herself, and actually nodded off, for a minute, her head against the side of the fireplace.

Vasco's voice woke her. "You may go, Manuel," he said. "Leave the wine ready on the side table." His voice rose to join in a babble of bidding. A few minutes later she heard it again, clearly. "That will do, gentlemen. The servants know their orders; we will not be disturbed again."

There was a rustling and a murmur of voices as the conspirators apparently threw in their cards and drew together for their real business. Juana had a clear picture of the room now. Vasco must be sitting at the head of the long table, close to the fireplace. The man who held the bank would be at the far end, so that she could not hear him. She set herself to listen.

An hour later, so stiff that she could hardly move, she crawled across the room to light a candle and take an anxious look at old Luisa. What she had heard tonight had taught her just how dangerous Vasco was. He did not deal in half measures. Suppose the sleeping draught he had measured for her should have proved too much for the old woman? But Luisa was breathing more naturally now. No need to be anxious about her. And that was just as well, Juana thought, as she climbed into her ostentatious bed. She had enough without that.

It was a sultry night, but she lay for an endless time, shivering with something that she preferred to think of as cold. She knew Vasco's plan now, and knew how right she had been to be afraid of him. Its very simplicity was the mark of genius. But a mad, frightening genius. There had been a moment, listening there, when she had found herself thinking that it might be best for Portugal if Vasco did succeed. He was a strong man, and that was obviously what the country needed. So far as she could see, he was the only person who had really faced the threat from France. His plan might well save Portugal. But to what end? Talking to these, his chosen few, his band of Brothers, as he called them, he had outlined, briefly, his plans for the country when it was his. They made her blood run cold. It was not just his casual dismissal of her: "We'll need a pompous wedding," he had said, "and an heir, of course, or, better still, a couple of the brats, but after that ... Well, you know what I think—what we all think of women, Brothers."

There had been a murmur of approval. Apparently they did.

He had returned to the larger issue. His intention was to come ultimately to an agreement with Napoleon, whom he described as "the other strong man of Europe." Juana thought the plan a diabolically clever one. Junot and the French army were to be lured farther and farther into Portugal by the apparent inertia of the country. Then, at the last moment, the Prince Regent and his family would be murdered, the country would rally behind the miraculous "Sebastian," and the army would march in from the coast and confront Junot's force, which would by then be worn out with its long march. "They'll be expecting nothing of the kind," Vasco had said. "And I saw Junot's army: it's composed mainly of raw recruits. They'll give us no trouble. Not when they know we mean business. Junot can act as my ambassador to his master."

Even if Dom John and his family decided to escape to the Brazils, Vasco's intention was that they should be killed, down to the last infant. "We've had enough of the Braganzas, my friends."

And there had been a muffled shout of "Long live the House of Aviz."

In response to a question put by a voice Juana could just hear, and, maddeningly, thought familiar, Vasco had explained his position further. The rank and file of the Sons of the Star, he said, were a sentimental, woolly minded lot who would boggle at murder. Much better that they should think Dom John and his family would be spared. They would be useful, were in fact essential for the destruction of the French army. "After that," he said, "it will be time to show our hand."

Someone must have asked him how the rank and file of the Brotherhood were to be persuaded to fight the French, with whom, as liberals, they had such sympathy. Vasco had given a great guffaw of laughter at this point. "I've news for you, gentlemen." He told them that ten days earlier the French and Spanish had signed a secret treaty at Fontainebleau, by the terms of which Portugal was to be divided into three parts, one to be given to the young King of Etruria, one controlled by the French, and one to be handed over as a kingdom to the infamous Spanish minister, Godoy. "When I tell them that, Brothers, our problem will be to make them wait until the French have walked into our trap."

As always, with Vasco, Juana had had the feeling that even now he was not telling his allies everything. It was fantastic, but she found herself even wondering whether he had not, in fact, some secret agreement, himself, with Napoleon. Certainly he planned, ultimately, to work hand in glove with the French, and a few casual words left her in no doubt as to what would be the fate of Strangford and his entourage if they should be so unlucky as to be still in the country when he took over. Her own ultimate fate, both as woman and as English seemed no less certain. After the birth, of course, of the couple of brats he had spoken of.

But there was still a little time. Junot's army would not walk into the trap for two weeks or more. The final arrangements would be made at next week's meeting of the Sons of the Star. "Precipitate action would be fatal, Brothers."

Most of the time she had been unable to hear anyone but Vasco, presumably because he sat at the head of the table nearest the fireplace, but at the end a question had come over brutally clear. "And the woman? Our future Queen? Marriage has made her cooperative?"

She had been right. Vasco had told his friends they were married. "I expect no trouble from her," he said now, repressively.

"And when do we expect an heir?" The question was part of a half-heard barrage of ribald comment, the gist of which seemed to be that marriage with her was a sacrifice Vasco had to make for the cause.

It was a long time before Juana slept that night.

CHAPTER 24

The days crept by. Listening to the meeting of the inner circle seemed to have exhausted Juana's luck. She was on the alert, all the time, for the slightest chance of escaping, or at least getting a message out, but none came. The ring of protective custody round her was absolute. In moments of near despair, she thought of trying to win old Luisa over to her side, but abandoned the idea as worse than hopeless. For Luisa, the sun rose and set in Vasco. To tamper with her was to ensure disaster.

Confinement was beginning to tell on Juana's health as well as her spirits. She slept badly, haunted by horrible dreams, and in the daytime made herself walk up and down, up and down the bedroom in a vain effort to tire herself out. An appeal to Vasco to let her walk in the courtyard after dark fell on deaf ears. "We must take no chances, my Queen."

She felt sick now, when he called her that, but luckily he noticed her less and less as the days wore on towards the November meeting of the Sons of the Star. He had never referred to her suggestion that she should act as Handmaiden, and she did not dare to bring the subject up, for fear of rousing his suspicions. Pacing her room at night, when Luisa was sleeping the deep sleep of the stupid, she saw the central courtyard filled with moonlight. Two days to the meeting . . . one day . . . tomorrow . . . tonight.

She had not seen Vasco for two days. Perhaps he would not even return before the meeting. She must not think like that, it was too close to despair. "I'm bored," she said to old Luisa. "When is the master coming home?" She had fallen into Luisa's habit of calling him this, because she could hardly bear to say his name.

"I thought you were missing him!" The old woman was delighted with the question. "I knew why you were moping, my Princess, better than you did yourself. Never mind, I've good news for you: it won't be long now. He sent word this morning that he would sup with you tonight." She had crossed the room to the wardrobe where hung the regal gowns Vasco must have had made in advance. "You are to

273

wear this. See! A gown for a Queen." She shook out crimson velvet folds lovingly.

"But I'll stifle in it!" These clothes, too, witness of Vasco's long-term planning, made her feel sick, and not only with fright.

"Never mind that. The master expressly said you were to wear it."

Why? Not, surely, just to sup with him. What did he care what she wore? Wild hope flooded through Juana. "Oh, in that case," she said, "of course I will."

"And the diadem too," Luisa went on. "Look, senhora, did you ever see anything so beautiful? It will hide that short hair of yours and make you look every inch a Queen."

"Yes, several inches too many." Juana made it a joke, but a cold finger touched her spine at the thought. Suppose she did not manage to get out of this; suppose she found herself, fantastically, Queen to Vasco's King Sebastian? How long would he bear the fact that she towered half a head above him?

The crimson velvet was a perfect fit. "How on earth did he manage?" asked Juana, as Luisa shook out the heavy folds of the skirt.

"Manage? Oh—to get the fit? Why, Maria, of course; she came every day for a while."

"Did she?" The ground shook under Juana's feet. Maria—her friend from childhood had been conspiring against her all the time. Was there no one she could trust?

"There!" Luisa adjusted the shimmering diadem on Juana's rebellious locks. "There," she said again, with complete satisfaction, and then, surprisingly, sank into a deep, awkward curtsey. "God save Your Majesty!"

It was at once moving and terrifying. "I hope He will," said Juana.

Her thoughts were racing. This regal costume must mean that Vasco intended to present her to the Sons of the Star tonight. It might give her a chance, a hairsbreadth, desperate chance to save herself, and Portugal. She must be ready to take it with both hands and use it with all her intelligence. That was her only weapon, she knew, against Vasco—the fact that he thought of her almost as a thing, not for a moment as an equal.

When he arrived, she became aware of another advantage. He was visibly taken aback by the regal figure she presented, and kissed her hand with a deference that had been notably

274

absent since he had had her in his power. When he said, "My Queen," she thought he almost meant it.

She would ask no questions. She had thought about this meeting all day and had drilled herself to impassivity. Whatever his plan was, she would make him broach it, would seem, herself, hardly interested, just the mindless female he expected.

She made herself eat heartily of a dish of chicken with rice and almonds, drank a glass of wine, and said nothing. As the silent meal dragged on, she began to be aware of his sideways glance upon her. When he had planned this conversation, she thought, it had begun with a question from her. He would have to replan it.

"It's the full moon tonight," he said at last.

"Good gracious, so it is! I had quite forgotten. One loses count of the days, shut up as I have been." And then, quickly: "Don't think I'm complaining, cousin; that would be ungrateful indeed. But is it really the full moon?"

"Yes." He took this, she saw with pleasure, as merely another proof of her expected stupidity. "It is indeed, and the last time the Sons of the Star will meet in secret."

"Goodness!" She tried to sound like Daisy. "Are you sure? Isn't it exciting?"

"I find it so. But, Juana, a while ago you said you would like to act once more as Handmaiden of the Star. Do you remember?" He obviously thought it quite possible that she had forgotten.

"Of course I do," she said warmly. "I thought it would be so splendid to do it when I knew it was for you, cousin. But I thought you didn't like the idea, so I rather gave it up." She glanced at him with what she hoped were large, adoring eyes and wished she could inconspicuously get herself slumped down still further against the table so that the difference in their height would be less apparent.

"You were right. I didn't much like it at the time, but now things have changed. Are you ready to do it once more, my Queen, for my sake?"

"But of course. Why should I be afraid when I know you are there? Only—in these beautiful clothes?" She left it, vacuously, in character.

"Luisa will find you a black robe to wear over them. The Sons of the Star will never know that a Queen has acted as their Handmaiden tonight."

Oh yes they will, she thought. It was clear now. He meant,

275

suddenly, somehow, to bring her forward and present her to the Sons of the Star as Queen Juana. That would be her chance. She must be ready for it.

But it seemed fantastic that he should risk it. Could she really have fooled him to such a point? She would like to think so, but could not. So, when he suggested a glass of madeira with dessert, she moved, carelessly, so that she could watch him in that invaluable looking-glass. And saw, once again, a vial produced from his pocket. What could it hold this time? Not a soporific, surely, but something that deadened the will? That would make her act as his puppet?

"Thank you." She accepted the glass enthusiastically. "I need this if I must really go down the winding stair once more. But how shall I get to it?" It was surely a natural enough question, but one, she hoped, that he would find it difficult to answer. At all costs he must be distracted for a few moments while she got rid of her dubious drink. "You'll never take me through the castle, surely?" If only he would.

"Leave all to me, my Queen. I have a secret way of my own. Only, for your own sake, you will let me bandage your eyes? It's safer for you that you should not know it."

"Of course, if you say so." She pretended to sip her drink, but merely let the liquid touch her lips. "Your madeira is delicious, cousin." He was sitting across the table from her, watching her every move. She pretended another sip, and, this time, was compelled to let a few drops into her mouth. She dared not swallow them but tilted her head back a little so that the sweet liquid settled under her tongue. "But strong." Her singer's training stood her in good stead. "Could I have one of those little cakes to go with it?" Her handkerchief was ready in her hand as he rose to fetch the plate of sweet cakes from the sideboard. When he returned, it was back in her lap again, soaked in madeira. But there was still the nearly full glass to be dealt with. She took another pretence sip and a bite of cake. "What time do we start?"

"Soon. Drink up your wine, my Queen." She could feel his impatience strong in the air between them.

"It's making me dizzy." Would he know what the effect of those sinister drops should be? "I must have a breath of air." She rose and moved over to the window. "How glad I shall be to get out of doors again." She felt that he was following her, but had a moment while her body screened what she was doing. It was time enough to tilt the glass against the heavy velvet curtains so that the liquid trickled slowly down them.

She left a little in the bottom and turned back to face him. "It's quite the most delicious madeira I ever tasted, but the strongest too. I feel ready for anything, cousin, even the winding stair. Look! The moon is up already." Still standing by the window, she kept between him and the telltale stain on the curtain.

"Yes. Time we thought about going. It's a roundabout route, I'm afraid, I have to take you to the cavern. The carriage is ready."

"But what about my cloak? The bandage for my eyes? Are you sure I ought to go down into that horrid cavern in this dress? It's the most beautiful one I ever had: I wouldn't want to spoil it." She sounded, and meant to sound, a complete fool. Anything to get those probing eyes off her for a moment.

"There'll be a hundred more where it came from. It's time to go."

"So soon?" She leaned towards him lovingly. "I've missed you so, these last two days. When can we be together all the time, my King?"

He backed away a little. "Very soon now. Tonight I launch my great enterprise. I only wish you could be there to see, instead of shut up in the Handmaiden's cell."

"So do I." Thank God—and Mrs. Brett—that he did not know she would in fact see and hear everything. She leaned a little nearer to him. "Your day of glory," she murmured.

"Quite so." At last he turned away, and on the instant the rest of the madeira was soaking into the curtain.

"I feel better now." She moved back to the table and grasped it as if for support. If only she knew what those drops were supposed to do to her. She must just hope that Vasco had not seen their effect before.

Luckily, he was impatient to be off. "I will take you up to Luisa. She has your cloak ready for you. We must lose no more time."

"Shall I really need a bandage over my eyes?" Juana asked as she rejoined Vasco. "I can't see a thing if I pull my hood together so." Would he trust her? It would be immensely encouraging if he did.

He laughed. "But suppose you forgot, my Queen. This is a secret too dangerous for a woman."

It is indeed, she thought: the secret of your treachery. And shrugged, and made a little moue: "You must be the judge, of course."

277

"Of course." He took her arm to lead her down the stairs. Down, at last, past the dining room to the central courtyard where she had longed to be for her two endless weeks of captivity. She had time to see that the great gates were still tight shut. Vasco was taking no chances.

He helped her into the carriage with all the deference due to a Queen, then took a silk scarf out of his pocket. "The time has come."

"So soon? And with the moonlight so beautiful. My first drive for two weeks, too!" She intended it merely as a token protest, and submitted with a good grace as he tied the scarf around her hood so that she was blinded with a triple thickness of material. She thought they were both glad when it was over. It was odd, and terrifying, to realise that he actually disliked touching her. And yet he intended that she should bear his child. It conjured up a picture so horrible that she found herself shivering inside the heavy velvet.

"You're cold?"

"No," she said with perfect truth. "I'm frightened. I hate going down that winding stair."

"It's the last time." He spoke tolerantly, as to a child, and she knew he was pleased. It was right that she should be frightened.

"How far can you come with me?"

"Not all the way. I will get you to a place you know: the bottom of the second flight of stairs. Then, I fear, I must leave you. It would hardly do for me to be late for my own entrance, tonight of all nights."

They drove for a long time, probably, she thought, round in a great circle. At last he made sure her blindfold was still in place before helping her out of the carriage. "Do exactly as I tell you," he said. "The way is dangerous."

A doorway ... a long narrow passage, with her skirts brushing each side as she walked behind him, her hand on his shoulder ... Then stairs, upwards, extraordinarily difficult to negotiate blindfold. "Don't speak from now on," he warned when they came to them, and she thought, with a pang, that they were no doubt entering the Castle on the Rock. Through the wall, one way or the other, Daisy and Teresa might be sitting mourning for her. Or Maria, plotting against her, as she had been all the time.

"Level ground now," he whispered. A narrow opening. They must be in Mrs. Brett's bedroom, the room from which she had been abducted. Suppose she were to scream? In all

278

probability there would not be a soul in the whole turret, now the old lady was dead. To scream would merely be to give herself away. But she longed to be sure. She pretended to trip, fell sideways, and touched material. Brocade. The curtains of Mrs. Brett's big fourposter?

"Shh." His angry arm was round her to hold her up. "Careful," he whispered. "This way. Wait."

She recognised the squeak of the wardrobe door as he opened it, heard him push clothes aside, and then waited, with strange amusement, while he had some difficulty in finding the secret spring at the back of the cupboard. He had known the other passage by heart; to this one he seemed, comparatively, a stranger. She had a frightened vision of the plunging steps they had to negotiate to reach the bottom of the second flight where he meant to leave her. It was bad enough on one's own, with a lamp, but to have to do it, blindfold, under his orders . . .

On the other hand it was a chance—a horrible one. She knew the winding stair much better than he did. She had only to pick one of the places where one side was open to perpendicular darkness. If she jumped there, and pulled him with her, they would both fall to certain death. It would save Portugal—perhaps. It would save her, at least, from the intolerable prospect of marriage with Vasco.

"This way," he whispered. He must have found the secret spring at last.

As she obeyed his whispered instructions and followed him down the stair through the castle, she carried on the dreadful argument with herself. If she killed them both, she would never know what she might have achieved by staying alive and taking her chance at the meeting.

"We can talk now," he said. They were through the bottom door and the dangerous stairs lay below. "Go very carefully." His voice was louder now. "A step out of line means death."

How well she knew it. Both their deaths. Was it courage, or cowardice, that kept her dutifully behind him, feeling her way down the endless flights, pretending that she did not know, by count, when they reached the landings and the tunnel where the bats were. At last, on the second landing, he stopped. "Just a moment," he said, "I must find the entrance."

There was a little business of his making her stoop to go under an imaginary archway, of leading her up and down the landing a couple of times. Then, at last: "Here we are," he said and untied her bandage.

They were standing, as she had expected, on the second landing and he was busy lighting a spare lantern that must have been left ready for him. "From now on," he said, "everything must be just as usual. You need have no fear of the acolytes, by the way. They are my friends. You know your way?"

"Of course."

"I'll watch you down the next flight. Go carefully, my Queen."

Of course he would watch her. He did not want her to see his lantern go twinkling back up the flights of stairs towards the Castle on the Rock. She was supposed to think he had brought her in by a different entrance. Starting obediently down the next flight, she thought about waiting and following him back up to the castle. Hopeless, of course. He would bolt the door at ground level and the one into the closet. Her chance must come, if it came at all, when he brought her in to present her to the Sons of the Star. Since she had not killed them both, she must stake everything on that moment.

After two weeks of constant surveillance, it was delicious to be alone, even down here in the dark heart of the cliff. She must have a long wait before her, since Vasco would have to go back up to the castle and so out to the cliff entrance. Would he go back the way they had come, or would Maria be waiting to let him out of the main gate of the castle? Maria? Or some other member of her family?

Horribly, anything was possible. And the acolytes were his friends, he had said, in warning or reassurance. So much for one of her plans. There was no hope of enlisting their aid against him. She passed through the door of the great cavern, then leaned against it for a moment, savouring the temporary feeling of safety. What would happen if she locked it behind her and simply did not open the great doors when the gong rang?

She dismissed the idea at once. That would be a coward's way. Besides, she had always been convinced that somewhere in the big cavern there must be a way out to the Pleasant Valley. Bitterly, now, she regretted that she had never made herself come down early and look for it. But among the rough rock and shadows of this huge place, what chance would she have had?

She made herself go about her usual duties, then, when all

was ready, found herself standing irresolute by the council table. Should she try, at this eleventh hour, to find the way out? It would at least be something to do, something to keep terror at bay. But would it? She remembered the first time, when she had slipped among the rocks making just such a search. If she was to have any chance of convincing the Sons of the Star of how Vasco intended to betray them, she must have a cool head and a calm voice. She put her lantern on the big table, sat down in the leader's chair, and rehearsed what she must say. She would not have long. A few moments of surprise, before Vasco or his gang silenced her, would be all her hope. She must use them well. But suppose, in this moment of crisis, she should find herself stammering, even in Portuguese? She did not dare think about it. How could she stop herself? She remembered Gair, back in the sunlit maze at Forland House, where it all began. He had fooled her finely then, and she had sung, that night, for him alone. Tonight she would speak for herself. Would she ever have a chance to tell him that he had been as much a dupe as she? That they and Mrs. Brett had all been Vasco's puppets, jerked here and there as he pleased? She would enjoy telling Gair that.

The sound of the gong knifed through her thoughts. Vasco had wasted no time. Did he not trust her alone in the cave? It was not a reassuring thought.

Strange to remember the simple fear she used to feel when she admitted the acolytes. Tonight's was compound, stifling ... And, for this very reason, tonight everything must seem exactly as usual. She was relieved to feel no trace of stammer as she spoke her ritual greeting. If Vasco had not told her the acolytes were his friends, would she have appealed to them now? But already the moment was past, and she was shut in her cell. Once again, listening to the key grate in the lock outside, she felt the temptation to bolt herself in and refuse to stir. What would happen? She knew Vasco now. He would leave her to die, alone here in the dark.

The gong sounded for the second time. She thought she counted more slowly than usual, but when she opened the secret panel the meeting had only just begun. As usual, the leader was speaking. It was odd to know he was Vasco.

And terrifying to hear how well he was putting his case. What chance had she, if ever she got a chance, of destroying his skilful argument? He spoke of Pombal, of Portugal for the Portuguese, and, at last, of Sebastian, the lost Prince and his own claim. In fact, she thought, he was really telling them very little; that was the genius of it. Without going into dangerous detail, he had whipped them up to a point where they were his to command.

"Sebastian!" The shout rang through the cave. "Long live the House of Aviz!"

Watching, she thought she saw Vasco hesitate, and was sure she could read his mind. He was wondering whether he needed her to back his claim. If he decided he did not, she was lost. Very likely she was lost anyway.

But one of the hooded figures had risen to ask a question. "Most Royal Star"—it was the Brother of the Silver Serpent—"are you, after all these years, the only descendent of the lost Prince?"

"No!" Vasco had reached his decision, or been pushed into it. "Brothers! Our Brother of the Silver Serpent has spoken well. There is indeed another descendent of the great Prince Sebastian, one with a better claim than mine to the throne of Portugal. She is my cousin, and my wife, Juana. She is also, thanks to the Star, mistress of the Castle on the Rock and Handmaiden of the Star. She waits now in the antechamber, as befits a woman, even a Princess. Is it your pleasure, Brothers, that she appear before you, the first woman worthy of the notice of the Star?"

There was a murmur of approval, but Juana did not dare to listen longer. She closed the secret panel and sat down on her hard wooden chair to wait, trembling in every limb, for the summons of the Star. And, humbug, she told herself bracingly.

It did not feel like humbug when the key grated in the lock and the cell door swung open. She rose to her feet, pulled the hood close round her, and faced the two acolytes.

"Daughter of the Star," said the one who had unlocked the cell door, "the Star summons you to his presence."

She was supposed to be surprised. "Now?" she said, and was aware of hearts turning at the big table.

"Yes, now." This was Vasco's friend. He had not been taken by surprise, but must pretend to be. "Approach the Star, and fear not."

Fear not? Lunatic advice. She moved forward with all the dignity she could muster. Too soon, now, to start speaking. She must await her chance—what did Vasco call it? Her moment of glory. Very likely her last.

The acolytes led her forward and round the long table to

where the Star—Vasco—was waiting for her. As she approached, he threw back the hood from his face in a dramatic gesture and stood there for all to see under the big star that hung above the table. He held out his hand to her, his attention still focused on the hooded figures round the table. She was his puppet; he did not need to look at her. "Brothers of the Star"—he pushed back her hood to reveal her diadem-crowned head—"I, Vasco de Mascarenhas, lineal descendent of the great Sebastian, son of the House of Aviz, present to you my wife, Juana, Lady of Aviz and Queen of Portugal."

Their shouts of approval echoed strangely through the cavern. then died away raggedly into silence. Now was her chance. She had thought of so many things to say. She said none of them. "Sons of the Star"—she pitched her voice as if she were singing, and it echoed back to her—"I am indeed Juana, Lady of the House of Aviz, descendent of the great Sebastian." Beside her, she was aware of Vasco's astonishment. He had not expected his puppet to speak, but so far what she said suited him well enough. She had a few seconds more. "And I warn you," she kept her voice clear and steady, "do not trust this man who will betray you as he has me. Ask him about the Treaty of Fontainebleau; ask him his plans for the Braganzas; ask—" Strong hands pulled the hood over her face, silencing her.

Beside her, Vasco was speaking. "The woman is mad," he said. "My brothers, I had meant, for the sake of the House of Aviz, to endure this and make her my Queen. I should have known that no woman is worthy of trust. Out of her own mouth she has convicted herself of treachery to us all. We cannot allow of a divided claim. Brothers, out of a grieved heart I call for the verdict of the Star."

Unable to move, blinded and stifling under the hood, she heard the ripple of condemnation pass round the table: "Death . . . death . . . death . . ."

Then, from somewhere across the table, a dissenting voice: "Brothers, should we not look further into this before we condemn the heir to the House of Aviz on one man's voice, even be it the Star's—and he her co-heir? Should we not ask, first, what she means by the Treaty of Fontainebleau, and what the Star's plans are for the House of Braganza?"

Juana held her breath as a little doubtful murmur ran round the table, but Vasco's voice quelled it. "All in good time, Brother of the Silver Serpent. As for the Treaty of Fontainebleau, it is true I had not meant to tell you of its monstrous provisions yet, but I see I must. We are betrayed, Brothers, betrayed by our false friends, the French." He rapidly outlined the provisions of the treaty as Juana had heard him describe them to the inner circle. "As to the House of Braganza," he went on, "it is not I, but Napoleon who plans its destruction. I hold in my hand, Brothers, a copy of the French gazette, the *Moniteur*, dated from Paris on October 13th. It says, in so many words, that the House of Braganza has ceased to reign in Europe."

"Long live the House of Aviz," said a voice somewhere to the left. The cry was taken up round the table.

"And death to the traitor." This was a voice from the other end of the table, and Juana had a horrid picture of the members of the inner circle, scattered at intervals where they could act as crowd-leaders.

"But is her treachery proved? Has she not shown herself careful for our good? I say this needs more investigation, Brothers. I will not condemn even a woman unheard."

"Brother of the Silver Serpent." Vasco's head must still be bare; his voice sounded more clearly than the others'. "You have tried the patience of the Star long enough. Ever since you first joined our Brotherhood you have been a quibbler and a questioner. Now I, who have revealed myself for the glory of the Star, demand that you be put to the ultimate question. Bare your face, Brother, and show yourself a man to be trusted." And then, mockingly. "See, Brothers, he dares not meet the challenge of the Star. Seize him and let us see."

There was a scuffle; an exclamation: "The Englishman!"

"You see, Brothers, how we are betrayed. This is one of Lord Strangford's people, set to spy upon us. At leisure, we will find out how he came to insinuate himself among the Brotherhood. But now we have lost too much time. I put the question to you all: death to them both."

"Death!" The unanimous shout echoed strangely from the cavern roof. Juana writhed unavailingly for a moment in her captors' grip, then made herself stand still. At least she could die like a Queen. She bit her lips under the hood, remembering the ruthless cord that had killed Father Ignatius in front of them all. But Vasco was speaking again: "The Star is merciful," he said. "For a traitor and a traitress the death in life will come fast. Take them away, Brothers."

No cord. Her captors were dragging her away from the table. She was aware of other struggling figures nearby. The

Brother of the Silver Serpent ... the Englishman ... It hit her like a blow. Gair. She stumbled, and was pulled along ruthlessly, rough rocks bruising her, then thrown to the ground. She lay for a moment, panting, sobbing for breath, then heard the unmistakable sound of the cell door slamming shut. The key turned in the lock outside. She pushed back the hood from her face and sat up, painfully.

The lantern was still burning on the table. Gair lay inert on the floor beside her, breathing heavily, unconscious ... Quickly, shakily, she felt his pulse and found it steady enough, nor did he seem to be bleeding. Merciful to have left her the lantern. Merciful? The only source of air to the little cell was from the door or the secret panel. With these shut, and the lantern burning, the two of them would not last long. The Star's merciful death in life was simply death by asphyxiation.

She rose shakily to her feet and moved over to the secret panel. Dared she open it? If the acolytes had been stationed by the cell door, it would destroy their last chance. But why should they be? No one knew about the panel. She thought she must risk it. Trembling convulsively, she blew out the lantern and pressed the spring.

Nothing happened. The acolytes were back in their places. The meeting was going on with extraordinary, blood-chilling normality. The episode of herself and Gair was over. The Sons of the Star were making their final dispositions for attacking the French and taking over the country.

It was frighteningly efficient. Vasco, still speaking with bare head, finished outlining his plans. "Remember, Brothers, not a word, not a breath till the French are in our power."

"And the signal?" asked the Brother of the Ragged Staff.

"I, Sebastian, will give the signal when I proclaim myself heir of the House of Aviz and rightful King of Portugal."

And once again the cavern echoed with cries of "Sebastian!" and "Long live the House of Aviz!"

"I thank you, Brothers. And now, we meet only to part ..."

Juana closed the panel. The meeting was over. She dared not wait and see how Vasco dealt with the problem of closing the cavern.

She found the tinder-box on the shelf, relit the lantern and knelt down by Gair, who was breathing more easily. Was she right about the death in life? Or would an executioner, any

285

moment now, unlock the door and drag them out to the torture? She began, breathlessly, to count. How soon did she dare reopen the panel?

CHAPTER 25

"Five thousand and five, five thousand and six . . ."

Gair stirred, put a hand to his head, and sat up. "Where am I?" And then, "Juana! How could you?"

"What do you mean?"

"You married him! That impostor, that . . ." He stopped himself with an effort, "I'm sorry. I shouldn't . . . But how could you, Juana?"

Of course. Vasco had let the meeting think them married. Well, for the moment, she would let Gair. "How do you feel? Did they hurt you much?" She put an anxious hand on his forehead.

"There's nothing wrong with me." He recoiled from her touch. "A few bruises . . . If they were all . . ." He pulled himself up to a sitting position, moving a little away from her as he did so, and looked about him. "Where are we?"

"In the Handmaiden's cell. The meeting's just over. I don't dare open the panel to look yet. I'm beginning to hope they've left us here to die."

"To hope?"

"Yes. Don't you see? They don't know about the panel. They think we'll die of suffocation. That's their 'death in life' that leaves no mark. In fact, I think I'd better blow out the lantern now I know you're better." The brazier had burned out and now the darkness was absolute.

"Better! I'll never be better, Juana. I don't care any more. When I think you let him fool you into marriage. But"—his voice changed—"poor Juana; you know now how little he cares for you. To leave you to die here in the dark . . . I suppose nobody knows you're here."

"Only Vasco. But what about you?"

"Nobody. It seemed safer so."

"You might have told *me* you were the Brother of the Silver Serpent!" It was absurd, perhaps, to be angry about this, here in the shadow of death, but she was just the same. Was this why she had not undeceived him about Vasco? "What a fool you must have thought me," she went on. "Solemnly reporting to you the things you yourself had said. No wonder you didn't always hurry to see me the day after

287

the meeting. It must have been vastly tedious for you to have to come at all."

"Juana! Don't say that. You must see I did it for your sake. I thought it safer for you not to know."

"You sound just like Vasco." Angrily.

"Vasco!" It brought him back to it. "Juana, what madness seized you? After all, I did warn you . . ."

"So you did." She was still too angry to explain. "I wish I knew how long it was since I closed the panel." She changed the subject. "We ought to open it again as soon as possible or we really will suffocate. I had counted to five thousand before you came to. We'd better wait a little longer, don't you think?"

"How big is the panel? Is there any hope we can get out through it?"

"None, I'm afraid. It will provide us with enough air to keep us alive, that's all. Have you any friends among the Sons of the Star?"

"Who might come to the rescue? I doubt if they will be able. Your cousin will see to that. I'm sorry; I should say, your husband. When did you realise your mistake, I wonder? At least you made the best amends you could. Too late. If only I had known sooner that Mascarenhas was the real leader . . . Surely you owed it to me to tell me that, Juana."

"Good God! You can't think—" He actually imagined that she had gone off with Vasco of her own free will. It made her, for a moment, too angry for speech. Then, "I shall open the panel," she said. "We need some air in here." Fury gave her courage. Her hand hardly shook as she worked the secret mechanism. The panel slid open, revealing darkness absolute. "They've gone." She whispered it, just in case, but it was hard to imagine that anyone would be lurking there in the dark.

"So it's to be a slow death, not a quick one. I'm sorry, Juana. Whatever you may have done, this is my fault for bringing you here in the first place. Can you forgive me?"

"That depends a little on what you have let yourself believe I've done." At least, talking in the dark like this made it easier to speak freely. She felt her way back to the chair and sat down. Gair was sitting at her feet: she could feel him move restlessly on the hard rock.

"Let myself believe? What do you mean? There was your letter after all. Your sisters showed it to me. That put it brutally enough."

288

"My letter?" Why had she not thought of this? "What letter?"

"Why, saying you had gone off with Vasco de Mascarenhas. That you loved him beyond reason, 'more than family, more than home, more than life itself.' You see, I remember every word of it. I shall never forget—not that it looks as if I'll have much time. But, poor Juana, what did he do to you to cure you so drastically and so soon?"

Another forgery. She should have thought of this. There had been no search parties. When she sang, hopefully, the old songs from Forland House, thinking Gair might be looking for her, he had believed her ecstatically married. "You believed I'd do that?" she said.

"What else could I think? Except that you might have sent some message, one word of apology, of explanation for me. I've been frantic, Juana, don't you see, worrying about you and wondering what would happen about the meeting tonight."

"That's all you think about!" Anger was warming in that cold cave. "Your spying!"

"It's all I've dared think about since I heard of your marriage, otherwise I believe I'd have gone mad. But you might have written me one line, for myself. After all, we've been comrades, haven't we, for more than a year? I trusted you, Juana." He too was finding the darkness conducive to free speech. "I loved you. I only realised just how much when I knew I had lost you. But to lose you to Mascarenhas —what did he do to you, Juana? Was it very bad? It must have been, to turn you against him so. You were splendid, out there in the cavern. That's when I really knew what I had lost."

"Lost? How can you lose something you never had?" But though she still spoke with surface anger, she felt a little incorrigible glow of happiness fighting the dank chill of the cave.

"I'm sorry. You're right, of course. It's all faraway, now, and long ago—a lifetime ago. But, Juana, remember the maze at Forland House—the sunshine and the scent of lavender—and tell me that then, if I had had more sense; if I had not been a career-mad young fool ... If I had spoken then, Juana, would you not have said yes?"

Of course she would have. "I was a child then—"

"A delicious child, fighting her stammer. I'll never forget that first night: Cesario in the moonlight, ready to plunge

289

into the river. Why did I not understand that I loved you from that moment? But, Juana, what could I do? I had my way to make in the world—still have, come to that—but now I'm sure of a seat in the House, the way is open before me. No use now. You're married to Mascarenhas."

"Worse than that. Have you forgotten? We are shut up here, waiting a slow death in the dark."

"I won't believe it." She heard him rise to his feet, and stagger a little as he did so. "My life may be finished. It ended when I heard of your marriage. But there is more than that to be thought of. We have to escape, Juana. We have to save Portugal from—oh, God—from your husband."

She really ought to tell him. Instead: "Try the door, if you like," she said. "Look, it's this way." She took his hand to guide him, and felt it tremble at her touch. She felt more than that. She had thought, once, that Vasco's touch was incendiary. This was an earthquake; a soulquake, she thought, and gave herself up to Gair's embrace. His lips on hers, not savage, as Vasco's had been, but pleading, loving ... His hands, now, palm to palm against hers, with their own message ... And her own mouth and hands, answering his with all the feeling she had so long denied.

As quickly as it had happened, it was over. He let her go, and she could hear him breathing—sobbing?—in the darkness. "Oh, God, you're married. I'm sorry, Juana."

Now, surprising herself, she laughed. "As a matter of fact," she said, "I'm not, you know."

"Not!" She felt him take it, in the darkness, like a blow. "You mean he didn't even— Oh, God, Juana!" And then, quickly, "It makes no difference: you must know that. But we must be married at once. Just in case . . ."

It was fantastic, but it was heart-warming too. "In case I should bear a bastard Aviz? Dear Gair, how you do jump to conclusions. But I'm grateful just the same—" She was close to tears, the first it had occurred to her to shed, and tried for a lighter note: "Don't you see, that's the last thing Vasco would want—any more suspicion of that kind. You're not thinking—"

"How can I, when it's a question of you? Juana, have pity on me: explain. Don't you see, I've been distracted since you disappeared: I've not made sense. But—you're really not married to him? None the worse? It's too good to be true. But how in the world?"

"I persuaded Vasco we ought to wait and be married, like

290

a King and Queen, in the Cathedral at Lisbon. In fact, he was glad enough to put off the evil hour. No, I'm none the worse, except for being shut up in the top floor of his house for two weeks, with no one but his crazy old nurse for company. But that's hardly the point now, is it? The question is, how do we get out of here? And—do you think they will come back? The Sons of the Star?"

"Eventually? Yes, of course. To remove our bodies. You remember how that man of yours—Tomas—was found. But how long will they leave it? Will we still have the strength to put up a fight? At least, the element of surprise will be on our side."

"Yes, and they're a superstitious lot: should we pretend to be our own ghosts, do you think? But there's another thing—you don't think Vasco may decide he can't do without me?"

"I hoped you wouldn't think of that. But, in fact, I don't think it's very likely. You were listening. You heard how he had the meeting with him—they were hailing him as King Sebastian before he even mentioned you."

"Yes, if you hadn't raised the question of other heirs he might well have decided to do without me. As it was, he didn't mean to let me live long. Gair, it was horrible—I heard them, you know, the inner circle. That's how I learned about the Treaty of Fontainebleau—"

It was delicious to hear him laugh there in the darkness. "You're a better secret agent than I will ever be, my darling. That's why I joined, you know, in the hope of getting into the inner circle. I never got within a mile of them. But tell me about it. God knows we've time. And first, sit down; there's a chair somewhere isn't there?"

"Yes." They had been standing, one on each side of the locked door, intensely aware of each other, but instinctively keeping a little apart. If they touched each other, if they talked about themselves instead of about their plight, anything might happen. Well, she thought, and why not? If they were to die here, trapped in the dark, why not their moment of happiness first?

"We're going to get out of this, you know." He might have read her thoughts. "Everything is different now I know you are free. We're not, for a moment, going to despair. You're going to sit down, very calmly, like yourself, and tell me everything that has happened to you. Who knows, it may help us to think of something?"

"Yes." Obediently she felt her way back to the hard little chair. "I wish we could light the lantern."

"We daren't. Not so long as the panel is open. This way, we will know the minute they enter the big cavern."

"You're right of course." She felt him settle at her feet again. "Oh, Gair, I'm glad you're here."

"So am I." He found her hand and kissed it, then let it go quickly. "We've got to keep our heads, Juana. Tell me what happened to you."

It was an order, and she plunged into her story.

"So there is still time to stop him," he summed it up when she had finished.

"Yes, if we can only escape. They'll do nothing until the French are almost at Lisbon. Then it will all happen at once."

"And he will give the signal, by declaring himself Sebastian. Juana, we have to escape."

"I do so agree with you."

"There's no secret way out of this cell?"

"No. I asked my grandmother once. I didn't much like the feeling of being locked in here; I thought my grandfather might have provided an escape route. She said he had considered it, but found it impossible."

"So there's nothing we can do but wait."

"That's it. How long do you think it's been?"

"I don't know. How long was I unconscious?"

She thought about it. "Not long. I had only counted to five thousand. Gair, I'm hungry."

Once again his hand reached up to find hers. "And cold, my poor darling. I suppose there's no more fuel for the brazier?"

"It's outside."

"Of course. It would be. Come and sit beside me, love, and at least let me try and keep you warm. Oh God, Juana, if only I'd left you in England."

What a strange thing. She had thought she looked forward to telling him that it was really Vasco who had arranged for her to come to Portugal, that they had all been merely his puppets, but when it came to the point, she had glided over this in her story. It would be intolerable for Gair to think he had been Vasco's dupe, and Mrs. Brett's. She turned towards him in the darkness. "Never think that," she said. "I'd rather be here, with you, for the rest of the time we have."

"Juana!" In a moment, the control that had kept them side by side, merely touching each other, was going to snap.

"Shh . . . listen!" Was it imagination, or had she heard the sound of movement in the big cavern?

He had heard it too. They were on their feet, moving silently to the open panel. And, far away to their left, they could see the flickering light of a lantern. "Should I close it?" she whispered.

"No. We must know . . . But it's too soon, surely?"

He was right. They had agreed that since the air in the Handmaiden's cell was supposed to last her through the meeting it must take some time for a prisoner there to die of suffocation. Juana shivered, thinking of Tomas, dying here, ignorant of the panel that might have saved him.

Gair's hand on hers was a warning. The lantern was nearer now. They could see that it was carried by one man, apparently alone. Vasco? Gair moved away, and she heard him pick up the heavy chair, the only possible weapon.

The approaching figure wore the robes of a Son of the Star. His hood was drawn close about his face and she could not see his emblem. But, surely, he was too tall for Vasco? She dared not speak to Gair, but touched him lightly in warning. The hooded figure was very near now. He put down the lantern on the rough floor of the cave and felt in his pocket. For a moment, the light of the lantern showed a pistol ready in his right hand. He bent to look at the fastening of the cell door. The panel was close beside it. Juana hardly dared breathe. If she had had a weapon, might she have been able to reach him?

He straightened up again, and spoke. "Juana! Can you hear me?" The voice, low and cautious, echoed unrecognisable in the big cave. Gair's hand on hers told her to say nothing.

"Juana! Can you hear me?" Again. "It's I, Roberto. I came as soon as I could. Can you hear me, Juana?" A little pause. "I've not got the key. I'm going to have to blow the lock off. If you can hear me, Juana, stand away from the door."

Vasco would have had the key. Her hand and Gair's communed in the darkness. "Roberto!" she whispered through the opening. "Is it really you?"

"Thank God!" He straightened up at the sound of her voice. "I'm not too late. And Senhor Varlow?"

"Is here too. Oh God, Roberto, but I'm glad to see you."

"We must lose no time. He may come back. Stand well

293

away from the door, both of you." The shot echoed horribly in the big cavern. Then the cell door swung open and Roberto entered, hood thrown back so they could see his face. "Juana, you're none the worse?"

"Not now you're here. But Roberto, how?"

"Later," he said. "First we must get out of here. It's a rough climb I'm afraid. Do you think you can manage, Juana? We can't go back through the castle; it's not safe. Uncle Miguel has been sleeping in the old lady's room since she died. You know he's the Brother of the Ragged Staff, Mascarenhas' right hand man? It's not safe for you there, Juana, not now."

"Miguel!" So many things suddenly, horribly, made sense. "But how do we go, Roberto?"

"Through the tunnel to the Pleasant Valley. You'll get wet, I'm afraid."

She could not help laughing. "Dear Roberto, just now, getting wet is the least of our worries. But, Gair, are you strong enough?" By the light of Roberto's lantern she could see the swelling bruise on the side of his head.

"Of course. And your cousin's right; we mustn't waste a moment. Who else knows about this entrance?" They were out already, following Roberto across the great cavern.

"The inner circle, I think. Not that I'm one of them. If I had been, I would not have let that liar Mascarenhas delude me so. Juana, we owe you a great debt for what you did tonight. Here's the entrance." He had led them swiftly but carefully over the increasingly rough rock of the cavern floor. Now he rounded one high pinnacle and showed them a dark opening concealed by the masking rock. "We have to crawl for the first bit," he explained. "I'll go first, then you, Juana, then Senhor Varlow. I'll feel much safer when we're out of this cavern. There was a good deal of talk, while the meeting was breaking up. They're not solidly behind Mascarenhas any more. I think it just possible that he will regret his decision about you, Juana, and come back. Now, follow me, do exactly as I do, and don't try to talk." He kilted up his robe with its cord, bent down, and crawled into the opening.

Juana had more trouble with her skirts, since the red velvet must be got out of the way as well as the cloak. "Here." Gair handed her his cord. "Use this too."

"Thank you. What shall I do with this?" She took off the diadem Vasco had made her wear and was about to drop it at the entrance to the tunnel when Gair took it from her. "We might as well keep it," he said, "as a souvenir of the day you were Queen."

"Hurry!" Roberto's voice from the tunnel. Juana bent down and followed him into it. The going was not, in fact, quite so bad as she had feared. At some point, this tunnel must have been the channel of an underground stream, and the water had smoothed away the rock. But it was awkward enough, working one's way along, half-crawling, half-crouching, and it was with a sigh of relief that she saw Roberto rise to his feet ahead of her.

"There." He helped her up. "That's the worst bit over. Except the stream. Can you go straight on, Juana?"

"Of course." She turned to Gair, who had joined them, and saw that he had taken off his robes and was carrying them in an awkward bundle. "And you?"

"Yes. Let's lose no time."

From now on they could walk upright, but the going was much rougher, and from time to time Roberto had to pass the lantern back to Juana so that she could light Gair over a particularly difficult bit. Presently he stopped and Juana heard the sound of water. "We're beside the stream now," he said. "The entrance is in the bank. One has to go straight across and up the other side. But, first, you two wait here while I make sure there is no one about. I can't think why they should have anyone on guard here, but we'll take no chances." He handed the lantern to Gair. "Hold this. If I don't come back, it means they've got a guard on the far side of the stream. You'll need to be ready to defend yourselves. You'd better have this too." He handed over the pistol, which Gair took without protest.

"All's well so far." Roberto returned a few minutes later. "Take my hand, Juana. The water's only waist deep."

"Is that all!" She followed him round a last turn of the tunnel and saw the glow of moonlight ahead.

"Quietly now!" He helped her out of the entrance and down into the cold, swift-running stream. For a moment, it was an effort to stand upright, then she was following him across, rocks shifting under her feet, the cold water rising to her waist. On the other side, they plunged at once into a thicket of myrtle and small oaks, through which, to her relief, ran the tiniest possible path. "Wait here," he whispered, and went back to fetch Gair.

She knew where they were now. This was the thicket just

below the pressing floor. Incredible to be so near home and so far from safety. Her velvet gown clung soaking round her legs and long involuntary shivers ran through her. What now?

"We have to walk, I'm afriad." Roberto's whisper, as he and Gair joined her, answered her unspoken question. "I dared not take horses from the stables. Thank God, the moon's still up." He had blown out the lantern and as they emerged from the thicket their shadows lay long on the path in front of them.

"Where to?" Juana fell into step beside him.

"I've friends in Guincho who will hide you while we decide what to do next. With luck we should get there by dawn."

"You're sure they're safe?" This was Gair, from beyond Juana.

"Yes. They're women." They were nearly up to the little village of peasant houses at the head of the valley. "Quiet now."

It was strange and horrible to walk silently through the well-known village, knowing it full of friends who might be enemies. But it was worse still to pass the castle, where it lay dark against the moonlit sky. Suppose they were to meet Miguel on his way back from the meeting? Miguel, who, Juana realised now, had been playing Vasco's game all along. It was Miguel who had delayed her, the day she was attacked by the bandits. Miguel, too, who had sent for Vasco on the day of her sisters' double wedding. And Miguel who had written to the lawyer. No wonder Gonçalves had never come. But there was worse than any of this. There was old Mrs. Brett. Could he have killed her, his own mother? She would probably never know.

CHAPTER 26

The moon had set. A pale glow of light along the horizon heralded the dawn, and still Juana walked like an automaton between her two companions. They were planning together in low voices, but she was beyond caring, beyond listening, numb with exhaustion and accumulated shock. Vasco . . . Miguel . . . even old Mrs. Brett . . . How tight the web of treachery had been about her. Miguel—of course:

"Gair?"

"Yes, love?" How naturally he said it.

"I've just thought of something. Uncle Miguel is one of the inner circle. That night I listened, I thought I recognised another voice besides Vasco's, but couldn't place it. Now, I'm almost sure it was Miguel. Will that help?"

"Immensely. It's what we need." And then, "Look!"

They stopped. Behind the hills, the sun must have risen. Almost before their eyes the sea had turned to silver and they could see a majestic row of battleships, all sails set, taking advantage of the dawn breeze to head down towards the promontory that hid the mouth of the Tagus.

"The English?" asked Roberto.

"Yes," said Gair. "I must lose no time. Lord Strangford has received his passports already; he'll go aboard the moment he can." And then, at Juana's exclamation, "Of course; you don't know what's been happening. England and Portugal have been almost in a state of war since Dom John signed his last set of edicts. Will your friends at Guincho have horses, Roberto? There's not a moment to be lost."

"Undoubtedly. But this won't change our plans?"

"Not if I can catch Lord Strangford before he leaves. I'm sure when he hears my story he'll stay to meet Dom John at Queluz and make one more effort at persuading him to escape to Brazil. Whatever happens, I'll meet you at Queluz tonight. You have the *Moniteur* safe? The one with Napoleon's statement that the House of Braganza no longer reigns in Europe?"

"Yes, thank God. I wonder if Mascarenhas has realised yet that in the confusion he never got it back."

"Lucky for us he didn't sooner," said Gair. "He might well have come back for it."

Juana was counting again, footsteps this time. Five hundred and five, five hundred and six . . . They were down off the cliff now, approaching the wind-tormented sands of Guincho. "Nearly there," said Roberto.

When had Gair put his arm around her? Would she be able to keep going if he took it away? Six hundred and three, six hundred and four . . . They had turned away from the coast road . . . There were trees at last, shading her from the morning dazzle of the sun.

"Here we are." A cool courtyard, the sound of a fountain . . . voices . . . Gair was explaining something. She made a great effort to take it in. "Safe here," he was saying. "Rest. I'll come for you as soon as I've made arrangements to get you out to the British squadron."

Now she was awake with a vengeance. "You're not staying?"

"We can't, Juana. The fate of Portugal may be settled today. Roberto's going to Queluz to meet Dom John, who is due there, at last, from Mafra. I must get to Lisbon as fast as I can to catch Lord Strangford before he leaves. But I'll be back for you, my heart." He kissed her hand, as he had done so many times before, pretending passion. Now it was real. How could the same gesture be so different? But there were people all round them. He let go of her hand. "You'll look after her, senhora?"

"Of course." A strange voice. "She's asleep on her feet, the poor child. Come, *menina*."

Sleep came in a flood, like happiness, like despair. It seemed no time at all until she was being shaken awake, gently at first, then harder. She fought her way up from the depths: "What is it?"

"He's come for you, *menina*. It's almost dark. You must lose no time, he says."

Gair was waiting in the courtyard beside a closed carriage. He was white with fatigue, the bruise showing dark on the side of his face. "Juana!" His voice was a caress. "You're ready? Thank God." She could feel his impatience to be gone, but he joined her, just the same, in the necessary, ceremonious thanks to her hostess before helping her into the carriage.

It was dark inside. "Juana—" The carriage moved heavily forward out of the courtyard. He was holding her hand in

298

both of his. "It was real, wasn't it? You'll laugh at me, I hope ... Do you know how I love you to laugh at me? Only—last night—down in the cave—you were afraid, distraught ... I had no right to ask you then."

She smiled at him lovingly in the darkness. "Well, if you're worried, Gair ask me again."

"Juana! I adore you."

Now she could laugh. "That's precisely what you've been saying for a year, and not meaning a word of it."

"But I did, don't you see? I just didn't know I did. Oh—what a fool you must think me!"

"I think you a very able secret service agent."

"Oh God, if I only were."

"What do you mean?"

"That I've resigned."

"Gair! But why?"

"There was nothing else to do. When I got to Strangford's house, he was ready to go. I couldn't persuade him to change his mind. He said it was too late for talking, time for action. He wouldn't even wait while I fetched you. He's aboard Sir Sidney Smith's flagship by now. He expected me to go too."

"But you're here."

"Of course I'm here, my heart. Where else?"

"You resigned for my sake?" She regretted the question the minute it was out.

"Partly," he said. "Juana, I love you too much to lie to you. Of course, nothing would have made me leave you behind, but I think I resigned as much for Portugal's sake as yours. You've not asked me where we are going."

"Why, I haven't, have I. Where are we going, Gair?"

"To Queluz, of course, to see Dom John. Since I can't make Lord Strangford see the danger Vasco represents, I must help Roberto persuade Dom John."

"I see. I'm glad you think me worth telling the truth, Gair." She thought of adding "at last," but did not.

" 'At last,' you nearly said? Bless you, love; you've every right to reproach me, but believe me, I only kept you in the dark for your own sake."

"Yes, just like Vasco. The less a woman knows, the better. And very dangerous to me it turned out to be. Gair, promise you'll never keep me in the dark again."

"I doubt if I'll be able to. But, Juana, you've not answered my question."

"That, dear Gair, is because you have not asked it."

"Juana! Will you marry me?"

"Oh, my darling, of course I will." Safe in his arms, there were a thousand questions she wanted to ask him, but she could feel his exhaustion. "Rest, love, while you can," she said.

"It seems such a waste . . ." She could feel him droop against her. It seemed the most natural thing in the world to settle his head on her shoulder. "Cesario," he said, and slept.

She had to rouse him when the carriage slowed down outside the palace of Queluz, where ranks of flaring torches lit up a scene of indescribable confusion. The royal cortège must have just arrived and sweating servants were busy unloading chairs and stools and ornate four-poster beds from wagons and carrying them into the elegant pink-fronted palace that was the Braganzas' Versailles, as Mafra was their Escorial.

"Keep well back in the carriage," said Gair, as their coachman drove on past the main entrance and round the side of the rambling palace to what was obviously a servants' entrance. "We dare not be seen here, either of us." He helped her alight and led her out into a moonlit formal garden. "No one knows how many of the Sons of the Star are about the Court," he went on as they approached the foot of a branching ornamental flight of steps.

"And to meet one of them would be enough," agreed Juana. "Do you think they know yet?"

"That we have escaped? I think we must assume so. Hush, there's someone coming."

"Roberto," Juana said with relief as he approached them down the graceful stairway, the torch he carried held so as to light up his face.

"You're punctual, thank God." Roberto wasted no time on greetings. "Dom John will see us now."

"Alone?"

"Yes, it took some persuading, but I managed in the end. I think, at last, he has realised how he is surrounded by treachery. I showed him the *Moniteur*. That shook him. That so many people should have known about it, and no one told him." He was leading them back up the flight of steps as he spoke. "Keep your veil well over your face, Juana, and you, senhor? Ah, I see . . ."

Gair had produced a large handkerchief from his pocket and held it in front of his face as they threaded their way quickly through a maze of corridors. At last, Roberto opened

300

a door, looked inside, spoke briefly, and ushered them into a small withdrawing room, still entirely devoid of furniture, where Dom John, unmistakably ugly, was standing by a window gnawing on a grilled chicken bone. At sight of them, he put it away in a small enamelled box, tucked that into the pocket of his brocade coat and came forward with a sudden and rather moving assumption of dignity. The fate of Portugal might lie in the balance, but the full ceremony of presentation, the bowing and curtseying must be gone through just the same. At last: "Senhor Brett-Alvidrar tells me you can substantiate this wild tale of his?" The Prince Regent fixed his pop-eyed, anxious gaze on Gair.

"Sire, in every detail, and so can the senhora." Juana had never respected Gair so much as now, listening to him describe the plot at once simply and dramatically so as to appeal to the limited intelligence of his royal auditor.

"*Deus*," said the Prince, and again, "*Deus*," and, at last, "But what can I do?"

"Sire, send for Lord Strangford. Believe that the English are your true friends, the only ones who can save you. And, in the meanwhile, order the arrest of Vasco de Mascarenhas and Miguel Brett. Without Mascarenhas, the conspiracy may be scotched. And the senhora here is sure that Brett is one of the inner circle of the Sons of the Star. Put him to the question and, if I know him, he will give you the names of the others. Arrest them, and you can breathe again. At least the domestic threat will be removed."

"I wish you could deal with the French one so easily." Dom John walked up and down the room, cracking his knuckles. "What do you advise there, senhor?"

"I am sorry to say it, sire, but I think you have no alternative to flight to the Brazils. But, I beg you, send for Lord Strangford. He can advise you better than I."

"How can I, when he has left me like this? My dignity will not permit it."

Juana knew what an effort it cost Gair to speak calmly. "Suppose Lord Strangford were to come to you once more, uninvited, Sire, to appeal to the ancient friendship between our two countries. What then?"

"That would be quite a different thing, of course." Dom John was delighted to let circumstances decide for him. "I am always happy to see Lord Strangford, the representative of our oldest ally." And then, to Roberto, with a sweeping bow for Juana, "You will conduct our guests to their carriage, and give the necessary orders. For the arrests, I mean, and a move to our palace at Belem tomorrow. If Lord Strangford wishes, he may ask audience of us there."

The interview was over. Outside, the three of them conferred briefly in the deserted corridor. "It's as good as we can expect," said Roberto. "I'll see to it that poor Miguel talks."

"And I'll get out to the British squadron and convince Strangford that he must come," said Gair. "A line from you would help."

"Of course. Come to my room and I'll write it for you."

Once again there was a tangle of dark corridors to be traversed, but at least, when they reached it, Roberto's room had a bed, two chairs, and a writing table. He sat, and wrote fast, then looked up at Gair. "But what about Juana? Can you take her with you?"

"To the squadron? I wish I could. But God knows how I'm going to get out to them myself. I'll have to bribe a sardine fisher; it wouldn't be safe for her. But I've been thinking: how does your brother stand?"

"Pedro? Clear of everything. That I do know."

"That's what I hoped. And he's at Ramalhao with the Princess?"

"Yes."

"Then I shall take Juana there immediately. Pedro must persuade his mistress to let her act as one of her ladies in waiting. Thank God, the Prince has faced facts to the extent of planning to move to the Belem palace tomorrow. Doubtless the Princess and their children will be moving there too. Juana can come in Carlota Joaquina's train without any danger of attracting notice."

"Admirable," said Roberto. And, to Juana, "You can trust Pedro in this. He's always been the Princess's man, and nothing else. While I—If you knew how I hate myself. You've seen Dom John . . . he's not brilliant, God knows, but he's a good man. And I've been conspiring against him all this time. I'm so ashamed . . . If you hadn't undeceived me, Juana, I would have connived at his death and all his children's without even understanding what I was doing."

"Yes," said Gair, "but she did undeceive you, and lord knows you've made handsome amends. Now, we must go. I don't need to remind you that Mascarenhas and Miguel Brett must be apprehended without delay."

"Oh, poor Uncle Miguel," Juana said. "You won't be hard on him, Roberto?"

302

"I won't need to be," said Roberto. "Don't waste your sympathy on him, Juana. He's a coward through and through. Once he knows he's lost, he'll betray them all to save his own skin."

"I suppose you're right. But it's horrible, just the same—" This was to Gair, safe once more in the darkness of the carriage. "Will they torture him, Gair? If they did, it would be all my fault ..."

"They won't need to, love. Roberto's right; your uncle is not the man to suffer for a cause. He'll talk without persuasion. If only they catch him, and Mascarenhas. That's what worries me. I had hoped Roberto would have persuaded the Prince Regent to give orders for their arrest long before we got there. As it is, they have had too much time ... If Mascarenhas has found we have disappeared, he must know the game is up. Juana, you will be desperately careful, won't you? For my sake."

"I wish you could take me with you."

"So do I. But we both know I can't."

"Yes. But suppose Lord Strangford refuses to make a last appeal to the Prince Regent."

"I don't think he will. But if he does, I shall go to Sir Sidney Smith, who is in command of the British squadron. By all reports, there is no love lost between him and Strangford. He might be glad to step in where Strangford won't. And, if all else fails, I'll come back for you, Juana. Never think I won't."

She smiled in the darkness. "I know you will, Gair. It's—comfortable. But what will we do?"

"Go to the Brazils, if necessary, but I hope it won't be. You realise Roberto and Teresa will have to?"

"I hadn't thought! But I suppose they will. It wouldn't be safe for him to stay?"

"No. Even if we round up the leaders, there are bound to be enough of the Sons of the Star left to take vengeance on a proved traitor."

"And you're one too, in their eyes. Gair, you must be careful. I shan't have a quiet moment till I see you again."

"Careful! I'll be relieved if I don't find myself cowardly. I've too much to live for, all of a sudden. Believe me, I'll take no unnecessary risks."

"Yes, love, but what about the necessary ones?"

He laughed, and quoted: "I could not love thee, dear, so much Loved I not honour more.' We both know, my heart, that we started this, and must see it through to the end. You do realise, don't you, that they killed your grandmother? I feel we owe it to her, if not to ourselves, to fight it out to a finish against them."

Here was another chance to tell him about old Mrs. Brett's double game. Now, strangely, it was for her grandmother's sake that she held her tongue. Gair would never understand how a lonely old lady might have been blandished and deluded by Vasco's charm. She herself understood only too well. If she had not met Gair first, she would have been clay in Vasco's ruthless hands. Mrs. Brett's secret, she promised herself, would be the only one she ever kept from Gair. "Just think," she said now, "but for Vasco, we might be married, you and I. Operatically, perhaps, but married just the same."

"I wish we were."

"I don't. I intend to stand on my rights now and be courted in good earnest. Besides, do you think it would have stood up, that operatic wedding?"

"Mascarenhas obviously thought so or he'd not have forbidden the banns."

"Yes. Poor Father Ignatius. I suppose he had no idea that what he was doing ran counter to his leader's wishes."

"No, why should he? The secret of 'Sebastian' was known to the inner circle alone. Ignatius was merely one of the rank and file."

"Like you? It'll be a long day, I warn you, before I forgive you for joining without telling me. And when I think how laboriously I reported your own speeches to you! I could shake you, Gair."

"Do," he said.

CHAPTER 27

Carlota Joaquina welcomed them with enthusiasm. Since her intrigues with the Spanish Government had been exposed, she had been living in compulsory seclusion at her *quinta* of Ramalhao, with only rumour to feed on. She agreed at once to add Juana to her train, and plied Gair with questions, which he answered as best he could before making his quick, apologetic farewells.

It all happened so fast ... so publicly. One minute he was there, kissing the Princess's hand, and Juana's, the next he was gone. "A brave man that," said Carlota Joaquina.

"Yes." Juana swallowed tears. If the Portuguese caught him, it meant prison. If the Sons of the Star did, death.

"*Deus,* but I'm glad to see you," the Princess went on. "Sing for me, child, but first tell me, do you not wish that our wedding had succeeded, that day last summer?"

The life of a lady in waiting on the Princess was one of a suffocating boredom that was exacerbated by Juana's gnawing anxiety for Gair. He had warned her that there would be no way he could let her know if he got safe out to the British squadron. "Don't worry," he had said. Absurd advice. She did nothing else. And as the long newsless days dragged by, she began to be horribly afraid that he had miscalculated, that Dom John did not intend to take his detested wife with him to the Brazils. But that, surely, was impossible? Carlota Joaquina had the royal children with her. Whatever he might decide about his wife, Dom John would never leave his children behind.

Worst of all was the lack of news. Carlota Joaquina lived in a kind of royal Coventry. Nobody came near her, nobody wrote to her; she was dependent for information on the alarming rumours picked up by her servants. Everyone knew by now that Junot's French army had crossed the border and was advancing with breath-taking speed on Lisbon. Everyone knew, too, that the Foreign Minister, Senhor Araujo, had sent an envoy to Junot and that the messenger had returned all too soon, having found the French army already on the river Zezere. He and Junot had conferred under a tree in the pouring rain, but nothing had come of it.

The rain was the last straw. When the order finally came for Carlota Joaquina to pack up and take her children and household to the Ajuda Palace in Belem it was coming down in torrents. The roads were all awash, and rain blowing in at every cranny of the huge old-fashioned royal carriages added to the miseries of the crowded journey. But Juana was relieved to be at Belem, with the Portuguese fleet a hive of activity farther up the Tagus, and the blockading British downstream off Cascais. She had still had no word from Gair and kept trying to tell herself that no news was good news. Pedro was a great comfort. Warned by Gair, he did his best to keep an unobtrusive eye on her, and also, most heartening of all, rode over to the Castle on the Rock and returned with loving messages from Daisy and Teresa, and with the expected news that Miguel had been arrested.

In the crowded Ajuda Palace, hysteria was never far away. With the other ladies in waiting, Juana was kept occupied packing and repacking the royal wardrobe under Carlota Joaquina's furious orders.

Roberto found her alone, one dull November morning, trying in vain to close a huge Spanish leather trunk crammed to bursting with tissues and heavy brocades. "There you are, thank God. I couldn't get away before."

"You're here at last!" His presence in the Princess's apartments was a grave breach of etiquette, but she was beyond caring. "Roberto," she hardly dared ask, "what's the news?"

"None good, I'm afraid. There's been no word from Varlow. None from Strangford. And it's over a week now. I'm sorry." He saw how hard it had hit her.

She sat on the floor, quite quiet, for a moment, then looked up at him, her eyes large with tears. "I should have known. He was so tired, Roberto. I shouldn't have let him waste his strength taking me to Ramalhao. You should have helped him—no, that's not fair: you had your own duties. It's my fault, all of it."

He let her cry for a few minutes. Then, "Juana, I can't tell you how sorry I am, but I'm afraid you're right: he must have been caught. It seems impossible, if he managed to get out to the British squadron, that we haven't heard something before this."

"Yes. Even if he couldn't convince Strangford, he said,

whatever happened, he would come back for me." She was making a great effort to master her tears.

"And he would have, if he could. But, Juana, you mustn't quite despair. It would be difficult for him. There's no communication with the British, you know. We're almost in a state of war. But there's worse than that, for us. Juana, Mascarenhas escaped."

"Oh my God." But she knew that in her heart she had expected this. "What's happened to poor Miguel?"

" 'Poor Miguel,' as you call him, has proved the double traitor I expected. Thanks to him, most of the inner circle have been arrested, but not all. And, of course, not the rank and file." Even though they were alone in the room he did not name the Sons of the Star. "That's why I came to warn you. For God's sake, Juana, keep always with the other women. I don't like to see you alone like this, even here, in the palace. We know nothing of Mascarenhas' whereabouts. It seems unlikely that he will have time to think of revenge, but if he should, you're the obvious target. Trust no one, Juana. Keep always with the others; remember that even the guards may be members. I've sent for Teresa, by the way. At least you can trust her. You do realise, don't you, that as things are your only safety, like ours, lies in going to the Brazils with the court?"

"I suppose so." If Gair was dead, nothing mattered.

"But, Juana"—his tone had changed—"we need your help."

"Mine?" Drowning in her private despair, it was an effort to pay attention.

"Yes. Don't you see? Since Mascarenhas is still free, he may try to give the signal, and strike his blow, even without the inner circle behind him. So, think as hard as you can, Juana. What did he say about the signal?"

She put a weary hand to her forehead. "Let me think. They were to wait until Junot and the French army were deep into Portugal ... till they were tired out ... They were conscripts, he said, raw troops ... they'd not stand up to forced marches as the Old Guard would. Then, when they were nearly to Lisbon, he would give the signal, the Portuguese army would march in from the coast, the royal family would be murdered ... It's horrible." She was crying again.

"Yes, Juana, but when?"

"I don't know. He didn't say."

"Then, what signal?"

"He would proclaim himself Sebastian. That was all he said. I don't think he trusted anyone, Roberto. That was his strength."

"And his weakness. With luck, since we have rounded up most of the members of the inner circle, his message won't get to the army."

"Yes. But doesn't it seem absurd that they should still be on the coast, as if the English were the enemy?"

"It may be absurd, but it's a crowning mercy, since we know that if they were here, they would be for Mascarenhas. That's all you know about the signal?"

"I'm afraid so. I'm sorry not to be more help." She reached into the open trunk, pulled out a priceless piece of silver tissue and dried her eyes with it. "What will happen, Roberto?"

"God knows. Dom John will decide nothing. He is waiting for Lord Strangford. It's just the excuse he needs to give way to his natural sloth. It would not befit his dignity, he says, to send again to the English. And, on the other hand, he can't make up his mind without consulting them. So—nothing is done. And, Juana, don't tell anyone—we don't want any more panic than there is already—but we had word this morning. Junot has left his main army behind at Abrantes and is coming on with the advance guard, by forced marches. They'll be here in two or three days."

"Two days!" The silver tissue tore in her hand.

"Yes. Now you see why we need to know Mascarenhas' signal. He may give it any time now, and once he does, frankly, I think we are all lost. It's not just Dom John and his wife ... it's their children ... all the other intended victims. You and I too, of course. I deserve it, for letting him fool me so ... But the others ... It doesn't bear thinking of. And we simply don't know who is loyal and who a member—" Again he did not name the Sons of the Star. "Even if I could persuade Dom John to go on board his fleet, there's no guarantee he'd be safe. His ships' captains themselves may be members."

"It's horrible."

"Yes. What is it?" Juana had stopped listening and was looking past him out the window which commanded a wide view of the Tagus.

"Look!" A British sloop was beating its way upriver, a flag of truce conspicuous at its masthead.

"At last," said Roberto. And then, "Don't let yourself be

308

too hopeful, Juana. It's been so long. It may be nothing to do with Varlow. But I must get back to Dom John. He'll need me."

"I can't bear it, Roberto. To wait. Not to know."

"Juana, you must."

She had to. Straining her eyes, she watched the sloop drop anchor well below the busy ships of the Portuguese fleet. She could see its boat pull to the Belem pier and a group of men disembark. Try how she would, she could not recognise their faces. She might pretend to herself that one active figure was Gair's, but she knew it for what it was, merely a pretence.

If time had dragged before, now it stood still. Word of the English arrival had run like wildfire through the palace. The ladies in waiting knew that their fate was being settled in Dom John's council chamber. Some were more frightened of the long sea voyage than of the French. As the note of hysteria grew, Carlota Joaquina sat motionless among them, like some ugly Eastern statue, waiting for news. Only when her adored children caught the general panic and five-year-old Dom Miguel burst into floods of panicky tears did she rouse herself from her furious passivity to comfort him and urge Juana to sing for them: "It will be better than this waiting."

The waiting was nearly over. Next morning, a messenger from Dom John's apartments at the other end of the palace brought his orders that the household prepare for immediate embarkation. Pandemonium reigned. Still, in the midst of it, Carlota Joaquina maintained a furious calm that held her ladies' hysteria in check. It was she who gave the orders for loading the huge coach that would hold herself, her eight children, their nurse, and two ladies in waiting. She singled out Juana for one of these: "You will keep your head, senhora."

"Yes, Your Highness." The English must be gone. There had been no word from Gair. It was the end. He was dead, had probably not survived the night they parted. She should have admitted it to herself a week ago. Today there was not even time for tears.

Teresa arrived at the last minute, and flung herself into Juana's arms. "I never believed it," she said. "Any of it. Oh, Juana, I'm so glad ... I'm so sorry ..." She was laughing and crying all at once. "Roberto told me," she explained. "Some of it. Is there any news of Mr. Varlow?"

"None."

A quick look at her, and Teresa began to talk quickly about affairs at the castle. "Do you know, it was the most amazing thing. When poor old Mrs. Brett died— You did know she had died?"

"Yes." Juana managed it through the tears that threatened to stifle her.

"Well, you can imagine the confusion when we found her. Maria had been sitting with her and had fallen asleep, you see." And Juana thought: of course, Maria. "So there was Maria having hysterics and Daisy not much better, and nor was I for the matter of that and in walked Aunt Elvira—" She paused impressively.

"Yes?"

"She looked at the old lady and said, 'Cover her face, mine eyes dazzle, she died old.' And then she kind of shook herself, and said, in quite a normal voice, 'Well, has anyone sent for a priest?' And she's been running things at the castle ever since. Just like you used to."

"You mean . . .?"

"I don't know what I mean."

And with that Juana had to leave her and take her place in the immense carriage shaped like a figure-of-eight that was to take Carlota Joaquina down to the Sodre Quay. As it waited to join the fantastic cortège of more than seven hundred vehicles that was needed to transport the Court, Juana had a glimpse of the old mad Queen leaning out of her carriage window, her white head bare, to shriek, *"Ai Jesus!"* And then, to her attendants, "Do not drive so fast. They will think we are running away!"

Carlota Joaquina said nothing, except to comfort her children. The rain came down in torrents. The journey seemed endless, since the roads were crowded with panic-stricken fugitives, and even when they got to the quays it was merely to sit in the carriage, and wait. Ahead of them, Juana saw Dom John alight from his coach, despite the pouring rain, and surrender himself to his lamenting people, who crowded close to kiss his hands. Piles of baggage lay everywhere on the quays. The silver plate from the Ajuda Palace, priceless books and manuscripts from the royal archives, and even the gem-studded robes of the patriarch all lay higgledy-piggledy in the rain.

Now, at last, she could see boats beginning to pull away towards them from the Portuguese ships. A chamberlain came running up to ask Carlota Joaquina to alight and prepare to embark. The quays were getting more crowded every minute. It seemed as if all Lisbon hoped to get away on those few ships. "You will come with me on the *Affonso d'Albuquerque*," Carlota Joaquina told Juana. Her oldest son, Dom Pedro, was to join his father on the *Principe Real*.

They were all on the quay now among the shouting, mourning, unpredictable crowd, where soldiers of the royal guard tried in vain to keep some kind of order. The royal children were crying and Juana picked up little Dom Miguel to save him from being crushed by the mob. She could see Dom John and his mad old mother quite near to them on the very edge of the quay, waiting for the first of the approaching boats. And with them, she saw now, was Lord Strangford and a little group of Englishmen. Not Gair.

Tears blinded her eyes for a moment. She brushed them away. There would be time for tears. A lifetime. She was distracted by a kind of eddy in the crowd beyond Strangford. A cowled priest was making his way through it, distributing blessings as he went. It was surprising, she thought, and in a way reassuring to see how the crowd gave way before him. He was quite near now to where Dom John stood among his weeping subjects. The first boat touched the quay and for a moment everyone's attention was on it save Juana's. She kept on watching the priest, fascinated by something . . . what was it about him?

Suddenly, horribly, helplessly, she knew. Short and strongly built, the cowl close about his face, the crucifix held up to the crowd . . . Vasco. And the signal?

She grasped the little Prince more tightly and looked about for help. But anyone, everyone in this crowd might serve Vasco. The Sons of the Star were probably everywhere, waiting for the signal to strike. Even if the royal guard should prove faithful, neither she nor Dom John and his family would have any chance of escape, once Vasco gave his signal.

And there was nothing she could do. To scream would be worse than useless. It might even act as the signal. At the very least, it would draw attention upon herself from whichever of the Sons of the Star stood nearest.

She watched, silent, horror-struck, turned to stone. Dom John was ready to get into the boat. The cowled figure reached him, threw back his hood and revealed the expected face of Vasco. The crucifix was in his left hand now, his right held a dagger. He raised it, gleaming dully as the rain

311

splashed on it, and for a strange moment the crowd was silent.

"I, Sebastian," he shouted, and one of the royal guard leapt at him from behind Dom John. The dagger flew from his hand and fell to the quay with a clatter of metal on stone. The two men fought like maniacs, like beasts, while round them the crowd stayed silent, watching, waiting ... The guardsman was handicapped by his ceremonial dress, the "monk" by his robes. They fought on, horribly silent, slipping on the wet stone, getting nearer and nearer to the edge of the quay. Now the "monk" had got the guardsman down and was banging his head on the stone. His helmet flew off. Gair.

Juana never knew whether she screamed, or whether Gair heard her. But he writhed out of Vasco's grasp, slipped sideways, was on his feet, and then, as Vasco rushed him, delivered a knockout blow to the chin. They were right at the edge. Vasco staggered backwards, fought desperately for balance, plunged down into deep water. The splash ... the widening ripples ... then ... nothing.

There was a long, tense moment with the crowd still strangely silent as Gair stood on the quay edge, looking down. Then he turned, lifted his hand, and spoke: "Sebastian is dead. Long live Dom John. Long live the House of Braganza!"

The crowd gave a kind of shudder, something between a groan and a cheer. Near her, Juana was aware of one or two of the royal guard slipping quietly away. The little Prince started crying louder than ever. Dom John got into his boat to be rowed out to the *Principe Real*. It was all over.

And Gair was coming towards her. "Juana!"

"Gair! I thought you were dead." Tears were streaming down her face.

"You were very nearly right. Your cousin was a mean fighter, God rest his soul. But he never trained with Gentleman Jackson, luckily for me."

"And for us, senhor." Carlota Joaquina interrupted the brief *tête-à-tête*. "Since my husband did not think fit to stay and thank you, I must do so on his behalf. Wear this for me." She pulled off one of the blazing diamond rings that encrusted her hands.

Thanking her, he explained that it had been by prearrangement that Dom John had embarked at once. "With him safe, the rest of you are so much the safer. But I have his orders that you, too, are to embark without delay."

"You will come with us, I hope, senhor?"

"Yes, Your Highness. Those are my orders." His words were for her, his eyes for Juana.

With him beside her, what had been hard was easy, what had been misery, happiness. Even the appalling conditions of the over-loaded, half-prepared ship could only make her smile. Besides: "We won't be here long." Gair seized the first private chance to speak to her on the crowded deck.

"No?"

"No. Strangford intends merely to see the Prince on board and then return to the British sloop *Confiance* and take the news of the embarkation out to our squadron. But he has asked me to stay with the Princess until the fleet sails, just in case . . . Roberto stays with Dom John. We will transfer to the *Confiance* when the Portuguese sail . . . She is to take the news to England. We may be there next week."

"It seems impossible."

"I hope it's not." He lowered his voice. "I wish I could have persuaded Strangford to take you off now, but he's still very much on his dignity with me. He won't forgive my resignation in a hurry. I thought I'd never get him to make a new approach to Dom John. I don't ever want to go through a week like this one again. I've been mad with anxiety for you, Juana. But at least, thank God, I didn't know Mascaren-has had escaped. If I'd known that, I don't think I could have stayed on board."

"You'd have deserted for my sake?"

"I'm afraid I would. As it is, it may have taken Strangford too long to make up his mind. The latest news is that Junot's advance guard is only twenty-four hours away, and, look, the wind is against us. We may be caught still, like rats in a trap. But at least it will be by the French, and we'll be together." And then, quickly, "Smile, Juana. Look like someone who knows she is safe at last. Just think what a panic would be like in this crowd."

She could smile now. "With you here, I refuse to believe I'm not safe. Oh, Gair, do you realise that for a whole week I have believed you dead?"

"That's nothing, my love. For twice that long I thought you married to Mascarenhas."

Night fell. The embarkation was complete, the ships crowded to danger point, and still the wind blew straight into the harbour. For another unbearable twenty-six hours it remained the same.

313

"It's going to be touch and go," Gair told Juana on Saturday night. "If you ever prayed, my love, pray for a fair wind tonight."

Something woke her in the blackness of the crowded cabin. A change in the movement of the ship? "Nothing good ever comes of the Spanish marriage or a Spanish wind." She remembered the proverb and the first Juana, remembered Gair, and prayed that tonight would be the exception.

She slept again and was waked at last by the shouting of orders and the rush of sailors' feet on the deck above. Teresa had the pallet nearest the porthole. "Look!" she cried. "We're moving."

Juana was one of the first on deck. The rain had stopped at last, and sunshine was drying the piles of baggage that still strewed the deck. Ahead of them, the *Principe Real* was well out into midstream, with all sails set.

"But look!" Gair joined her at the rail and pointed back to the Castle of Saint George on its hill above the river. As they watched, the Portuguese flag disappeared from its tower.

"Because the Prince Regent is gone?" she asked.

"If it were only that." The tricolour flag of France streamed out on their saving wind.

Gair turned to look downstream to where Fort Saint Julian lay ahead of them, its guns commanding the river. "Will Junot think of that?" he asked, and answered himself. "He's bound to. After all, he was here as ambassador. He knows all about Lisbon. Thank God, we are next in line."

In fact the bulk of the Portuguese fleet was safely beyond the fort when Junot's advance guard got there. One shot was fired at the last frigate, but it was too late. Already the main fleet was being greeted by the British squadron with a royal salute of twenty-one guns.

"We're safe." Juana tried to believe it as the Portuguese guns roared out their answer.

"Do you know, I really begin to think we are." The two fleets were level now, and they could see a boat being lowered from the *Confiance*. "Strangford didn't forget," Gair said. "We had best say our farewells to the Princess."

"Were you afraid he might?"

"Where you are concerned, my darling, I am afraid of everything."

"Oh dear"—she made a little face—"how tedious for you. What shall we do about it?"

"We'll marry," he said. "At once. I'm not sure I won't get

314

the chaplain of the *Confiance* to do it before even we get back to England. I don't ever want to let you out of my sight again."

"You say that! You, who let me go on thinking you were dead!"

"Juana, I had to. You must see that."

"I may see it," she said, "but that doesn't mean I like it. There's one thing I want to have clearly understood before there is any more talk of marrying, on the *Confiance* or anywhere else."

"Yes, my fierce and only love?"

"Gair!" Her voice broke. "You must understand. I couldn't go through it again ... Couldn't bear it ... It's been too much." She managed a smile. "I must have cried enough, these last few days, to keep an orange grove going. Please, Gair, must you go on?" And yet, how could she ask it of him? It was his life, after all.

But he was laughing. "You don't want to marry a secret agent?" he asked. "Well, I can't say I blame you. We've had enough adventuring, haven't we, love? But I'm not a spy any more. I resigned, don't you remember? Since then I've been— I suppose—a free agent. That's what I mean to stay. You must see, I had to finish this, but now ... Juana, you said you would marry me when our most likely prospect was death. Even if I lived, then, I had little to offer. Now things are different. The British squadron brought me letters. Poor Forland is dead. Vanessa has a boy, and I am his guardian. She wants me to live in the Dower House and manage the estate for her. And, presently, there will be a seat in Parliament. Juana, tell me that is the kind of husband you want."

"You know perfectly well what kind of husband I want, and I'm not going to flatter you by telling you again. But, oh Gair, poor Vanessa."

"She's got the boy."

"Yes. Look—the boat's quite near now."

"And here is the Princess."

The farewells and thanks were almost over, and the English boat was at the side, when Teresa came running up from below. "Juana, you left this behind." She handed her Vasco's diadem.

"Oh, so I did." Juana took it indifferently.

"Let me see," said the Princess. And then, *"Dues!* Do you not know, child, that each of these stones is a diamond of the first water?"

315

"Good God," said Gair. "And I thought I was marrying a penniless wife I could bully."

"Oh, you did, did you?" said Juana. And she said it in English, without a trace of a stammer.

Notes

Portugal. In Juana Brett's time it had long been known as England's oldest ally. An English fleet bound for the Second Crusade paused there to help capture Lisbon from the Moors in the twelfth century, and the Portuguese king, John the First, founder of the Aviz dynasty, married Henry IV of England's sister. English invalids went to Lisbon for health, merchants for profit. By the eighteenth and nineteenth centuries, there were thriving English communities at both Oporto and Lisbon, the centres of the wine trade.

Sebastian. The last of the House of Aviz, he became King of Portugal at the age of three. Growing up mystic and ascetic, he led an unlucky expedition against the Moors in Africa, was killed and his army annihilated. Portugal's old enemy, Spain, seized the chance, and the country. Although Sebastain's death was, in fact, well authenticated, rumours that he had survived persisted, and various pretenders appeared during the years of Spanish domination. These ended with the successful revolt led by the House of Braganza in 1640, in which the Sebastianists played an important part. They were active during the Napoleonic wars, and still in existence in the early twentieth century. Of course, the real Sebastian never married. It was a *revenant,* a kind of King Arthur figure, that the Sebastianists looked to, not a descendent.

Pombal. By the mid-eighteenth century, Portugal and the House of Braganza had gone to seed. A brilliant, self-made man, with a grudge against the aristocracy, Pombal completed his domination of the negligible King Joseph by his vigorous action in 1755, when an earthquake destroyed half Lisbon. Virtual dictator of Portugal, Pombal seized on the so-called Tavora plot as a chance to destroy two of the aristocratic families that opposed his reforming rule. It is not known whether the Tavoras and the d'Aveiros were really involved in the attempt on the King's life, though he had tampered with women in each family. Anyway, Pombal's torturers wrung out plenty of evidence. The chief members of both families died horribly, the others stayed in prisons or nunneries until King Joseph's death in 1777 and Pombal's consequent fall from power.

Joseph's daughter Queen Maria had the case reopened and the Tavoras at least cleared, and it was rumoured that her sense of her father's guilt helped drive her insane. In 1806 she was shut up, quite mad, at the Palace of Queluz, and her not very bright son Dom John was ruling as Prince Regent. His Spanish wife, Carlota Joaquina, disliked him intensely, had plotted against him and was living, in disgrace, at her country house—or *quinta*—of Ramalhao at Sintra. Marcus Cheke has written fascinating books about both her and Pombal, to which I am deeply indebted, and which I recommend to anyone who would like to know more about this extraordinary period of Portuguese history.

Britain and France. In the early nineteenth century, Britain was fighting a war of survival against Napoleon Bonaparte, who had made himself Emperor of France, and conquered most of Europe. Pitt, the great leader of the Tory party— the war hawks—had died in January 1806. His party fell into disarray and the Whigs—or doves—came into power in a patched-up government called the Ministry of All the Talents because it could boast so few. Its outstanding member, Fox, died in September 1806, but the ministry staggered on through the winter, to be replaced by the Tories in the spring of 1807.

In the summer of 1806 the Whigs were still hoping to make peace with Napoleon and had sent Lord Lauderdale to Paris to negotiate. Napoleon kept him in play while preparing to attack Portugal. The Portuguese dithered; the British sent a naval squadron under Lord St. Vincent, and two generals, Rosslyn and Simcoe, to try and organise resistance. The Portuguese went on dithering, but luckily for them Napoleon had to change his plans at the eleventh hour because of a sudden threat from Russia, whose Tsar kept changing sides.

Napoleon marched east, defeated Russia and her Allies, made peace at Tilsit, and was ready, by the autumn of 1807, to have another go at Portugal. He sent a rather scratch army under Marshal Junot, who had been French Ambassador at Lisbon and had managed to create a considerable pro-French party there. It is not known whether the Portuguese ministers were actually treacherous or merely incompetent, but first they did nothing, and then they panicked. Once again the British sent a naval squadron to their help, this time under the flamboyant Sir Sidney Smith; but despite all he and the Ambassador, Lord Strangford, could do, the Portuguese submitted so tamely to the French demands, and showed so little sign of defending themselves, that there was a time when Britain and Portugal were almost at war. Junot's army was actually approaching Lisbon when Dom John saw a copy of the French official paper—the *Moniteur*—with the flat statement that the House of Braganza had ceased to reign in Europe. Recognising his danger at last, he agreed to flee with his court to his rich overseas domain of Brazil. He got away just in time, as described in the last chapter of the book, but not much good came of it.

The Portuguese Scene. Many English travellers have left their impressions of Portugal in the late eighteenth and early nineteenth centuries, but those of William Beckford—author of *Vathek*—are outstanding among them. His Portuguese *Letters* and *Journal* provide bad-tempered, brilliant sketches of the priest-ridden and lethargic society of the time. More recently, Rose Macaulay's *They Went to Portugal* gives a fascinating picture of the continuing relationship between Britain and Portugal.

The Sons of the Star are as imaginary as the rest of the story.